Finding Elvis

Leslie Asbill Prichard

A One Nosey Broad Book

ISBN: 979-8-9889480-0-1 (paperback)
ISBN: 979-8-9889480-1-8 (ebook)

Cover design by: Leslie Prichard/One Nosey Broad
Library of Congress Control Number: 2018675309
Printed in the United States of America

To Elvis - Thank you!

To my parents in heaven, for an endless amount of love and for introducing me to Elvis when I was six years old. You were the best parents a girl could have. Miss you so much!

To Marcie, for your unwavering friendship, support, and encouragement and being a valuable sounding board and reader. To Cindy for your clever edits. And a special thanks to Jacky-Lynne for your valuable feedback and input. It's appreciated.

To all the Elvis fans out there, I hope this book makes you smile, and you enjoy reading it as much as I enjoyed writing it. There are a few hidden tidbits throughout that only you will appreciate. Thank you for keeping Elvis alive in your hearts and minds. Never stop loving him.

And to my amazing kids - thanks for your support and love and listening to my Elvis trivia - he's the King of Rock-n-Roll, you know!

And finally, to all my sixty-year-old compadres, no do-overs, we don't need them; we have a lot of life to live. Let's get to it!

Chapter 1
The Big Birthday

The restaurant was fairly empty when Jackie arrived. A few families still lingering after church, possibly, but she knew by four p.m. the hustle and bustle would descend and the patio and dining room would be bursting at the seams with hungry patrons. Sea View was the most popular restaurant in Seattle, after all, with its prime view of the Puget Sound. And now that the warm summer air had settled in nicely, it would bring the masses looking to taste the catch of the day or sample the raw oysters: Cliff Points, Westcotts, Pacifics, and Olympians. Her favorite were the Westcotts, even though she tried hard to like the native Olympians. The Westcotts won out; they were plump and buttery. Add a little mignonette sauce and, voila, it made the perfect treat with a Bloody Mary.

The beginnings of rumbling in her stomach with the thought of the tasty treat reminded Jackie that it was two o'clock and she'd not eaten all day. There was no particular reason for her unintentional fasting other than her mind had been full of life contemplation, and she'd simply forgotten. Turning sixty over the weekend prompted an unforeseen questioning of her entire existence, so much so that it consumed every waking minute, causing her to be rather preoccupied with growing old. She didn't feel old necessarily, but numbers don't lie.

"Do you have a reservation?" The young hostess interrupted Jackie's thoughts.

"Yes, at two. It will be under my friend's name. Roberts is the last name," Jackie replied, noticing how many visible tattoos the young girl had.

It was interesting how times had evolved over the span of her lifetime, which was one of Jackie's most distracting thoughts during the past few days, halting her from doing simple things, like eating. When Jackie was the age of the hostess, she didn't know anyone with a tattoo. It was only hippies or military that donned them. There were no tattoo parlors on every street corner, no reality shows about ink, no reality shows at all.

Her own son had one solitary tattoo, but nothing like the sleeve the hostess wore. At least Jackie thought a "sleeve" was what it was called when your entire arm was an art gallery. Who knew, it seemed the Gen-whatever had their own terminology for everything, even if it made absolutely no sense and insulted the construct of the English language. She wondered if the art of completing a sentence with whole words was even a "thing" anymore. Social media and texting had reduced conversation to emojis and abbreviations. Lol… she thought as the hostess steered her to the table.

"Follow me. We have a very special table reserved for you. It says it's a birthday celebration. Is that for you or your friend?"

"That's me. I'm the birthday girl, turning forty again," Jackie joked and started to giggle, instead producing an awkward garbled sound, something between a squeak and a laugh.

The girl was sweet, Jackie admitted to herself, feeling very judgy about her thoughts and a bit like her mother, which was not a good thing. Thinking back, as a teen herself, she had drawn butterflies on her wrist in pen until her mother scared the wits out of her with talk of ink poisoning. And if she were being honest, if tattoos had been accessible when she was that age, she would be displaying a butterfly with the word "free" across her wrist today.

Taking a seat on the patio overlooking the water, she sighed and lost herself in the sparkles of the sun glistening and dancing off the inlet like a sea of diamonds. Watching the ships float casually away from port, loaded with who knew what but all of it necessary to keep the economy moving and growing. The country had learned the hard way about supply and demand over the past couple of years during the pandemic. Jackie was glad that was behind everyone for the most part. It was nice to sit in a restaurant and gaze at the beauty of the world.

She watched the sailboats dart and glide across the glassy water off to destinations unknown, longing to sail away with them. An adventure is what she needed to shake off the blues. It had been a long time since she'd let herself relax and enjoy life. Being on the hamster wheel at her law firm was her main focus for what now could truly be defined as a lifetime. Juggling raising kids and building a successful law practice had not been easy.

Jackie's grandmother used to say, "her bones were tired." Jackie agreed, hers were too. She was also troubled by a nagging feeling there were plenty of loose ends she needed to tie up. If only she could figure out what they were.

Her eyes were drawn to a sea lion bobbing up and down not far from shore, diving and resurfacing, seemingly suspended and unaffected by the drift. It was serene and captivating, coaxing her to relax and release her worries as she waited for her best friend Maggie to appear for the big birthday lunch. Checking her watch, it was ten past two, which meant the criteria for being fashionably late had been met, so it shouldn't be long until Maggie arrived. Lateness was part of who Maggie was. There was no expectation she would ever arrive on time. It was something Jackie was used to after so many years, besides she was enjoying the moment of distraction from her own unexpected tortuous thoughts.

Birthdays had always come and gone with little effect on Jackie, normally easily rolling through them with a fun celebratory day. But this birthday shocked every fiber of her being and saying the number out loud was akin to foreign words rolling off her tongue that she didn't quite comprehend. How could she be sixty...6–0? Wasn't she just turning twenty-five, finishing law school, taking the bar exam, and off to set the world on fire? Was that really thirty-five years ago?

Life had sped past her like a blur, blotting out time and space with smudged images residing in her memory, all a bit out of focus. Now that her days sat empty, the lens was clear with nothing to consume her thoughts other than being squarely focused on the years gone by and the fact that she felt time was running out.

The deep melancholy mire returned and slid over her before she had a chance to push it away. Fortunately, it didn't sit with her long as the commotion making its way through the restaurant forced her to refocus. She recognized the exuberant sound of the person traipsing towards her in orthopedic flip-flops. It was Maggie, with gift bags in hand, along with her bubbly enthusiasm for the celebration. Jackie pushed away the emptiness dogging her soul.

"Happy Birthday," Maggie exclaimed so loudly that the few patrons sitting nearby turned and smiled, some issuing a happy birthday out of politeness. "How are you?" Maggie embraced Jackie, bags and tissue paper smashing into Jackie's ear.

"Other than turning sixty, I'm fine, but it beats the alternative. So, what are you going to do?" Jackie joked. "Thank you for the gift. You didn't have to do this. You're always so thoughtful." Jackie extracted the bag out of her right ear and took it from Maggie's hand.

Maggie was the most thoughtful person Jackie knew. They'd been friends for over thirty-five years, meeting at college in Lubbock, Texas, when Jackie was pre-law and Maggie was studying psychology. Solidifying their friendship during law school and Maggie's pursuit of her master's in counseling. Both born and bred in Texas, Maggie grew up in West Texas and Jackie in Dallas. How they had both ended up in Seattle was a happy coincidence happening only a few years after Jackie began practicing law.

They temporarily lost touch after graduation, but one day Jackie ran into an old mutual friend and heard Maggie had married and moved to the Pacific Northwest. When Jackie found out Washington had reciprocity for attorneys, on a whim she pursued getting licensed there. It would prove useful three years later when the Texas firm she worked for sent her to open the West Coast office. She landed at the airport, took one look at the sound, and felt an immediate escape, then fell in love with everything else the city offered and never looked back.

It had been a good move, but the South was part of her and that would never change. Once she and Maggie finally found each other and reunited, they picked up their friendship where it left off and had been best friends since. She even ended up marrying Maggie's husband, Charlie's old college roommate and business partner, Bob. The marriage was perfect for a while until it wasn't. But her and Maggie's friendship never faltered. Maybe since neither of them had a sister, they simply adopted each other as faux sisters. Whatever it was, it worked, and they were inseparable. A real Thelma and Louise without the murder, running from the law, the hot young con artist, and certainly no plans to drive off a cliff.

"I'm so excited for you Jackie. It's a big birthday. What did the kids do for you? Did you have a fun family dinner Friday night?" Maggie wanted to hear every detail.

Jackie smiled. If there was one thing she could count on, it was Maggie's enthusiasm for her life. Maggie never seemed to tire of hearing about Jackie's day. "It was fun. The kids came over early, wouldn't let me do a thing, and cooked me an amazing dinner. I'm always so shocked when I realize they can do things like cook. There were days when they were young, I thought I'd end up taking care of them forever. But suddenly, they're these amazing adults who handle life with ease.

They made all my favorites instead of me making their favorites. It was really quite sweet. I didn't even know they knew I had favorites." Jackie and Maggie giggled. This time Jackie's laugh was relaxed and normal. Maggie's presence grounded her.

"That's wonderful. Did you get your present?" Maggie had a lilt in her voice as she asked the question, cluing Jackie to what she already suspected, that Maggie had helped her kids, Susan and Toby, pick out her present. A full set of Elvis record albums to be played on Jackie's antique turntable with gold lilting, the one nobody is allowed to touch.

"Oh my gosh," Jackie exclaimed, "you helped Susan and Toby with that, didn't you? You know they are grown, right? I'm sorry they dragged you into that."

A wide smile grew across Maggie's face. "Are you kidding? I offered to help. It's a special birthday. And you and I both know your lifelong love and deepest crush of your life is Elvis Presley. How could you have a sixtieth birthday without Elvis?"

Maggie signaled the waitress, who seemed to be having a difficult time pulling herself away from her cell phone to wait on them.

It was true, Jackie had a deep love and admiration for Elvis Presley, spending hours watching his movies, collecting his albums, and listening to his records non-stop. A crush that began at the tender age of six, the first time she saw Elvis on TV in the 1968 Comeback Special. A flame was ignited and grew more and more every day of her life. Seeing him live in concert when she was thirteen sealed her obsession with all things Elvis.

She was barely fifteen years old when he died. She had dropped to her bedroom floor, slung her embroidered flower headband across the room, and cried her eyes out when her mother broke the news. Lying on the floor for hours thinking she would die of heartbreak, madly in love with the superstar. The day he left her was the day she gave up on fairy tales.

6

After that, Jackie tucked her Elvis obsession away for years, sharing it only with Maggie and the kids and keeping her collection of memorabilia to a minimum. Recent sleepless nights tempted her shopping gene as the anniversary of his death approached. Under the covers, cursing the reasons sleep was elusive, she would pick up her phone, login to Amazon and begin shopping, adding items to her cart only to click 'save for later' before finalizing her purchase. Not committing was a theme in her relationships too, not that there had been any recently.

"Oh, my sweet Elvis. I've listened to those albums non-stop, in between binging Elvis movies all weekend. I could hardly wait for the kids to leave so I could put those records on and break out a bottle of wine."

A dreamy, faraway look settled on Jackie's face as she thought of the days when Elvis movies were only on television or at the theater, she relied on her records to keep him front and center, playing them endlessly, locked away in her room, starting the record over and over to hear that silky voice crooning the most pleasant sounds she'd ever heard.

"I'm so happy you love your present. I knew you would. And I didn't even call you yesterday so you could remain in your dream world of everything Elvis." Maggie laughed.

"Kids these days don't know how lucky they are being able to stream movies at the touch of a button," Jackie told Maggie.

"I know. Remember when we got VCRs and could rent movies?" Maggie said. "We thought that was the greatest invention ever made."

"Except for the late fees, my dad hated those. Now I can stream movies at the push of a button no matter where I am, even in the bathtub. Isn't technology grand?" Jackie added.

It took Jackie some years and maturity to realize her love for Elvis that started when she was young was because her mother loved him too. She and her mom never really saw eye-to-eye on much, but on Elvis, they both agreed. And any conflict they had fell away when they sat in the living room on the dark red carpet, spinning Elvis records. In those moments they were best friends who laughed together and saw eye-to-eye on the most important thing in her world, Elvis was the King.

"Can I take your drink order?" The waitress finally appeared tableside.

"Yes, you may," Maggie said, looking at the waitress, who had apparently missed a gap in service. "We don't have any menus and we're going to order lunch, but you can start us off with a bottle of Prosecco. We're celebrating this amazing woman's birthday."

The waitress was clearly lost in her own world and barely acknowledged Maggie or Jackie. Instead, she mumbled, "Prosecco, I'll get menus," before walking away without looking up.

"Well, she's really loving her job," Jackie added when the server was out of earshot. "Remember when we had those awful summer waitress jobs at that BBQ place off Highway 84 in Lubbock?" Jackie raised her eyebrows. "We were so awful. How did Guy ever hire us? I don't think we ever mastered that job."

"Because we didn't want to be there. It was stifling hot in that narrow little run-down restaurant in the sweltering summer heat, and the floors were always sticky. And the only reason we worked there was your fault because you had a crush on that cook. That looker we met, you know, the one you insisted had eyes like Elvis. What was his name? Tex? Billy Bob? Johnny Jack?" Maggie rolled through a list of stereotypical Texas names, laughing hysterically.

Jackie blushed at the thought of that summer and how silly it all had been, but she still remembered that boy.

"Deke," Jackie said through the laughter. "That was his name, and he was the sweetest guy ever. But, yes, his name was Deke."

"He could two-step like nobody's business and swept you off your feet and right into a job at Guy's BBQ and you dragged me along with you. You were so boy crazy, you made our life insane." Maggie rolled her eyes dramatically.

"Yet, fun!" Jackie added, raising her water glass in a mock toast to herself.

"He'd stay in the back humming that song. I think it was an Elvis song, I can't remember. The only time he came outside was when y'all were headed to his old, broken-down, pickup truck, to make out."

"Oh, geesh, how do you remember these things?" Jackie smiled at the memory of Deke. "The song was, *Loving You*, I think. That feels like another lifetime it was so long ago, it's hard to remember. Although he was hard to forget at the time, but we had very different life rhythms."

The thought of how terrible they were as waitresses and their horrible work ethic at that point in their young lives was amusing. She had to wipe away tears as they roared with laughter at a season of their past. And how she had been so in love with Deke, those bedroom eyes and that blonde hair. Although she rarely saw his hair, since he wore a ball cap all the time.

As sweet as he was, he hardly talked, but on the rare occasion he did, he was thoughtful and articulate. His greatest life ambition was to stay right there in the Texas Panhandle and cook BBQ. How life had changed quickly when she graduated law school. It became serious and grown up in a flash. That summer fling with Deke was a distant memory and one of life's little lessons in perspective and priorities.

The waitress appeared and set the Prosecco and two champagne flutes on the table, along with two menus. Then turned and walked away without a word.

"And she's off." Jackie poured the Prosecco perfectly, keeping the foam at a minimum, and raised her glass. "What shall we toast to?"

"You, it's your birthday," Maggie reminded Jackie.

"No, no, that's too easy. I mean, yes, of course we will toast my birthday, but what is my annual, profound, mystical, life-directing toast that will guide me through this year? Because, Lord knows, I'm going to need some guidance to get through it. I usually have some good ideas, but I can't seem to dig out of my despair of turning sixty to set my compass to true north." Jackie set her glass down.

"Well, what do you want to do this year? You're free from work and have all the time in the world to do the things you like. What's something you've always wanted from the bottom of your heart? What would make you happier than you've ever been in your entire life…other than having your parents back?"

Maggie reached across the table and put her hand over Jackie's. The loss of her parents was Jackie's deepest sorrow. And Maggie knew all too well how she felt, although she was still blessed to have her father and visited him as much as possible. It was difficult at times to manage everything with her job, her husband, and her life. Even though he was spry, he lived in an assisted living residence and seemed to be thriving with a full week of activities and the company of people his age. It helped ease Maggie's guilt.

"That's putting a lot of pressure on me. I can barely figure out what I want for breakfast these days, when I remember to eat," Jackie half-kidded.

"Let's think of something fun, something crazy, something we would have wanted when we were those reckless young, terrible waitress girls we used to be!" Maggie suggested.

Feigning a smile, Jackie paused to think about her birthday wish. "Well…," she started to say, twirling her champagne glass, staring at the bubbles rise to the top and pop as she considered what she wanted. "What would bring me joy? What would be fun and crazy?"

"Make it good," Maggie urged.

It came to her in a flash and Jackie knew what she wanted more than anything in the world. She raised her glass and Maggie followed, raising her glass too. "I know what I want. Here's to my sixtieth birthday... and this year...I want to Save Elvis!" The women clinked their glasses together to seal the toast.

"Here's to Saving Elvis and to you. Cheers!" Maggie echoed as an unsettled feeling gnawed at her gut. She had no idea what Jackie meant by saving Elvis, but she was sure it was going to be an unforgettable adventure and Jackie was going to drag her along for the ride.

Chapter 2
A Plan is Born

Maggie set her glass on the table, waiting to hear about the plans she could see swirling around in Jackie's head. She recognized the flashes of mischief in Jackie's green eyes. Maggie was used to that look, though mostly years ago when they were young and wild. Jackie was the wild one and she semi-wild, to be accurate. It had been years since she saw the old light in Jackie.

The past twenty-five years had been stern and serious, with Jackie walking around with the heavy weight of responsibility on her shoulders. But something had sparked in Jackie with this milestone birthday and not in a good way. There was a restlessness, a need for more.

Not only had Jackie turned sixty, but she'd also retired four months earlier after winning the case of a lifetime, providing her with more money than she could spend in the next twenty to twenty-five years that were left in a life on countdown. The backside of sixty was a slow ride to nothingness that had to be capitalized on and not wasted, time was precious and fleeting. Maggie heard Jackie enumerate these thoughts more and more lately.

Maggie herself was a couple of months away from sixty and a few months ago couldn't really understand this anxiousness Jackie was emoting, but as her own birthday crept closer, Maggie was beginning to relate.

"Well?" Maggie questioned, letting the word linger in anticipation of the plan Jackie must have to "Save Elvis." Jackie always had a plan after all, and was defined by being organized, contained, in charge, and driven. All qualities that elevated her to senior partner of a successful law firm and led her to become the owner of that firm for the past twenty-five years.

Drawing in a breath, Jackie said, "I love Elvis. We all know that. But…" she hesitated.

"But?" Maggie urged the conversation on as Jackie sat silent, pensive almost.

With a slow exhale, Jackie laid out her thoughts. "I love Elvis, but have you ever considered what the world would have been like without Elvis in it? He was a visionary, a trailblazer, an instrument of progress. He changed the world in a flash." Jackie snapped her fingers to make her point. "And half the world, these young kids, do you think they even know who Elvis is? What he did? How important he was to the world culturally and, of course, to music?"

"I know how important he was," Maggie replied, "but I'm not following Jackie. What are you going to do? How are you going to save Elvis? Does he need saving?"

The passion Jackie had for anything Elvis was always very well known to Maggie and she loved Elvis too, but not like Jackie. Elvis had been the heartbeat of all young girls when she and Jackie were growing up. Everybody wanted to be loved by Elvis and Elvis was loved by everyone, girls and boys alike. But Maggie wasn't following what Jackie was planning to do.

"Elvis had a fear of being forgotten and I'm worried the world is evolving so rapidly and kids are so disconnected to the true history of past generations that they might be missing the importance of that era. Like the destruction of segregation, the breakdown of social constructs, life-changing societal progress. How Elvis attempted to meld the black and white culture and brought it together with music.

13

How he made it okay to accept black music and entertainers. Let's face it, he created rock-n-roll and made it cool! It's important." Jackie delivered a closing statement in her well-embedded attorney mode.

Maggie sat back and took a sip of Prosecco, reflecting, before she said, "I think you may be right. Elvis may be starting to be forgotten, but aren't there foundations and Graceland? Isn't the family promoting him and keeping him alive? What about that new movie that recently came out? It was spectacular. I bet that has spurned new interest and new fans."

"Maybe. I can't explain it. I wish I could resurrect him and bring him back to life. It's tragic, and such a loss that Elvis died the way he did. I feel like he was broken. I would love to go back in time and fix it. To warn him about the vultures, to help him, to keep him alive."

Jackie was serious in her desire to bring Elvis back to life, a fantasy she'd entertained since 1977, but she knew it was a dream, a longing, and not a reality. She sighed heavily and took a long draw of her Prosecco. Even she didn't understand what she wanted to do to save Elvis. Her heart longed to undo his death as unreal as that sounded, even to herself.

"How can you miss someone you never met?" Jackie said. It was a question she had asked herself over and over since that fateful day in August.

"I'm not sure, but I know you aren't the only one who misses Elvis," Maggie said.

"I think I'm going to take a trip and try to figure this out. I know I need to do something, but I don't know what. Maybe a trip to Graceland. I've never been there if you can believe that!"

Maggie realized that Jackie didn't really have a plan to save Elvis, and she also knew that when Jackie set her mind on something and there was no plan, it could lead to trouble. Jackie worked manically under unorganized constraints.

"No, I can't believe you've never been to Graceland. I haven't either, it's on my list. I think you should take a trip as a birthday present to yourself. You deserve to get away and relax, begin living the second act of this life of yours. Have fun," Maggie encouraged. "You don't have to save the world, Jackie. It's okay to enjoy your life and take care of yourself. Look at all the good you did in your law practice, how many people you helped representing the little guys against the big guys. You've done enough saving."

"Thanks. I honestly can't remember the last vacation I took," Jackie admitted.

"The last vacation you took, I distinctly remember both Susan and Toby telling me you worked the entire time. That's not a vacation Jackie," Maggie reminded her. "You deserve to go have some fun and relax."

Over the past ten years, as technology developed, it made it nearly impossible to escape office connections and demands. Maggie knew Jackie would be in heaven in Memphis. It was perfect. She still didn't understand and was a little concerned about how Jackie was going to "Save Elvis," but she wasn't going to push it any further. Jackie was at loose ends since retiring. Maybe this was a good project to help her ease into a new routine.

"I think I'll take several days and tour the entire area, really get a feel for where Elvis grew up. Who he was, where he walked, what he saw as a kid in Tupelo and as a teen and adult in Memphis. Then when I get back, maybe I'll create a music foundation or something to aid underserved children. I've got enough money to do some good." Jackie filled her glass again.

"That's a great idea. But please put relaxing on the agenda." Maggie tipped her flute, signaling to fill her glass and finish the bottle. Maggie knew Jackie was not the type to sit at home and putter around the house. She had been on the fast track for far too long to come to a screeching halt. It would drive Jackie crazy.

The waitress finally reappeared so the women could order. A second bottle of Prosecco was at the top of the requests, along with a dozen oysters and the salmon dish, their standard fare at Sea View. Whatever adventurous spirit had been sparked in Jackie for this new beginning, it didn't extend to her appetite. The old regulars were safe and dependable. Baby steps.

"When are you planning on going?" Maggie asked, hoping her schedule was open so she could go too and start marking off items on her own bucket list.

Sometimes Maggie envied Jackie's freedom. Jackie had no attachments. The kids were grown, and she was free to go anywhere whenever she wanted. Sadly, it seemed she rarely did and instead spent a lot of time alone or working. Her practice had kept her tethered to the office for many years and the kids had consumed the rest of her time, with the balance skewed in favor of work. Now that the kids were adults and the law practice gone, it was time Jackie got out and explored the world.

"I was thinking about going next week," Jackie said, looking hopefully at Maggie. "Any chance you're free?"

"Oh darn, no, I can't go then. Charlie is having his hernia repair surgery later this week. He's put it off for months. I don't dare ask him to put it off any longer. It's been causing him a great deal of discomfort." Maggie was torn at the thought of missing out on fun with Jackie, but she and Charlie were devoted to each other and had been for most of her adult life. She loved Charlie. He came first.

"Oh, shoot, I forgot about that. No, you should be here with Charlie. I'll have fun and I'd probably drive you nuts with my Elvis trivia iterations. It seems right that I should make this trip alone. It will be a cathartic experience." They both laughed.

Jackie admired Maggie's relationship with Charlie. And Charlie had supported Jackie in more ways than she could count throughout the past thirty-plus years.

"Do you realize Elvis was only forty-two when he died? The same age as Bob, my amazing husband, when he died," Jackie commented.

The extreme sarcasm did not go unnoticed by Maggie. "I knew Elvis was forty-two, seems so young now but seemed so old when it happened, which is an interesting perspective about age when you think about it. And, by the way, Bob didn't die, you divorced him. As if you needed reminding of that awful nonsense."

"Wishful thinking!" Jackie murmured. "Bob is dead to me and to his children. Here's another similarity: since our divorce, I've heard from Bob the same number of times that I've heard from Elvis since he died."

The women broke out in hysterics. The waitress who had been coming to check on them immediately did a U-turn with annoyance at the outburst of laughter.

"Guess she doesn't appreciate our exuberance," Jackie whispered in between giggles.

Maggie sobered for a moment. "I'm so sorry that jackass put you and the kids through all that he did. Such a jerk!" Maggie withheld the true description and curse words she would normally assign to Bob, since a family with young children had been seated near them.

"I've never heard you describe him that kindly," Jackie said, knowing Maggie was restraining herself.

It was Jackie who felt awful for what Bob had done, even after all these years. Scamming them all. Cheating on her while she slaved away to provide a plush life and cheating Charlie out of money, almost breaking Charlie and Maggie when he disappeared with customer account funds. It had taken all of Jackie's resources to track him down after he fled the country. It took even longer to find out how much had been stolen, get a divorce, and put her kids back together when their dad absconded.

"I'm thankful the kids were young, so they had plenty of time for a normal life," Maggie told Jackie.

Jackie nodded in agreement. "Me too."

She ultimately used her own money from an inheritance to make Charlie and Maggie whole again financially, something Maggie never knew then or today. Jackie had passed it off as an insurance recovery when she handed them a check. The fact that Bob almost got away with the scam still chapped Jackie, it paid off that her firm had the best private investigator around to track down her slimy ex and prove Charlie was innocent.

Thankfully, Charlie was resilient, and it quickly became clear that he was on the long list of unsuspecting victims. True to Charlie's good nature, he felt guilty for setting Jackie up with Bob, and Jackie felt guilty for not noticing Bob was cheating them all. Bob was a liar and a cheat and Jackie never forgave herself for not realizing that sooner. Trusting any man after that was not on her agenda. The main thing that stood solid and firm was her friendship with Maggie. There was never any option of choosing Bob over her friend.

"It's your birthday. Let's not talk about those dark days," Maggie redirected. She'd seen the look in Jackie's eyes dozens of times over the years, time-tripping to difficult days.

"Yes, let's plan my trip to Memphis," she agreed. Grabbing her cell phone, she began searching travel sites to book a flight and purchase a VIP tour ticket and make her dreams come true. Immersing herself in Elvis's life was just the medicine Jackie needed to push away the "turning sixty blues." It was something to look forward to, and she was ready to have fun.

"It needs to be a once in a lifetime blow out. I can't believe I'm going to miss it," Maggie lamented.

"I know, it's okay though," Jackie responded, trying to be gracious. "If it's fun, we'll do it again together and then I can plan the trip, line up everything, and be your personal tour guide."

Maggie chuckled inwardly at Jackie's instinctive need to plan. "You need to make this trip over the top. Elvis wouldn't want it any other way! The best of everything for his Jackie."

The festive mood was restored as their Prosecco giggles kicked in again.

Chapter 3
Too Beige

Jackie arrived home in high spirits. The Uber ride went by like a flash while she dreamed away the time, lost in thought of her impending trip to Memphis. Usually, she would have chatted up the driver, but tonight she enjoyed being absorbed in her daydream.

She had spontaneously purchased a flight leaving in a few days that was priced better than the flight a week away, surprising herself since impulsiveness was not part of her character. More than once she'd heard an office reference her secretary used to make, that she was "buttoned up." Jackie bristled at the thought, not because she doubted it, but because it was true. The other office gossip designated her as being wound tight as a top. Also, true.

"Humpf," Jackie huffed. "I'll show them who can relax and have fun."

It was really herself she needed to show, since none of those colleagues were around anymore to see the transformation she was willing herself to make. Taking this trip was a great first step. Although in the back of her mind, Jackie was starting to categorize these things as her "Bucket List," which took her to a place she didn't care to go. Age and time were inevitable and moving at the speed of light, no matter how hard she tried to hold on and slow it down. Jackie cleared her head, pushing past the negative thinking, focusing on the fun ahead of her this week, not the years that would descend on her whether she wanted them to or not.

Going against her frugal nature, without a plan and doing it in style, she booked a room at the highly acclaimed Memphis Manor Hotel, reserving the King of Rock suite. Feeling proud that it was done without research, price shopping, checking calendars, filing motions, rearranging schedules and hearings, and rethinking and second-guessing it all a dozen times. Miraculously, she found what she wanted and clicked "Add to Cart," entered her credit card, and would be headed to see Graceland soon. Another bold step.

Everything was falling into place, and she congratulated herself for mimicking Elvis's way of life and taking care of her business in a flash. All her life, she had taken care of business for everyone else. Now it was time to take care of herself.

Moving past her jolt of spontaneity, there was true planning that had to be done. She had to pack. What in the world was she going to wear? Yanking clothes from her closet, she tossed them on the bed. Elvis was singing in the background, the rich sound of his voice coming from the vinyl in clear, round notes that melted in the air around her.

Do kids these days even listen to records anymore?

Such a tragedy they'd never know the excitement of a new release and beating it to the record store waiting for the shelves to be stocked. Then hustling back home to get the record on the turntable as fast as possible. Or the sheer devastation when you accidentally left a record in your car while you ran into a friend's house for a minute and took too long getting the week's gossip, coming out to find your new vinyl record had warped in the hot car, waves of vinyl undulating all around. There was no fixing that. It was a reminder of how valuable and protected those records were.

Vinyl had all but disappeared with the advent of CDs and now, with streaming and every option for downloading apps and listening to music, it seemed it was going to be a difficult resurrection. For Jackie, the new technology didn't compare to the excitement and hype of a new album release when she was young. Holding that vinyl record in your hand, you felt the artist; it had weight and value, and importance in your life. Plus, and most importantly, the sound was second to none.

She clicked the remote and slid the volume up on the spinning record. The sound growing and filling the room; the sultry tones, the clarity of the instruments, and the mesmerizing, lush and seductive voice that was unique and unmistakable as the King of Rock-n-Roll singing his heart out to her as he had done so many nights before. Joy ebbed through her.

Staring at the pile of clothes on her bed, her joy was cut short by the mountain of beige. The task at hand dragging her away from the smooth intoxication she felt from the Prosecco and her daydreams of Elvis. Frustrated, she sorted her clothes, organized, packed, and re-packed, then unpacked. And, after an insightful evaluation of her dreary wardrobe, called Maggie.

"Hey, Maggie, thanks for dinner tonight. It was so much fun," Jackie told her.

"You're welcome. I had a blast too. Are you packing?"

"Nope. I can't go."

"What are you talking about? Why?"

"I have nothing to wear. My clothes are terrible. How have I been walking around the past twenty years with such a drab wardrobe? Why didn't you tell me I was old and boring?"

"You are not old and boring. There is this place you can go; it's called a mall. Go shopping Jackie and buy some fun clothes. Remember the clothes you wore back in college? I know you have shopping skills. It's time to dust them off and put them to work," Maggie encouraged.

"I need you to go with me like we used to do. Tomorrow? Noon? Meet me at the mall? I'll buy lunch," Jackie proposed.

"Deal. I'll see you there. So, can you go on your trip if we get you new clothes?" Maggie asked.

"Nope! I look terrible. My hair is gray, and I've started biting my nails again." A terrible habit she'd broken over two decades ago and recently caught herself falling back into. "I'm stressed," Jackie admitted. "I'm a mess."

"You're not a mess. You have a couple of days until you leave, go do a spa day. Pamper yourself Jackie, you deserve it," Maggie told her, surprised by Jackie's admission. She was a woman who was always put together and unflappable until recently.

Jackie sighed and agreed, "I know you're right. I'll find a spa and treat myself. It's long overdue. How did I let this happen, Maggie?"

"Life, Jackie. We all get busy and forget to prioritize ourselves. I do it too. Hell, almost everyone we know gets this way. Everyone other than Marilee. She's always at the spa. She only knows how to prioritize herself," Maggie said, adding a spark of gossip to amuse Jackie.

"That's so true. I guess there's a happy medium out there somewhere."

"Okay, go make your list of what you need. I know you are dying to do that."

"You know me well. First, I need to tackle this mountain of old lady clothes on my bed and find a spa. I'll see you tomorrow. And, thanks Maggie," Jackie said sweetly.

"You're welcome. Happy Birthday again. See you at the mall. Goodnight."

Tomorrow would be the eradication of beige. No more court clothes were needed in her wardrobe. Life had gone off track, evidenced by not one stitch of fun clothes hanging in her closet. Shoving the pile of clothes into the corner of the room, she vowed to donate most of them after her trip.

Readying for bed, Jackie stared in the bathroom mirror, barely recognizing the woman looking back at her. Not only had the gray taken over, so had time. She contorted her face, assessing the frown lines and the laugh lines, noting the furrowed brow lines were getting deeper than the last time she'd paid attention to them. No doubt a gift from worrying. It wasn't only work stress; she was witnessing and evaluating the barrage of time, the drag of gravity, the effects of walking around on this earth for sixty years. By some measures, she was holding up well enough, but it was time to pay attention and fight back a bit against the inevitable. Maybe hold it off a little longer. She wasn't old; she tried to convince herself, just a little worn.

In a few days, she would be visiting the King, which gave her time to get primped, primed, and pretty. Maggie was right, she deserved it.

Scrolling through website after website, it was apparent getting the spa day set was more challenging than booking the trip. Losing hope, Jackie scrolled through her contacts looking for her last hairstylist, instead coming across a former client who owned a spa. She had represented the spa a year ago against the corporate landlord and had prevailed in a big way. The owner told her at the time whenever she needed a massage, a pedicure, a haircut, or any other service, to call her private cell number and she would make sure Jackie was pampered. She had tucked it away in her contacts, never thinking she would actually use it, but now it was time to call in that favor.

Yes, it was Jackie time! She couldn't remember when there had ever been Jackie time, but she was about to find out what it was all about.

Chapter 4
Spa Day

The gurgling rock fountains on the exterior of the building told Jackie she was in the right place to begin her transformation. She arrived at the spa with enthusiasm and a deep hope there were talented miracle workers inside. Her client was more than happy to fit Jackie into the schedule and give her the VIP treatment on such short notice. If there was one thing Jackie was certain of, it was that her clients loved her, opposing counsel feared her, the partners respected her, and she got results. It all seemed so purposeful for all those fleeting years, but now she wondered if she had given up too much of herself.

The latest craze was work-life balance. Jackie barely knew what that was. Making your way in the corporate world in the eighties was a challenge she wasn't sure some of the younger generation could appreciate. Women were the ones who had to balance it all; home life, kids, work, and battling to the top in a male-dominated workforce. Spread thin on every front, something had to give, and it was usually yourself. You became the last priority. She was proud watching her own daughter set stronger boundaries between the work woman, mom, and wife roles.

Being the first woman in her family trying to navigate and juggle the multi-faceted demands with nobody to guide her had been another trail Jackie had to blaze. Her mother never understood why Jackie wanted to work so hard, attributing it solely to Jackie's need for material things: the house, the cars, the nanny, the expensive furniture, all received the blame from her mother who never had a need for anything other than what Jackie's parents had from the beginning. The conversations were endless, trying to explain to her mother that the drive for success was more than accumulating possessions. It was a need to prove to herself that she was smart and could do anything the male partners could do.

Back then, women didn't talk about kids or husbands at work. You were the work, a force, or you didn't become partner. The men were never judged for working long hours, being dedicated to their jobs, ignoring their families to get ahead in a corporate world that absolutely cared more about billable hours than whether you missed PTA or little Johnny's soccer game. You bit your lip and stayed tough.

The unending criticisms many times were from other women as well. When Jackie started her career, there was a divide between women who worked and women who stayed home, criticisms flying across the chasm. Fortunately, over the years, that gap was bridged somewhat, and the importance of individual decisions and personal situations made both lifestyles acceptable. She felt judged many times when the kids were young, the most painful criticism coming from her own mother, who simply didn't understand Jackie's life.

The most difficult memory of those early years, was knowing how she pretended she was happy and in control, not sitting in the tub at midnight, turning up the music, and crying about how she was going to get up and do it all again the next day, and bake three dozen cookies by morning for the bake sale she only heard about at bedtime. "Having it all" was a phrase thrown around casually without thinking about how it could be accomplished. Jackie didn't know how to have it all and take care of herself. She made sure the kids were taken care of, and she damn-well made sure her job was taken care of. She never thought of taking care of herself beyond the basics, but was learning that life and work were different now.

"Good morning, Ms. Sawyer. We were told to expect you," the receptionist said pleasantly.

"Hello, thank you so much for working me in. I really need this," Jackie confessed.

"Absolutely! We want you to relax and de-stress today. We have you booked for a full day. Massage first, mani/pedi, and a cut and color. You're welcome to use the sauna or the saltwater tub after your massage. You'll have about an hour before the mani/pedi. Then a delightful lunch and your cut and color. You'll be transformed when you leave. We have wine, coffee, tea, and flavored water available. Please let your hostess know what you need at any time. Any questions?"

"No, that sounds amazing. I can't wait," Jackie responded, overly impressed by the white-glove service.

"Is that Jackie Sawyer?" Maria, the spa owner, came out of her office.

"Maria, so good to see you. Thank you so much for working me in. You're a lifesaver." Jackie hugged her former client.

"Are you kidding? If it weren't for you, the spa would be out of business. You saved me. I was happy to make the arrangements. You deserve this. I know how hard you work," Maria said.

"Worked, past tense. I retired in April," Jackie told her. It felt strange to admit her new status.

"Really? I thought you would work forever. I'm thrilled for you. I hope you are loving every minute," Maria replied, shock planted on her face.

"I thought I'd work forever, too. It's been an adjustment, that's for certain," Jackie admitted.

"I'm happy for you Jackie. How are the kids? I think I remember your daughter had a baby, a little girl, and was starting her own business?" Maria asked, recalling their conversations from a few attorney-client lunches that drifted into personal matters.

"Yes, Rosie is two now, and feisty, but Susan handles it with ease. Susan is a UX Designer and works part time from home. Her husband Rusty is a computer programmer, and he takes good care of them. Their life seems well orchestrated. I certainly couldn't have done that when my kids were young. For one, we didn't have the option," Jackie said.

Maria's case had dragged on for over two years, so she and Jackie had become more than attorney and client. They weren't exactly friends, but they enjoyed lively conversations.

"What's a UX Designer?" Maria asked.

"I didn't know either. I had to Google it. She enhances websites to make the consumer experience more pleasant and user-friendly. I'm still not sure I understand. Those types of jobs weren't available when you and I were in college." Jackie laughed.

"You're so right. We had about twelve career choices when we were young. Owning a spa wasn't my first choice, it's a second life career. Maybe I'll hire her to take a look at my website," Maria said.

"You should. She's good at what she does."

"And your son, is he still in banking?"

"Yes, Toby is still a banker and still a bachelor. He's living his best life. Hopefully, one day he'll meet someone that he'll keep around longer than a few months, but as long as he's happy."

"That's all we can hope for. Well, I'll let you get your spa day started. I'm so glad you called me. I'm running out to a meeting soon. I'm not sure if I'll be back before you leave, but please have a great day and relax," Maria said. She gave Jackie a long hug.

"Thank you, Maria. I can't wait and I'll be making this part of my regular routine." Jackie smiled. Her heart lifted. She turned back to the receptionist, who had been waiting patiently.

"What type of water would you like? Cucumber, lemon, or orange?"

"Cucumber," she replied, thinking it sounded refreshing.

"Wonderful. Your hostess is Amanda. She will take you to the changing room and get you situated. Please enjoy your day and have fun relaxing." She smiled.

Amanda delivered Jackie to the spa locker room, which was a far departure from the gym she briefly joined twenty years ago, a membership she rarely used. Elegance surrounded her as she slipped into the plush robe, and with shaky hands, pulled on the matching cushioned slippers. For someone so stoic and solid in the courtroom, the thought of relaxing set her nerves in overdrive. It was going to take time to get used to the downshift, to prioritize existing without guilt for standing still and not doing something productive. It would be a process.

Picking up her cucumber water, she made her way to the solitude room, where ladies waited to be scooped up and whisked off for relaxation. Her muscles felt tight and tense. She quietly managed some relaxing breathing she learned in the three yoga classes she took two years ago, like then, her body fought back, and her mind continued to whirl and click into fast gear.

Amanda appeared on cue. "Ms. Sawyer, if you will follow me to the Sunset room, I think you'll find it the perfect space to meditate and surround yourself in calm," Amanda instructed, leading Jackie down the dimly lit corridor with soft, pastel carpeting and faint, tinny music lofting through the hallway on the route to relaxation.

Exhaling the breath she realized she was holding more loudly than she planned, Amanda turned, looked at her, and smiled. It was a foregone conclusion that Amanda would be sorely disappointed by Jackie's meditation skills, something she'd never perfected or achieved. Zen remained allusive. All she ever accomplished was manufacturing a headache from working diligently to put thoughts out of her mind as they battled and pushed their way back in, splitting her head in half. Ultimately, she had given up. Maybe she would try again now that her mind was free of clients and cases, and right and wrong weren't

29

permeating her brain. Perhaps now she could control her thoughts and reach that tranquil state of mind. Doubtful!

"Enjoy your day," Amanda directed her to the chairs.

The Sunset Room was nothing like Jackie had imagined ten minutes ago. It was filled with overstuffed leather recliners, Frans chocolates, and magazines with luxurious travel destinations on the cover perched symmetrically on hand-carved wooden tables, with Himalayan salt lamps situated strategically next to them. The entire room was submerged in rolling waves of music from an indigenous flute, prodding her to release her stress.

Sinking into the recliner several chairs away from the other younger women who seemed to be pros at relaxing and pampering, Jackie decided she wanted to be one of those women instead of a woman waiting for an invitation from the world to give her permission to unwind before she could permit herself such an indulgence.

The only thing she had done over the years to distract herself from stress and work was to grow roses. Her garden was bursting with award-winning roses, but even caring for those required assistance by her landscaper from time to time, mostly when she had been in the middle of a trial, which was often.

Scolding herself for thinking of work, she pushed her shoulders down and tried to disappear into the recliner, propping her feet up, sipping her cucumber water, and pretending to look through a travel magazine. Maybe she would go somewhere tropical. Who was she kidding? She couldn't even focus on the words and had forgotten her glasses, so there was that.

Thinking back to the conversation with Maria, Jackie had to admit how well Susan seemed to handle motherhood and working from home. It was a blessing that Rusty was so helpful and involved. When Susan and Toby were young, there had been plenty of mornings when Jackie wasn't even sure she had the same color shoes on when she left the house. That nightmare happened on one occasion when she showed at work with one blue shoe and one black shoe. To make it worse, they weren't even the same height heel. By luck, she worked downtown, where there were department stores so she could rectify the humiliating moment. Only her paralegal had noticed and with what Jackie paid her, keeping confidences was ensured. That's when she realized how out of control her world was. It was a pivotal moment, forcing her to restructure her life. Become more organized, maintain strict plans, keep schedules, and eradicate chaos. She started sleeping less to be up early enough to make sure the mornings were not an explosion of bedlam. A drastic change from her true nature of a hippie mindset, thriving on adventure and curiosity about life, growing up with dog tags and a crush on Elvis.

She'd always been responsible, diligent, and productive, but she managed it all with soulful freedom until she came face-to-face with adult reality. Looking back on it, she became rigid. If Bob had helped, life might have been easier, but some things were impossible where he was concerned. Maybe it was her laid-back, accepting nature that caused her to become the wife that rolled with his shortcomings and accommodated them. The multiple conversations with Bob about restructuring their lives were futile, and she had simply acquiesced.

It was also then when she had been forced to admit she needed outside help with the kids, so she did the only thing she could, and hired a nanny who was a saint, and the support Jackie needed. Armed with her new regimented schedules, her Day-Timer, her Blackberry, and her new nanny, life became a bit more manageable, but it also made it easier for her to stay later and later at work and go in earlier and earlier, and for Bob to increase his extra-curricular activities. It was the perfect setup for her to become more forgotten and the beginning of the end for her marriage, and herself.

A flash of anger struck her as she revisited the memories, not anger at Bob, but at herself for not standing up and insisting Bob participate in their lives, and for modifying her personality, becoming hardened to survive. Anger at herself for marrying Bob, a decision she would gladly reverse if possible.

The marriage imploded quickly after that, and Jackie didn't want to salvage any part of their life. Desperately wanting out and away from Bob with the least financial destruction as possible. Thinking about those days brought tension to her brow and she could feel the horizontal lines deepen. Jackie forced the thoughts away. The last thing she wanted was for Bob and the past to cause her new worry wrinkles. The most important fact was she made it through with healthy and happy kids who never wanted for anything, except maybe her time. She pushed away the guilt, which was another rabbit hole she didn't want to go down. She was supposed to be relaxing, damnit.

"Jackie?" The voice of the massage therapist shocked her into the present and away from continued self-deprecation.

"Yes, I'm Jackie," she answered.

"Are you ready for your massage?" The girl led Jackie to another quiet and calm room, a private room, where they sat to talk about what Jackie wanted to accomplish with her massage; the pressure she liked, any concerns or areas that needed extra attention.

"I think I mainly want to relax," Jackie responded. Her goal was simple.

"Perfect. I can do that. You'll feel wonderful when we're done. I'm going to step out so you can get undressed. We'll start face down, make yourself comfortable under the sheet. The table warmer is on low, is that okay?" the massage therapist asked.

"Sure, that's fine." Jackie didn't know if it was okay or not but went with it.

She positioned herself on the table, overwhelmed by an awkward and vulnerable wave of anxiety as she lay naked under the thin sheet, waiting for this experience to begin. How she had gone through her adult life without a massage was preposterous. They weren't en vogue most of her life, except as an indulgence. Now it seemed spas were everywhere. Mostly, she blamed it on her lifestyle. Work, work, work…what was it all for now?

Taking a deep slow breath, hoping to force herself to relax, concern grew that her body had been in such a heightened mode for so long that she couldn't power down. Intensity had been her most common emotion for decades. Maybe she was broken, permanently.

"Are you ready?" A knock came at the door.

"Yes," Jackie mumbled against the face rest. She was ready and deserved to unwind, jumping at the initial touch of hands on her back that were now smoothing her neck and shoulders. Perhaps after a little deprogramming, it would become routine.

"Let me know if the pressure is too much," the massage therapist said.

"It's perfect right now," she mumbled.

Her thoughts faded away as the calming voice and soothing music swam over her, forcing the tension to subside. The warm oil on experienced hands gliding and pressing into the deep knots in her shoulder blades coaxed her to relinquish her senses. It had been a long time since she'd felt another person's touch. Now these magic hands were urging and pulling her into a tranquil place long forgotten. She transcended into a new home of relaxation, with thoughts of Elvis floating past as she drifted into a light state between sleep and awake. It was an experience she knew she would need again soon.

Chapter 5
The Adventure Begins

Jackie tapped her foot impatiently as the passenger in front of her in the aisle struggled with hoisting her luggage overhead, squishing and squeezing bags into spaces that weren't quite large enough to accommodate overly packed carry-ons. Jackie had checked her bag at the ticket counter and was done thinking about it other than how much she packed for this short trip. Her shopping jaunt had been a grand success. Although her wardrobe had taken a significant upgrade from business suits, she was beginning to second guess some of the more risqué tops Maggie had convinced her to buy.

A new energy to try out life was slowly reviving her. It was as if she had not been alive for decades, caught in a drab beige, buttoned-up world, and now she was stripping it all away. She touched her newly styled hair, the fresh modern cut made her feel lighter. The color was sublime, deep caramel with a few blonde highlights wisped in between. It made her green eyes pop; the stylist had said. She felt ten years younger, coifed and primped, as in her younger days. The new jeans with the built-in stomach flattening fabric looked good and gave her a bit of confidence. She had at least been able to stay somewhat thin over the years, mostly because she never had time for lunch and ate dinner on the run, but the widening-middle was a constant battle. Menopause was a bitch.

"Excuse me," Jackie said to a tall, slender man who was straightening his jacket, just so, but blocking the aisle so nobody could pass.

"I'm so sorry," he said in the most lyrical voice, a slight southern drawl notable.

Meeting his gaze, she noticed his face, his shoulders, his Prada slacks, and everything else about him, which was put together in perfect synchrony. Staring at a man and letting it impact her was something she'd not allowed herself to do in the many years since her divorce, instead securely adopting bitterness to protect her against the evil of the world. It was better that way. Bob had always wanted a pair of Prada slacks. That was an indulgence she never obliged. He would have destroyed their elegance. A slight satisfaction came over her watching the handsome man wear them so well, stirring something within her.

"It's fine," Jackie stammered. "I'll try to squeeze by."

She attempted to pass as the man moved to step into the area in front of his seat. They collided briefly, face-to-face. Jackie felt the warmth of the handsome man's body pressed against her. His smile was seductive. She froze momentarily, smiled awkwardly, then quickly gathered herself, thrust her shoulders back and moved past without a word. She glanced back at the man, feeling the flush of embarrassment rise in her cheeks. The man smiled enticingly, his lip curling slightly on the left side, very Elvis-like. The image catapulted her back to her mission, Elvis; he was her target for this week.

Turning back around, she felt her smile grow, absent-mindedly she touched her lips as she made her way to her seat. As soon as she was safely buckled, she immersed herself in the Elvis book she bought for the trip and put the real man three rows up out of her thoughts. Well, almost out of her thoughts, rising slightly to peer over the seat one last time, noting the attractive gray streaks visible on the top of his head, bringing another smile before she returned to her book and got back on track.

"We'll be landing in Memphis in twenty minutes."

The announcement by the pilot jolted Jackie from the dream state she'd sunken into, having dozed off twenty minutes after the flight began. She never napped, but this sleep had been easy to sink into, not even recalling falling asleep. It simply grabbed her and took her under. The last memory she recalled were her eyes feeling heavy, thinking about how good those Prada slacks looked. Her next awareness was waking to the flight attendant asking for empty cups as she oriented herself to where she was and struggling to decide if this relaxation was good or bad. It appeared to be skewing her perception of the reality of who she had been all these years and the new life she was embarking on. It felt enticing and pleasant, yet simultaneously artificial and unreal.

Exiting the plane, she went into autopilot and made her way to baggage claim and the car rental desk, her excitement growing as she mapped the drive to the hotel while waiting in line for her car.

"Yes, I made the reservation two days ago," Jackie argued with the car rental attendant.

"I don't have the reservation. I'm sorry. Let's make a new one," the attendant offered.

Jackie sighed impatiently. "Let me check my email. I have a confirmation number." She pulled her phone out and showed it to the man.

"Ma'am," the young attendant started.

Jackie bristled at the word ma'am. It stung.

The attendant continued, "You're at the wrong car rental agency. You need to go down two stations. I'm sorry." He stared at Jackie with a consoling look that said, *it's okay, it happens.*

Jackie hesitated, but couldn't say anything except, "thanks, sorry!" She turned on her heel and got away as quickly as possible, hoping nobody could see the crimson evidence of her error.

What was wrong with her? She never made mistakes. She was known for having every "t" crossed, every "i" dotted. All. The. Time. Now it was as if she had lost her ability to function. The immersion into relaxing had gone to her brain and turned it to mush. Pushing her annoyance away, she gave into her excitement and hustled to get to the Memphis Manor Hotel.

Turning off Elvis Presley Blvd., she stopped and snapped a photo of the street sign. The man had a street named after him; she had to have a picture. The images on television of a packed street when the funeral procession made its way down the thoroughfare seeped into her mind. Masses of mourners lined up for miles on that fateful day, crying, wishing it weren't true, hoping beyond hope that Elvis lived. Conspiracy theories flew about and grew wild with people saying Elvis faked his own death and was alive. If only it had been true.

Driving past the security shed on the long white stone drive to the entrance, lined perfectly with hydrangeas and ornamental grasses that appeared to be swaying in time to music, she pulled into the hotel and parked under the soaring portico at the entrance. She was in awe of being a block from the house where Elvis once lived.

She opened the massive wooden door to the hotel and was instantly greeted with rich and wonderful music. Elvis's sultry crooning of *Love Me Tender* wafted over her gently as she rolled her new suitcase to the brightly illuminated check-in desk with the oversized Elvis sign in fluorescent red lights hanging behind it. The immersive atmosphere sent a spark of pleasure through her. Thinking about the weekend ahead, she could feel her anticipation growing, she was certain this was going to be a life-changing weekend.

"Hello, I'm checking in, Jackie Sawyer," she told the young man at the desk.

"Welcome, to the Memphis Manor Hotel. You're in The King of Rock Suite. You're going to love it! It's one of my favorites," he said. The animated young man gave her details about all the amenities, the live music, the reels of Elvis movies playing at seven. "Sorry, it's already started tonight," he said with disappointment after checking the time. He handed her a map of the restaurants and bars, noting there were also peanut butter sandwiches available until nine o'clock.

"It sounds like I'll be in heaven," Jackie said, thanking him and gathering her key card and pamphlets.

"Oh, by the way, the restaurant will be closed for a private event tonight from eight until nine-thirty. We're having a memorial for a long-time hotel employee," the desk clerk whispered as he told Jackie about the sad inconvenience. "But there's a restaurant at the end of the parking lot, the Jailhouse Rock, if you turn right out of the main doors. It's fabulous, you'll love it. It's a sister property, but it's all about Elvis too."

"I'm so sorry for your loss," Jackie responded. "Thanks for letting me know. I'll give that a try." Jackie smiled and left rapidly. She couldn't wait to see her room.

The over-the-top hotel overwhelmed Jackie in the most delicious way. It was everything Elvis, everyone talking about Elvis, Elvis music everywhere. The furniture was dripping in seventies style, something Elvis would have loved, plush and opulent. Large photos adorned the walls as she headed to her room. They were of Elvis in various jumpsuits, all cut off at the neck with no face to see, only the toned body in sparkling sequins and flashy designs, V-cuts showing that flawless chest. She couldn't resist touching the photo as she waited for her elevator. Elvis was alive here.

It was late, and Jackie was starving. Quickly freshening up, she changed her clothes, exited the hotel, and walked the short distance to the Jailhouse Rock restaurant. Entering through the faux prison doors, she beamed at the theme. The employees were dressed in black and white prison uniforms, mimicking the movie costumes. Behind the bar, a replica of the dance scene from the movie made Jackie feel as if Elvis himself would soon appear. It was perfect.

She opted for a seat at the bar, making casual banter with the chatty female bartender as she perused the menu. The young bartender was bubbly and eager to strike up a conversation. Jackie relaxed into their chatter, which felt more like high school gossip with the bartender telling her about some of the regular fanatics that Jackie would most likely run into during her stay. The conversation tickled her. It was an interaction she had never really imagined herself having with anyone. Between the talk of Elvis and the drink, she felt light as air.

With her first drink almost finished and contemplating drink number two, she was taken aback when a young, gorgeous bar manager appeared behind the bar. He sported a tweed newsboy's cap, the light growth of beard adding to his captivating look. He spoke directly to Jackie.

"Hi, are you a guest at the hotel? Are you having fun?" he asked.

His haunting, gold-flecked eyes drew her in. "Yes, oh yes, it's absolutely fabulous," Jackie gushed.

"Do you have an Elvis story?" he inquired. "Nearly everyone who comes in here has an Elvis story."

Jackie thought for a second and said, "I guess my Elvis story is that I saw him in concert when I was young. Our seats were far away, so I wasn't close to him or anything, but it was an amazing concert, and I have been obsessed ever since."

What she didn't say was her other reason for loving that concert. It was the one time she saw her mother enjoy herself like she'd never seen before. It was hard to know if her mother was happy or sad. On a typical day, her mother's face revealed a simple expression with a hint of sorrow, but when she watched Elvis, her eyes lit up and her smile became real, exuding a joy rarely seen. Jackie tried not to think about her mom often, but there were times when the memories were too good to push away.

The non-stop gossip of Elvis was light and fun. Jackie relaxed into the mood, watching the bartender's expert mixology doling out

Pink Cadillacs, Hound Dogs, and Blue Hawaiians, as the bar filled with Elvis fans, most wearing Elvis t-shirts or hats. The bartender leaned on the bar on crossed arms when he was caught up, devoting his attention to Jackie.

"So, are you on vacation?" he asked.

"Yes, I always wanted to see Graceland," she told him. "What about you? Are you from Memphis?"

"No, I moved here a few months ago. I went through a divorce and felt like I needed to go somewhere to heal and start over. This felt like a good place to reinvent my life."

"I'm so sorry. Divorce is hard. I went through one myself. I wish I could have started over, but I had to push through. But I retired recently and I'm starting a new chapter." Telling him more than she planned to.

As they spoke, it dawned on her that he was the first man in a long time that had given her any attention; it felt nice, and she felt pretty, even if he was at least twenty, maybe thirty years younger. She didn't want to do the math. While they talked, an elderly woman entered the restaurant. He immediately went to her, taking the fragile woman's arm and leading her to a corner table before returning to the bar.

"That's Doreen," he explained on his return. "She's a celebrity around here. Her story is fascinating, she knew Elvis when she was a teenager, and he was just getting his start. You should meet her."

Jackie watched after him as he walked back to Doreen's table, again trying to calculate how old he was while attempting to convince herself he was not as young as she originally assessed. She scolded herself for her rampant thoughts.

It was true, her post-divorce recovery had no time to recreate her life. She simply dove in harder at work, continuing down her steady path with several budget saving tweaks. There was no about-face, though she could relate to that imbalance now as she embarked on this phase, teetering on embracing her newfound freedom or falling into a weeping puddle of regret and misery.

In her daydreams of retirement, she had seen things differently, feeling relief at reaching a milestone and patting herself on the back for a job well-done while thumbing through an imaginary stack of accomplishments. Instead, her days were filled with empty calendars and empty rooms she walked in and out of without any fanfare, no praise for her accomplishments, no requests for her wisdom, it was only her, ambling through the day taking in the décor and the quiet of her beautiful house. When the kids were little, she had longed for quiet. Now it was consuming and unnerving and reinforced that she was alone.

The biggest struggle of her divorce had been letting go of her dreams and creating new ones while placing her trust in some cosmic power that those dreams would stay in place. She had been cautious since then about invoking any dream that would cause her disappointment and instead constructed her dreams to revolve around her children and their well-being. Work was the means to that end. Now, here she was, sitting in a bar in the middle of Memphis, Tennessee, trying to conjure new dreams, and wondering who she really was and what she wanted. It was daunting.

The young bartender was motioning toward Jackie as he talked with Doreen, who had to be close to eighty but seemed energetic as she walked with the bartender to come meet Jackie.

"I hear you're an Elvis fan?" Doreen commented, greeting Jackie with a calming smile.

"I am. And I hear you're the Elvis expert," Jackie responded, returning the friendliness.

"Oh, I sure am. Let me show you some photos."

Doreen pulled her phone from her purse and began showing photo after photo. The walls of her home were covered with Elvis memorabilia. Shelves were stacked with Elvis themed gifts and a couple of gifts from Elvis himself given to her when she was a teen. Those were mailed to her, she said, probably from his PR team, but the notes were handwritten by Elvis and her prized possession. Doreen was delighted with how her home had become her own private museum dedicated to Elvis and keeping his memory alive.

"You know I met Elvis several times when I was a teenager," Doreen said before launching into a story that captivated Jackie. "I was only fifteen. I worked at the movie house on Main Street. Elvis had recently become famous and couldn't go around town anymore without a crowd coming after him, so he'd rent out the skating rink, or the theater, or the mini golf in the middle of the night, so he and his friends could have fun." Doreen's eyes danced as she told Jackie all the details of her job, the first time Elvis came into the theater, and the strict instructions employees were given by their boss to not talk to Elvis. They were told to wait on him and be courteous, but not to engage him or ask for an autograph.

"Wow, that must have been something," Jackie responded, visibly impressed.

"You can't even imagine," Doreen gushed, "that man was the most gorgeous man I've ever laid eyes on. Seeing him in the movies or on television was nothing compared to what he looked like in person. You couldn't stop looking at him. He was magnetic. I loved every second he was near, so there was no way I was going to break the rules, partly because I couldn't even manage words when he was around. His beauty left you speechless." Doreen's eyes glistened as she recounted days gone by.

"I can't even imagine." Jackie wanted to hear more.

"Although, I regret now that I never spoke to him. He was so kind. But I was a teenager, and I needed my job. Times were tough for my family back then and I loved my job because I knew working there was my best chance to see Elvis from time to time," Doreen added.

"That sounds like a once-in-a-lifetime experience that many would be envious," Jackie said sincerely.

"I regret that I never spoke to him," Doreen repeated her words.

"Well, I'm sure you did the right thing," Jackie told her, patting Doreen's hand. "You saw Elvis up close and personal, not many people were that lucky. I wish I'd been two feet away from him like you were so many times. It's incredible," Jackie reassured Doreen as they looked once more at the photos. "Thank you so much for telling me about Elvis." Jackie hugged Doreen, thanking her again for sharing her stories and her love for Elvis.

It warmed Jackie's heart talking to others who loved Elvis as much as she did. She'd found her people, she joked silently with herself. Mouthing the words "thank you" to the gorgeous bartender, who was tenderly taking Doreen's arm and leading her back to her table where dinner had been served.

Finishing her drink, Jackie went back to her hotel and up to her suite to dream a little before mapping out her journey to Tupelo, Mississippi, set for the next day. Her plan was to track Elvis's life from the beginning to the end, following his rise from poverty to stardom. It was a fact that Elvis was born with a God-given talent, but it was his own ambition that lifted him above and out of extreme poverty, taking him higher than perhaps he even imagined. There had been a cost though, Elvis had paid for stardom by sacrificing his freedom, his health, his love, and ultimately...his life.

Elvis rambled through Jackie's subconscious, seducing her into thoughtful slumber. Wishing she could have warned him of the pitfalls and sacrifices, so he could have made different choices and perhaps he'd still be alive. Maybe it was a mutual wish aimed at herself also, wishing someone would have warned her of the mistakes she would make, the pitfalls she would succumb to, and though they were eclipsed by those Elvis faced, maybe if she had known what was in store she would have made different choices. Not that she wanted to erase her children, they were her greatest love. But she couldn't help wondering how her life might have been different if she'd taken another path and made different decisions. Mostly, she wished she had known she was important too. Hopefully, there was still time to prove that to herself.

Chapter 6
Tupelo and Beyond

Jackie studied the map on her phone while she waited for her breakfast to be served. She hadn't noticed the couple who entered and sat at the table next to her, but when she looked up, she was startled by the gold sequined jacket the man wore. He was in his fifties easily, with a combover.

"Good morning," his wife said to Jackie.

"Hello," Jackie replied.

"Are you enjoying Memphis?" the woman asked, clearly wanting to engage in conversation. Her husband appeared to be lost in an Elvis magazine he was studying intensely.

"I am. I'm going to Tupelo soon though, to see where Elvis was born," she told the woman, unsure why she was engaging, but she was relaxed and loving conversation about Elvis.

"Oh, you will love that. We've been there many times. It's a sad little house that he lived in when he was young," the woman told her, practically making a tsk-tsk sound.

"Really? I knew he grew up in poverty. It's amazing how he pulled himself out of it." Jackie couldn't criticize Elvis for his unfortunate situation as a child.

"You know, they had no running water in his house, it was such a little thing they all lived in. I don't know how they managed. His poor mother tried her best, but they were evicted and had to live with relatives and moved a lot when he was young. That's why Graceland meant so much to him." The woman wanted to share all her knowledge with Jackie.

Jackie noticed the woman's tennis shoes, which appeared to be hand-painted with Elvis's face all the way around the edges.

"Sounds like you know a lot about Elvis," Jackie said.

"Oh yes, we collect records and magazines all devoted to Elvis. We travel around in our RV from town-to-town hunting Elvis collectibles." The woman smoothed her over-bleached hair out of her face.

"Really?" Jackie didn't know how to respond. "Is it hard traveling in such a little thing?" Jackie sarcastically posed.

"Oh, not really," the woman replied. Jackie's irony going over the woman's head. "You see the jacket my husband is wearing? That's an exact replica of the jacket Elvis wore in Viva Las Vegas. He has several more, but this is his favorite. We have a group of Elvis fans that are getting together tonight for a big celebration. We meet up at Graceland every year for it. It's a blast," she bragged.

"I hope you have a great time. It sounds fun," Jackie said, trying to be gracious.

"You're welcome to join us. You know, you'll hear about Elvis as a little boy today in Tupelo, what you might not hear is that he was an anxious little boy, never able to sit still, that might be what led to his insomnia, he battled it his whole life evidently," she said.

"I hadn't heard that." Jackie was becoming annoyed.

"And he went hungry, too. That poor little boy never had good nutrition. Being poor and hungry, it's no wonder he spent money helping others like he did. He was a generous man, despite his rough childhood," she added.

Jackie was glad the woman at least tried to redeem herself at the end. The woman's husband never uttered a word. Paying her bill quickly, Jackie left the restaurant, ready to get to Tupelo and away from the well-meaning fan.

The drive to Tupelo wasn't far. Jackie tried to focus on the scenery but was caught up in a daydream about what she would discover and what it had been like when Elvis was making the trip from Tupelo to Memphis in the 1940s as a thirteen-year-old with nothing except his guitar, a dream, and his parents' hope for a better life for the young boy.

She tried to push away the conversation with the woman at breakfast, but the deeper picture of the degree of poverty: no running water, his dad in prison, moving constantly, poor nutrition and hunger, was foremost in her mind. She hadn't heard many stories like that other than a general picture of poverty, but not the private details the woman disclosed. Not that anyone would have known, as the world was different back then. Private affairs were just that, private. There was no splashing every bit of your life across social media for others to offer advice or criticism. Whether too much sharing or not enough sharing is better is debatable.

The details of a dismal life were difficult for Jackie to listen to. A pain sat heavy in her heart, thinking of young Elvis and all the other children that went to bed hungry. How was it that there were still so many children in a civilized nation that were hungry? Thinking about young Elvis and those children weighed heavily on her mind.

Merge on to U.S. 45 in one mile.

The British GPS man interrupted her thoughts. She loved his enticing accent; it was a fun distraction. The quippy little voice was directing her to the exit to Main Street in Tupelo. A wave of excitement washed over her as she steered to the hardware store where Elvis received his first guitar at the age of eleven.

Arriving on Main Street, she wasn't disappointed. It was as she had imagined; one street, scattered storefronts, all modernized now, Elvis nostalgia, and a few hotels. There were no tourists. The streets were empty but adorned with musical tributes to the days when people would crowd into Tupelo to celebrate Elvis. Today was not one of those days. Elvis week had passed, and the crowds were long gone. Metal guitar structures painted with bright colors and designs were anchored to the sidewalks lining the main street, which was appropriately named Rock-n-Roll Road. All reminders that Elvis was a part of Tupelo.

The town décor included a wall mural of Elvis, an uncanny likeness and a further tribute to the man who created rock-n-roll and to his humble birthplace. Everywhere Jackie looked there were musical notes, plaques memorializing Elvis's history, and subtle tributes to the music and the man. The town square revolved around Elvis with a statue to memorialize the first concert he played in his hometown. Jackie loved it all, snapping photo after photo and texting them to Maggie.

The hardware store was a two-story, multi-colored red brick building that had stood the test of time. Large white letters were anchored across the front and under that, the name of the man who owned it, George H. Booth. Jackie's eagerness grew as she waited patiently for the crosswalk signal to turn green. The purpose of her waiting escaped her since there was no traffic on the small four lane road. Tupelo was simple, a bit desolate, but she was fine with that. It gave her space to explore without crowds.

Her mind buzzed happily as she pulled open the glass door, triggering the jingle bell, alerting the employees she had entered. Instantly, she was overtaken by the history that was on display. High two-story ceilings soared above her. The white tin ceiling had to be original. The weathered and scratched slatted wood floor was undeniably born with the building. Gifts, gadgets, photos, guitars, cut outs of everything, covered every wall, and filled every wooden shelf all the way to the top of the room. There was more to look at than Jackie could take in, and she tried to lock it all in her memory before being welcomed by a pleasant employee.

"Can we help you find anything?" he chimed eagerly.

"I'm here to see where Elvis bought his first guitar," Jackie replied, certain she was not the first person to say that, probably not even the first person today.

She scrutinized the merchandise surrounding her, mentally noting items she wanted to take a closer look at though there were too many to count. It was going to take all her resolve not to leave with a bag full of unnecessary trinkets. Fighting the urge to begin her shopping spree, she made a deal with herself, to find a few select pieces of memorabilia and that was all, limiting the number of tchotchkes coming home. She knew she was lying to herself and by the time it was all said and done, she would need an extra suitcase to get her bounty home.

"Let me give you the grand tour," he said. "Come over to this counter. As you can see, this is where the guns are sold. It's the same counter and set up as it was back in 1946."

Jackie looked at the glass counters and all the photos on the wall behind it that memorialized that day and days after when Elvis had stopped in after becoming famous.

"So, is that a photo of the guitar?" Jackie asked, pointing to a photo of a grown Elvis holding a guitar at the store years after the purchase.

"Yes, he stopped by on occasion. The story is written down as well," the clerk told her, showing her a typed-up version of the events.

"That's fascinating," Jackie said.

"Elvis's mom was markedly protective and didn't want him to have a gun, so the salesclerk working that day offered the option of a guitar. Evidently Elvis threw a little fit about it, but eventually they convinced him it would be a better birthday present than a gun," he told her the story that had obviously been told a million times over the years.

Jackie had a hard time believing Elvis threw a fit about the gun. Thankfully, Gladys was protective and bought the guitar instead. How the world might have been different if Elvis never got that guitar. The next day Elvis went to church, and the pastor taught him a few chords and the magical musical journey began.

"You see that X on the floor?" the clerk asked Jackie, pulling her thoughts back to the here and now.

"Yes, what's that?" Jackie asked.

"That's the spot where eleven-year-old Elvis stood when he bought that first guitar."

Moving to the X, she stepped on it, closed her eyes, and tried to feel what it must have been like when that young boy began a journey he could not have comprehended on that special day. As she took it all in, she imagined that fortuitous day in 1946, the time, the era, the culture. The day a spark was lit that would become a wildfire and the beginning of a music revolution. Jackie opened her eyes and stared at the other photos, overcome with loss.

"Show me more," Jackie told him, eager to learn all she could.

He grinned as he led Jackie around the store, most likely envisioning the haul of merchandise she would be buying. Jackie followed him, listening intently, soaking up everything. Gathering t-shirts, guitar pics, and other memorabilia, it was impossible to avoid thinking of Colonel Parker and the merchandising he created around Elvis. It was all there, the merch machine in action to this day. Jackie's stomach turned as she thought of how the Colonel robbed Elvis of huge amounts of money over the years. She was grateful he wouldn't be getting any of her money now.

After selecting several books to quench her curiosity, the salesclerk handed her one more, a book detailing Elvis's family and medical history, telling her it was illuminating. With her purchases complete, the clerk walked her to the door, but before she could exit, an older man, his skin browned and leathered from the Mississippi sun, entered.

"I'm sorry." Jackie stepped out of the way to let the man pass.

"Hello, Joe." The salesclerk greeted the man with a hearty handshake and turned to Jackie. "This is Joe. He's famous around here as Tupelo's self-designated Elvis expert. Ask him anything. He knows everything about Elvis." The salesclerk thanked Jackie and left to assist another customer.

"Are you having fun exploring our little town?" Joe asked.

"Yes, it's fascinating. I love hearing the history around Elvis," Jackie replied.

"You headed to Elvis's birthplace now?"

"I am. Anything else I should see while I'm here?" she asked, making polite conversation.

"As you heard, I'm Joe, and you are?"

"Jackie. Jackie Sawyer."

Joe extended his hand and took hers in his and held it, momentarily closing his eyes.

"Nice to meet you, Jackie. Are you staying in Memphis?"

"Yes, I'm headed back later this afternoon," Jackie explained, perplexed by his behavior.

Joe paused, then said, "There's a place not too many people know about, but I think you'll like it. It's a little off the beaten path. Take Highway 30 west at New Albany on the way to Memphis. You'll be headed to an old cemetery called Southern Trail. Enter it in your GPS and you'll find it. It's not that far out of the way. When you get there, you'll find the gravesite of John Mansell, who was Elvis's great-great-grandfather. It's rumored that Jesse, Elvis's stillborn twin may also be buried there, but I can't say whether that's true or not. John was the son of Morning Dove White Mansell, Elvis's great-great-great-grandmother on Gladys's side. The talk over the years is she was a medicine woman."

51

The intriguing stranger had Jackie's full attention. "I've never heard about this."

Joe continued, "Most people haven't. There's a legend surrounding Morning Dove, that she was caught between the spirit world and the earthly world and revisited the earthly world after Elvis passed. I've heard it from many tribal elders and others I've known over the years. She walked the Earth with restlessness, seeking to find something or someone. There are those that say Elvis was trapped between worlds as well and she was trying to bring him home."

"You don't really believe that Elvis is still alive, do you? That's crazy talk by wishful thinkers." Jackie scowled and took a step back.

"Oh, no, I am certain Elvis died all those years ago. But people close to him reported unusual things in the days after his death. According to some, there's a connection between the earthly world and the spiritual world that can crossover each other. I can't say that I understand it or even know what it is, but it's one of the many stories talked about consistently over the years in these parts." The elderly man squared up with Jackie and smiled.

Unable to tell if the man was serious or telling her a tall tale, she decided it was the latter. This lineage was new to Jackie, never having heard these stories. After Elvis died, talk of him faking his own death and being alive irritated her, knowing it wasn't true because she felt the profound loss when she was fifteen years old and heard the news of his death. It was real, she was certain of that. But as Joe spoke, it felt as if a small thread had been pulled and a mystery was starting to slowly unravel. She smiled as she calmed her curious thoughts.

"Well, thank you so much for the information. I'll definitely stop by the cemetery now," she said.

"You're welcome," Joe replied. "You know, I was there the day before."

"The day before?" Jackie didn't understand.

"The day before he died."

"I'm sorry, you were where?"

"At Graceland. I was there the day before he died. Never thought it'd be the last time I saw him." Joe shook his head in sorrow.

"You saw him?" Jackie wanted to know more.

"I did. Elvis and I were friends. I was young, and he taught me a lot. He'd call me for special errands from time to time."

"Oh, wow, that's really special," Jackie told him.

"Saddest day of my life." Joe's eyes grew misty as he spoke.

Jackie wanted to hear more about Elvis but wasn't sure if Joe was telling her the truth or if his memory was intact as he periodically stopped talking and stared into space.

She excused herself so she could stick to her schedule to see the house Elvis was born in, especially now that she was going to detour to the cemetery. Joe's words and the story of Morning Dove were swirling in her mind along with the thought of Elvis and his great-great-great-grandmother being trapped between worlds.

Stepping out into the sunshine, the intense Mississippi summer heat instantly swallowed her, but despite that, an unexpected chill came over her, raising goosebumps on her arm. She rubbed her arm hard to push the eerie feeling away and continued her tour.

Chapter 7
Where it Began

Jackie made her way to the home where Elvis was born, which was only a couple of blocks away, arriving in time to join a small tour group. The home was as she'd heard it described; a small, white shotgun house. Named that because if you stood at the front door and fired a shotgun, the bullet would go right through the front door and out the back door.

The house was constructed of only two rooms, one in front of the other. The front room was a bedroom with the original beautiful, hand-carved wood fireplace mantel, painstakingly sculpted by Elvis's dad, Vernon. It was lovingly placed in the one bedroom shared by the family, making for a cozy upbringing. The second room, adjacent to the bedroom, was the kitchen.

When Elvis was a child, Elvis's grandmother, Dodger, as Elvis affectionately referred to her, lived with them. Elvis's father was still serving time for the forty-dollar bad check, so it was the three of them: Gladys, Dodger, and Elvis. And it was true, as the woman at breakfast claimed, Gladys did what she could to pay the bills but fell short and, ultimately, she and little three-year-old Elvis were evicted. It was post-depression in the sleepy little town of Tupelo, Mississippi, and Jackie could only imagine the difficulty of earning a living when the entire country was struggling. It was another sad story imparted by the tour guide, who explained it all in intricate detail. Jackie fought to keep her tears at bay with each story, the next sadder than the last.

After the tour, Jackie stopped in the chapel and took in a moving musical show at the church Elvis attended as a child. It had been relocated to the property some years after his death. Jackie's throat tightened as she walked through the little church where hymns from the past with strong, stout lyrics filled the room and images of worship and exaltation played out on the walls through a movie reel from the past that clicked away. Jackie pictured little Elvis performing the hymns proudly before the congregation.

Before she left the grounds, she passed through the gift shop, having long ago lost the agreement with herself to keep her purchases under control. Her mind was still mulling over the conversation with Joe as she typed the cemetery name into her GPS to see how far it was.

"Have you ever heard about Morning Dove, Elvis's great-great-great-grandmother?" Jackie casually asked the salesclerk.

The older woman behind the counter let out a huff before she spoke. "Well, there are many rumors, but I think they're just that. Supposedly, she haunted the woods around here after Elvis died. I wouldn't give it too much thought. Did you run into Joe down at the hardware store? Sounds like he was filling your head with stories," the woman asked Jackie pointedly.

Jackie looked at the woman, who was giving a side glance to a tall, older woman that also worked at the gift shop. She'd seen that look before, one which told the story of keeping lies. Jackie had dislodged the truth from many witnesses during heated trials. She was sure she could crack the woman.

"Yes, I believe that was his name. He was quite full of colorful information. It was easy to see it was probably nonsense, and it's obvious the two of you are not taken in by old wives' tales." Jackie waved her hand to indicate she was talking about the two women, pretending to be disinterested while browsing for more items.

"It's a far-fetched story and while I may believe in another world, I'm not sure I believe in ghosts!" the older woman responded.

"Ghosts?" Jackie repeated, her interest now piqued. "You mean it could be real? It could be true?" Jackie was nearly whispering.

Stepping closer to the older woman and maintaining eye contact, she strategically sucked her into a private space so she would forget about the tall woman who was uncomfortably trying to send a signal with her pursed lips and wide eyes. But Jackie had captivated the older woman and continued to speak softly to her, reaching out to touch the woman's arm gently to keep her drawn in.

The older woman leaned in as she brushed a gray curl from her face, and matching Jackie's near whisper, told her more, "Yes, the stories are always the same. I think it might be true. But please, don't spread it around."

The woman immediately started back-peddling on the conversation, telling Jackie brusquely, "We don't want any publicity for Elvis about this. It would create a firestorm of crazies and ghost hunters. They would destroy our woods and the graveyard. Nearly forty years ago, the rumors got out, and they practically dug up the graves at the old cemetery and there was no social media back then, can you imagine what would happen now? We love Elvis here in Tupelo, we don't want people damaging his legacy or our land."

Jackie understood now why the women were so reluctant to give the story credence. "I promise I would never destroy anything about Elvis." Jackie patted the woman's arm and stepped back.

"I know you won't. Joe needs to keep his mouth shut. It's surprising that he told you about that. He usually keeps that quiet. You must have impressed him in an important way."

"Or he thought I was a gullible tourist," she said, holding up her full-to-the-brim bags as evidence.

On her way out, a young boy around four was enthusiastically purchasing "Elfis" sunglasses. He wanted to be like the "Kwing." Jackie couldn't suppress her smile; it warmed her heart that a new generation was loving Elvis and assuaged her worries of Elvis being forgotten.

Jackie primed her GPS again before heading to the old cemetery to see for herself what the hoopla was about. The mention of the word "ghost" was certainly unsettling, prompting an inner reminder that she didn't believe in such things, before finally forcing herself to brush it off as an overly dramatic tale. If there was another gift shop at the cemetery, she would know she'd been set up.

The highway was empty as the GPS guided her to the exit, delivering her onto a two-way road with considerable potholes that wove its way around through dense groves of native loblolly pine trees lining the road and stretching tall on either side. The GPS began circling, indicating a confused signal as she pressed on, not knowing exactly where she was going. She slowed the car and finally located the turnoff and a partially hidden sign worn by time with the words, Southern Trail Cemetery - one mile ahead.

The narrow road twisted its way deeper into the pines before finally emerging in front of a run-down old cemetery. Remnants of a black wrought-iron fence remained but lay on the ground, bent by years of neglect. Jackie evaluated the area surrounding the small cemetery with maybe two dozen headstones sparsely set among the rows of trees. The sun was barely able to peek through the canopy of leaves atop the trees, which only increased the darkness and sense of loss.

She parked on the deserted road and assessed her surroundings. The uneasy feeling in her heart was begging her to stay in the safety of her car and causing her to question what the hell she was doing taking a trip to Memphis, stalking the life of a man she'd never met, and now standing in the middle of an abandoned cemetery. Had she lost her mind? Jackie half-screamed as she rubbed her hands over her face, trying to make sense of how her life appeared to be taking a direction completely out of her control. She wasn't adventurous anymore. She should be back in Seattle, staring at the sound, sipping wine and eating oysters, not gallivanting across the country chasing ghosts she never knew about.

Opening the car door and climbing out with caution, viewing her surroundings again, she confirmed there was nobody in sight. With a slow exhale, she pushed away the trepidation, chalking it up to her imagination getting the best of her, feeling silly for letting herself become nervous. She stepped onto the broken sidewalk and began her pursuit of finding the grave marker for John Mansell. The uneven ground and decaying piles of debris made it hard to navigate as she walked strategically through the markers, pulling a tissue from her purse to wipe time-hardened dirt from the headstones so she could read the names.

Going from marker to marker, searching for the long-lost relative of the King was slow work. She stood and stretched, her knees aching and tired from stooping to uncover buried markers and trying to make out names on the worn stones. Sweat dripped down her back, making her consider that it was time to give up. The next marker stood deeper into the trees. It was large and sitting askew on the concrete burial stones. As she looked harder, she felt her excitement rise. She pulled her phone from her pocket to take a picture of the gravestone of John Mansell: 1828-1880.

Jackie was lost in her discovery and distracted by taking photos of the marker when she heard a familiar sound. Having lived in the dusty plains of West Texas, it was not a foreign sound but one you recognize right away as instincts kick in automatically, alerting your brain to danger. When the rattling grew louder, she froze where she stood. Without looking, she knew there was a rattlesnake nearby. Fear overtook her when the sound repeated itself. From the location of the ominous rattling, she knew the snake sat somewhere behind her, but she couldn't see if it was coiled or traveling. Looking around the best she could, her eyes came to rest on it. Unfortunately, it was perfectly coiled and ready for trouble. All she could do was hope it was far enough away that even if it struck from its protective spiral, it couldn't reach her, the calculation not giving her the slightest comfort.

The only move that made sense was to jump and get behind the headstone, ensuring the slithering beast didn't come closer and strike her. She'd never be found at the remote cemetery if it did. She would die right next to Elvis's great-great-grandfather, and nobody would know until her bones were all that was left of her. That was not how she wanted her sixty years to end. Surely, she had many more exciting years ahead of her and a new life she was beginning to explore, and to top it off, she'd spent a fortune on her spa day. All that expert work wasted; she was far from relaxed now.

She drew a tight breath, moving as slowly as possible while she tried to estimate the distance between her and the snake. Then counted down, looking at the angle to the headstone, three…two…one. Jackie leaped as far away from the snake as possible, grabbing the stone as she flew through the air, her feet not finding the ground and sending her tumbling backwards, the massive headstone rocking wildly as she hit hard. The snake, being more startled than Jackie, lurched up and slithered rapidly in the other direction. Jackie struggled to get her footing and upright herself. All she could think was if there was one snake, there was probably another. The headstone was still rocking. Jackie tried to stabilize it to keep it from falling over, but its weight was too much and it fell backwards, barely missing her hand. Fortunately, the stone didn't shatter. She could only guess that if it had, it would bring many years of bad luck. She didn't need that.

I've got to get out of here! Jackie shouted at nobody. *This is crazy. I'm going to get myself killed.*

Jackie scrambled to find her phone, which had gone flying in her daring snake escape. Digging through the pine needles on the ground, hoping not to unearth another reptile, she ran her hand along the ground at the base where the headstone had been perched, locating an object in the dirt. Sadly, it wasn't her phone. It was a round object that appeared to have been lodged under the stone; she picked it up and dusted it off. It was old, engraved, and darkened with age, a medallion of some sort. She wiped it against her new khaki pants, which were covered with dirt and grass stains, resigning herself to their destruction.

As she polished the medallion, it revealed engraving which looked like a labyrinth with an eagle etched at the top. It was difficult to tell if it was stone or petrified wood. Its weight was light, and it was hand-carved with impeccable craftsmanship. She turned it over in her hand and noted some writing, but was unable to read it without her glasses, the print practically disappearing as she extended her arm to try to make the letters come into focus. She hated not being able to see without reading glasses; it was one of the worst inconveniences.

Finally spotting her phone, she grabbed it and slid the medallion into her pocket and headed quickly to her car. The wind kicked up, the tree branches swayed and parted, the sun came darting through, shining brilliantly on Jackie. It shocked her as the darkness disappeared in an instant, shielding her eyes and peering up at the light. She thought she heard an owl screech, but that couldn't be possible. Owls are nocturnal, and it was the middle of the afternoon. As quickly as the light blasted through the treetops, the wind stopped and the darkness resumed, dropping an unsettling stillness over the area. She looked back at John Mansell's burial site, shocked to see the headstone had mysteriously righted and sat back in place. Jackie froze on the spot as she cautiously eyed the area. There was nobody in sight.

The chill returned and rose slowly, then dropped rapidly down her spine as she sprinted to her car and left the area as quickly as a sixty-year-old woman could move. She didn't want to think about what had happened. Her mind was focused solely on getting back to Memphis, to the safety of her hotel.

By the time she reached the freeway, her pulse had settled, but her mind had not. As soon as she arrived back at her hotel, she planned to take a hot bath, drink a glass of wine, possibly a bottle, and forget this craziness. She had to call Maggie!

Chapter 8
The Land of Grace - Finally

Maggie was silent for a split-second before nearly screaming, "Oh, my goodness, Jackie. You could have been bitten by that rattler." Maggie was not happy that her friend had put herself in harm's way, plus she had an irrational fear of snakes.

"Yes, but I wasn't," Jackie pointed out.

Jackie knew she had made the right decision not to call Maggie last night, considering the state she was in herself when she arrived back at the hotel. It had taken the full forty-mile drive to Memphis from the graveyard to stop shaking and convince herself what happened was real. After that, it took nearly a bottle of wine, a hot bath, a couple of Elvis movies, and finally a sleeping pill to force herself out of panic mode long enough to settle her brain and sleep. She was calm now that it was morning. Not quite the relaxing vacation she'd envisioned when she spontaneously booked her adventure.

"Please be careful. I thought you were going sightseeing, not treasure hunting. It's a good thing I didn't go. I don't want that as part of my tour when we go back there together." Maggie was mortified.

The visual image of them both running from snakes and ghosts made Jackie laugh. Maybe it was the lack of sleep, but it tickled her, and her laughter spread uncontrollably.

"What's so funny? It's not funny, Jackie, this is serious," Maggie insisted.

When Jackie continued, Maggie finally relented. The contagious laughter infected her, causing her to start laughing herself. Jackie's hysterics finally subsided as she wiped away tears the laughter brought. With her stress released and in the sober light of day, she remembered the medallion she found at the gravesite. Grabbing her purse, she fished it out of her wallet where she'd placed it for safekeeping. Being too unnerved last night to examine it or even think about it.

Holding it in her hand now brought anxious curiosity. Turning it over and over, but unable to make out the pattern or words etched on it she frantically searched her purse for her reading glasses, dumping it upside down on the bed when she couldn't easily find them, and realizing her purse was holding more items than necessary for anyone's survival. Finally spotting them on the nightstand, she exhaled and regrouped, then popped them on for a closer look at the etchings.

"How much time do you think I waste searching for my reading glasses?" she asked Maggie.

"I know, me too. I try to keep them everywhere, but I can't ever find them," Maggie added.

"Last week I had them on my head and was searching for twenty-minutes before realizing the obvious." Jackie confided, releasing a heavy sigh. Pretty soon she'd have to start wearing them on a chain around her neck and sink right into the old age persona. She didn't want to go there today and refocused on the medallion.

"I wish I'd seen that." Maggie snorted a laugh.

"It was amusing. This medallion I found is interesting," she told Maggie. "It's etched with a pattern and some text on the other side. I don't have time to research it. My VIP tour is scheduled to start in about twenty minutes. If you're late, you don't get to go."

"Well, don't be late. You don't want to miss that tour. That will be so much fun for you," Maggie said, trying to stifle a yawn. It was early in Seattle, but Maggie had been eagerly awaiting Jackie's update on the vacation, so she hadn't minded answering when the call came in before the sun was up.

"It could be an artifact of some kind, I'm not sure. I'm going to send you a photo of it. If you have time, maybe you can see if you can dig up any information on it," Jackie suggested.

"Send it to me. I'll see what I can find out. No promises though, Charlie's pretty high maintenance right now; you know how men are when they are sick or hurt. We women can still run the world when we are recovering from surgery, but men, oh my, the drama!" Maggie sighed.

"I know. What is it about them? Such babies," Jackie lightheartedly agreed. "I'm going to head out. I was going to take the shuttle, but I think I'll drive. It's right down the block."

"Okay, send pictures. And have a calm visit without any ghosts or snakes, please," Maggie urged.

"I intend to. And, sorry I called so early. But I had to tell you about this misadventure," Jackie said, assuring her friend she would be safe. She ended the call, snapped a photo of the medallion, texted it to Maggie, and headed out to enjoy her day.

"Elvis purchased Graceland in 1957 for a smidge over one hundred thousand dollars," the tour guide said. The reactions of shock rolled through the tour bus as they headed through the musical note gates at the entrance of the house.

The guide continued. "Yes, that sounds insane compared to today, but you must remember, in 1957 the average annual income was around five thousand a year for a family and for women, it was around eleven hundred. A typical home cost twelve thousand dollars, so his investment was substantial and far exceeding the norm," the guide explained.

Departing the tour bus, Jackie looked around with happy satisfaction. A woman at the airport had warned her that Graceland wasn't as grand as you would think, but to Jackie, it was exactly as she had envisioned. The house was a time trip back to her childhood in the seventies: avocado-green countertops, mustard-colored appliances, and patterned linoleum. She could feel the spirit of days past, especially as she stood and admired the Jungle Room where green shag carpet hung on the ceiling from wall to wall, the Hawaiian style furniture bringing a sense of adventure to the room. It was the perfect depiction of Elvis's humorous personality.

"Elvis's favorite spot to sit in the Jungle Room was at the far end of that long brown, mohair sofa. He liked to keep the room extremely cold." The guide pointed out the sofa and told them more details. Jackie could swear she felt his presence and sensed his black velvet smile flashing around the room as he sat back casually, enjoying the people he loved. Maybe she had lost it after all, she considered.

"The Jungle Room was also used for recording sessions later on near the end of Elvis's life when he didn't like leaving Graceland," the guide said, shuffling people down the corridor before they headed to the main living area.

Jackie took photo after photo, not wanting to forget anything, periodically texting them to Maggie to let her know she was safe and sound. Admiring the family photos, lost in her thoughts, an Elvis enthusiast cornered her.

"Have you ever been here before?" A friendly woman trying to wrangle bored kids asked Jackie.

"No, it's my first time," she told her. "How about you?" Jackie wondered why the kids were on the tour. It was a VIP tour, and they were obviously disinterested.

"Oh yes, we come every year. I just love Elvis," she replied.

"Really? Do you live in Memphis?" Jackie asked.

"No, we live in Florida. It's our annual family trip," she told Jackie, grabbing the oldest boy by the collar and pulling him to a standstill beside her, sealing the warning with a threatening look. He straightened and calmed himself.

"I love Elvis too. This is a dream come true for me to see this," Jackie told her, smiling covertly at the young boy who was eyeing her, wanting to bolt like a wild horse.

"Elvis the Pelvis," the boy added to the conversation. His mom jerked him up again, handing him over to his father, who led him away from the group.

Moving away from the family, Jackie put a little distance between herself and the tour group. She felt a little anti-social, but she wanted to stay lost in her daydream and absorb the full effect of walking around in Elvis's home; the elegance of the white carpet, the stunning white grand piano where Elvis sat and played masterfully, the stained-glass windows filtering the light and sprinkling drops of color throughout the room, the rich blue velvet drapery framing the numerous windows, and the soaring staircase leading upstairs to Elvis's bedroom, it was off-limits of course. Only select family members were allowed into Elvis's sacred bedroom.

Jackie peered up and down the stairs, her eyes coming to rest on the captivating photo of teenage Elvis at the bottom of the pristine staircase; blonde hair and bright blue eyes stared back at her. It seemed out of place, especially with the signature black hair missing. Her heart arrived at the same tortuous question that haunted her for years...how could she miss someone she never met so very much?

The tour concluded at the memorial circle where the Presley family now laid in eternal slumber: Gladys, Vernon, Elvis, Minnie, the newest graves for Lisa and Benjamin, and a marker for Jesse. Jackie thought about Joe's words; it was rumored baby Jesse was buried with John Mansell. Jackie bristled, not wanting to think about the cemetery at all, snapping more photos and taking a video. A wave of emotion came over her with the acceptance that Elvis was forever lost to the world, the certainty of that was reinforced by the evidence of that undeniable fact sitting right in front of her covered in fresh, colorful floral bouquets.

Standing beside the long stone monument that held the body of the icon she had discovered at six years old, she read the marker: Elvis Aaron Presley: January 8, 1935–August 16, 1977. Jackie well remembered the day when Elvis left this world. The sorrow never left her heart while she mourned silently for years. Perhaps she still was. She cried uncontrollable tears when her mother broke the news; it was her first real experience of loss.

The stone was engraved with a touching epitaph partly reading: He had a God-given talent that he shared with the world. Going on to say that he was admired as a great humanitarian and generous, and revolutionized music and became a living legend, then God called him home for some rest.

Battling her tears all day and now sitting at his final resting spot, those tears spilled, along with the wish that Elvis could have lived longer. She wanted to tell him how his legend persisted years past his untimely death. Bending down to take a photo, the medallion slipped from her pocket; she retrieved it quickly. She'd been so focused on the tour she hadn't had time to carefully examine it. Now she thumbed it, turning it over and over, tracing the engraving, turning it to the backside to read the words as she stooped at Elvis's grave.

A steady rain began falling, the air hung heavy and muggy over her, anchoring her to the ground. The crowds were moving rapidly to the shuttles to go back to the main tour area and get inside the museums and restaurants as the rain intensified.

"The shuttles are running double-time to the main grounds due to the rain and tours will be ceasing for the day. Please board a bus quickly," a woman walked around telling everyone, ushering them to waiting shuttles.

67

The quiet and the thinning crowds were a relief to Jackie, giving here some solitude to reflect. Putting her reading glasses on, she tried to make out the words on the medallion, reading them aloud as a clap of thunder shattered the air.

There is no death, only a change of worlds,
with some lost in between.

When the last word left her mouth, she felt herself tumble backwards from where she had been kneeling and looking at Elvis's beautiful grave marker. Dusting herself off, she sat up as the sky opened up and rain poured down. Wiping the rain from her eyes and struggling to see, Jackie looked around, but everything was different. Nothing looked the same. The gravesites were gone, they'd vanished. No people were running for cover or even present. It was where Graceland sat, yet it was stripped of everything modern. The white marble Presley Family monument was gone. All that remained was a new white wrought-iron circular fence surrounding the concrete paving where she sat in the rain.

Confused and disoriented, she wiped her eyes again as she tried to make sense of what she was seeing. A draft of wind chilled her now bare legs, her jeans from the morning replaced by a dress. A style Jackie had not seen since she was a child; white linen speckled with tiny red flowers, white bobby socks, and red Mary Jane patent-leather shoes. Jackie wondered if she hit her head when she fell back, if not, she was surely delusional.

Nothing logical could explain what was happening. She reached for her phone in her pocket, but there were no pockets and no phone. Still clutched in her hand, the medallion was warm, nearly hot to the touch, with heat still radiating from it. The circular pattern on the front was more visible and clearly revealed the shape of a snake with an eagle etched above, talons extended.

"Are you okay?" a male voice shrieked from the porch of the antebellum house.

Jackie couldn't speak. She examined her hands. They were young; the age spots there this morning gone, her nails short and manicured, painted light red. Her legs felt young again and lighter than when she bent down to take a closer look at Elvis's gravesite minutes earlier. Struggling to stand, the elder man came to her side and helped her up.

"Here, here," he said, extending his handkerchief to her to wipe her wet face. The rain began tapering to a drizzle. "My goodness, how did you get over here? Were you lost in the storm?" he inquired.

"The storm?" Jackie's confusion continued.

"Yes, young lady. Your car is in my drive. I assume you were trying to take cover in case there was a tornado. We were lucky this time. Are you okay? You seem confused. Are you hurt?" The man took Jackie's arm and guided her toward the house.

Young lady? Jackie knew the man was older, but he wasn't much older than Jackie and certainly not old enough to call her a "young lady." She looked again at her arms and legs, unbelievably she was not sixty anymore. Forcing a smile, attempting to keep the look of shock off her face, Jackie tried to mask her distress.

"Is this Graceland?" she questioned.

The man looked puzzled. "Well, I've never heard it called that. It's my home."

"What year is it?" Jackie asked as she rubbed her head.

"I think you may have hit your head when you fell. I'm a physician. Why don't I do a quick exam and make sure you're okay? You don't know what year it is?" He looked quizzically at Jackie as he pulled a small penlight from his pocket and did a quick check of her eyes.

"I'm okay," Jackie reassured the doctor, her voice sounding strange as she spoke, solidifying her notion that she was young again.

"Well, to answer your question, it's July 1956." The doctor was not convinced the young girl was as fine as she insisted. "Where is your home? Miss…"

"Jackie. Jackie Sawyer," she replied.

"I don't think you're from around here, are you? I've never seen you before and I know most people around this area," he said, his questions coming more slowly now. A look of concern sitting firmly on his face.

"No, I'm passing through. Somehow, I managed to get turned around in the storm. I may have hit my head when I fell, but I'm feeling much better, thanks." Jackie knew she wasn't all right. Nothing she saw or heard made any sense at all. How could it be 1956? All she knew was she needed to stop asking questions and pretend she was okay.

"I think you need to sit down. Where were you headed?" the doctor said.

"I'm headed to Nashville to see my aunt. I'm going to spend the month with her before I go back to school." Jackie was spinning lies as fast as she could. As a trial attorney, she had years of practice in constructing stories on the fly, now tapping into that skill.

"Can I call her for you? I'd really like for you to come inside so I can make sure you are okay," the doctor implored.

"I'm so embarrassed. Really, I'm fine, I assure you. Thank you so much for your hospitality. I should get going and back on the road."

"I wouldn't do that if I were you. There's another storm expected later tonight, and you'd get caught in it. You're welcome to stay here. Let's go check with my wife." The doctor turned to go up the front steps.

"Oh, no, thank you. I couldn't impose. I'll find a hotel in town. I have money that my aunt sent me in case I needed to stay overnight on the journey." Jackie lied more, caught up in her own tale as it grew and with every false word, her determination and anxiousness to leave multiplied.

"Very well, I understand, although you shouldn't be driving. There is a new Holiday Inn near town, just off the highway, as you head back toward Memphis," the doctor replied.

"Thank you so much," Jackie said. She dug in her purse, hoping there were car keys for the old car sitting on the gravel drive. Her modern-day rental car was nowhere in sight. And if she found the keys, she hoped the car was automatic. It had been a lifetime since she had synchronized a clutch, accelerator, and gearshift.

Easily locating the keys in what appeared to be a nearly empty purse, something new for Jackie, she quickened her steps, moving hurriedly toward the car. Waving at the doctor and shouting her thanks, she frantically tried to get inside the car and find somewhere to be alone to figure out where she was and how she was not sixty years old. How could it no longer be 2023? The pounding in her head was making it hard to think clearly.

Inserting the key into the lock, she fumbled awkwardly, finally releasing it, letting her climb inside the safety of the large interior of the Chevrolet Bel Air. The piped white leather seat stuck to her legs as she tried to smooth her damp dress and start the car. She rolled the key quickly, coaxing the loud engine to life, then slid the gear into reverse and maneuvered the car, cranking hard on the steering wheel to get it to respond. She eased the car around the drive and sped away, passing the area where the famous musical note iron gates once stood. No fencing was in sight now, just tall trees and a gravel road that ran away from the house.

She followed the road, not knowing which way she was going, trying desperately to remember the directions, but it was difficult without landmarks or houses anywhere around to keep her oriented. There were only fields of oak trees as far as she could see. After driving for a good ten minutes, she finally stopped on the shoulder and put the car in park, her hands shaking as she sat still, hoping to get her bearings. The houses in the distance had to be Memphis. How had she lost the cunning sense of direction she had half her life before GPS? Relying on her phone for directions and locations for so many years had dulled her ability to navigate.

Staring at her surroundings, she caught her reflection in the rear-view mirror and gasped. Looking again, and focusing intently, did not make it any more believable. Her eyes had to be deceiving her. She took a long hard look at herself and saw her daughter's face gawping back at her and then realized it wasn't her daughter at all; it was her own reflection from many years ago. She was a young girl again, about twenty-one, she guessed, remembering what she looked and felt like at that age.

As her head cleared and she accepted it was truly her own reflection in the mirror, Jackie was hit with a new thought, an exciting thought, a miraculous thought. It was 1956 and Elvis was alive, and he would be twenty-one years old. It was obvious from her encounter with the doctor that Elvis didn't live there, but Jackie knew he lived in Memphis, and he couldn't be far away. And if he wasn't living at Graceland, then he had to reside at his Audubon house, the first house he bought for the family.

Jackie's hands still quivered as she smoothed her damp hair, the curls starting to pop out as it dried. She had all the memories of her life already lived but was here in 1956, young again. Could this be her do-over? And if so, what about her other life and her kids? Without a doubt, she loved her kids, but what if this was the chance she had fantasized about for the past several years? A chance to re-live her life, do it all again without making foolish decisions. Jackie's thoughts tumbled.

Taking a deep breath and trying not to get ahead of the moment, she forced herself to think logically about where she was, possibly a parallel universe or a traversable wormhole or other cosmic phenomenon. Admitting to herself that her knowledge of time travel was limited. In fact, it was non-existent with the bulk of it coming from catching a few episodes of *Outlander*, some partial episodes, not even adding up to a full season, so she wasn't sure that provided much insight. Feeling crazy for even thinking about the possibility, she kept coming back to an undeniable fact: she was here, sitting on the side of the road in 1956.

Jackie knew what she needed to do, which was what she always did, the thing that had driven her life for the past thirty-plus years as an attorney, a practical analysis of the facts and situation. She was an excellent attorney because she used facts to prove her cases, then used persuasion to show juries how her facts formed the truth. She reviewed the facts.

Fact one: She was alive in 1956–fact!

Fact two: She was not sixty years old anymore. Jackie checked the mirror again to see her smooth and wrinkle-free face–fact!

Fact three: She could see her own face in the mirror without glasses–fact! She loved that fact.

Fact four: Graceland is not Elvis's home yet, it is 1956–fact!

There was only one conclusion from the facts she laid out–she had traveled back in time. It was 1956 and Elvis was alive and young and the most brilliant part of all of this was…she was too! Jackie felt a long-forgotten thrill of excitement, knowing exactly what she had to do…she had to find Elvis tonight! Maybe she really could save him.

Chapter 9
Memphis - The Search

Urging the car back into motion, driven by her new purpose and the possibility that her mission was coming closer to being a reality, she headed towards town. By whatever means she'd arrived in 1956 and for however long the stay in this new world lasted, she knew what had to be done. Saying a quick prayer that Elvis was in town and not on tour somewhere. That would be a great tragedy.

Finally finding her way back to Memphis, she spotted the large green hotel sign and went straight to the Holiday Inn. She checked her purse and took inventory, not finding any credit cards or driver's license, which was understandable since she hadn't even been born yet. She did find two hundred dollars cash, thankfully.

Also, lying in the bottom of the purse, sat a gold lipstick container. She picked it up and examined it. It was foreign to her; she hadn't worn lipstick for decades. Pulling the cap off, she turned the tube, coaxing the red wax high enough to apply it on her lips. Checking her reflection in the mirror, she traced her lips, which seemed much fuller than she remembered. The technique to apply the lipstick was still fresh in her memory, rubbing her lips together, blotting the red lipstick expertly. It had been years since red lips stared back at her in a mirror. It looked pretty, but she questioned if it was her anymore, but the longer she stared at her reflection, the more convinced she became that it was a perfect time to recreate herself.

The beauty of this new world was that it allowed her to be anyone she wanted and fix the flaws she had at twenty-one, the insecurities, the self-doubt. The wisdom gained after attending the school of life for sixty years was certainly going to serve her well. Not only was this a second chance, but an opportunity to revise pieces of life that only brought discontent.

Perhaps Maggie was right. It was time to live a little and have some fun. Grab this second chance at love, find the man that truly loved her and not make the same stupid mistake as the first time around. Look for the right ingredients and not ignore the red flags. There were no excuses to accept less than she wanted because she knew she could succeed on her own. She had proven that to herself already. It would be nice to be lucky at love, just once. She smiled at the girl in the mirror with the red lips.

Jackie checked the back seat for her suitcase but found nothing. Remembering the trunk button from her childhood (that hadn't occurred yet), she leaned over and opened the glove box and pushed the trunk release, popping it open on command. It had been a long time since she'd done that. It was her favorite thing to do as a child when she drove with her grandparents in their big Cadillac. Maybe it was silly, but there was comfort in tiny, pleasant recollections of grandparents who were full of joy and love. It was a sharp contrast to her mother's subdued and quiet personality.

She liked to think she was more like her grandfather, who "never met a stranger," at least she used to be. The past ten years weren't exactly reflective of anyone she recognized, as her exhausted by life demeanor became more like her mother, less social and somewhat withdrawn. The pop of the trunk was an excellent reminder of who she once was.

Exiting the car and lifting the heavy trunk, she found a rectangular box, her suitcase. The old design was a sharp contrast to the sleek, four-wheeled roller case she had left Seattle with a couple of days ago. Instead, it was reminiscent of her grandmother's luggage. She hoisted it out of the car and headed to check-in, not sure what would transpire when the clerk learned she had no credit card or identification.

"Welcome to the Holiday Inn," the middle-aged woman sing-songed as Jackie entered.

"Thank you," she replied, still not used to her own voice. "I'd like to get a room for a couple of nights."

"Of course. I've got a double available. That will be thirty dollars for two nights. Would you like to pay for this with cash or a check?"

"Thirty dollars? For two nights?" Jackie asked in shock.

"Yes, it's the weekend rate, so it's a little higher than weekdays." The clerk assured Jackie the price was excellent.

Jackie was in disbelief. In her world, people spent more than that on lunch. "That's perfect. I'll pay cash," she replied happily.

"Wonderful. If you'll sign the register and write your name and address, please."

"Sign the register?" Confused at first, she quickly remembered there were no computers in 1956 with every transaction done with pen and paper. Jackie wrote her address in Seattle, wondering what stood there today. It wasn't her house since it hadn't been built until the 1980s.

The clerk took out the receipt book, carefully placed the carbon paper between the sheets, and wrote Jackie a receipt for the room, ripping off the top white page and handing it to Jackie while retaining the yellow copy in the tidy little book.

She was most certainly not in 2023.

The room key hung on a plastic keyring with the room number printed on it. Jackie opened the door and plopped the suitcase on the bed, pushing the gold buttons to release the locked latches to reveal her 1956 wardrobe.

She examined the foreign contents. There were multiple color coordinated outfits with matching scarves, perfectly folded into tiny squares and stacked on top of each outfit. Jackie pulled a light-yellow scarf out and tried to remember how to affix it on her head. She'd only worn them a time or two as a child but loved watching her grandmother and mother put them on, covering their beehive hairdos, protecting them from the elements as they left the house.

Removing more items from the suitcase and laying them on the bed, she looked over the high cut polyester panties that she was sure came straight from her grandmother's dresser. *Is this what young ladies wear?* Jackie thought she might have to do some shopping. She'd never been a granny-panty girl, regardless of her mature age, and certainly not as a twenty-one-year-old. The material looked restrictive and uncomfortable. She supposed she should be relieved they were only panties and not a full-blown girdle.

Examining the bra, or the brassiere, as they were called in the fifties, the cups were not soft and flexible; they were pointy and stiff, someone could lose an eye with a little horseplay. Jackie scowled at the strangeness of the lingerie.

The last item buried in the suitcase was a large rectangular make-up bag with the basics, including make-up, a can of hairspray, a brush, and heavy moisturizing cream. She looked warily at the hairspray. *Wasn't this banned for destroying the ozone?* She studied the ingredients, none of which she could pronounce other than water and fragrance. The moisturizing cream smelled like time gone by, nights at her grandmother's house, and fleeting days of childhood giggling as she played in her grandmother's makeup. Revisiting the long-lost memory warmed her heart. She hadn't thought about those days in decades. Sadly, she thought she would never forget the memories of her grandparents, but somehow, she'd misplaced them.

Taken under by nostalgia momentarily, Jackie brought her thoughts back to the present and refocused on the mission at hand. The first priority was to address her appearance, which now resembled and was beginning to smell like a drowned rat. She started the shower, eager to rinse off the rainwater and dirt. Catching her reflection in the bathroom mirror, it shocked her again to see the young face looking back at her. Her shorter hairstyle was more obvious as it dried.

She stood, staring at her reflection; the new body, the new face, the old soul weathered by years. She liked what she saw; it was exhilarating to feel and look young again. She stepped into the shower and stood under the hot water, trying to understand this day and what it meant. It was confusing and her logical, fact-driven brain was battling with reality. Her breath quickened as she accepted where she was and forcibly shifted her confused thoughts to the hope of finding Elvis.

Choosing the light blue pedal pushers and a coordinating top, she slipped on the white tennis shoes, grateful for practical shoes. She'd forgotten how well people dressed back in the 1950s, at least according to all the photos of the era that she had seen.

Attempting to style her hair in a fifty's hairdo, she wished for her cell phone to Google the styles, but that wasn't going to happen. Cell phones were decades away. Her only choice was to revert to her life skills before cell phones. She had managed for nearly forty years without one and knew she could do it again. She only hoped the reflex to check her phone would subside soon. It was like an itch she couldn't scratch, and it was gnawing at her a little more than she wanted to admit. Maybe that was a sign she spent too much time on her phone, although lately there had been few calls received or made.

Jackie padded down the hall and down the stairs, her energy finding new life as she began her quest to meet Elvis. There were two days until the flight back to Seattle. Those two days had to be productive. She hopped in the car and steered towards downtown, making sure to ask for directions from the hotel clerk, not trusting her directional instincts had been restored yet.

The day was winding down as it neared six p.m., but the summer sun was still high. Unsure if Memphis was safe or not at night, she was glad it would be light for a while. She needed to get her bearings before nightfall. The era she found herself in was far different from what she knew, having been born in 1962. There were cultural issues she recalled from her childhood; the civil unrest and clashes talked about by the adults with caution and fear permeating conversations when discussions of race riots arose, but she hadn't really understood the impact at that time as a child, only a general sense of violence. Now, it was 1956, twelve years before Martin Luther King, Jr. would be assassinated. In fact, he'd only started his cultural movement for race equality the year before, in 1955. Jackie cautioned her younger self to be smart and observant.

As she drove into town, she spotted the Main Street Theater. She knew from her conversation with Doreen that it was a place Elvis frequented. She pulled the large car along the curb, parked, and stared at the storefronts lining the street. People strolled along the sidewalks, men in suits, women in dresses with stylish matching hats, and children smartly dressed and in lockstep with their parents. With a twinge of envy, she watched families walk hand-in-hand.

Reaching in her purse, she retrieved the lipstick and adjusted her mirror to apply it. When she finished and looked up, she saw a police car next to a beautiful new white Cadillac. The officer stood next to the car, pulled a ticket book from his pocket, and began writing. Jackie's mind was clicking to action. She'd seen this image before, a photo perhaps, maybe YouTube, it was a scene that had already happened playing out again. Jackie racked her brain. A white Cadillac, could that be?

The door to the barbershop opened and a tall, young man walked out and began talking to the police officer. Jackie grabbed her purse, locked the car, and hurriedly stepped onto the sidewalk and moved toward the Cadillac. Her heart lurched as she got closer and could see clearly who the young man getting the ticket was. She recognized the telltale hair instantly; it was none other than Elvis…Elvis Presley. Jackie froze where she stood.

She couldn't stop staring as Elvis joked easily with the policeman. She drank him in as she watched them both smiling and chatting like they were old friends. Jackie was close enough to hear speaking but couldn't quite make out all the words. What she could hear was a silky voice dripping with a smooth southern drawl. It was familiar and enticing.

"Yes, sir, I understand," Elvis politely said to the officer.

Jackie took in every detail as she inched closer. The most obvious thing she noticed was how sharp he looked in black trousers, a white button-down short-sleeve shirt, with the sleeves rolled into a cuff, and his muscular arms appearing deeply tanned next to the crisp white shirt. Jackie felt her knees weaken. She'd never gone weak-in-the-knees over a man in her life. Taking a deep steadying breath, she continued watching the King of Rock-n-Roll get a parking ticket.

The reality rolled over her unexpectedly, sparking uncertainty and a nervous flutter in her stomach, something she'd only experienced in court, never from looking at a gorgeous man. After years of admiring him and knowing his entire life story, his personality, and what a stellar man he tried to be, she should feel comforted, and yet, as she looked at the handsome star, a jittery feeling she couldn't fight ran through her. All she could do was gawk and continue observing him take the ticket and chat jovially with the officer. Then he opened the car door, and the officer walked away.

Jackie stood motionless, gazing at him. The boldness she imagined in her head hours earlier had evaporated. Elvis started to climb into the car but stood back up and turned to look over his shoulder, spotting Jackie staring at him. He raised his hand and gave a wave and flashed a killer smile her way, then the King got back in his shiny car and drove away.

A solid minute passed after watching him drive off before Jackie moved. With trembling hands, she concluded this day had more excitement than she'd felt in many years. A sway of faintness and an ache in her stomach confirmed she needed food and a quiet place to sit and calm herself. She had come all the way to Memphis to visit the life of a dead man, now somehow finding herself in his world was making her dig deep for the gumption to meet the idyllic man who was very much alive and somehow, she had to warn him of the downfalls he would face. She walked toward the theater and found a little hole-in-the-wall diner, a perfect spot to figure out this alternate existence and make a new plan.

Chapter 10
Best Laid Plans

Jackie slid into a booth next to the window. She wanted to watch the town and secretly hoped Elvis would drive back down the street. That's what she and her friends would have done when they were young, drive up and down the main drag looking for friends, finding trouble, and learning life lessons, like the one she learned today and was struggling to process. She had never been a shy and unassuming person, even at twenty-one, and couldn't comprehend why she couldn't speak to Elvis, chalking it up to being star-struck. Or maybe she wasn't as brave as she thought she was or used to be in another life. It was overwhelming and even though she wanted to believe it was all happening; it was difficult not to feel like her mind was playing tricks on her. The fact that Elvis was alive, and she was in 1956, left her reeling.

"Honey, you, okay?" the waitress asked, breaking into Jackie's thoughts. "You look a little peaked."

"What?" Jackie faced the cheery waitress, who was dressed in a light pink uniform with her name monogrammed on the left chest that read - Betty. Jackie felt a tingle of amusement in the stereotype which fit perfectly into what she would have imagined being popular in 1956. She assumed that Betty had happily worked at the diner for a lifetime. "Sure, I'm fine. I'm starving though."

"Here's a menu, hun. Whatcha doing staring out the window so intently? Looking for anyone in particular?" Betty drawled sweetly and slowly.

"Oh, people watching, I guess," she replied weakly, a bit embarrassed by her true mission.

"If you're looking for Elvis, he left the barbershop not long ago. But if you're living right, he might be back later to watch a movie with his friends. It's Friday night and those boys usually head down here late on Friday. But don't tell anyone. We try to let him have his fun." The waitress winked at Jackie.

"Really? That would be incredible," Jackie replied without thinking. She heard the excitement in her own voice, reminding her of her present age.

The waitress took Jackie's order, tucked her pencil into her back-combed and piled high double-stacked hairdo before hurrying off to wait on another table. Jackie resumed her window watching as she formulated a plan. The theater was the most promising location to find Elvis. Even if she had to hide in the bathroom, she intended to be there tonight. It was a solidly weak plan, but she was determined to find Elvis.

The streets were becoming more crowded as the evening light faded and darkness moved in. Lights powered on, vivid colors popped to life, spurring the activity of a Friday night to unfold. Surely Elvis would be down on Main Street before the town rolled up the sidewalks.

The music grew louder as clubs opened. Beale Street sat one block away, and the town started to swing loudly. Instead of being bothered by the racket as she might have been in her usual life, the activity was intriguing and exciting, a new urge to socialize crept into her thoughts. It had been a long time since she'd felt like mingling in a crowd of strangers. She welcomed the feeling back. The day had come for her to shrug off the past life, which was sedate and calm, and let the music awaken a long-forgotten part of her that had been securely buried.

Relishing the last bite, Jackie finished her fried green tomato burger, acknowledging how much she loved southern cooking. Living in Seattle all these years, she'd pretty much eliminated those comfort foods from her diet. But now that she was twenty-one, fried food was acceptable, she told herself. She straightened a bit and looked around the diner, noticing a couple of young men glancing her way, who quickly looked away with slightly embarrassed smiles at being caught staring. Instinctively tucking a stray hair behind her ear as a pleasant warmth washed over her, amplifying that she felt svelte and young, she returned the flirtatious glances.

Sipping her soda slowly, savoring the drink and staring at the faces of people strolling the sidewalks, taking in the fashions, she was mesmerized by what she saw as the bustle of the night continued. Her eyes were drawn to a young blonde woman hurriedly crossing the street, holding her hat as she rushed. Pulling herself from her haze, Jackie stared harder, focusing on the details of the woman who looked strangely familiar. As the girl came closer, Jackie saw she couldn't be more than fifteen or sixteen, the uniform making her age more apparent. The girl was walking toward the theater before disappearing.

"Doreen?" Jackie spoke loudly as the girl reappeared, passing right by the window, unknowingly glancing quickly at Jackie but not seeing her through the tinted glass. A stressed frown was firmly fixed across the girl's face. It was Doreen, the woman she had met at the hotel. She was at least eighty when they met, but here she was, a teenager working at the theater. Summoning Betty, Jackie quickly paid her bill and darted out of the diner to go to the theater and find Doreen. Knowing someone in this alternate world made her feel strangely comforted and connected to her new life, even if Doreen had no idea who Jackie was in this day-and-age.

Jackie found the theater, opened the heavy, leaded glass door, and was instantly greeted by a rush of moviegoers exiting in mass. She made her way through the crowd, which were mostly couples holding hands, lost in each other. A group of teen boys blocked her movement inward, each flipping the other's baseball cap off and laughing in hysterics while paying no mind to Jackie, who was standing stalled before them.

"Excuse me," Jackie said to the boys.

It was a standoff until one of them whistled at Jackie and said, "Hello, beautiful." The wolf whistle from the cocky teen was immediately followed by a sharp elbow to the ribs from his friend standing next to the obnoxious boy. Jackie found no flattery in this exchange.

"Sorry, Miss. My friend has no manners." The tall boy tipped his cap and made a path for Jackie to squeeze through to escape the crowd. She thanked him and finally moved forward.

Tired of fighting the mass of people, Jackie stepped to the side and stood impatiently until the crowd cleared. She could see Doreen behind the ticket window at the top of the steps of the theater's grand lobby. Red carpet ran across the entrance, the walls behind the ticket booth were anchored with gold, velvet drapery hung high on either side, swept back with tasseled swags. Red pleated fabric soared in between the golden drapes, folded into pressed pleats, making it look like a massive stage. Two marquees hung at the entrances of each theater, lit with bright round bulbs, directing movie-goers to one of the two features. The names of the movies showing were affixed in plastic letters across the white slatted boards. Tonight's features were *The King and I* and *The Giant*.

Curved stairs ran along the right side of the entrance and disappeared at the top. A large gold braided rope with a sign in capital letters reading PRIVATE blocked the entrance. A small concession stand stood on the opposite side of the large foyer area; the familiar smell of buttery popcorn delightfully permeated the air.

She waited until the congestion finally thinned, then crossed the lobby toward the ticket booth as a man approached Doreen. Jackie was close enough to hear the man talking.

"Why haven't you locked the doors yet?" the man stammered. He slapped Doreen across the bottom and handed her the keys and told her to, "get to it!"

"You can't do that to her." Jackie instinctively inserted herself between Doreen and the man. Smelling a familiar odor of whiskey and cheap cologne brought a wave of the past to Jackie. The pungent sulfur smell rolling her stomach. Memories of Bob grabbed at her, but she forced them away. Having seen the end of her own story in that regard, it no longer caused her fear.

"I can do anything I damn well please," the man snarled at Jackie as he spoke.

"You most certainly cannot. This is a young girl, don't touch her. You are her boss, that is sexual harassment!" Jackie's blood was boiling as her legal fangs came out.

"It's okay, Miss," Doreen spoke with anxiety, trying to calm the situation.

"It is most certainly not okay, Doreen," Jackie said, forgetting where she was. She moved into full attorney mode as she turned back to the man. "Doreen can sue you and own this theater," Jackie warned.

"How did you know my name?" Doreen seemed perplexed. "He's not my boss exactly," Doreen said. "He's my boss's brother, passing through and learning the business."

Jackie realized her mistake using Doreen's name but gave it no acknowledgment, hoping she could glaze over it, returning her attention to standing her ground with the drunk man. She looked back at Doreen, who was hurriedly locking the front doors to the theater.

"I don't care who he is. He can't treat you that way, Doreen. It's not right!" Jackie faced the man again.

He was approaching her, his face bright red with anger. "Who in the hell do you think you are? You don't get to come in here and tell me what I can do."

"For your information, there are laws regarding this kind of behavior," Jackie insisted. She wasn't certain what the laws were in 1956. Most likely there were no protections from this behavior, but she wasn't relenting.

"Ha!" The man snorted. "There are no laws saying I can't pop that gal on the behind to get her to do her job. I've done it before, and I'll do it again."

"She's a minor," Jackie said.

"Well, miss smarty-pants, she's fifteen, the age of consent in Tennessee is fourteen. This country really messed up when they gave you women the right to vote. Stay in your place, young lady, or you'll learn the hard way," he slurred, weaving back and forth.

There was no fear of this man. She'd faced worse plenty of times. A fierce fighter was what she trained to be for the past thirty-five years, but she had no knowledge about laws in 1956 protecting women from workplace harassment. Feeling a bit out of her element, she knew that without missing a beat she could revert to her "fake it until you make it" self she used to build her career in the early years.

"Yes, consent being the key word. She did not consent and there are laws. I'm a lawyer. I know what protections employees have against this type of harassment. And as far as the right to vote, you have the State of Tennessee to thank for passing the 19th Amendment in 1920 and being the thirty-sixth state to do so, thus ratifying the Constitution." Jackie could tell by the perplexed look on the man's pudgy face that he had no clue what she was talking about. Little did he know she'd aced Constitutional Law and taught a class on it a few years ago.

The drunken man made no verbal retort. Instead, he launched into action, coming upon Jackie faster than she expected. She stepped back to avoid being hit, when out of nowhere, a big burly man appeared and grabbed the drunk man by the shoulders with both hands and pulled him away from Jackie. Her ankle rolled as she stumbled backwards, feeling herself falling for the second time today. But this time she didn't hit the ground, instead strong arms wrapped around her and steadied her.

"Whoa, there, honey! Careful, did he hurt you?" A melodic southern drawl fell warmly on Jackie's ears. The powerful arms using great care to right her until she was stable. Jackie's ankle pulsed with pain, which eased substantially as she looked into the most crystal-clear blue eyes, the unmistakable eyes of Elvis Presley. This time Jackie was not going to be silent.

"Thank you. No, he didn't hurt me. I twisted my ankle, that's all. He slapped Doreen across the rear-end and it made me furious. Nobody should behave like that." Jackie's voice was stern and serious.

"You're right. You okay, Doreen?" Elvis turned to check on the young girl.

"How do you know my name?" Doreen was flustered.

Elvis chuckled, his entourage smiled coyly, obviously used to the effect Elvis had on all women, young or old. Jackie put weight on her foot and winced. She attempted to hide her reaction to the pain, but it didn't escape the attentive singer's notice.

Elvis gripped Jackie's arm and braced her. "Hold on there, honey, you aren't going anywhere on that ankle. I can see it's already swelling. You need to get off it. How about watching a movie with me and the boys and give it a little time to settle down?"

"It's nothing, really. Some ice might help," Jackie protested meekly, but nobody seemed to be listening.

Elvis didn't argue the point, instead he scooped her up and headed to the stairs. Jackie instinctively wrapped her arms around the gorgeous man and let him whisk her away, making no effort to insist on being independent. She wanted to be rescued for the first time in many years, even if it was only for a moment.

He looked at her, turned toward Doreen and said, "Would you be a sweetheart and bring a bag of ice to the viewing room for me? It seems Miss...?" Elvis paused, waiting for a name.

"Jackie, Jackie Sawyer," she replied, trying not to stammer as his strong arms held her tightly, wondering if he could feel the rise of heat from her throat to her forehead.

"Miss Jackie needs some ice for her ankle," Elvis said, his smile widening, his lip raising slightly at the corner.

Jackie couldn't stop staring. "Thank you," she said.

"Didn't I see you earlier today, on the street?" Elvis asked as he continued up the stairs with Jackie in his arms.

So much for not being recognized. She nodded and quipped, "Yes, I believe you were getting a parking ticket."

Elvis grinned, entrancing Jackie as she stared into his steely eyes. The grown-up Doreen was right when she said Elvis was the most handsome man she had ever seen in her life. It was undeniable. Not only were his looks captivating, he appeared wiser than any twenty-one-year-old boy she'd ever met in her actual life. His chiseled features and sultry smile would make anyone fall hard. She smiled back at him, feeling a burst of electricity rise between them.

He stopped on the landing and stared at her. For a heart-stopping second, she thought he might kiss her, but he turned and continued up the stairs and followed his boys into a private viewing room with three rows of red velveteen theater seats. Seats, she would later learn, that Elvis purchased for the owner of the theater as a thank you for letting him and his boys use the viewing room to watch movies.

Elvis lowered Jackie gently into a seat, kneeling and taking her foot in his hand. He untied her shoe and placed her swelling foot on the wooden handle of the seat in front of her. It was a simple but sensuous act, which set Jackie's skin alight.

"There you go, honey. You sit back and relax and let your foot rest. We'll have you dancing the Jailhouse Rock again in no time," he teased.

"I'll need a partner," she replied boldly, feeling spellbound.

"I'm sure that can be arranged." He flashed a wicked smile. "I'm sorry, we haven't met officially. I'm Elvis Presley," he introduced himself, as if she didn't know who he was.

"I know. Everyone knows who you are." Jackie grinned.

He responded humbly, "Even so, manners are important, and a proper introduction is only polite."

She continued to be mesmerized, unable to look away at his dazzling blue eyes peeking through dark, thick lashes. Fortunately, Doreen arrived with the ice and broke her lock on the hypnotic expression that was pulling her under, trapping her in his spell.

"Thank you, Doreen."

He stood to take the ice and turned to face Doreen, partially blocking Jackie's view, but she could see enough to watch him pull a wad of money from his pocket and squeeze it into Doreen's hand. She could barely hear what he said to her, but the gist of it was she didn't deserve to be treated badly. Doreen didn't say anything other than a hushed "thank you," her eyes wide with adoration and gratitude.

Elvis took the seat beside Jackie, the lights dimmed, and the projector whirred to life.

"Have you ever seen this movie?" he whispered.

"No, I haven't," she replied, even though she had seen it as recently as last week on the classic movie channel.

The film began flipping around the large metal wheels. Elvis slid his hand over Jackie's as images of a Texas ranch and James Dean's name appeared across the wide screen. *The Giant* began.

"It's going to win awards," Elvis leaned close to Jackie to say.

A budding surge of happiness pulsed through her as she sat next to Elvis. She'd never known a man who exuded such strong masculinity in such a casual and modest way. She watched his fingers that were wrapped around hers. Even his hands were beautiful. Sensing he knew she was focused on him instead of the movie, he squeezed her hand gently, signaling he was thinking about her too.

Jackie thought this must be what heaven felt like. A warm feeling of contentment smothered her, making her pause to notice the smallest details about the night and embrace this moment that had her heart fluttering and her pulse quickening. It was the missing piece she'd been searching for.

It was impossible not to embrace the wonderful and natural feelings she thought lost to her: feeling attractive, getting attention, someone holding your hand. She didn't want it to end, as images overtook her of it being ripped away in a flash like it started. And reluctantly, she entertained the idea that she might never be able to return to her real life in 2023, losing the people she loved and the life she created. The next thought surprised her more…*would that be so terrible?* Guilt washed over her for even considering the idea. If she didn't return, what would happen to the people she left behind…*could they be erased?*

She turned to look at Elvis and was met with seductive, focused eyes, deepening her emotions, and removing any space between them. He leaned in and gently kissed her. His smile followed, as did hers. It was a simple, light kiss with the promise of more to come in time. It left her wanting to know everything real about this man, not the compilations from friends and former girlfriends, but the truth; what he thought, felt, liked, and dreamed. He focused on the movie while she tried to absorb this new reality that was making her head spin…and as cliché as it sounded…it felt as if it was meant to be.

As the doctor warned, a near torrential rain was slamming the town. Elvis whisked Jackie out of the theater to his waiting car at the back of the building. The theater owner's drunk brother had spilled the beans that Elvis had rented the theater. A crowd gathered out front like turkeys with no sense to get out of the rain, waiting for the hip slinging singer to emerge. But he wouldn't emerge tonight, something he would have normally done for his fans. He had to perform the next night, and standing in the rain would not be good for his voice. The theater owner apologized profusely to Elvis for the breach, and Elvis graciously assured him he understood and, not to worry.

Elvis carried Jackie to his long black car, her ankle still a bit swollen. He didn't want her to take any chances with the rain, even though she insisted she was fine and the car was only a few yards away. It was a meek protest on her part, not wanting to leave Elvis.

"How's the ankle feeling?" Elvis asked as he shut the car door.

"It's much better. My car is on Main Street if you want to drop me there," Jackie offered.

"We're all going back to my house. Do you want to join us? Where are you staying?" he asked.

It was past midnight and normally she would have been ready for bed, but she didn't feel sleepy, instead she was energized by the whirlwind that had scooped her up.

"I would love to join you. I'm staying at the Holiday Inn."

"Wonderful, it's settled then. I'll drop you off later," he told her.

"If you're sure you don't mind," she smiled.

He squeezed her hand.

"James Dean is a great actor, don't you think?" Elvis asked, putting his arm around her shoulder, pulling her closer.

"Yes, he is. You're going to be a great actor too," she told him.

"I'm excited, but nervous. I want to be seen as a serious actor like James Dean," he confided.

Jackie watched Elvis. His knee bounced up and down as he stared out the window. She wondered where his thoughts were. His life was changing rapidly, with so many new things happening all at once.

"I predict you'll make many movies," Jackie said.

In her mind, she told him there would be exactly thirty-one movies and the Colonel would trap him into the contracts. She bit her lip, resisting the urge to tell him everything.

His eyes met hers. "I hope so. I don't want to disappoint my fans."

"You won't," she reassured him.

As they talked about the movie and James Dean, Jackie also wanted to tell him about his gut-wrenching love scene performance at the end of King Creole, when he and Ronnie were trying to escape Maxie Fields. It was moving and Elvis had revealed his acting chops, solidifying for her that he could have been a serious actor. She blamed the Colonel for killing Elvis's dream.

"So, where are you from?" Elvis asked.

"I'm from Dallas, but I live in Seattle now. I'm on my way to visit relatives in Nashville," she partly lied.

"I've played several times in Dallas, haven't made it to the west coast yet, but I will soon. I head to LA in a week or two. They haven't pinned down the schedule."

It was hard to sit next to him and not tell him how he would be betrayed by the studios and his slimy manager. What if she altered everything? She tried to ease her frustration by looking out the window as they passed street after street, watching large puddles forming in the gutters.

Needing a diversion from all the thoughts of Elvis's career racing through her mind, she said, "I love real thunderstorms, don't you?" Although it rained a lot in Seattle, there was nothing like a strong, southern thunder and lightning storm and the fresh, crisp air that followed when it bellowed its way across the countryside.

"As long as it clears up by tomorrow, I don't want the concert canceled. We're raising money for the children's hospital," he replied.

As his thigh pressed against hers and his shoulder came across her chest when he leaned over to look out the window at the rain, his cheek next to hers, she realized she'd stop breathing. His fresh scent triggered a need deep inside her to touch him. Out of self-preservation, she avoided meeting his seductive eyes, mostly because she desperately wanted to kiss him and never stop. She tried to calm herself and continued staring at the rain. When he readjusted and sat up, she met his eyes. Shockwaves trembled through her stomach as she fell into the blue pools locked on her. Surging rapidly, then dropping hard into disappointment as her mind took over, questioning why he hadn't kissed her again.

"I bet it will stop by tomorrow. I'll think positive thoughts." Pulling herself together, meekly offering a smile.

Elvis grinned, then turned his attention to his driver, joking and talking about life, sharing details about California and his upcoming movie deal. Excitement filled the car, his laugh sultry and animated. Feeling glad she had held her tongue about the truth, for as much as she wanted to tell him what was coming, she couldn't destroy his happiness. She gripped his hand tighter. Relaxing her muscles, she sat back, forcing herself to dismiss her pressing anxiety and enjoy this new freedom and the new Jackie living in 1956, sitting next to Elvis Presley in his car, with her hand in his, driving to his house.

Chapter 11
Falling Hard

Elvis's house on Audubon was lovely and modest. It reminded Jackie of the house in Texas where she grew up. A house that had not yet been built for a life that had not yet begun. Regardless, it felt like home with its brick front entrance, white siding, and the wrap-around porch with enough space for a few rocking chairs, allowing a friendly hello to the neighbors strolling in the evenings.

"Are there always this many fans waiting for you?" she asked, as they drove up to people lined up outside the brick wall near the street.

"Yes, most days. I hate that they're standing in the rain tonight. I'll send one of the boys out with some gifts and tell them I've gone to bed. They'll go home eventually," he said.

Elvis waved at the fans as they pulled into the long drive and went straight to the back for safety and privacy. Jackie could hear the screams continuing out front as she stepped out of the car.

"The neighbors won't be happy in the morning," he said casually. "Are you okay to walk?" He took her hand.

"It's feeling better, thank you. I think your celebrity status may have outgrown this neighborhood," she offered.

"I know. I've been looking for a new house with more privacy," he told her.

Jackie smiled to herself, knowing the perfect home for him.

He led her to the house. The comfortable feel of his hand in hers made her smile turn outward. His boys were already inside engaged in typical horseplay when they entered. Elvis joined in enthusiastically, his eyes finding her periodically as she sat on the plush, curved, blue velvet sofa, still trying to nurse her ankle without anyone noticing.

When the chaos subsided, Elvis settled at the grand piano and began playing, causing Jackie's breath to catch as she listened to each note, drawing her further into the world she'd so pleasantly and unexpectantly landed. All of it brought her emotions to life as Elvis slid his hands over the keys with expertise. The boys gathered round, something Jackie was sure was a regular routine.

He began singing in a low and light, unassuming tone. The voice of an angel in Jackie's view, the vibrato smooth and silky. Hearing it live made Jackie realize the recordings never truly captured the perfection of Elvis's voice. It exceeded Jackie's imagination; it was a voice that made you fall in love.

Gladys appeared from the kitchen with a tray of food for the boys, smiling sweetly, which Jackie knew her own mother never would have done, particularly at one in the morning and with a house full of raucous boys and one girl dragged in like a stray cat. It did not appear to faze Gladys in the least. Jackie got to her feet immediately to assist with the tray and introduce herself, but before she could move to help, Elvis rose and took the tray from his mother and kissed her on the cheek.

"Thank you, Momma. You're the best," Elvis said. "This is Jackie Sawyer. She's traveling to Nashville. I met her at the theater where she was saving a young girl and injured her ankle. She'll be around for a while, I hope." Elvis gave a side glance to Jackie, accompanied by a grin that nobody could refuse.

"Pleasure to meet you, Mrs. Presley." Jackie extended her hand.

Gladys sized her up and shook her hand with a forced smile. "Welcome to our home. Are you hurt?" Gladys asked.

"Just a bit of a twisted ankle. It's feeling much better now thanks to your son." Jackie tried not to gush over Elvis.

No doubt Gladys was used to it. Pride sat on her face, hearing the compliment of her adored son. Jackie knew the look. She recalled having the same glow many times directed at her own children and their plentiful accomplishments. Jackie had been blessed with children who were driven and successful. Perhaps her own example of hard work hadn't been the curse Jackie attributed to her career. She always tried to be available emotionally to her children, but she still feared she had fallen short, especially with Toby.

Even though Toby was successful in his career, like Elvis, he tended to have many short-lived relationships with women who always had some disqualifying flaw which eliminated them from consideration in Toby's mind. Jackie knew her son had unrealistic expectations for the women he dated, and she suspected it was a defense mechanism to keep from getting hurt, but Jackie also knew her son was still young, only twenty-seven, and still figuring out who he was in this complicated world.

"Is it like this all the time?" Jackie tried to make conversation with Gladys.

"Oh, yes. They have a lot of energy. But it's fun and Elvis is happy. They'll settle down soon enough," Gladys said, standing to clear empty cups.

Watching Elvis, she couldn't help but think of Toby and how he would have been right in the middle of the group of boys across the room. The thought shot arrows through Jackie's heart, making her feel much older than Elvis. And for a quick moment she saw him only as a twenty-one-year-old young man, not someone who was taking on the role of a person who should be much older to manage the journey he had embarked. He was the family provider, a performer, an artist, a heartthrob, an icon–The King…the weight of success sat squarely on his shoulders.

In some respects, it was similar to the responsibility she carried for her own family and her law firm, but clearly at a much lesser degree. Nobody swarmed her when she went to the grocery store, her name wasn't splashed across the news, she had never been stalked, she didn't have to close theaters to see a movie, not that she'd been to a movie for many years until tonight, but that was beside the point. Her saving grace for managing the responsibility was the benefit of age and maturity when she went down her path to achieve her life plan.

"I overheard you tell that drunk at the theater that you're a lawyer. Is that true?" Elvis said, as he plopped on the sofa next to her.

"I'm in law school, not quite finished, only one more year and then I'll take the bar and be a lawyer." Jackie wasn't sure what to say, digging in deeper to cover her blunder. She was only twenty-one in this reality where women lawyers were uncommon, so her story needed to be believable as her lies continued, something she didn't relish doing personally. Honesty was the part of herself she cherished most, but the ramifications were too unknown and possibly attached to far-reaching consequences.

"Did you always want to be a lawyer?" he asked.

"I guess. I used to watch Perry Mason with my dad when I was young, and he told me I would make a good lawyer. So, it kind of stuck in my mind and my dad reinforced that plan every year, and it led me to law school," she explained.

"Hmm, I don't remember that show," Elvis remarked.

She froze, wondering when Perry Mason aired. She had never verbalized how her path started and barely remembered. Why that moment had become crystal clear as they spoke was a mystery to Jackie. Maybe nobody had ever asked.

"So, is being a lawyer something you wanted or your dad?" he posed.

"I've never really thought about it. It seemed like a good idea and my dad was right. I'm a good lawyer, or I will be." Jackie pondered if her path was predestined. She had idolized her dad. He took care of them and was a kind man. She never wanted to disappoint him.

"What kind of law do you plan on practicing?" Elvis was curious.

"I originally thought I wanted to be a corporate lawyer, but I like litigation. I want to help people fight against corporations," she admitted.

"Fighting the man," Elvis joked.

Jackie smiled. "Yes, something like that."

The altruistic version of being an attorney was the catalyst that drove her trajectory as a starry-eyed college kid with no concept of the reality of what being a lawyer meant, or how it would morph and take over her life. There had been other dreams in her mind as well, like being a mother and raising children, a white picket fence, and baking cookies, all firmly implanted in that vision, but over time and out of necessity, those imaginings slipped by the wayside.

"Did you always want to be a famous singer?" she asked.

He grinned. "Yes, I started singing when I was a little kid. I've dreamed about it all my life. I think people sometimes think I came from obscurity and overnight became famous. Truth is, I've worked tirelessly at this for several years. I got a lucky break, but now it feels like my destiny."

"I can't disagree. Please don't let it change your dreams," she cautioned.

She wondered if the same thing happened to Elvis, the life and career superseding the dreams. Whatever it might be for him, she admired Elvis, a twenty-one-year-old kid handling a huge, enormous, over-the-top life.

"I hope you'll stay for Elvis's benefit concert tomorrow night," Gladys remarked.

Jackie looked to Elvis for his reaction. He hid a smile and looked down. She replied, "Certainly, I would love to, thank you. I would be thrilled to see Elvis perform. He's so talented." Jackie knew she had lost the battle within herself not to gush over Elvis. She'd morphed into full fan-girl mode.

Laughing, he told her, "Yes, tomorrow will be fun. So, we better get you to the hotel and I'd better try to sleep some. I've got a fitting at noon, but I'd love to take you for a picnic tomorrow afternoon, if you'd like to go. The concert isn't until seven, so we'd have some time together. I don't know how long you plan to be in town." Elvis stood, helping Jackie from the couch.

"I'd love that. I'm not sure how long I'm staying, but at least through the weekend," Jackie admitted, having no idea whether her time in this dimension was limited or infinite.

As he took her hand, her heart was beating out of her chest. She was certain he could hear it. It had been a long time since she felt her heart wanting to soar with happiness.

"We can figure that out later, after our date," Elvis confirmed with a wink.

Gladys smiled, but Jackie sensed a reservation behind her tight lips. Elvis ignored it, gripping Jackie's hand tightly as they left the house.

The rain had slowed to no more than a mist and the fans had finally given up and gone home. Elvis opened the car door for Jackie and tucked her safely inside, touching her face with his hand as he closed the door. He dropped in behind the wheel and off they flew to Jackie's hotel. The thought of parting from him for any amount of time bringing a small sadness to her heart.

"I'll come by and pick you up at one," Elvis told Jackie as he leaned against the car in the hotel parking lot, his arms wrapped around her waist, pulling her close to his taunt body.

Jackie relished the safety she felt. Her shoulders were more relaxed than they'd been in years as she melted into him. Fixating on his lips, she wondered why he hadn't tried to kiss her again since the theater, overanalyzing what it might mean, while also trying not to place any importance on it, fighting the twenty-one-year-old insecurity which snuck back into her self-esteem. Her emotions were receding to being young and unpredictable again, and unexpectedly, eagerly anticipating love and longing and finding it all a bit confusing and scary.

She should be able to navigate this considering she had lived an entire life, but standing with Elvis's arms around her, logical thinking lost out to want and desire. The life she had already lived felt distant, like a dream moving in and out of her memory. The longer he held her, the more it faded. She was twenty-one. There was no reason to be practical. It was time to be young and carefree...and...she wanted him.

"One will be perfect. Thanks again for such a fun evening and taking care of me. I can't wait to spend the day with you tomorrow and watch you perform. I've seen you so many times." Jackie caught her mistake, reversing course quickly, hoping he didn't notice. "I've seen you so many times in the papers and clips on television. You're incredibly talented Elvis. I hope you know that and believe how much you are loved by your fans," she clumsily explained.

Jackie wasn't sure she would get a chance to tell him more. For all she knew, she would go to sleep and wake up back in 2023. It could all be gone in a flash. Her fear rose again.

Elvis blushed. "Thank you. Thank you very much. Although there are some that don't like my style, I can't please everyone," he said. "I bet law school hasn't been an easy road."

"It's a lot of work, a lot of studying. I feel like life has passed me by and my youth is slipping away more quickly than I thought it would." Jackie was sincere. It was nice to express it to someone who wanted to listen, even if he didn't understand the reality of how much life had passed her by.

"Everything worthwhile takes a lot of work."

"You're sweet, thank you. I've never felt so connected to someone," she told him as she stared into blue eyes that she could swear saw right through her insecurities and regrets.

He stopped talking, stared at her with magical eyes and, as silence enveloped them, placed a lingering kiss on her lips, taking her thoughts to a pleasant space that she didn't know existed. When he lifted his head, he gave her a contented smile.

"My Lady Lawyer," he said with the same cadence as she'd heard him use many times in interviews and appearances when he said, *My boy, my boy—My Lady Lawyer.* Jackie played it over in her head…*My Lady Lawyer…* she grinned ear to ear.

Elvis pulled her in tighter, ran his hand along her cheek, their eyes locked, then he leaned down and kissed her again, softly and tenderly, before saying goodnight. Again, leaving Jackie wanting more.

The anticipation for the day to come and the next time she would be in his arms hung on her, setting her soul on fire. It was a slow burn; one she welcomed back and didn't want to end. Tonight would be a sleepless night, a happy sleepless night.

Chapter 12
He's A Star

Jackie was up before the sun even though Elvis wouldn't be picking her up until one. Unable to sleep more than a couple of hours with thoughts of everything crashing down on her the minute she climbed into bed, she had spun into maximum overthinking mode in expert style. Insomnia hadn't plagued her since her retirement, before that her sleeping patterns were abysmal, but last night the thoughts of where she was and what she was doing tortured her.

In the cool of the morning, Jackie decided to take a walk to Main Street to retrieve her car and hopefully quiet her thoughts. Afterwards, she changed clothes twice, contemplated going shopping, unsure what to wear to the picnic, and finally sat down to count her money and think about her plan. The two-hundred dollars in her purse would go far in this century, but without credit cards there was a finite limit to her resources.

Already having spent forty-five dollars between the hotel and dinner, five dollars for dinner and a tip felt frugal, but in a time when the average salary for a woman was around eleven-hundred dollars a year, comparatively it was not a lot. Her guess was two-hundred dollars in 1956 was equivalent to two thousand in 2023. Which in 2023 wouldn't last long with the cost of housing, food, internet, cell phone, streaming services, cable, expensive car payments and insurance, and the other monthly obligations paid without too much thought. In 1956, people lived with what they needed, not what they wanted.

Uncertainty set in as she pondered how to get back to her era. That was the big unknown, sparking questions about how she was going to survive. Did she need to get a job? What was she going to do if she ran out of money? How would she get home? Could she get home? If she couldn't get back to 2023, where would she go in this world? Her life didn't exist yet. And to top it all off, to her surprise, with each passing hour in this time period, she wasn't quite sure she wanted to go back. Her thoughts were laced with heavy guilt.

As was her habit, she decided to weigh the pros and cons.

Cons: being cut off from everyone she knew and loved, having limited resources, rebuilding a new life from age twenty-one (that was a pro also), and she had no legal identity.

Pros: being cut off from technology brought a calmness to her body. She had a chance to build a new life, create a brand-new person, and she could make thoughtful and better decisions. Among all the pros, the most obvious and most important was Elvis and love.

If only she could call Maggie.

How she had lived until her forties without a cell phone was another question she had needlessly pondered in the wee hours of the morning: No Google, no GPS, no online orders and deliveries, no immediate knowledge of the entire world. Being dropped back to the days of her youth with three television stations and a newspaper, with the bulk of the news centered around the local area, life moved slower. The pace suited her right now and brought a much-needed change from the rat race she'd been living, one with many technological luxuries which weren't all bad, but being forced to disconnect and sit in a quiet world was nourishing her soul and forcing anxieties to slip away with calmness replacing the buzz.

Until this morning, she had been so caught up in the novelty surrounding her that the long-term ramifications hadn't been forefront in her mind. Elvis was going to be launched into stardom soon and off to Hollywood, then the Army and Germany, and lots and lots of girlfriends. Unfortunately, she knew about all the other women and also knew she wouldn't fit in. Her life wouldn't even officially begin until six years into the future. Jackie rubbed her temples and lay across the bed. She revisited the double-underlined pro...this new life had Elvis. Maybe a drive to town and breakfast would do her good, but before she could move, she fell asleep.

The knock on the door startled Jackie and brought her from a deep sleep she hadn't visited in years. Maybe a twenty-one-year-old body is better designed for sleep. It felt good, but she was groggy.

"Jackie?"

She heard the familiar sensuous voice through the door. Jackie sprang from the bed. What time is it? Glancing at the clock on the nightstand, she saw it was one p.m., on the dot. She straightened her clothes and ran to check herself in the mirror.

She was a mess.

"One minute, sorry. I'm almost ready!"

Moving frantically and dropping things, she tried to brush her hair, remove the smudged mascara, and quickly reapply what was needed to make herself presentable and not a crumpled mess with bed sheet lines across her cheek. She was keeping Elvis Presley waiting outside her door, geesh, this is not how she imagined this day going. Pinching her cheeks to circulate the blood, she finally decided she looked acceptable enough to open the door. She took a deep breath to calm herself.

"Hello." She tried to sound nonchalant as she swung the door open, hoping he didn't notice how frazzled she was.

He was waiting patiently, leaning with his back against the wall, one long leg outstretched with the other crossed over, the black, short-sleeve shirt half-way unbuttoned drawing her eyes down his body. Jackie stared at his chest, wanting to move closer and run her hands over it. Stunning…was all she could think, so stunning that words escaped her.

"You look beautiful," he replied, moving toward her. "Shall we go? I've got a picnic packed. I want to take you to this private little lake not far away. I need to be back at the house by four or four-thirty so I can rehearse and get to the ballpark." He was all smiles.

Jackie beamed. "Let me grab my purse."

Elvis was driving the stunning white convertible Cadillac, sending an excited thrill pulsing through her as he opened her door. The day was cloudy, keeping the temperatures down, making it a comfortable day for a ride in a convertible next to Elvis Presley. Being windblown would be a great excuse as to why her hair was even more unkempt than it should be. A fact she was hoping he hadn't noticed. If he did, he didn't seem to care. She wasn't sure why she was still dwelling on it and feeling embarrassed.

She soaked in the day as they skirted down the freeway. Being near Elvis made everything else seem insignificant. The drive to the small lake was short. He held her hand the entire way, other than changing the station when one of his songs would begin to play.

"Why do you keep changing the station off your songs? I like hearing you sing," Jackie asked.

"You're sweet, but I hear my songs a lot and you're going to the concert tonight. I don't want you to get sick of me." He rubbed her finger with his and glanced over at her, looking for reassurance. Those gorgeous eyes couldn't possibly be seeking confirmation, she thought, but Jackie sensed it was true.

"I don't think I could ever tire of you. You're an intriguing man." She winked at him.

He laughed a hearty, easy laugh as they arrived at the lake.

106

"Oh, Elvis, it's beautiful." She took a slow breath, looking at the lake, unsure if it was real or a masterful painting by a famous artist. Perfect strokes of beauty were inserted into the exact spot necessary to catch the glint of the sun and the sparkle of the water. Jackie noticed every detail, trying to imprint it in her memory, wanting to remember this moment forever. Never wanting to forget the rows and rows of trees surrounding the perimeter of the lake, the shoreline covered with sunflowers and blue Indigos swaying in the light breeze in perfect rhythm, or Elvis standing at the water's edge picking a beautiful bouquet for her, and how her heart set afloat when she took it from his hand, and he kissed her cheek. It seared into her memory, hopefully forever.

"I'm glad you like it. It's one of my favorite spots. I usually come here alone. I've kept it private; nobody knows I come here. It's my thinking spot," he confided.

He spread the blanket under a tree and opened the wicker picnic basket, pulling out item after item.

"I don't blame you. It's an idyllic place to think or dream," Jackie agreed.

Everything had been planned perfectly: the blanket, the food, cookies for dessert, fruit, potato salad, fried chicken, plates, napkins and Elvis's favorite drink, Pepsi. Elvis fed her grapes and with each one told her a detail of his life, like how the gourmet picnic was courtesy of Dodger, his romance partner in crime.

After they ate, Elvis packed everything back in the basket, took out his Bible, and stretched out on his side. Jackie turned to her side, facing him and watching him page through the scriptures, selecting a few and asking her thoughts. Elvis touched his gold cross that hung around his neck as he spoke. The sweetness with which he approached the conversation was endearing.

"I can't think of a day that I've enjoyed more than this one with you," Jackie told him.

She rolled to her back to watch the clouds dance and design above them.

"Me either. I've never fallen so quickly for someone," he replied.

She turned her head, her eyes meeting his. Elvis put the Bible away, moving closer with intent, hovering over her before he stroked her cheek and finally kissed her with the passion she had been waiting for. It dove deep into Jackie's heart, her breath faltering, the intensity catching her off guard as she lost herself in the kiss and his embrace. It had been worth the wait.

When they finally broke apart and took a breath, it was obvious Elvis was as consumed by Jackie as she was by him. They didn't speak; she didn't want to release him or let any space come between them. Their bodies were touching, but as close as they were, it was still too far apart.

In her day, this kind of passion would've led to much more, but Elvis remained respectful. Jackie couldn't stop the thoughts running through her mind, which included wanting to make passionate love to Elvis Presley on the blanket beside the adorable painted lake. But she followed his cue, he settled and began kissing her again with less intensity. Elvis finally checked his watch; it was nearly four o'clock. He groaned.

"I hate to say this, but we have to go back so I can get ready for the show." He rolled on his back, his arm over his eyes.

Jackie thought if he could have chosen, he would have stayed there with her until the stars came out. And even though they were in the shade of a tree, it was a sticky day, and she needed a shower…a cold one, preferably. She stared at Elvis as he lay there, every part of him was perfection, his handsome jaw, his tall physique, his long muscular legs, she absorbed it all not knowing if this would be the last time she ever got to witness his beauty other than watching him in a movie years into the future. She had seen him from far away in 1976, but miles away on a stage and by the time Elvis lived those years, he would have no awareness of her as she would be only thirteen. If she left him now, the two worlds would swallow them up and he would be lost to her and she'd be a stranger to him, a child.

"Okay, we should go," she said, not wanting to ever leave his side.

Before she knew what she was doing, she touched his chest she had been eyeing all day and ran her hand down his side and down his leg. Elvis lowered his arm and moved it around her, pulling her on top of him to resume kissing, full of want, stopping only when there was no choice as time was ticking away. Elvis picked up the basket, helped Jackie stand, kissing her one last time, and hurried to the car.

Realizing they weren't far from Graceland as they headed back to town, Jackie suggested a quick detour. "Wait, turn off. Turn right on that road up there and head up about a half mile. I want to show you something. We have enough time to make this detour, please?" she begged.

Elvis smiled and kissed the back of her hand and did as she requested. "Where are we going?" he asked.

Jackie didn't know exactly what to say about the destination. Saying we're headed to your future home and you'll eventually live here with a wife and child was probably not going to fly, so she told him the bare minimum. "I found this place the other day when I got lost in a storm. It was so stunning, I wanted to show it to you. I think you'll love it."

Continuing up the road, they arrived at the circular drive leading to the front of the house. They got out and started to walk around, looking at the house and the property. Elvis was quiet, scanning the property from one end to the other. He was captivated. Jackie watched him as he soaked it up, taking in every detail of the house and the expanse of the acreage. She witnessed him fall in love with the home the same as she had, albeit in different lifetimes.

"This is the place," he said with his hands on his hips.

The doctor came out the front door and greeted them. "Well, if it isn't Jackie Sawyer. You're looking much better," he said, embracing Jackie.

"Hi Doc. I feel great, thank you. I'm sorry to stop by like this. I thought Elvis would love to see your beautiful house. Hopefully, we aren't intruding."

"Hello, Doctor. I'm Elvis Presley," he introduced himself needlessly.

The doctor's eyes were wide. "Yes, Elvis Presley. Of course, I know who you are. It's a pleasure to meet you, my boy," the doctor said, shaking his hand enthusiastically. "I'm happy to give you the tour of the house."

"Thank you," Elvis replied. "We don't have much time, and we wouldn't want to inconvenience you, showing up unannounced like this. I've got to get home soon and get ready for the show tonight. I hope you're coming?" he added.

"We were planning on it, but my wife has taken ill, but we did see you down in Tupelo not long ago. You are incredibly talented, son. Those kids were going crazy." The doctor laughed as they approached the front door.

The tour was quick, but exciting. Elvis and Jackie didn't want to intrude, especially since the doctor's wife was feeling poorly so they moved quickly through the house. Jackie noted the differences were discernable from when she took the tour in her lifetime. Elvis would make it his own, she knew that for certain. When the doctor excused himself to tend to his wife, Elvis and Jackie promised they would show themselves out.

"If you ever decide to sell the house, please let me know," Elvis told the doctor.

"My wife may need to move to a drier climate soon. If we do sell, you'll be the first person I call. Take a look at the grounds before you leave and good luck with your show tonight. Oh, and Elvis, thank you so much for the donation you made to the children's hospital. It did not go unnoticed even though you wanted it to remain quiet," the doctor said before disappearing upstairs to help his wife.

"You're mighty welcome." Elvis beamed with pride.

It was easy to see how much Elvis enjoyed helping people without any fanfare. There were no social media posts since there was no social media, no articles extolling his virtue, no press release, only a quiet check put in the mail that would make a difference to sick children. He was generous because that's how his heart worked; it beat for others. He wanted to share his good fortune with the less fortunate. He understood the unfortunate life from having lived a life of misfortune, at least until he turned nineteen and showed the world his talent.

"I love this place." Elvis held Jackie's hand as they walked to the back of the property through the tall trees. "How'd you know I'd fall in love with it?"

Jackie smiled, knowing she could contently listen to his sweet southern drawl for the rest of her life. "It felt like you."

When they reached a large tree, Elvis pulled Jackie behind it, out of sight of the house, and pinned her against the tree, his hand on one side, the other holding her hand tightly before he leaned in with an urgent and raw kiss. The passion between them erupted like lightning, leaving them both breathless once more. Elvis pulled away to control the situation. Jackie smoothed her hair, and they both giggled at themselves, each knowing exactly what the other was thinking and wanting.

"Okay, we really have to get home," Elvis said with insistence. "The Colonel will have the police looking for me. He has no idea I'm with you, and I don't want him interrogating my mother. But, before we go, I plan on owning this place one day, so I'm going to carve our initials on this tree to memorialize this perfect day with the perfect girl."

111

Elvis pulled his pocket-knife from his trousers and carved a heart with their initials, EP plus JS. After enjoying more kisses, they finally headed back to town.

Reluctantly, Jackie climbed out of the car when they arrived at the hotel. Not wanting him to leave, even if it would only be an hour until she saw him again. Whatever force was pulling them together, it had strength Jackie wasn't sure she could fight. Elvis backed her against the car for one last kiss before he had to leave.

"I'll send one of the boys to pick you up at six sharp. You've got a tad bit over an hour to get ready. Hopefully, that's enough time." He grinned a crooked smile.

"I can drive my car over to Audubon if that would help," Jackie offered.

"No, there'll be a crush of fans at the house. You'll have to park down the street. It will be a zoo. It'll be safer if I send someone for you." Elvis traced his finger across her lips and followed it with a light kiss. "As much as I want to stay here with you right now, I've got to get home before everyone gets frantic." It was obvious to Jackie that Elvis was feeling nervous, his calm demeanor of the afternoon gone, his speech pressured.

Maybe he noticed it too, he pulled her close and kissed her again and again until he abruptly released her, jumped in the convertible, and drove off with a happy shout, "I can't wait to see you at the show tonight," then disappeared down the street.

Jackie stood watching him drive away, waving goodbye long after he was out of sight. She was falling hard. Correction, had fallen hard. She exhaled a deep, happy sigh and ran to get ready.

Chapter 13
Heartbreak Hotel

Jackie was overrun with excitement as they arrived at the field. She'd accompanied Gladys and Vernon and avoided the glares of the Colonel, who demanded to know who she was. Georgie, one of Elvis's old childhood friends who worked for him, warned her about the Colonel on the drive over to Audubon but told her Elvis instructed her to ignore anything he said.

Fighting the urge to put the Colonel in his place, she exhaled. Her hatred for what he was about to do to Elvis in the coming years was more than she could bear. But in the current reality, up until now, the Colonel was the one making Elvis a star. She had to find a better way to solve that problem and convince Elvis the Colonel was not his savior and not to be trusted. It was a better plan than confronting him outright; the Colonel was too manipulative and dishonest.

"I'm simply giddy about the show tonight," she told Gladys as they exited the car.

"Stay where the boys put you. They'll come get you afterwards," Gladys instructed. "Georgie, take Jackie to a safe spot."

Georgie did as he was told.

"Be careful," Georgie said. "Things can get excitable during Elvis's performance. If you feel like you need help, I'll be standing to the left of the stage near you. Just holler at me. I'll be watching to make sure you're okay."

Confused by the concern, Jackie watched as the Colonel led Gladys and Vernon away to their seats. Georgie delivered her to the front of the stage on Elvis's orders.

Trapped in the buzz around her as she stood waiting for the King to appear, she realized she hadn't smiled this much in too many years to count. It seemed to come easier now that she was twenty-one.

"Elvis wanted you to have a prime spot," Georgie told her.

"Thanks, Georgie," she replied.

"I'll be right there," he told her again, pointing to his station.

Looking around, feeling more happiness than she remembered possible, she tried to recall when her joy for life had been lost. It couldn't be attributed to one fatal event. It was more an avalanche of disappointment that buried her. She considered all the factors in play. Maybe the loss of joy was a sorrowful partner to aging, or as work intensified and responsibilities grew, there was simply no time for happiness anymore. Whatever logical scapegoat she tried to devise; the reality was it had been her own fault for letting the joy disappear. She should have tried harder to ensure there was more than work making her get up in the morning, finally accepting the blame. But none of it mattered now as she waited to see Elvis. Joy was decidedly back in her life.

The crowd was screaming before Elvis even took the stage, forcing the police to hold their line and keep hordes of young girls from storming the stage. Jackie had seen almost all the movies and even YouTube videos of Elvis performing and his fans going wild but seeing it in real-life was surreal. The recordings didn't capture the volume of the deafening shrieks and cheers.

Georgie watched her as the crowd became more intense. "You, okay?" he mouthed. She nodded. All of Elvis's boys were focused and intense and monitoring the crowd, a far departure from the wild horseplaying boys from last night. They looked grown up and official as they tackled their jobs of protecting Elvis.

The swarm of girls behind her pushed harder, making her think her spine might crack. It was going to test her resolve to stand her ground or be smashed by girls with raging hormones and dreams of ripping Elvis's clothes off his body. She wasn't going to allow that; she wanted to announce to them all. Squaring her shoulders and setting her feet firmly on the ground, she pushed back against the inching crowd. Many girls were already crying, and Elvis hadn't stepped a single foot on stage.

Feeling like she was watching the world in slow motion, she locked in all the magic of the night; the glimmer of the instruments perched on stage ready to come to life, the electric anticipation hanging in the air, the stern looks on faces of police eyeing the crowds, and the wide eyes of girls giddy with excitement, lust, and love. She took it in with amazement as the crowd erupted into thundering, mind-blowing screams.

Elvis had taken the stage.

Elvis spotted Jackie and winked at her. Girls next to her stared at her with dagger-like eyes, clearly wondering who she was. A couple of girls became physical as they tried to push Jackie back.

She caught Georgie about to make a move; she shook him off. "I'm okay," she mouthed.

Little did the girls know Jackie was skilled at dealing with aggressive people. You don't become a successful trial attorney by being a wallflower. Jackie had prepared for the onslaught and dug her heels in deeper in the dirt, raised her hands and pushed the girls away with equal intensity. Thankfully, they relented and moved on. She wasn't sure Elvis would approve of her starting a brawl before he'd even sung the first note.

Looking at Elvis standing on stage, her pulse fluttered. He was clad in a black suit, red tie, red socks, and shiny black loafers with custom red stitching. He had been transformed into a cross between the ultimate bad boy and southern gentleman, his black hair dipping

115

over one eye, his smile detectable as he stared at the stage, waiting for the band to ready. The guitar strap cut across his chest, the guitar swinging aimlessly over his soon to be gyrating hip. Jackie couldn't take her eyes off him, he'd infected her soul and buried himself deep in her heart, she had been charmed.

Images of their day together raised her intensity, which she didn't know could climb higher, and now seeing him standing on the stage with thousands of fans wanting to get to him, screaming at the top of their lungs, she thought her heart might explode. When he began bellowing out the first words to Heartbreak Hotel, the crowd lost its collective mind. Press flashbulbs popped in rapid-fire.

There were no cell phone cameras, reminding Jackie that the concert goers would go through the old routine of dropping their film off at the Kodak hut and waiting several days for the photos to be developed, all the while hoping the pictures would be good, with nobody's head cut off or their finger over the lens. Jackie failed at taking photos as a teen, with most images blurred or accidentally exposed before she ever dropped them to be developed. It was a crapshoot back then. On the positive side of it, without a camera in everyone's hand, the crowd was attentive and tuned in. Elvis had their full attention.

The distinctive chords of *Heartbreak Hotel* began loudly and with power as Elvis crooned the lyrics and swiveled his hips to the beat. Jackie watched every move. He was skilled and talented and knew what he was doing to wild the crowd, whipping them into a frenzy with every gyration. His voice carrying the fans to places they never knew existed. When he threw in the leg shake, the hip thrust, and the twist of his feet and legs as he propelled himself across the stage, there was no containing the masses of people.

The police earned their money protecting Elvis from the crying, shrieking women wanting to touch him. Even the men in attendance were screaming with delight. Jackie understood and knew what they felt. She felt it too. And even more than that, she felt like the most fortunate princess having spent the last two days being close to this talented man, not because he could perform on stage, but because he was so much more than that. She had begun to see his full personality and wanted to know all of him; he was complex, and his emotions ran deep. Speaking to him for only a few minutes, anyone could see what a thinker he was. She wanted to protect him from what was coming. She would set her plan into action tonight. Jackie screamed with excitement, and it felt good. Elvis winked at her again.

The throng of fans reached levels of pandemonium Jackie never knew existed as the concert closed. Elvis was hustled away by the police when the concert goers rushed the stage as the last note dropped. The physical exhaustion of the performance visible on Elvis, who was soaked with sweat and out of breath. Small circles of perspiration spotted the stage like raindrops.

"Let's go." Georgie was at her side with a couple of other boys. They grabbed her, surrounded her and rushed her to a waiting car to escape the madness.

Fans lined the street in front of the house by the time they arrived. Jackie was only starting to understand what Elvis's life must be like every day, and now understood why he didn't want her driving her car to his house. She was exhausted from watching it all. How had he done it year after year? He was stronger than she'd given him credit for. Knowing his future, she knew this was the happy beginning and there would be pain to go along with that fame, but how could you not be caught up in the contagion of the birth of rock-n-roll, it was infectious.

"Sorry, baby, it took me a while to get cleaned up," Elvis said quietly when he walked up behind Jackie as she stood on the porch watching the fans in front of the house.

She thought the crowd would subside, but it had multiplied as the night wore on. Elvis stayed behind her in the shadows so there wouldn't be more commotion; his body pressed against her back, his hands resting on her shoulders.

"Let's go out back where it's more private," he whispered in her ear.

Jackie turned to him and followed his lead to the back patio. The night was warm and comfortable. When Elvis reached for her hand and pulled her down onto a plush chaise lounge chair next to him, she felt like she had come home to a place she'd missed for years.

"How'd you like the concert?" he asked, nibbling her neck.

Trying to concentrate on her response and stop the buzzing of her skin, Jackie managed to answer, "You were a superstar. I'm so amazed Elvis. I've never seen anything like it. The sheer physical energy was out of this world."

Jackie had seen him in concert once in her life, but from so far away she could barely see him and with no appreciation for the physical exertion it took to perform a full concert since she was only thirteen at the time, with a skewed perspective. She snuggled against him, feeling his muscles relax and his heart beat slowly and rhythmically, melting into his exhausted state.

"Thank you, baby." Elvis pulled her closer. "I love performing," he confessed.

"I know you do. It's what you were born to do." Jackie saw her chance to try to warn him without telling him about the future. "Remember that feeling and don't trade it for anything you don't want to do. Don't let the Colonel or anyone take your career in a direction that doesn't make you happy," she pleaded.

Elvis looked at her with confusion. "The Colonel can be grumpy, but he takes care of my career and he's doing a good job, I think."

Jackie sat up a little so she could look at him face-to-face. "I'm serious Elvis, there are going to be people in your life that will take you for granted and try to use you for money and fame. You must remember that you're the talent. Everything is driven by you. Don't let anyone make you believe less of yourself or tell you that you have to do things you don't want to do. Okay? Promise me you will take care of yourself and your business."

"My Lady Lawyer," he said softly. He smiled and closed his eyes, laying his head back on the chaise.

"Promise me you will take care of yourself. Your health is important. I know you have trouble sleeping. I get it, I do too. And I know there are not many options, but pills are a trap and there are other ways to help you sleep." Jackie couldn't stop talking. She feared she wouldn't have much more time with Elvis and needed to get it all out.

"Like what? I've tried everything. My brain is on fire after I perform. I'm settled now because I'm wrapped around you, but the minute I try to sleep I'll replay every minute of the performance, analyzing how I sang, my moves, what the paper will say tomorrow, will the label be happy, will they want to arrest me. It doesn't end."

"I'm so sorry. I know there's a lot of pressure on you. Maybe try Chamomile tea or Sleepytime Tea." Jackie stopped mid-sentence, were either of those things available in 1956?

"Sleepytime, what?" Elvis opened his eyes.

"I meant chamomile tea, to sleep," she quickly corrected, being fairly certain Sleepytime tea wasn't created yet since it wasn't even available during her teen years now that she thought about it. "And there is meditation, yoga."

She wanted to say white noise, apps for sleep, sleep stories, melatonin, spa music, all the things she had tried over the years, none of which had been invented yet, plus, most had failed to alleviate her insomnia. Wine...but she knew Elvis didn't drink and didn't like it when people drank, so she skipped that suggestion.

"I've tried everything I can think of honey, even the pills don't seem to do the trick sometimes." He closed his eyes again and pulled her close as to say, let's quit talking about this.

Circular thoughts were her specialty, so she understood not being able to stop them, especially at night. She did the same when prepping for a trial, during a trial, after a trial, wondering if she could have argued a case better, differently, if she said anything to go up on appeal, was it her words that turned the jury, or her demeanor, was she too icy, not friendly enough, too friendly, didn't look at the jurors, looked at them too much. All those things buzzed in her head and affected her body, her sleep, her eating. It consumed her and it wasn't anywhere near the level of having the whole world analyze every part of you constantly and write lies in the paper. Her exposure was limited to a single courtroom of people. It was terrifying enough.

There was one more thing she wanted to say to him before the night ended, but she chose to lie next to him and relax while she measured the words in her mind. She was keyed up, and she knew it, a proficient skill of hers from time to time. More so when she was young and starting out as an attorney and was worried about every single little misstep, eventually she evolved into a calmer force. She hadn't felt this young and excitable in decades.

Gladys appeared and brought Elvis's favorite cookies and lemonade. Jackie sat up briskly, embarrassed to be laying so close to her son. Gladys pretended not to notice.

"It was another perfect performance tonight," Gladys told Elvis.

"Thanks, Momma," Elvis said.

"How did you like it, Jackie?" Gladys asked.

"It was unreal. I'm so thrilled I got to see it. He's extraordinary," she said honestly.

"I'm glad too. I thought the police did a great job controlling the crowd. It was calmer tonight than other nights," Gladys told Jackie.

"You're kidding?" She expressed her shock. "It was pretty crazy."

"There's been worse. Sometimes a crazed fan gets on stage and gets hold of Elvis, he's been scratched up a few times," Gladys described the chaos.

"It's not that bad," Elvis said, downplaying the danger.

The chatter between mother and son moved easily with a sincere connection reflecting a pure and sweet fragrance of love, lasting for about an hour or more before Gladys retired to bed. Jackie wished she and her mother had enjoyed that type of connection.

The talk of the concert reminded Elvis of his performance and moved him back to a hyped mood. With his tiredness gone and his energy revived, he was ready to kiss, much to Jackie's pleasure, her energy level growing to match his for various reasons.

As the night wore on, she tried to move him back to calmness. Jackie engaged him in conversation; thoughts on religion, growing up in Tupelo, his first performance, the people he admired, his dreams, his fears. With Elvis, conversation flowed naturally as he tried to satisfy his curious mind. There were no awkward silences. The conversation was one-sided by design. When he tried to ask deeper questions about her life, she didn't bite, dodging questions she knew she couldn't answer. Employing her skills at redirecting, she kept Elvis on track, peppering him with more questions, interrupted periodically by long stretches of kissing. Her favorite part of the night. The topic of Graceland finally rolled around.

"I think I want to buy that house one day. I thought this house would be perfect, but the fans stand outside sometimes all night. In fact, they're still out there right now, more of them even. The neighbors were complaining to my dad today about the traffic," Elvis told her.

"I think a new home would be a wonderful idea," Jackie agreed, knowing it would come to pass. "Elvis, I want you to know how much I admire your generous heart. I think it's wonderful how much you give to charity."

Elvis started to speak but Jackie put a finger to his lips. "Let me finish before you say anything. I know you love to buy cars and gifts for people, even strangers, but you need to be smart about your finances. So, promise me when you buy a car or other elaborate gift, that you deposit an equal amount of money into a savings account. Nobody needs to know. Pretend you're buying it for a future child or something. That way, there will never come a day when you're broke. And please, have a lawyer look over every single contract you sign. Don't trust the Colonel, don't sign anything without legal counsel. Promise me!" Jackie moved her finger from his lips.

He yawned. "I don't bother with the finances. My dad takes care of all of that, and I trust him," he started to explain.

"I know, and that can still happen, but you need to know what's going on or people will take advantage. Not your dad, of course, but others." Jackie searched her heart for the magic words to convince him without a direct warning. "I've read court cases where managers have taken advantage of stars and stolen all their money. I don't want that to happen to you. Can you promise me that you will protect yourself? Simply deposit the money in an account nobody knows about. You don't have to touch it, squirrel it away for a rainy day, as they say. And get a lawyer to review the contracts."

Elvis pulled her close again. "If I need more money, I'll go out and make it, but thanks for caring about me. I'll think about it," he promised. Then he kissed her until they both dozed off in each other's arms.

Chapter 14
Sunrise and Gone

The pain in Jackie's shoulder woke her before she spotted the sun peeking over the fence. Elvis adjusted his arm underneath her as she tried to get comfortable but not wake him. They'd slept tightly against each other, neither moving all night, even if it was a short night. For two people who battled demons to sleep soundly, they had achieved the feat together. As the day broke, she realized Saturday had turned to Sunday, the day she was scheduled to go back home to Seattle, but that was a conundrum she'd not yet solved. Even if she wanted to go back, she didn't know how.

Elvis shifted, nearly sending her sprawling on the concrete patio as she tried to free her arms and legs and get the feeling back in her hands. Her shoulder tingled as it came alive and the blood started flowing again. Elvis didn't want to get up, but Jackie nearly falling off the chaise had him awake now.

"Sorry, didn't mean to knock you off the chair," he apologized.

"It's okay. Guess we were tangled up."

"The conversation we had last night, I hear you and I'll promise I'll take care of it. I haven't slept this well in a long time. I think you're my magic cure," he said with a yawn.

"I agree, you're mine, too," she replied sleepily.

"There's something I want to ask you?" He put his arms around her and pulled her into his body.

Jackie pressed against him. "Sure, what's up? Good morning, by the way."

He kissed the back of her neck. "It is a good morning. Hopefully, it will get even better, depending on your answer."

"I'm intrigued now." Jackie smiled as she settled against him.

"I want you to go to California with me. I leave in a few days. I'll begin shooting the movie soon and will be there several months. I don't want to leave you. It's like you know what is in my heart, like you can see my life and my future. I know you make me happy, and I think I make you happy, too."

She turned to look at him. The blue of his hopeful eyes lured her to the sweetest place, blocking out the rest of the world.

He continued, "I know this is out of the blue and it seems a little crazy. I know you want to finish law school. Can you transfer schools? What do you say? Will you go with me?"

Jackie agreed it was crazy, probably the craziest thing she'd ever heard, but before she could think it through or stop herself from speaking, she said, "Yes, yes, I'll go to California with you."

Elvis kissed her, a long deep kiss sealing the decision. "Let's go tell Momma. She likes you. She told me that last night." He jumped up like a kid on Christmas and pulled Jackie up by two hands, tipping the chaise and nearly spilling them both on the ground this time. "Momma." She heard him holler. "I have some great news."

Shocked by the invitation, yet intrigued with thoughts of a life with Elvis, Jackie felt alive for the first time in years. Even more shocking was the fact that she didn't weigh the pros and cons before blurting out she would go. As far as transferring schools, she didn't even exist in this world yet, so there was no school to transfer from. She wasn't sure how to explain that.

She followed Elvis, struggling to keep up as he darted through the house looking for his mom. When Jackie finally arrived in the kitchen, Gladys was there, smiling a real smile this time, hugging Jackie and telling them to sit at the table while she got dressed and would be back to make breakfast.

Elvis did as his mom asked. He took Jackie's hand in his, telling her excitedly, "This is going to be perfect. We'll go get your car and your clothes after breakfast. You can stay here until we leave for California."

Jackie nodded in agreement, afraid if she spoke again, she might back out. Already swept up in the thrill of the day, images of their life flashed in her mind. Maybe this was the key to protecting him. Although she hadn't thought it through, knowing if she did, it wouldn't make sense and she would have to say no, which she didn't want to do. This was what she wanted, pushing away the logical thoughts and ignoring the cons, and rationalizing that she had no choice. She was stuck in 1956 and didn't know how to get back to her world. Soon she would need a job, the hotel life would never suit her. The thought of living with someone who sent her pulse racing and gave her hope for love was a much better option.

"You want some orange juice?" Elvis asked, his adrenalin pumping, making it impossible to sit still.

"Sure, that would be great." Jackie patted his knee before he jumped up and headed to the refrigerator.

Even though Jackie had made her decision and knew it was what her heart wanted, thoughts of her kids, Maggie, and her true life were trying to wiggle their way into her mind. She forced herself to stop thinking of that life and think about what she wanted for once, pushing back against herself. The new life in front of her was what she wanted. And the man standing at the refrigerator looking for the orange juice without any success was part of that new life even if he couldn't find the juice which sat motionless on the second shelf. Some things never change, a man looking at something right in front of his face but not seeing it at all.

As she watched him with amusement, she pictured many other happy days like this. He struck a level of excitement in her that she'd never felt. Maybe it was the lifestyle, or perhaps his charming personality and sex appeal. She hadn't quite pinpointed the source of her heightened existence. The truth was, aside from her logical placating to herself, she was in love and wanted this life being offered to her. She didn't want to go home. Damn the consequences, especially if it meant she could save him.

The one hitch in her plan which could undo everything she was envisioning was...the truth! She had to tell him the truth. Her mind quickly categorized all the possible reactions, none of them good: panic, psychiatric hospitals, police. With mere words, it could all fall apart, but she knew it was the right thing to do, otherwise the lies would continue and eventually the truth would come out. It always did, no matter how good the lie. She took a deep breath.

"Elvis, before we go to California, there's something I should tell you," Jackie said cautiously.

Elvis continued looking in the refrigerator and tapping his foot to an unknown beat. "What's that, honey?"

"It's about where I come from. I'm not from here," she continued.

"I know, honey, you're from Seattle." He turned for a second and looked at her with confusion before returning to the endless OJ search.

"Yes, that's true, but I am from the f...."

Jackie heard the thunder crash against the sky. She felt herself slip from the chair and the next thing she knew she woke at the Memphis Manor Hotel, her cell phone lying on the nightstand was ringing nonstop. She rolled over and grabbed the phone. It was 2023. The blurred name on the caller ID was her first clue. There was one way to confirm it. She stumbled to the bathroom and reluctantly looked in the mirror, where the truth stared back at her, mocking her with reality. She was sixty once more. Her life had returned to normal, and Elvis was gone–again.

Chapter 15
Truth or Insanity

Jackie answered the phone simply to stop the ringing, knowing it had to be Maggie.

"Hello!" she said abruptly.

"Where have you been?" Maggie yelled into the phone. "I've been worried sick. You haven't answered your phone for three days. Three days, Jackie! Why not? Are you okay?"

Swallowing hard and internally berating herself for being caught up with Elvis and 1956, she hadn't thought about being missed or that Maggie could be trying to reach her, not that she could have done anything about it. Fighting the natural urge to blurt out all that she'd experienced, they were best friends after all and she told Maggie everything; she sucked it in and apologized. The true conversation had to wait for the appropriate time.

"I'm so, so sorry. I lost my phone, and I just got it back," Jackie lied, a skill she seemed to be perfecting.

"Good Lord, Jackie. I almost called the police. Susan or Toby hadn't heard from you either. They told me not to worry, that you were probably having a great time, but it's not like you to ignore your phone. I know you're on vacation, but I was frantic."

Jackie could tell Maggie was on the verge of bursting into tears. Little did Maggie know Jackie was on the verge also, but for a different reason. The confusion and guilt were overwhelming. She had to get off the phone. She couldn't have this conversation right now.

"Again, I'm so sorry Maggie, it was out of my control. I had no idea you would be so worried. I didn't bring my laptop and couldn't email or anything. I was simply trying to enjoy my time here in Memphis. Speaking of, I need to get to the airport soon. I have to pack and check out. I'll explain everything when I get home," Jackie tried to soothe Maggie.

"It's okay, Jackie, I understand. I'm sorry for yelling at you. I was so worried. Do you need me to pick you up at the airport?" Maggie had calmed down.

"That would be great if you could. I don't get home until seven this evening. I'll text the details. I can't wait to tell you about my trip." Jackie tried to turn the mood.

"I can't wait to hear about it. Oh, I discovered something about that medallion you found. I'll tell you more when I pick you up. It's incredibly interesting," Maggie said.

Jackie had forgotten about the medallion with the shock of being back in her world. She ran to her purse and opened it, searching frantically, breathing a sigh of relief when it was there. Maybe she could get back to Elvis after all.

"Okay, I should go. I'll see you tonight and we can talk about everything," Jackie said.

She hung up the phone and crawled back into bed. Her flight wasn't for a few hours. Maybe closing her eyes would ease the pounding of regret and longing to be back with Elvis. Pulling the blanket over her head, she melted into the plush mattress, forcing herself to ignore reality. It wasn't a truth she wanted to accept yet.

After pretending to sleep for forty-five minutes until she thought herself ridiculous for the charade, she reluctantly threw the covers off and got out of bed. There were only two hours before check-out and time to get to the airport. She rubbed her temples and paced the room, trying to make sense of all that had transpired over the past three days and how she was going to tell Maggie the truth.

This great adventure was not something her kids were going to find out about, though. They'd never believe it and it might crush them knowing their mother wanted a life do-over and planned to leave them behind for that second chance. However, it all seemed rather irrelevant, since her foremost thought was how to get back to Elvis. He must have been so confused when she disappeared. Frustration set in.

Jackie showered, but even the hot water that usually revived her mind had no effect on helping ease her thinking about the situation. She went through the motions of dressing in her new clothes she'd bought in Seattle, 2023 fashions, and styled her hair, also 2023 style. Checking her watch, she knew there was time to take a quick look at Graceland if she hurried. Tossing her belongings in her modern suitcase with wheels, she checked out with her chipped credit card and headed to the hybrid rental.

Driving past Graceland, she spontaneously made a U-turn and pulled into the cut-away in front of the massive gates, debating buying a ticket to get on the grounds. She needed to know why the time warp dropped her back in 1956 and if she could get back. If she bought a ticket, she could at least check the grounds for the tree with her and Elvis's initials as proof the past three days were real, but the odds were that the tree was gone. Perhaps Elvis had been so angry that she vanished he simply cleared the tree. The reality was, there were no options left. She climbed back into the rental and headed to the airport.

The flight was uneventful. Jackie's mind was preoccupied with too many thoughts for her own good, but it made the flight pass quickly. She stepped off the plane in Seattle in a daze. The passenger pickup was crowded as usual as she waited for Maggie. A more settled feeling washed over her as she looked around at her familiar surroundings and tried to ground herself to sink back into her life. But the disheartened feeling in her gut would not budge, neither would the feeling that she had to fix this situation and get back to Elvis somehow and explain. He deserved that much. They were making plans to go to California and poof; she disappeared.

Hearing the conversation with herself about plans to live in 1956, she looked around at the present day. It was official; she had lost it, that was all there was to it. She'd finally gone over the edge. What in the world was she thinking? She had kids, live kids, a granddaughter, friends, and a semblance of a life that she intended to start living instead of pining away for a man who had died years earlier. She was fifteen, for Pete's sake, when he died. Screaming silently at herself and feeling skeptical about the reality of the past few days, she wrestled with telling Maggie about Memphis.

A familiar honk focused Jackie's thoughts as to why she was standing on the curb, suitcase by her side, with Maggie appearing from the line of cars stacking up one behind another at the curbside pickup.

"Jackie, hello," Maggie hollered through the rolled-down window, "here I am!"

The warm embrace from her best friend was much needed as the women exchanged hugs, which almost made Jackie cry. Maybe it was the dichotomy of emotions tugging her heart apart, but she knew she had to pull it together and put on a brave face, unsure if Maggie would comprehend the strange emotional turmoil she was feeling.

"Thank you so much for picking me up. Saved me an Uber ride." Jackie forced a smile.

"I'm so happy you're back," Maggie said with sincerity.

"Me too," Jackie replied, trying to sound enthusiastic despite her internal battle.

"Oh, I discovered some interesting things about the medallion you found. It's a gorget. I remembered it from helping with Native American studies at the school. The kids made them out of construction paper. I had to punch a gazillion holes and string them with yarn, they are typically worn like a necklace. I did a bit of research

131

about them. They're usually carved from seashell and sometimes a symbol of rank, or could be an amulet of protective medicine," Maggie explained to Jackie.

Jackie pulled the gorget from her purse and showed it to Maggie. "That would make sense."

Jackie thought about the medicine woman whom the gorget must have belonged. Perhaps Morning Dove was walking at the cemetery, caught between worlds like old Joe had told her. She wasn't going to relay that theory to Maggie yet, but it had to be the key to her own journey between worlds. Somehow, she had slipped in and was trapped between dimensions, like Morning Dove had been.

"And here's an interesting tidbit. I found a picture of Elvis wearing it during one of his concerts, maybe not this exact gorget, but something similar. It's a bit hard to see but look at this photo." Maggie handed Jackie her phone, primed with the image.

Jackie studied the picture, deciding it had to be near the end of Elvis's life as she focused on his beautiful face; he wore a gold jumpsuit, and a medallion hung from his neck on a chain. It looked eerily similar to the gorget Jackie held in her hand. How could he have it?

"It's hard to tell for certain, but you're right Maggie, it's similar. I wonder what that means," she posed. Jackie had no answers, only more questions and one more reason she had to get back to Elvis.

"You should hold on to it. It could be extremely valuable if it's an old necklace that belonged to Elvis," Maggie suggested.

Jackie wasn't interested in an heirloom. She was interested in what it could do.

"I'm glad you're home," Maggie said when they arrived at Jackie's house.

"Do you have time for a glass of wine?" She invited Maggie in, knowing she would accept and giving herself a little time to work up the guts to tell Maggie about the Memphis adventures.

"Of course, I always have time for wine with my bestie," Maggie grinned as she pulled into the driveway.

Jackie poured them both a glass of wine, knowing they would soon need it. The conversation began easily as all their talks did, without effort or pretense. Jackie eagerly laid out everything she did until Friday; the hardware store, Tupelo, a brief mention of the graveyard and finding the gorget, even details about older Doreen, which brought more giggling over the hot bartender, and more details of what she did before going to memorial circle on her tour. She stopped short of telling her about Elvis, though her heart was bursting to share how they fell in love, as crazy as it sounded. She had always confided in Maggie, but this was different and made no sense. Still, she was confident it was safe to confess to Maggie; she was the one person she trusted with all her heart.

"On Friday I toured Graceland. The weather was terrible, it rained steadily all day, it kind of felt like Seattle. I was at memorial circle kneeling by Elvis's gravesite. People were running for cover." Jackie took a deep breath and a sip of wine before she continued. "This next part is going to sound crazy and you're the only one I can tell this to. Everyone else would think I've lost my mind. But you know me and we always tell each other the truth." Jackie looked at Maggie's face and saw the perplexed look staring back at her.

"Jackie, what did you do? Is this going to be like the time we were on spring break in Galveston, and you almost got into a fight over a parking space and nearly got us arrested for disturbing the peace? Oh my gosh, is that why you were missing in action for three days? Did you get arrested?" Maggie asked with shock, her hand to her mouth.

"No, no, I didn't do anything. And I didn't get arrested. Really, Maggie? You think the first time I go off on a vacation, I'm going to get arrested? I'm a lawyer Maggie, I don't break the law, at least not anymore. And, technically, it was only two days." Jackie laughed, stalling to collect her thoughts. "It's something that happened to me at Graceland. I can't believe you brought up Galveston, that was decades ago. And I was waiting for that parking space. You know we were there first," Jackie insisted.

"Yes, I know we were, but there were three other spaces we could have parked in and you didn't have to jump out and pour your Slurpee on their window. Those women were as old as we are now. They were so shocked. I think they called us 'young hooligans' or something. Today we might have gotten shot or become a viral video," Maggie countered.

"I disagree. I did have to pour my Slurpee on their window. You know I had my signal on and was waiting for that space. They totally zipped in around us," Jackie argued.

Maggie raised her hands in surrender and smiled. "Okay, you're right. Let's continue the talk about Graceland."

Jackie giggled at the old memory of that day when youth and passion took over sanity and logic momentarily. She would have loved to trip back to memory lane with Maggie and recount all the stories from that week in Galveston, but now wasn't the time and she wanted to tell Maggie about Elvis before she lost her nerve.

"Let's not get off track here. Like I said, I was at Graceland, and it was raining. I was examining the gorget and wishing I could save Elvis when this loud thunderclap boomed and ear-splitting lightning cracked. When it did, I was knocked back and what's even crazier is when I got up, the present day was gone, and I was in 1956." Jackie watched Maggie's face, waiting for her reaction.

Maggie stared at Jackie and then burst out laughing. "Are you serious? Come on Jackie? That's hilarious. You almost had me until the part about 1956. Seriously, what did you do on Friday and Saturday?"

"I'm serious Maggie. That's why I missed your calls. That's why I couldn't call you. I went back in time. I met Elvis and spent time with him, made out with him, went on a picnic," Jackie confessed everything.

"Whoa, wait a minute. You went back to 1956? How old was Elvis, like twenty-one or something? You're a sixty-year-old woman.

You're telling me you hung out with and made out with a twenty-one-year-old and nobody thought that was bizarre? Particularly in 1956?" Maggie set her glass of wine on the table and turned to Jackie.

"No, I wasn't sixty when I was back in 1956. That was the weirdest part. Well, it was all weird, but all amazing as well." Jackie ran her hands through her hair as she continued explaining, "I was Elvis's age. I was twenty-one, Maggie. It was incredible. You can't imagine what it felt like to be young again. It was so freeing. I was given another chance at life to make different decisions, better decisions. To live a life that I've never dreamed of, but not because I didn't want this life, but because I had tunnel vision when I created my dreams the first time around. I didn't know there could be other dreams."

"Jackie, there's nothing wrong with your life. You've been blessed in so many ways. Look at your home, your kids. Why would you want to do it all over differently?" Maggie was flustered by Jackie's revelations.

"I don't know, Maggie, but I feel like I missed something the first time around. Listen Maggie, not only did I go back and meet Elvis and fall in love with him, but he asked me to go with him to California. He was going to film *Love Me Tender*, his first movie, and he wanted me to be with him. It had a different title back then. I didn't tell him that, but they did change it later after they started filming," Jackie rambled as Maggie stared at her in disbelief.

"Jackie, none of this is funny. I told you I'm over that I couldn't reach you. I understand about you losing your phone. You don't have to make up this story. Are you making fun of me because I was worried about you?" Maggie was indignant.

"No, Maggie, I'm telling you, I was transported to 1956 and then sent back to 2023 and I'm not sure why or how. I don't know how it all works. I have no answers, but I'm telling you the truth. It happened! I've never lied to you, Maggie. Why would I start now?" Jackie felt her anger rising. Of all the people in her world, Maggie was the one person she truly believed would be on her side and would believe her.

"How do you know? How do you know it's real? Maybe you hit your head or got roofied. When we talked Thursday night, you were hanging out with that young, good-looking bartender. Maybe he slipped something in your drink, and you don't remember anything. Maybe you're having a health issue, Jackie." Maggie moved closer to Jackie and took her hands.

"No, none of those things. And we spoke Friday morning, so that's not possible," Jackie said flatly. Her annoyance had peaked. She expected a little pushback but not complete denial.

"Jackie, you've been under a lot of stress for many years. Perhaps something is causing you to have hallucinations or maybe you slept hard and had an incredible dream," Maggie offered.

"I slept for three days?" Jackie pulled her hands back from Maggie's grasp. "I did not imagine this, Maggie. It all happened and more that I've not told you yet. But, since you clearly don't believe me and think I'm having some…some…medical issue, I'll spare you the details. If you don't mind, I'm tired and I'd like for you to leave."

Jackie stood to show Maggie out. They'd never fought in their long friendship, never even disagreed with any significance, but something had shifted tonight. Maggie was in disbelief, and Jackie felt abandoned. Jackie knew it sounded unbelievable, but Maggie wasn't even trying to hear what she was telling her. She expected more from their friendship.

"Look, Jackie, it's a lot to take in, you must admit. You're telling me that you traveled back in time? That's not possible. There is a logical explanation. I promise we will figure it out together."

Jackie crossed her arms and glared at Maggie. "I don't have to figure out anything. It happened Maggie. I'm not like the guy in that movie with a brain tumor that altered his perception of reality and made him able to hear colors or do complex math or whatever it was. I met

Elvis. I was there. And we were in love! And all I want to figure out is how to get back there so I can finish what I started, to save him."

Staring at the tile floor in the entryway, Jackie held the door open for Maggie to leave. She blinked hard, battling hot tears. It had been years since she'd cried in front of anyone. She clenched her teeth, hoping not to begin now, not because she didn't want to, but in fear that once she started, she wouldn't stop, and would look a bit unhinged. Maggie never saw her cry; it would worry her if she melted down now.

Gathering her purse to leave, Maggie paused in front of Jackie before she did. "Please meet me for brunch tomorrow over at Rounds near the hospital. I have to drop Charlie for a post-op check, which takes a while. We can have brunch and a Bloody Mary, your favorite, and talk about this some more. Okay? Around ten-thirty?"

Maggie stood stoically in front of Jackie, who finally relented and agreed to meet, albeit reluctantly. With the assurance they would talk tomorrow, Maggie did as she had been asked and stepped onto the porch. The door slammed hard behind her.

Maggie climbed in her car, looking at the house and searching her mind for a single day over the past thirty-five years that she and Jackie hadn't been friends. She knew her reaction of disbelief was warranted, fearing something was terribly wrong medically with Jackie. Maggie also knew Jackie's stubborn streak and that once she set her rudder, she'd as soon crash into rocks, then admit she suffered any health issues.

There was only one person who could help and answer the medical questions, her friend Glenn, who was a neurologist. He would know what was wrong. The only problem standing in the way was Jackie and Glenn had a falling out after his wife Robin died some years ago, but she had no choice. Glenn was her only hope.

"Siri, call Dr. Williams," Maggie spoke to her car.

"Calling Dr. Glenn Williams, Neurology," Siri announced.

"Hello, Maggie, is everything okay?" Glenn answered his cell on the first ring, disregarding the late hour.

"Hi, Glenn. I don't know if everything is all right. I'm concerned about Jackie. I want her to come see you. I'm worried she's imagining things and losing time. Maybe she's getting dementia, or a brain tumor, or having a stroke, I don't know. I'm so concerned. She's talking nonsense." Maggie's calmness left her. Panic set in as the possibilities of her friend's condition poured down on her.

"Let's take this one step at a time, Maggie. I can tell you're upset. Is Jackie lucid and oriented right now?" he asked.

"Yes, there's no emergency. She took a trip to Tennessee, went missing for three days, and has this crazy story about traveling back in time." She chose to leave out the part about Elvis to protect Jackie somewhat.

"Hmm, that is odd. You and I both know that Jackie is not going to come see me voluntarily. As you know, she's not a fan of mine. But I'm happy to help if she'll let me. Is there a way you can get her to my office around four p.m. tomorrow? I can run some tests if she'll cooperate," the doctor offered.

"I don't know how I'll get her there. We're having brunch at Rounds around ten-thirty. Could you casually stop by? I know you are terribly busy, but maybe you could come talk to her for a minute and help me convince her to have the tests run?" Maggie knew it was a big ask, but she was desperate, and Glenn owed her a favor and she was calling it in.

"Sure, Maggie. I'll move some things around. I won't have much time, but between both of us, hopefully we can get her to my office. I can probably walk over to Rounds at ten forty-five or eleven, depending on how long my first appointments take."

Maggie breathed a sigh of relief. Something was terribly wrong with Jackie whether she wanted to face it or not and Maggie was going to get to the bottom of it. She hoped it didn't break their friendship.

The look of betrayal on Jackie's face burned in Maggie's mind. Optimistically, she hoped Jackie would thank her one day for this. She had her own mission now... Save Jackie.

Chapter 16
The Scam to Scan

Jackie was still angry at Maggie when she woke up. She was having second thoughts about meeting for brunch, but she had promised, and she was true to her word. Sometimes she hated that about herself, particularly this morning.

Flashes of being twenty-one a couple of days ago passed through her mind. The person staring back at her today in the bathroom mirror was unknown; the youth evaporated. Looking at her reflection, she wondered who she really was, the girl with the red lipstick or just a woman searching for a bit of her old self in dreams and wishes and hoping to reclaim a bit of lost time. Jackie tried to smile, but it was pointless. She got dressed and headed to Rounds. On the drive over, she constructed her plan to talk it out with Maggie, even though she preferred to disappear and figure out how to get back to 1956.

"I already ordered the Bloody Marys, no spice," Maggie told Jackie as she sat at the table. Maggie handed her a menu.

"Thanks," Jackie mumbled, leaving her sunglasses on and raising the menu high enough not to see Maggie across the table. It was juvenile, but in many ways, Jackie still felt like she was twenty-one; impulsive and emotion driven. She didn't want to be mature and logical; it was tiresome.

"Jackie, you're going to talk to me. Stop acting like a spoiled child." Maggie was irritated, reaching across the table and pushing the menu down. "Let's go through it again. Tell me what happened and let's figure this out. You're an expert in analyzing cases, so let's examine this one."

The waiter set the Bloody Marys on the table and turned to leave.

"Bring me another," Jackie told him.

"Umm, yes, ma'am," he replied before scuttling away.

"Please," Maggie added to Jackie's command to the waiter. A disappointed scowl planted firmly on her face as she stared at Jackie.

"Sorry," Jackie said flippantly. Jackie looked after the young waiter with irritation at hearing the word ma'am. She preferred to hear endearing monikers like honey or sweetheart or baby, not ma'am.

The Bloody Mary provided some temporary relief to her foul mood as she nursed the drink and avoided looking at Maggie. Raging publicly wasn't her method, especially directed toward Maggie. Something was off. Perhaps a trip to the doctor might be a good idea, but she wasn't going to admit that to Maggie, the feeling of betrayal sat too comfortably in her heart.

She had tossed and turned all night, trying to reconcile Maggie's reaction with the sturdiness of their friendship, only concluding that she was tired and preoccupied with thoughts of everything. It was as if she'd been running fast and far and abruptly stopped, but the world was still whizzing by. The notion it was a hallucination, or a dream, was ridiculous. How had it lasted for three days? Her memories were clear and crisp.

It was real.

"Explain it to me again," Maggie asked gently.

"I'm not going through it again. I told you all the details already. Oh, I did leave out the part about going to see Elvis perform at a benefit concert. I've never seen such a show, there are really no words to describe it, you had to be there, and I was, on the front row to be exact, being winked at by the King of Rock-n-Roll." Jackie calmed herself by saying it out loud.

"Wow!" Maggie had nothing else to say, choosing instead to pull her phone out and Google benefit concerts in Memphis in the summer of 1956. One popped up. It had to be the same one. She scrolled through the photos from that night. If Jackie really was there, maybe there would be proof.

Jackie watched Maggie staring intently at her phone, her annoyance rising. She removed the book she bought in Memphis from her purse and laid it on the table and put her sunglasses away. Incorrectly assuming Maggie would be late, she'd planned on reading a little, but Maggie was early today, which was odd. She flipped opened the cover of the book, trying to make a point that Maggie was being rude, looking up with a glare, but Maggie was still scrolling. The cover synopsis said Elvis inherited medical conditions that pre-determined his untimely death. Jackie was even more curious. If there was medical information, maybe she could find a doctor to treat him and extend his life.

"What are you doing?" Jackie was fed up with Maggie ignoring her.

"I was looking at the photos from the concert you're talking about. I'm sure you've seen them a dozen times," Maggie confessed, setting the phone down so they could order.

"You thought I might be in a photo?" Jackie said. Sitting back and crossing her arms.

"It was just a thought." Maggie picked up the menu.

"I'm not sure that is how it works, Maggie. I was there, whether I was in a photo or not," Jackie said with exasperation. She finished her first Bloody Mary and started on the second.

Maggie lowered her menu and rolled her eyes as Glenn came around the corner. She hadn't prepared Jackie that he was coming.

Inhaling slowly, she braced for the fallout that was headed her way, considering Jackie's foul mood.

"Good morning, ladies." Glenn arrived at the table and pulled out a chair and sat down with the women.

Jackie glared at Maggie, lips pursed, wondering what the hell was going on.

"Glenn," Jackie finally acknowledged him.

"Jackie," Maggie broke in, "I asked Glenn to come here so we can try to figure out what happened in Memphis."

"Jackie, I'm only here to help if I can. I have an opening at the end of the day. I could run necessary tests, do bloodwork to make sure there is no underlying medical issue," Glenn said, trying to explain.

"You told him?" Jackie put her drink down with emphasis. "I had to. He's a neurologist and you're having some strange symptoms. Hallucinating, believing you've traveled back in time, losing three days. Jackie, please, something is terribly wrong," Maggie pleaded, big tears forming quickly.

Jackie took a deep breath. Logically, she knew how it all sounded. She'd even questioned her own sanity around two in the morning. Could she really blame Maggie for thinking she had gone off the deep end? But if what happened to her in Memphis was a dream, then she wanted to get back in bed, pronto.

"Fine, fine, you win. I'll get the tests," Jackie said, knowing that once Maggie began crying, she would agree to it sooner or later. It might as well be sooner.

"That sounds great, Jackie. And, if you could stop with the Bloody Marys, I need you completely lucid for your tests." Glenn smiled.

Waving her hand, Jackie motioned him to go away and ordered coffee to appease him. Glenn left the women to enjoy their breakfast.

"Thank you, Jackie." Maggie was lighter now. "I'm sorry I had to call Glenn. I know your last encounter with him many years ago was not pleasant."

"Maggie, he cornered me at your house, in the kitchen, was drunk, and I had to rack him to get away."

"I understand, but you know he had recently lost Robin. He was lonely, and it was the Fourth of July, and you know he doesn't drink and had one too many." Maggie pled his case again, as she'd done a hundred times over the past seven years. "He felt terrible about it all, still does. Why do you think he's doing this today?"

"Yes, I know. He sent flowers every week for two months until I told him I forgave him. But that doesn't mean I've forgotten. Robin was my friend. I'd never be with Glenn. It was insulting, not to mention creepy and weird. And frankly, I wasn't thrilled that I had to rack him. I hadn't done that since junior high school." Jackie was annoyed again, with no adult beverage in sight.

Maggie began giggling. "I don't need the visual."

Jackie stared at her, waiting for her to stop laughing and glowing with satisfaction, until she finally relaxed and let the laughing lessen her mood. "It's only eleven a.m., don't you think I could have one more Bloody Mary?"

"No! Waiter, more coffee, please."

"You're absolutely no fun. You know Maggie, just because we're sixty doesn't mean we can't have fun."

"We have fun," Maggie insisted.

"Do we? Like what? When I was working, I spent a zillion hours at the office. I'd come home, stand at the refrigerator and eat dinner, watch a movie which I never heard the dialogue of because I was too preoccupied thinking about work, hop up to get a glass of wine and end up checking my email and reading briefs, and finally fall asleep at midnight and get up at five-thirty and start all over again. I should have been more than my work. I let years slip away and now I'm sixty and my knees hurt if I stoop too long and it's a crapshoot if I get down on the floor whether I'll be able to get back up again. I'll be shopping Amazon for a life alert before you know it. I want the years back. I want to have pure, unadulterated fun."

"Jackie, you did what you had to do, what you needed to do for the kids. You still have time to enjoy life and it's going to be a long time before your life alert days are here. And if you want fun, start having it, like the trip to Memphis. That was a great start. I think." Maggie tried to reassure Jackie time hadn't run out even though she'd been having her own thoughts of life slipping through her fingers.

"And what do you do, Maggie? You come home from counseling children at school and making everyone feel better about themselves and then take care of Charlie and the house. Who takes care of you? You were the most incredible artist when we were young. When's the last time you painted anything other than a bedroom wall?" Jackie inquired.

Maggie stammered, "I enjoy taking care of Charlie."

Maggie had nearly forgotten her artistic ability, which was never going to earn her a living, so it fell by the wayside. And so what, if she took pride in keeping her house, "just so." It was hard work to juggle it all sometimes, but she was happy most of the time. She wasn't unhappy, maybe a little bored now and again, but slowing down is a natural part of getting older. Her parents had lived long lives; they watched television every night, read the paper, watched the news, and went to bed. Admittingly, she always thought they were old and boring. It hit her square in the jaw. Jackie was right. She had officially become old and boring.

"There's nothing wrong with taking care of Charlie. I think we should mix in taking care of ourselves, too. That's all. You don't have to shake up your world, but I'm going to shake up mine. I need to find out who I am and what I want, not who I was supposed to be, or expected to be." Jackie picked up the check and paid the bill. "By the

145

way, you're coming to Dr. Williams' office with me. This was all your idea, and I'm not doing this alone."

Maggie nodded; she expected no less. "I planned on being there. Besides, if I weren't, you probably wouldn't tell me the truth about the tests," Maggie scoffed, "then I'd get Glenn in trouble for HIPAA violations to find out."

Jackie couldn't help but laugh, even though she tried to hide it. "And it was two days! See you at four."

"Wait, Jackie, you forgot your book," Maggie called after her, but she had already turned the corner.

Maggie picked up the book and stuck it in her purse. For now, mission accomplished. Although thoughts of an incurable ailment afflicting Jackie were lodged in Maggie's brain. She wouldn't rest easy until the tests were done.

"Thanks for coming, Jackie." Glenn handed her forms to complete.

Jackie looked at him with annoyance but completed them anyway and handed them to the nurse.

"Please try to be nice. Your irritation is obvious. Glenn is doing us a huge favor. Do you know how difficult it is to get an appointment with a neurologist? He's doing this to make up for what he did seven years ago. So please let him off the hook? And after this, can you and Glenn call it even and be friends again?" Maggie whispered to Jackie.

"Fine, I'll be nice, but I'm not happy about any of this. It's a huge invasion of my privacy having to be here and fill out this paperwork, change into a hospital gown, and have an MRI on my brain. You didn't say anything about an MRI," Jackie whispered back through gritted teeth.

"I know, I know. I'm sorry. I had no idea what he would do. I'll make it up to you," Maggie offered.

"Yes, you will! In fact, I know exactly how you're going to make it up to me. There's a tribute to Elvis in Hollywood this weekend and you're going with me."

"Hollywood, California?"

"Yes, is there another Hollywood?" Jackie asked sarcastically. "Tell Charlie you're going away with me for the weekend. He can man up with the hernia recovery. We're going on a girls' trip. The flights are booked, we leave Friday morning. We'll be there mid-morning in time for the ribbon-cutting at two of the statue honoring Elvis's philanthropic ventures." Jackie had already planned every detail.

Maggie smiled. It seemed Jackie was fine and acting like her old friend again, large and in charge, and as soon as the doctor confirmed it, then she could breathe easy. "I'd love to go. But first, let's make sure your brain is still intact, and you're cleared to fly to Hollywood."

Jackie rolled her eyes dramatically, then followed the nurse to see what her future held.

Chapter 17
Hollywood Here We Come

Jackie handed Maggie her boarding pass. "I told you I was fine, and nothing was wrong with me. Glenn ran every test he could think of and then some," Jackie told Maggie for the second time as they walked to the gate to board their flight.

Jackie reviewed the itinerary with Maggie once again. She'd gone over it three times already after she pre-ordered the program for the Elvis tribute, which listed all the movies to be displayed and the schedule for special events. It took over an hour mapping it out so they could see every bit of the show.

"I know and I'm so grateful you're in tip-top shape." Maggie tried to keep up with Jackie's quick pace. There was nothing wrong with her stamina.

"So, do you believe me now about Memphis?" Jackie asked.

"I'm trying to, but I'm struggling," Maggie replied.

"Oh, my gosh." Jackie stopped in her tracks and grabbed Maggie's arm. "Look, see that man up there, grayish hair, snappy dresser?" Jackie pointed him out to Maggie.

"Oh, yes, I see him. My, he's quite handsome."

"Come on. That's the man I saw on my flight to Memphis. We sort of ran into each other on the plane, physically, I mean." Jackie smashed her hands together in demonstration. Slowing her pace, she tried to walk casually and not be seen while she assessed the situation.

"Really? You didn't tell me about that! That I would have believed." Maggie laughed to herself.

Jackie sped up, following him more closely and more conspicuously, her curiosity about this man boiling over. Fortunately, he was headed the same direction they were, straight to the B gates.

"Come on," Jackie urged, pulling on Maggie, forcing her to pick up the pace.

"I'm hurrying. He's going to see us, or do you want him to see you?" Maggie was intrigued.

Maggie knew after the divorce Jackie had sworn off men. College was the last time she'd seen the true boy-crazy girl. Back then, wild horses couldn't drag her away from every good-looking guy that passed by, and guys were drawn to her like a moth to a flame. Who could blame them? Jackie possessed model-like beauty and piercing green eyes, and she was aware of the power she held in those years of youth. As an adult, her confidence waned, as she shifted to being a supreme lawyer, downplaying her looks to be taken seriously as an attorney. Maggie never understood and was thrilled to see the shift. Maybe the real Jackie was coming back.

The women caught up with the handsome man who did an abrupt about-face, Jackie nearly crashed into him again. "Oh, sorry," Jackie apologized.

The man produced a lip curled smile. "So, we meet again. Are you following me?" he asked slyly.

Jackie didn't miss a beat. "I think you're following me," she responded with a smirk.

He laughed, his light-blue eyes twinkling as the slight wrinkles around his temples came together, enhancing his masculine charm. Jackie tried to examine his perfectly set jaw and high cheekbones without staring, a tricky feat from two feet away.

"I'm sorry to be so rude. I think we sort of met on the plane to Memphis. I'm Jackie Sawyer. And you are?" Jackie extended her hand.

149

"I'm Garon," he replied and shook her hand.

She mentally recoiled when his hand touched hers, making her hold on a bit too long. "And this is my friend, Maggie." She yanked Maggie next to her.

"Pleasure to meet you, Garon," Maggie said.

"You as well," he replied.

"Are you from Seattle?" Jackie was intrigued.

"I live here part time, the other half I live in Memphis," he answered easily.

Searching her memory as quickly as she could was giving her nothing in placing where she knew him from. She hated that at times pulling names and faces together seemed like a never-ending puzzle, forgetting names she thought she shouldn't. At least she'd had a full neurological work-up, so she didn't have to put memory loss on her worry plate.

"I feel like we've met before. I don't mean on the plane to Memphis, but somewhere else," she told him again.

"I was thinking the same thing, but I haven't figured it out yet," he agreed.

Jackie wasn't sure she believed him, detecting a tone that seemed to be on the placating side instead of being sincere. "You aren't a lawyer, are you?"

He laughed. It was a pleasant sound, one that Jackie thought she could listen to for a lifetime.

"No, I'm a retired music broker. Now I buy and sell horses. It makes me happy and keeps me out of trouble." He smiled at Jackie.

Garon had to be the most interesting man she had met in a long while, at least in this era. Surprisingly, her curiosity about this handsome stranger was growing.

Maggie broke in, "Jackie, they're calling our flight. We're headed to Los Angeles. Where are you going?" she asked Garon.

"I'm headed back to Memphis. Are you going for the weekend?" he asked.

"Yes, we're going to the Elvis tribute." Maggie wanted to say more, but Jackie interrupted.

"We better get going. Nice to meet you, Garon. Enjoy your flight. I'm sorry, but what is your last name?" Jackie couldn't let it go.

"White. Garon White. It was a pleasure to meet you Jackie Sawyer," he said, taking her hand and kissing the back of it. "Enjoy your trip and say hello to Elvis for me."

Jackie stood, watching Garon walk away, feeling a sense that something she didn't quite understand had happened. Was there a meaning behind the comment? Was he making banter? Was he flirting? It'd been so long since anyone had flirted with her, she wasn't sure she would recognize it when it happened. With Elvis, it had been magnetic, with no need for pretense; he was easy to show his attraction without diluting it. She'd been a master at flirting four decades ago. Now she felt rusty, but maybe Garon was the perfect person to brush up on her skills.

"What did he mean?" Jackie turned to Maggie.

"I have no idea. Let's go, we're boarding. We'll figure it out later. Seems later will be super busy with all we have to figure out."

Jackie and Maggie didn't have a chance to discuss Elvis, Memphis, or anything else on the flight as they had planned. The woman seated next to them never stopped talking, dominating the conversation so neither could get a word in edgewise. Jackie was fortunate to be in the aisle seat. She finally opted for a magazine and dozed off briefly. Poor Maggie was exhausted from being polite to the woman and nodding in agreement and throwing in some "oh, really?" every so often.

By the end of the flight, Maggie knew everything there was to know about the woman's life, from her husband's affair back in 1974 to every job each of her children and grandchildren ever held. The woman had worked as a teacher for fifty years, so naturally the conversation blossomed since Maggie was a counselor at a school and they had much in common. But, after two hours of non-stop conversation, when Maggie wanted to grill Jackie more about Memphis, Elvis, and the handsome man, Maggie was out of conversation energy.

"I need a nap," Maggie told Jackie as they made their way to baggage claim.

"I bet you do. Sorry, I abandoned you. I wasn't a good wing-woman, but I couldn't stay awake. I had to check out of that conversation somewhere between the drama at the bridge club in 1985 and the hailstorm at the graduation of her youngest child."

"Well, you missed a lot after that. I'll be happy to fill you in if you're really interested," Maggie joked.

"Maybe later, much later. What did you tell Charlie about this weekend?"

"I told him we were going to the Elvis tribute, and I wasn't sure if I'd have cell phone reception, but not to worry if I didn't call him back, just like you told me. He wondered why I wouldn't have cell reception in the middle of Los Angeles. I said it would be crowded with poor reception. I'm not sure why I had to tell him that, but I guess it was necessary since the last time you left town, you disappeared," she reminded Jackie.

Maggie never lied to Charlie, and it didn't sit well with her that she stretched the truth. She thought about saying they were going to a yoga retreat, but that didn't feel right, and she rarely did yoga, despising it if she were being honest. She never bought into the trend of wearing yoga pants on every outing and around the house, didn't even own a pair, so it would have been a terrible lie. Charlie would have cut right through it. She also felt guilty that she'd not told Charlie about Jackie's time jump to 1956 and Elvis. The words to explain it still hadn't formulated in her mind.

"How much money did you bring?" Jackie asked. She knew they had to be prepared in case a miracle happened, and they went back in time again, assuming she wouldn't have credit cards like the first time. To be safe, she'd tucked away five thousand cash, which could sustain her quite a while.

"I did as you asked and brought two thousand. I don't know why we need cash. I feel vulnerable, and it seems incredibly dangerous. We have credit cards and our bank cards. It's not necessary to carry cash these days. Especially headed to crime-ridden LA. Have you read what's been happening there?"

"I know. I get it, but I have my reasons," Jackie explained, not telling her that she hoped they'd end up in a different, less crime-ridden year. "It's only mid-morning. Let's get to the hotel, check-in, change, eat some lunch, and then go to the studio before the first event later today."

Maggie agreed. "Where are we staying, by the way?"

Jackie smiled a devious, yet proud, smile. "The Wilshire!"

"Are you serious?" Maggie's eyes lit up. She had dreamed of staying at the pricey hotel all her life but gave up that fantasy long ago. On hers and Charlie's budget, The Wilshire was a far-away fairytale that would never happen. Rooms were somewhere upwards of a thousand dollars a night. Even if they could have afforded it, her tight-wad husband would never splurge on an overpriced hotel. Charlie thought Motel 6 was overpriced. Maggie's enthusiasm climbed higher as they headed to the most luxurious hotel in Los Angeles.

"This is incredible, Jackie. Thank you for this trip. I hope we can figure out what happened in Memphis, but let's have some fun, too."

"Yes, we will. Did you know Elvis had a suite at the hotel? Fans used to send messages to him hoping to get an invitation to the penthouse accessed only through his private elevator," Jackie divulged the trivia.

153

Jackie's hope for this trip was two-fold, which she didn't tell Maggie. First, that this trip was as fun as Memphis, and second, that her prayer would be answered and she'd find Elvis. Leaving the past hanging would gnaw at her for years to come, closure was the only thing that could soothe her aching heart. It seemed a longshot, and she promised herself not to be disappointed if it didn't happen, at least that was the lie she was telling herself this week.

She missed Elvis desperately and hoped beyond hope that she could find him again to explain. The gorget was safely tucked away in her purse waiting for the right time; she pulled her purse a little closer and prayed again; she had to find Elvis.

Chapter 18
Spinout

The opulence and history of The Wilshire was impressive. Maggie and Jackie gushed and fawned over every detail from the crystal chandeliers to the walls covered in beveled edged mirrors, the imported marble floors with gold-flecked veining, and the gold statuettes surrounding the large waterfall fountain in the center of the soaring four-story foyer. A visit to Los Angeles wouldn't be complete without this experience, a necessary expenditure Jackie rationalized, handing over her credit card to the clerk. Jackie regaled Maggie with more Elvis trivia as they stepped into the elevator.

"It's perfect," Jackie exclaimed when they entered their suite through the wide double doors. For someone who had never been concerned with décor and plush surroundings, she couldn't stop carefully hovering over the baubles and furnishings, trying not to touch anything as if she'd walked into an exclusive showroom.

"I've never seen anything like this, Jackie. It's quite impressive. I don't want to break anything. It's so clean and exquisite. Look at the beds. I can't wait to climb between those sheets. What do you think the thread count is?" Maggie asked Jackie as she sat gingerly on the bed and smoothed the duvet. "How about a quick nap before we go?" she pleaded.

"I would have absolutely no idea about thread count. You know I have zero decorating knowledge. And I wish we had time for a nap, but let's keep moving. Lunch will help revive you. It's supposed to be a beautiful, sunny day and the tribute should be full of fun. I promise we won't stay out late, and you'll be snuggled in bed before you know it."

Jackie pulled Maggie up off the bed, where she'd collapsed.

"Okay, if you insist, I'll rally. Let me go wash my face and change." Maggie relented wearily.

After lunch, Jackie and Maggie battled the traffic to get to the studio. Jackie had forgotten how crazy the traffic in Los Angeles made her.

"I hate the traffic here," Jackie mumbled through a clenched jaw, trying to listen to the GPS direct her to the correct exit, the British accent speaking way too fast for her to understand the unfamiliar street names.

"I'm glad you're driving," Maggie managed to say, grabbing the frame of the door as Jackie dodged cars traveling well over the speed limit, switching lanes as if it were a death race. "You're doing a great job, looks like we're almost there." Maggie commended Jackie.

They finally exited and arrived at the studio, following the large signs directing them to the event parking, opting to pay the fee to get the closest parking possible to the studio lots, which was still a bit of a hike. Both women climbed out of the car, frazzled by the effort to get to where they were. Between airplanes, rental cars, and the Los Angles traffic, it felt like a long travel day. Maggie thought about the plush bed waiting for her at the hotel and sighed.

Jackie noticed Maggie's exhaustion. "I know. It's been a full day already. You need one of those rally caps we used to have in college."

"Yes, it's weird how those worked, but I think they were most useful for those weekend music fests we used to go to for the sole purpose to keep drinking from breakfast to the wee hours of the morning," Maggie said, reminding Jackie of their sturdier selves.

The music grew louder as they approached the event, the upbeat mood of the tribute palpable, lifting their energy and shaking the travel weariness. Gigantic banners of each Elvis movie hung high across the buildings, tracing his acting career from beginning to end. His handsome face was plastered everywhere. Jackie drew in a happy, deep breath and smiled. Maggie shook off her exhaustion and let herself get caught up in the celebratory atmosphere.

Sound stages were set up with movie memorabilia, and crowded tours were ongoing. A few stars that worked alongside Elvis were present for special appearances. Jackie wanted to talk to those that knew Elvis and get their impression of the man she'd desperately fallen for. The songs Elvis sang in each film were playing on mocked-up sets. At the main exhibit area, they collected their souvenir booklet replete with unknown movie facts that had never been told. Jackie had one already but picked up another, just in case.

"It's Elvis everywhere," Maggie said, turning slowly in a circle, taking in all the banners.

"I thought we should start with his first movie, *Love Me Tender*," Jackie replied.

"The set stage from *Love Me Tender* is over there." Maggie pointed the way.

Opening her purse to put the booklet away, Jackie saw the gorget and slipped it in her pocket. They walked to the first set and admired the guitar Elvis used, the costumes, the staged house with the porch where Elvis sang the famous title song, and the hat he wore.

The feeling of loss came upon Jackie as she stood in front of the set, knowing she would have been living in Los Angeles with Elvis when he filmed the movie if she hadn't been sent back to 2023 so abruptly. It hammered at her as she toured the set before moving on to the next one for the movie, *Spinout*.

The outdoor exhibit was filled with race cars Elvis drove in the movie, a total of four, all in pristine condition with new paint jobs.

Jackie circled the cars lined up on the lot, periodically crouching to admire the details on each, stopping to notice the etching across the bottom of the McLaren.

"Maggie, look at this," Jackie said.

"What am I looking at?" Maggie bent down to see what Jackie was noticing.

"It appears to be a scrolled design, but if you look closely, it's writing, cursive writing. The production assistant probably had no idea what it said since they don't teach cursive anymore," Jackie remarked sarcastically. Maggie nodded in agreement and annoyance at the education system today.

"Dang it, why is writing getting smaller every year?" Maggie dug her glasses from her purse but became distracted by a small dark cloud hanging over the women that seemingly appeared from nowhere. "Do you think it's going to rain?"

A familiar shiver of trepidation moved through Jackie as she took a quick glance at the ominous cloud. She continued examining the writing, then pulled Maggie close and hooked her arm tightly in Maggie's.

"It says the same thing that's on the gorget." Jackie held the gorget tightly in her hand as she read it.

There is no death, only a change of worlds,
with some lost in between.

The ground shifted as the shrill clap of thunder boomed in Jackie's ears. Feeling herself falling briefly, she held tightly to Maggie. Landing forcefully on the ground with Maggie sprawled half-way on top of her, Jackie knew instantly they had been sent back to the place her heart wanted to be, back to Elvis.

Jackie gathered her senses, and the meager contents of her purse, which had scattered across the pavement. Sitting on a concrete expanse between sound stages, she assessed the activity. People were moving and running everywhere, some pushing carts of costumes, others setting up catering tables, men with clipboards barking orders, and women with pencils stuck behind their ears moving quickly. The lot was packed with cameras, booms, lights, sound systems, trailers, pop up canopies, and more and more people, all walking with intent and dressed in fashions that clearly stated this was not 2023. They had landed on a hot movie set.

"What in the hell happened? Jackie, where are we?" Maggie scrambled to her feet, looking around, trying to understand the upheaval of the world around her.

"Now, do you believe me? I told you." Jackie laughed. "Maggie, we're back in time. We are on a movie set. And look at that sign." Jackie pointed to a sign designating the set.

"It's *Spinout!*" Maggie's mouth hung open. "If this is *Spinout*, it's got to be 1966. I saw that in the promotional magazine at the tribute."

"Ten years after I last saw Elvis, he's thirty-one now. I wonder if he'll remember me. I wonder if I can even get to him. He's a huge movie star now, not like the young upstart I met in 1956. I'm sure he has security all around him."

Jackie tucked the gorget back in her purse and checked the contents, finding no driver's license and no credit cards. It made sense, in 1966 she was technically only four years old. Her cash was there. Thankfully, her plan had worked.

Maggie turned in circles, not speaking, observing the activity with wide eyes. Jackie could relate. She'd been similarly stunned the first time herself.

"Maggie, look at me," Jackie told her.

Maggie turned around and took one look at Jackie, and almost fainted. "You have go-go boots. White ones. I always wanted white go-go boots as a kid. And my-oh-my Miss Jackie, wow, those legs go on for days under that mini-dress. Oh, my Lord. What is happening,

Jackie? Look at you, you're so young. You can't be more than thirty." Maggie stepped closer to Jackie, touching her auburn shoulder-length hair flipped up at the ends, trying to absorb the inescapable surroundings.

"It's not only me, look at yourself. Your long blonde hair like back in college. Your blue eyes even seem brighter," Jackie told her, pointing out the obvious.

"What the hell?" Maggie couldn't stop the word 'hell' from sputtering from her mouth, a word she typically never uttered. She examined her arms and legs, gave her backside a few pats to confirm the solid structure lost a few jiggly parts that she'd left Seattle with that morning. There were no complaints about that. "I'm young and hip!" she said, tossing her hair over her shoulder with flair.

Jackie giggled. "Isn't it spectacular, Maggie? We get to be young again. I don't know for how long, but we can enjoy it while we're here. And do you know what else? Elvis is alive. We need to find him, Maggie," Jackie said, taking Maggie by the arms, shaking her in delight.

Maggie smiled as she peeked down her own shirt, admiring her breasts; they sat upright and perky like they had years ago. "My body is rocking. I have abs!" Maggie announced.

"Yes, I can see that." Jackie knew it would take some time for reality to sink in, she also knew Maggie would have fun in the short-term but would soon miss Charlie and her life back in Seattle, abs or no abs. Jackie's only thought was to find Elvis and discover what her heart held.

"Why aren't you two where you're supposed to be? What are you doing here?" A bald man with a red face and clipboard in hand began shouting at the women as they stood admiring their firm backsides and frontsides.

"All extras are supposed to be behind that barricade and seated in the speedway stands. Didn't you get the notes for your casting call?

We have exactly five minutes before we begin the scene. Don't stand there, move it." The man was not messing around.

Jackie looked at Maggie and they both looked at the man pushing them toward the barricade before hustling off to corral other wandering extras.

"Extras?" the women exclaimed together.

"Guess we better take our places. Maybe this means Elvis is on set. This is perfect. Come on Maggie." Jackie grabbed Maggie's arm as they fast walked to the set as commanded by their new "boss."

They claimed two spots on the third row of the staged stadium bleachers for racing fans, wanting to ensure a prime view of Elvis as they pretend-cheered their favorite racer, Mike McCoy. Jackie couldn't believe her good fortune. Soon she would at least see Elvis, even if it might be from a distance. The production assistant appeared and read the casting instructions to all the extras seated in the bleachers: silently cheer, watch the race, no speaking, no sounds. In other words, be seen and not heard, an instruction they could easily follow. After all, they were Gen-X.

"Do you think it will alter the future if we're seen in this movie?" Maggie whispered to Jackie.

"I have no idea, but I can't wait to see it in present time and see how great we look. I mean, look at you in those slim capri pants and that mid-drift. When is the last time you wore a mid-drift?" Jackie whispered back.

"I think I was probably eight." Maggie couldn't help but giggle.

The production assistant turned and glared at the women and put her finger to her lips to indicate "quiet." No action was underway on the set. The filming had ceased long ago, so the reason for being shushed was unknown. The only activity on set was a handful of sweaty extras fidgeting and grumbling about the intense afternoon heat. A bead of sweat dripped uncomfortably down Jackie's back, rolling from her mid-back all the way down. She could feel the wetness in her go-go boots growing. The last thing she wanted was to be sweaty in case she saw Elvis.

"Better be careful, we can't get kicked out of here until we find Elvis." Jackie leaned close to whisper to Maggie.

"This is getting boring. I'm hot and I'm going to melt into a puddle soon," Maggie responded as quietly as she could, wiping her forehead, attempting to keep the sweat from melting her makeup.

Finally, the production assistant announced that shooting had suspended for the day and to take a break. The bald, sweaty man came running back, his pudgy face glistening with perspiration. He spoke franticly to the production assistant, who shrugged her shoulders in response. Most of the extras had fled to the hospitality area to find some shade and cool off and wait for a recall for another scene or be dismissed for the day.

Maggie and Jackie were still sitting on the bleachers trying to locate Elvis, fanning themselves with the production schedule left behind from overheated extras. The lot behind the main camera area where the trailers were located looked the most promising as a hideaway for a star. They watched the area with focused precision.

"You two," the bald man shouted at Jackie and Maggie.

The women looked at each other, thinking they were getting banished from the set. "Yes," Jackie responded with authority.

"Come with me. Can you dance?" he demanded.

"Dance?" they said in unison.

"Yes, dance! We have two dancers who called in sick. We need two fill-ins. They want to shoot the pool party scene today and I don't have time to get the casting agency to send over replacements. So, can you dance?" he demanded.

"Yes, of course we can dance," Maggie announced confidently.

Jackie's eyes widened. A naughty smile slid over her face. Nodding at Maggie, she turned to the man and affirmed, "Yes, we can dance."

The man had stopped listening, consumed by his mission to deliver his two new dancers. A jolt of excitement surged through Jackie's veins, thinking of how she used to love dancing. She had danced plenty in her life: classes as a kid, cheerleading, dancing with Maggie in college, and practicing the Hustle, the Twist, and the Pony for hours locked away in her room as a pre-teen.

As an adult, she and Bob used to go dancing with Maggie and Charlie at least once a month. But with the divorce, the dancing stopped, literally and figuratively. And thus far, Jackie never had the inclination to start dancing again. Sadly, she'd abandoned too many things she loved, whether out of necessity or bitterness, possibly not even a conscious decision, but one thrust upon her by life and demands. Though now, dancing was back in her world and this time, she would dance with Elvis.

"Follow me," the man ordered.

The little round man sped off. Jackie and Maggie double-timed it to keep up. Jackie's go-go boots swished against each other with each step she took. Maggie and Jackie were trying not to burst out laughing at the annoying sound. They arrived at Lot 12 where the out of breath bald man spoke to another man with yet another clipboard while the women leaned against a trailer trying to catch their breath. Large fans were positioned to cool the set. They welcomed the rush of air on their faces while they listened for instructions.

"The scene will be shot here. Follow Ross and he'll take you to your mark. All you have to do is dance through the song. Elvis will be walking through all the dancers as he sings. You are to smile at him as he comes by. Do not touch him or sing or talk to him. You are dancers, fourteen and nineteen, and you only dance. They will give you more specific instructions when you're on your mark. Got it?"

"Got it," Jackie mirrored as she squeezed Maggie's hand.

A make-up girl refreshed their make-up with the expediency of a pit crew. Ross hurriedly directed them to the set where actors were positioned and ready. Jackie noticed the annoyed and bored looks of the other dancers as they waited impatiently for dancers fourteen and nineteen. Once they were set up, the Director shouted instructions and movement began and then, Jackie saw him.

He entered the set, dressed immaculately in a dark blue suit that fit perfectly over his firm body, standing stone-faced and focused as he waited for his cue. He was more handsome than when she'd seen him as a fledgling bright star at twenty-one. It showed on his face that he'd lived life since then; lost his mom, been in the Army, made gold records, and acted in dozens of movies. So much time and life had raced by. He was a super-star, his light burning bright, and he looked good in the glow. Jackie fell in love all over again as she stared at him, hoping he would look her way. He didn't.

They'd been instructed to stand and dance next to opposite ends of a bench for approximately one minute of the song, then to sit on either side of the bench still dancing while they sat. Elvis would come to the bench, step on it, and dance between them, sit down and look at each of them while singing, stand and continue dancing through the rest of the girls. Jackie thought she would explode, she couldn't speak to Maggie, they had been given the "quiet on the set." She looked back and forth at Maggie, raising her eyebrows and making dramatic facial expressions in an attempt to send a message saying.....OH MY LORD...ARE WE THE LUCKIEST WOMEN ALIVE OR WHAT?

In total shock and disbelief of the day, Maggie raised her eyebrows back at Jackie. She desperately searched the recesses of her brain, trying to remember the dances from the sixties she had promised she could perform. Hopefully, all the hours of dancing in her bedroom while watching American Bandstand and Soul Train would pay off.

The set remained quiet. Only the Director's voice and callouts for the scene set up by the assistants could be heard. Then Jackie heard the word "action" and watched as Elvis jumped up on the fake flowerbed bricks and began singing and dancing, snapping his fingers, moving those enticing hips, interacting with the dancers, smiling at girl after girl swiveling their bodies, doing the twist, the mashed potato, and the pony.

Jackie's body instinctively kicked into motion as she began moving her hips, shoulders, arms, and legs, smiling, and getting lost in the beat and the sound of Elvis's perfect voice. She felt freer than she'd felt in years. She moved her shapely body in perfect rhythm, casually twisting in the direction of Maggie to see her dance moves. Maggie appeared equally caught up in their roles as dancers, a broad sincere smile radiating her glee.

Fighting the urge to scream out to Elvis, Jackie saw the signal from the technical director that a minute had passed and to sit on the bench, which she and Maggie executed perfectly as they sat down simultaneously, like pros. Nobody would ever know they were fake dancers numbers fourteen and nineteen. They performed as if they'd been dancers in Elvis's movies all their lives. Their faces reflecting pure excitement.

Jackie could hear him approaching from behind her as his voice grew louder the closer he came, the cameras following him tightly as he moved around the set. She saw his shiny Oxford step on the bench; she looked up; he looked down at her from where he stood, then without missing a beat, he looked at Maggie, then sat between them, looking back at Jackie again. Their eyes met.

Unable to read his gorgeous face, whether his thoughts were good or bad, she sensed he recognized her. He drew a long breath, which paused the lyrics for an extra beat; the band covered the break in tempo. His eyes were locked on Jackie and hers on him. Forcing herself to continue smiling at him enthusiastically as directed, her thoughts behind the smile were one of apology for disappearing and begging for forgiveness. Elvis broke the look and caught the beat, delivering the lyrics expertly so nobody could detect they weren't as scripted. He stood and continued the scene, moving away from her.

Watching the entire exchange with bewilderment, Maggie wanted to get off the set as quickly as they could so she could talk to Jackie.

Jackie tried to remain in the moment with a smile on her face, but a sick feeling lay low in her stomach, her eyes trained on Elvis as the song neared the end. Elvis gave one last glance back at her before delivering the final masterful notes of the song. Jackie heard the Director yell, "Cut!" and "That's a wrap." Everyone began dispersing. Elvis disappeared with his handlers and out of sight.

Chapter 19
Time to Talk

Jackie didn't want to leave the lot, but she knew she'd be forced to in a matter of minutes. The production assistant began aggressively directing all extras to the hospitality area to facilitate the set exits. Tomorrow's call lists were handed out as the extras passed through the gate.

"Are you okay?" Maggie asked as she rubbed Jackie's shoulder. She saw the pained look on Jackie's face after she and Elvis came face-to-face. Only Maggie knew what her expression meant.

"I'm okay. He was right here, Maggie. I must talk to him and explain. We can't leave until we find him. It could be my only chance. I couldn't tell if I saw anger or happiness when he looked at me." Jackie sighed. She suddenly felt thirty-one and like a woman in love, or worse, a woman in love, about to be heartbroken.

"I couldn't tell either. I was so in awe that he was here in front of me, that we are here, all of it. And you were right Jackie, he is gorgeous, even more so in person. I've never seen someone as perfect as that man," Maggie gushed. "Can you forgive me for not believing you?" Maggie grasped Jackie's hands, hoping to make amends for doubting her best friend.

Jackie had lost concern about her fight with Maggie. Her only worry now was whether Elvis would forgive her. Jackie looked at

Maggie and hugged her. "It's forgotten. We have a more important mission to execute, Maggie. I must talk to him."

Maggie took Jackie by the hand, dragging her toward the trailers, determined to get her to Elvis. "You will. We'll find him. Come on, let's go to the trailer area, nobody is watching anymore."

"You can't go back there," said a big, strong-looking man who stood crossed-armed in front of them, blocking their path.

"Georgie?" Jackie exclaimed in relief. "Georgie, it's me, Jackie Sawyer."

Georgie stood stoically, not responding. Finally, he spoke. "I know, Jackie. EP told me he saw you. He told me to make sure you stay away from him."

"No, Georgie, I have to see him. You don't understand. I need to explain."

Georgie uncrossed his arms, his exasperation showing. "You broke his heart. He had me looking everywhere for you. I liked you with him, Jackie. You brought out the best in him and he was calm and happy with you around those few days. After you disappeared, he didn't sleep for weeks. I've never seen him so upset. He even hired a private investigator to go to Seattle and find you. But guess what? He couldn't find you. You didn't exist. There was and is no Jackie Sawyer. So, I don't know what game you were running on EP, but you're not getting to him this time. He's doing fine, he's happy. Stay away from him, whoever you are." Georgie crossed his arms again, frowning, his anger simmering as he blocked the women.

"Please look at me, Georgie, I can explain." Jackie had never seen Georgie angry. His temperament was typically steady as a rock, which told her that Elvis had been hurt.

Georgie turned his head, refusing to acknowledge her.

Maggie jumped in to defend Jackie. "Georgie, I'm Maggie. I've known Jackie most of our lives. She's my best friend. There was no game being run on Elvis. She loves Elvis, and has for years. You have to believe that she had no choice. I promise, it was completely out of her control."

Usually, Jackie took on the role of handling stressful situations, especially when dealing with upset people, her negotiating skills coming naturally. She was the one who would confront the manager if the service was bad, or send back an ill-prepared meal, or complain loudly for more cashiers when checkout lines were insanely long with only one cashier working. Watching this new side of Maggie blossom and being assertive in the most ingratiating way touched Jackie.

Georgie looked at Maggie, then looked at Jackie again, rolling his eyes as he softened.

"Please?" Maggie pled in her soothing tone. "Please talk to Elvis. All she needs is a half-hour and if he wants her to leave after they talk, then he'll never have to see her again. But don't you think he should know what happened the day she disappeared and why?"

Georgie succumbed to being rolled by Maggie's soft manner and logical words. "He's probably going to fire me. Let me go talk to him and see what I can do. Wait here! Don't move! And don't disappear Jackie," he lectured, wagging his finger at her.

"I promise I'll wait right here. Thank you, Georgie. Please tell him I only want to explain. And Georgie, tell him I'm so, so sorry, and I want to tell him in person so he'll know it's from my heart." Jackie laid her hands on Georgie's crossed arms.

"Wait here!" Georgie ordered before marching off in a huff to Elvis's trailer.

"Maggie, thank you. I hope Elvis will listen to Georgie."

"Who is Georgie to Elvis?" Maggie asked.

"One of Elvis's old friends from grade school. He took care of me when Elvis was busy with the concert. Is it weird that Elvis and I fell so hard for each other after only three days? Well, three days for him, a lifetime for me," Jackie reflected.

169

"The counselor in me says it's hard to know if your love is a culmination of a lifetime of appreciation, nostalgia, his talent, his looks, what could have been for him, and his star power. But for him, you came out of nowhere and he fell for you, that feels real. Your love for him is real, but you loved him before you met him based on descriptions and stories. You tell me? Who did you fall in love with, the image of the man or the man? Only you know if you love him and if it's real," Maggie said, laying it out logically for Jackie.

"I can only say that I've never felt happiness like I felt with him. The man I experienced gave me everything I hoped love would embody," Jackie said sincerely.

Jackie thought Georgie had been gone way too long. The set had emptied. All that remained were security and Elvis's entourage gathered protectively in his trailer.

"He's not going to agree. If he were, it wouldn't be taking this long," Jackie said, feeling deflated.

"Have faith," Maggie encouraged.

Jackie turned and walked in the other direction, pacing as she always did before court. Wondering what she was going to say if Elvis did agree to talk to her. She couldn't tell him she was from the future. How would that conversation go? She repeated her path back and forth until Maggie grabbed her arm.

"Stop! It's not going to help."

Jackie shook her arms, forcing her nerves to settle.

"What am I going to say to him if he agrees? Oh sorry, I was zapped back to 2023 for some unknown reason. I was watching your rock hard, perfect ass while you stared into the refrigerator looking for the orange juice, which sat on the second shelf, by the way. I was thinking wicked, dirty thoughts of what I wanted to do with you and God or some higher power or maybe a medicine woman's magic, punished me for those salacious thoughts and sent me packing."

Maggie's smile turned to laughter at the absurdity of the situation and Jackie's admission of sexual fantasies about Elvis. It was about time, Maggie thought. "You and a million other women have had those thoughts. I for one, am happy you wanted to jump Elvis's bones." Maggie continued laughing.

It had been years since Jackie heard those words from Maggie's mouth, probably as far back as college. Her smile grew wide. The situation spurned elation and heartbreak at the same time. Jackie's emotions were spiraling, which appeared to be her usual state within any proximity of Elvis.

Georgie opened the door to the trailer and walked down the stairs. A serious look covered his face as he came back to the women to deliver the verdict. Georgie heaved a tremendous sigh before he spoke. "EP has agreed to see you. You will have half an hour. Where are you staying?"

"We're at The Wilshire," Jackie offered, resisting the urge to violently hug him.

"He'll send a car for both of you at eight tonight."

"Okay, that's it. That's all he said?" Jackie clarified.

"Yes, that's it? Pick up at eight at your hotel, you'll be brought to EP's house, you can apologize and explain, then you'll go back to the hotel, and go your separate ways. That's exactly what he said."

"Okay, thank you, Georgie." Jackie had to hug him. She'd been given a chance to apologize, but she feared it might be too little too late. It seemed to be written in the stars that Elvis had predetermined their path, and their relationship would be over, each going their separate ways to their own dimensions. Perhaps he didn't love her anymore, maybe he never did. Her heart began to crack.

"Don't break his heart again," Georgie added. "He's different today, but he's still that same kind-hearted guy who carried you upstairs with an injured ankle and stayed up half the night planning a perfect

171

picnic. There's been a lot of women in his life, but he thought you were different, that you really saw him."

"I understand Georgie. I'm not here to turn his life upside down. But I need to tell him what happened."

"You better make it good," he sniped, before turning and retreating to the trailer.

Maggie and Jackie grabbed each other's hands. Jackie didn't know if she should shout for joy or begin to cry. Forcing herself to be optimistic, she chose to embrace excitement. She would see Elvis tonight, explain, apologize, and hopefully, not be sent on her way. Maybe he didn't feel the same about her anymore, but she could continue with her mission and try to change the future. His future. Hers appeared to be destined to stay the same. She would give it her best persuasive argument.

"Let's go to the hotel, get ready, and take that nap." Maggie's pace picked up. Even though she desperately loved Charlie, the quick minute she saw Elvis had her wanting to spend time with him and discover more. He was captivating. She now understood Jackie's lifelong crush.

"We have to find the car first," Jackie told Maggie when they arrived at the parking lot. They stared at a never-ending field of cars, all from the 1960s. When they parked earlier that day, they were driving a 2021 model rental, it was no more.

"Can't you click the remote and honk the horn so we can track it down?" Maggie asked.

"Maggie, darling, we are in 1966, the era of cars with no remotes. No TV remotes either. Remember?" Jackie looked at her, then back to the cars, and assessed the daunting task ahead.

"Right! It's super inconvenient," Maggie half-joked. "Let's think about this. What kind of car would you drive in 1966? Did you have a favorite car?"

"I was four in 1966. My favorite car happened to be a pink Barbie car. At sixteen, I drove a Honda Civic, standard, with a faded paint job and grateful to have that." Jackie pulled the car keys from her purse to examine them. "Look, Maggie, the key is a Ford. That narrows it down."

"Sure, we only have to try the key in the door of a hundred cars instead of two hundred," Maggie said with a loud sigh.

Dangling the key in front of Maggie's face, she said, "But you may be onto something. How about my dream car at sixteen when I got my license? That would be Eleanor."

Maggie broke into a smile at the reference to *Gone in 60 Seconds*. In chorus, they both said their signature, "I'm a little wired and tired. Or something like that," before giggling wildly. Jackie's memory instantly flashing to a wine filled movie night decades ago, maybe one of the last nights they had really laughed with abandon before Bob had entered the room and ruined it with a scowl. The women had continued torturing him by repeating the mashed-up phrase, following every word he uttered by "or something like that." Bob had stormed out of the house. It was weeks before they tired of saying, "or something like that."

With a lift in spirits, the women split up, searching row by row for Eleanor, the Ford Mustang GT500. The color they were looking for was still a mystery, but Jackie's dream color was Candy Apple red; they would start there. They prayed they were on the right track, or the evening would be desperately long, and they didn't have time to waste. After finding the car, they still needed to get to the hotel, change, and eat dinner. Searching for a needle in a haystack was going to undo everything if they didn't find the car quickly.

"What if we aren't there when he comes to pick us up?" Jackie said in a panic. "He'll never forgive me if I disappear again."

"We'll make it. Any luck?" Maggie shouted as she took a break, wiping the sweat from the back of her neck. The heat was unforgivingly radiating up from the black tar pavement, making Maggie feel like she was standing on a hot skillet.

Jackie responded with dejection, "No, nothing."

"Okay, I've covered these five rows. I'm going to move to the end and work my way back," Maggie told Jackie.

"I'll do the same. I need water, too bad there's no bottled water in 1966. We've been searching for more than thirty minutes, we must hurry," Jackie complained as they resumed their search.

"It's here," Maggie shouted from eight rows over, pronouncing it as if a BINGO had been announced, feeling like a winner.

Jackie broke into a jog, wiping her brow as the salty sweat began to trickle down her cheek. She saw the car. The same one she'd dreamed of for months when she learned to drive. Jackie inserted the key. It slipped in perfectly; she turned it, popping the lock with ease.

"You found it, Maggie!" Jackie whooped.

Maggie told Jackie, "Wait, you have to say it!"

Knowing instinctively what Maggie meant, it was their old college party day routine, Jackie put her hands up, shook the keys, and said, "Let's ride!"

Jackie and Maggie slipped into the new, slick 1967 model Mustang in mint condition, as shiny as if it had recently rolled off the assembly line, sporting silky leather seats, custom stitching of the Mustang emblem on the steering wheel, duplicated on the headrests and, of course, on the floor mats.

"Oh, she's lovely." Maggie ran her hands over the soft cream color Italian leather seat.

The engine came to life with a roar and settled nicely into a warm purr. Jackie adjusted the A/C, then studied the gear shift for a moment to reorient herself to a manual transmission. She'd learned to drive on a standard, but decades ago, slowly it started to come back to her. Maneuvering a manual transmission was essentially a lost art in 2023. It was the opposite when she was young, and everyone learned to drive a standard. She pressed the clutch and expertly eased the gear into drive, then stepped on the gas.

Chapter 20
Forgive Me

Jackie changed clothes three times before finally deciding on the pale-yellow baby doll dress and yellow slingback sandals. She fussed over her sixties flip style hair, finally believing the rich auburn color did compliment her green eyes, applying more mascara, hoping Elvis would be entranced and want to stare lovingly into them. Her hair had been perfect five minutes into styling it, then she spent the next forty-five minutes trying to improve it, only to arrive back at the original style that had taken only five minutes to fix. Maggie assured her she looked beautiful.

She transitioned from worrying about her looks to worrying about what she was going to tell Elvis; the truth wasn't an option, but she didn't want to lie. She'd already lied to him enough for two lifetimes and she was living both.

Watching Jackie pace again outside the hotel while they waited for the limo to arrive was beginning to make Maggie dizzy. "It's still ten minutes of eight. You might as well sit down and relax," she urged.

"I know. I'm not nervous, I feel unprepared as to how I'm going to explain all of this. I can't even explain it to myself. I don't know the rules of this new universe. I'm not sure if what I say will undo some event yet to come and I don't want to mess this up. And I don't want to say something that might send me back and leave you stuck here."

Jackie took a seat by Maggie on the rock ledge filled with the most perfect red roses, the sweet fragrance floating in the air.

"Yikes, me either. Can that happen?" Maggie had been thinking about getting home for the past hour, but that was not a possibility she considered. She already knew she wanted to go back. Staying in 1966 was not the life for her. As much fun as the trip had been, her dreams didn't consist of being an Elvis groupie. "I don't know the rules either, but I guess tell him what you can without saying you're from 2023 and sixty-years old."

"Maybe it doesn't matter what I say. Maybe he's not going to forgive me, and it's all done. I go back to my world, and he continues to live the life we know he lived."

"Maybe it's the grandfather paradox," Maggie said.

"The grandfather paradox?" Jackie questioned.

"Yes. I did a little time travel research when I thought you were crazy. The paradox goes: Can you time travel back in time and kill your grandfather? Because if you did, your dad would not have been born and you would not have been born to go back in time and kill your grandfather. So, it's not possible. You can't go back in time and change something that erases you because you wouldn't be there to do it in the first place," Maggie explained. "Maybe this is some kind of paradox."

"That is truly a paradox. And it makes sense, and fortunately, I don't plan on killing anyone, so I'm not sure it's the same."

"But what if you go back in time and do something that erases someone else? Like what if you and Elvis get together, profess your love for each other and you're with him for the rest of time. What happens to his family? It would change Elvis's life and erase his family. And what happens to your children? Does your life cease to exist? Are you erased and your kids erased? Or is this a parallel universe and everything still goes on?"

"I'd like to believe we're in a parallel universe because my life in 2023 still goes on, but if it erases me, does that erase my children?

And if I'm erased, I won't be there to go back and save Elvis to begin with. I see what you're saying. Maybe if we can fix this parallel universe, change Elvis's trajectory, then maybe when we go back to our lives in 2023, he will have lived a long life and not die in 1977. So, do you think the trick to saving him is that I can't stay with him? I need to sacrifice my happiness in order to save Elvis! I don't want to erase anyone, especially my kids or his. I only want to keep Elvis alive as long as humanly or mystically possible." Jackie turned to Maggie. Neither knew the right approach. The consequences of the wrong action or wrong words seemed catastrophic.

"Here's the limo. The best course of action is always the truth. Tell him what you feel and what happened and let the chips fall where they may. By the way, I really love our new car. I get to drive it tomorrow," Maggie said. She took Jackie's hand and led her to the limo, where Georgie stood with the door open.

"You ladies look beautiful tonight," Georgie said with sincerity.

"Thank you, Georgie." Jackie patted his cheek lovingly. "Is Elvis in a happy mood tonight?" Jackie asked.

She needed to prepare herself for the situation she was walking into. Being prepared in court always gave her an advantage. With every case, she tried to find out in advance about the personality of the Judge, opposing counsel, the client, the witnesses. It had served her well in developing her delivery style and strategy.

"EP is in a good mood, surprisingly. His mood was awful this afternoon when he saw you, but tonight he is laughing and joking around, his usual demeanor," Georgie told the women.

Jackie smiled at the thought of the happy, cheerful Elvis. That's really all she knew. She never experienced his anger or bad mood. He loved to have deep and serious conversations, but he had an elevated spirit of life and felt blessed to be the King, at least in 1956 he did. She wondered how he'd weathered the last ten years. From media accounts she'd read over the years, there were career woes, and in two years he would perform the Comeback Special and begin touring again, catapulting him on the way up once more. Jackie stared out the window as they drove, so lost in thought that she didn't even notice the limo had stopped and parked.

Maggie stood half out of the car, gently pulling Jackie's arm. She said, "Jackie, we're here. Are you coming?"

"Oh, yes. Sorry, I was thinking about something," Jackie replied.

"Yes, I know what you were thinking about. Let's go do this," Maggie encouraged.

Jackie wasn't afraid to talk to Elvis, she didn't need preparation for that, she couldn't wait to see him again. Her fear was she would simply run into his arms and beg forgiveness when what she really wanted was a mature and purposeful conversation impacting his future in a meaningful way. She had been lost in thought, trying to formulate the words to change the course of history, and didn't know what she was going to say in the limited time she had.

Exiting the limo, she was struck by a sharp pang of disappointment when she didn't see Elvis there to greet her. Georgie directed Maggie to the living room, where food and drinks were laid out. Jackie was to be delivered to Elvis's office alone.

"This is a beautiful home," Maggie told Jackie, who agreed wholeheartedly.

The style differed greatly from Graceland. This house reeked of Hollywood with décor for a movie star with high coffered ceilings, mirrors, chandeliers, and massive windows with long white sheers pleated perfectly on either side of the beveled edged glass. Jackie imagined the light would stream in from every direction during the day, creating a cheery atmosphere. Dark fur rugs lay on top of the dense light carpet. Long-stemmed multicolored roses soared from voluminous crystal vases strategically placed on dark wooden tables.

The colors were not as bold as Graceland, but were pastel and demur, the epitome of chic, clearly a decorator's signature.

Jackie arrived at the office and took a seat in a chair facing Elvis's large mahogany desk. The room exuded tranquility with a different décor than the rest of the home. With oversized furniture suited to the manly design and Elvis. The dark green walls with matching mahogany panel wainscotting commanded the room. Perfectly aligned photos of Elvis with other celebrities hung on the wall behind the desk with symmetry, clearly measured by an expert, not by eyeing it like Jackie did. Bookcases were stuffed from edge to edge with collections of books amassed and organized from top to bottom. Gold accents and hardware on cabinet doors and the feet of side tables added a touch of elegance.

Jackie heard the door open, but she didn't turn. She waited until she heard him walking toward her and stood as he passed, as if the King of England walked by and she, the loyal subject, was paying respect. He moved behind his desk, where he sat in his large leather chair. He hadn't looked at her yet. She focused on his face. He looked amazing: fit, handsome, healthy, and more mature. It seemed impossible, but he had grown more striking than the last time she saw him ten years ago. Jackie couldn't look away, sitting quickly, feeling her knees weaken as she watched his face. He remained silent. When he finally looked up, their eyes locked, but neither spoke. They sat in silence for what seemed like an eternity until Jackie couldn't take the standoff anymore and broke it.

"I'm sorry," she said as they stared at each other.

Her simple words released him, and he sat back in his chair and closed his eyes. With a heavy sigh, his shoulders relaxed.

"Where did you go?" Elvis asked in a steady, matter-of-fact voice. He placed his arms on the desk and leaned toward her, studying her.

"I had to go back to where I'm from. I didn't have a choice," she said, feeling a quiver in her words.

"We were talking, and you disappeared. How should I have reacted other than with confusion and fear? You were just gone. We looked for hours. I went straight to the hotel. Nobody had seen you and when we checked your room, there were no signs you had stayed there at all. Not one thing in that room looked used, and the housekeeper hadn't cleaned it that day. Your suitcase was gone too. It's impossible that you could have come and gone in the time between when you left the house and when I sped to the hotel. I assumed you planned to leave and had your suitcase with you. But nobody saw you. I asked everyone outside. None of the boys saw you. None of the fans. Nobody gave you a ride. Your car was at the hotel, so how did you get it? How did you disappear so quickly?"

Jackie let him talk because she knew she had no explanation or answers to any of his questions. "I hadn't been to the room since the day before, so it was cleaned from the prior day, I assume. We were together, remember?" She wanted to remind him of that blissful night.

"I remember," was all Elvis said.

"I didn't have any choice, Elvis. We are from two drastically different places. I wanted to stay with you, but the universe had other ideas, and I had to go back," Jackie tried to explain, without actually explaining.

"You said you wanted to come to California with me. Did you panic and run? You could have talked to me and told me. We could have talked it through."

"With all my heart, I wanted to come. I was ready to go. I wanted a life with you."

How was she supposed to tell him the truth? Her own best friend questioned her sanity, and Maggie had known her for decades. Elvis barely knew her after only three days together. He would never believe she lived in the future. He'd have his security carting her off before she knew it.

"So, you're saying you went back to Seattle?" he asked, rocking back in his chair, a tight expression sitting on his beautiful face.

She wanted to see him smile. That's all she cared about, that magical smile of his that set her soul on fire. "I did go back to Seattle."

"I hired a private investigator to find you. There was no trace of you, no records. There was no Jackie Sawyer to be found in Seattle or in Dallas, Texas. Not a Jackie Sawyer that was you, anyway. We found plenty of people that shared your name, but we didn't find you. My PI searched for nearly a year."

"Sawyer is my married name," she said without thinking.

"You're married?" Elvis levelled a look at her, then stood and walked to the far side of the room.

Jackie was on her feet, trying to explain, saying, "No, I'm not married. I was married, but not when I met you, and I'm not married now. My maiden name is Carpenter. Born in Dallas, Texas to Scott and May Carpenter."

She knew it was enough information that a good private investigator could find her birth certificate if he wanted to, but it would show she was born in 1962, only four years earlier. He'd never believe it was the same person.

"I still don't understand how you were gone. We were talking, you said you wanted to tell me something. You said you were from the F.... and that was it. I turned around, and you were gone. What were you going to say? Where are you from? Seattle does not start with an "f.""

So that's what had happened. Jackie hadn't recalled every detail. She was going to tell him the truth, that she was from the future. It was the word "future" that sent her back. She needed to tell Maggie. It was the key to getting back to 2023 or, in her case, not getting back.

"I know what I was going to say," she told the truth. "I can't explain it, Elvis. If I do, then I'll be catapulted away again."

"I'm supposed to accept this at face value?" he said and looked away.

"Please understand, I need you to trust me," she begged, hoping he understood there was something larger going on than a girl disappearing.

"So, you were married and divorced before you met me? What you're saying makes no sense."

"No, I wasn't married and divorced when I met you. It happened later in my life. I can't explain it Elvis, it's complicated, but I can't say anymore."

"How can I trust you? I don't even understand what you're trying to tell me. Are you saying it's a cosmic thing, a magical phenomenon, like Houdini you can vanish into thin air?" Elvis smirked.

"Yes, it is, and that's all I can say."

His eyes narrowed as he paused and gathered his thoughts. "I've been reading a lot of books about different religions and different beliefs. Some are far out, but others are more believable. There's one book I read that talks about past lives and how people have memories of their past lives that help them solve problems in their current life, but sometimes their past life takes over their present life and they end up back in their former life. Do you believe in those things?" Elvis asked.

"Well, if you'd asked me a couple of weeks ago if I believed in souls between worlds, or reincarnation, or any other supernatural concept, I would have said no and insist you prove it with facts. But now, I would think there is truth in that."

"I'm not sure if I believe it, but it's interesting reading. Were you married in a past life?" Elvis stared at Jackie.

She wanted to say that it felt like a past life, but she didn't respond. She stopped herself from crossing the room and taking him in her arms, but she knew she had to press on with her mission. "Do you know anything about your great-great-great-grandmother, Morning Dove?" Jackie watched Elvis's reaction but saw nothing in his face.

"Yes, some. I only know she was loved by everyone and lived in South Texas."

"Did you know she was a medicine woman, maybe had some special powers?" Jackie pressed.

"I've heard a few stories of her being a healer, but that's it." Elvis closed the distance between them and stood in front of Jackie. "I don't really want to talk about her, though. What I need to know is if you still love me? Did you miss me as much as I've missed you?"

Jackie was taken aback. It was the last thing she expected to hear from this man who had aged majestically over the past ten years and developed a sexual power that hung in the air like lightening ready to strike her and electrify every cell of her body. There was a maturity and worldliness wrapped up in his presence, yet he somehow was still able to maintain an edge of innocence. He was thirty-one, with greater weight of the world bearing down on his shoulders then the last time he held her in his arms, and here he sat, relaxed and sensual, apparently handling it with ease.

"Of course, I do. I didn't leave you by choice," she said, her voice breaking with the words. She moved closer, knowing she'd not really explained her abrupt leaving at all.

He moved to her and took her in his arms, pulling her close to him. She couldn't tell if it was anger or passion she saw in his face, but when he leaned down and kissed her like they'd never left each other's side, she knew exactly what it was. Returning the kiss feverishly, she wanted him to understand how sorry she was, how much she wanted to be with him, all the thoughts that were running through her mind a mile a minute, she tried to transfer it all to him in that kiss. It was imperative that he understood what she felt, which was that she never

184

wanted to let him go. When they finally paused for a breath, Elvis moved her to the sofa and pulled her on top of him to resume kissing.

Elvis finally stopped the kisses and spoke. "The Colonel said you were working for the government. He said you were the reason I was drafted."

Jackie recoiled. He hadn't accepted what she said, and why would he? She hadn't offered any reasonable explanation, and he was still thinking about her leaving. "He said what? That's absurd. I've never worked for the government. I can assure you. And I wouldn't have done that to you. I'm sorry you were drafted. I don't think the Colonel has your best interest at heart, Elvis. Please don't trust him," Jackie warned.

In this moment, with her head buzzing from his kisses, she thought if he'd not gone to Germany that maybe his career and his personal life would have taken a different path. She reprimanded herself for the thoughts; it was ridiculous for her to be jealous of his life. A life that had already been lived and one she knew about in detail.

"He has a suspicious mind. I told him he was crazy. The boys all had their own theories, too. A few thought you were a journalist, and they searched newspapers daily for an exposé to be printed. A couple thought you were a runaway. And there were those that thought you were a criminal and planned to steal from me, but changed your mind," he told her all the tales.

"What did you think?" she asked, while tenderly planting tiny kisses on his neck.

"I thought you were terrified of how quickly we fell for each other and how strong my feelings were. And, frankly, after you left, and I thought about it logically, it scared me too and I might have run if I were you."

Her heart surged. She wanted this man more than she'd ever wanted anyone in her life, in both lives. It was real for him, and her heart confirmed what she already knew. She sorted that out the moment she saw his frown in the office a few minutes ago, never wanting to see him sad or worried. She wanted to help him.

"How's your insomnia?" She stroked his hair lightly.

He closed his eyes. "It's problematic when my schedule is crazy. I get hyped up when I'm working and it's hard to tone it down to sleep. I tried the suggestions you made. Some have worked, others didn't."

Jackie understood, struggling with the same battle in her life, too. "Are you still relying on the sleeping pills?" She tried to ask in the least judgmental tone she could muster.

"Yes, and no. Sometimes I need them and sometimes I don't. When I'm on vacation, I don't need them at all. I heard what you said about the pills, and I've been mindful. I'm trying to be selective when I use them, and only in times of great need."

"Good, thank you."

"Did you finish law school? I searched every law school and there was no Jackie Sawyer enrolled in any law school," he asked.

"I did finish law school, but under my maiden name." It wasn't exactly a lie. When she attended law school, she was Jackie Carpenter.

"My Lady Lawyer," he teased.

It felt like heaven to hear his beautiful voice say the words. She kissed him again, forcing her love through her lips into his heart. I need to save you, was all she could think. She wanted to believe she could, and was going to try everything possible, but before she did, she intended to explore this incredible man's body and mind during the time they had left with each other.

"One last question," Jackie said.

"What's that?" he whispered.

"Did you find the orange juice?" she said playfully.

He responded by moving on top of her, pinning her arms above her head and kissing her with a passion that set her soul on fire. She was never letting him go.

Chapter 21
It's In The Stars

Maggie was fully engaged in conversation with Georgie when Jackie and Elvis finally made an appearance. Walking hand-in-hand and a little ruffled, Jackie tried to smooth her hair when she saw Maggie motion that it was a mess. She wanted to beam with pride in looking a bit disheveled. Oddly, she hoped people noticed. She straightened her dress, too. Clearly, she and Elvis weren't tending to business.

Jackie looked at Elvis and sidled closer to him. She noticed the red lipstick on his neck and reached up to smudge it away. He responded with a wink and a squeeze of her hand, making a smile form instantly on her face. The room was momentarily silent upon their entry until one of Elvis's boys masterfully broke the silence, as if he had years of experience with Elvis walking into a room with a woman on his arm and lipstick on his neck.

Soon, all that could be heard was talking and laughing as more and more people filled the room. Jackie had no idea where they came from. They appeared and multiplied. Elvis sat on the sofa and pulled Jackie onto his lap. A content smile crossed his face as he joked with his boys, his arm locked firmly across Jackie's legs. Beautiful women continued to arrive, evidently dancers from the film Jackie deducted after hearing them talk about the scene they shot today. Their side glances toward Jackie were not hidden, but glaringly obvious. Maybe they recognized her as dancer fourteen and wondered how she secured a coveted place on Elvis's lap.

Ignoring the looks, Jackie excused herself and went to freshen up. When she returned, Maggie and Elvis were locked in a deep conversation about trauma and loss and ways to work through grief. After multiple interruptions from barely dressed ladies holding on to Elvis and producing annoying giggles, they excused themselves to have a more private conversation. Elvis kissed Jackie on the cheek as he left the room and the swarm of people, his bodyguards forming a protective line to keep the giggling women from following him.

"I'm going to try to talk with him about not letting people take advantage of him," Maggie whispered to Jackie as they passed.

"Good," Jackie softly replied. "He said the Colonel thought I worked for the government and arranged to get him drafted. We need to make him understand the Colonel is bad news. I know he's done a lot for him, but we know about the lawsuit and that he's a crook. I hope he had attorneys look over his contracts, but I'm doubtful."

Maggie nodded in agreement. "Come find us in about twenty-minutes," she added and left to join Elvis on the patio.

Jackie moved toward Georgie, wanting to test the waters and find out what crazy stories he had heard and let him know she wasn't a reporter, a runaway, a thief, a government spy, or whatever else the boys had dreamed up, and prove to him that she had Elvis's best interest at heart.

"So, I guess he forgave you?" Georgie leaned over sideways so only Jackie could hear him.

"Yes," Jackie said, grinning, "he did, and we are both blissfully happy."

"I'd like to know where you went and how you disappeared so quickly too but, if the boss is happy, then I'm happy." Georgie raised his hands in resignation.

"You know, Georgie, there's going to come a day when you may have to tell Elvis that there are some bad people in his circles who could take advantage of him. A perfect example is the Colonel. Who is not a colonel and not a U.S. citizen, he's in this country illegally. I've done some research about him." Jackie stared hard at Georgie.

"Really? He's got his claws into EP. He keeps making decisions that EP is not happy about, but EP doesn't think he has any choice. The Colonel signed a deal with the studio for a series of movies that EP hates," Georgie explained.

"Hmmm, I need to see those contracts. I'd like to know what the Colonel is up to. Has Elvis used attorneys for all of this? Or relying on the Colonel?" Jackie asked, fearful of the answer.

"I'm not sure. I think he trusts the Colonel with the contracts between them. I know attorneys participated in the contracts with the studios and the label because Vernon complained about the bills. I'd ask Vernon about it, but I'm not sure he'd go against the Colonel."

"No, don't mention it to Vernon. The fewer people that know I'm asking, the better, and less chance it will get back to the Colonel. We have to protect him, Georgie, or the Colonel will drive Elvis to an early grave," she said with emphasis.

"I worry about EP. He burns the candle at both ends," Georgie replied.

"Yes, and when Elvis starts touring again, and he will, you can't let the Colonel overwork him and push him beyond what's humanly possible. Elvis's health will suffer, and he'll be gone. We could lose him forever, Georgie."

Georgie looked at Jackie with concern. She hoped she hadn't said too much, but she feared her subtle warnings to Elvis were being brushed aside, overruled by his intent on providing for his entourage and family. Right now, his workload was heavy but manageable, so Elvis couldn't see the truth yet. Jackie excused herself to Georgie and went to find Maggie and Elvis. She hoped Maggie had imparted some wisdom that Elvis would embrace.

"Hello, you two," Jackie greeted them.

The sparkling city lights across the horizon behind the property pulled her in. *All that glitters is not gold*, came to mind. It was mesmerizing and hypnotic, she couldn't look away. The glitter of gold seemed to summarize all that was Hollywood, the promise of fame and fortune sitting right in the backyard, waiting to be grabbed. She'd never been much of a dreamer of fame, even with the touch of it from being a standout attorney. How it was manageable on a superstar level was something she couldn't really comprehend.

Elvis reached out and pulled Jackie into his arms.

"We've been having the best conversation," he told her.

Maggie smiled. "It was fascinating. Elvis is a deep and thoughtful man, not just a pretty face and magical voice," she teased.

Elvis laughed a hearty laugh. "We were talking about mama, about you leaving, grief, responsibility, life, I think we covered it all."

"Maggie's a great person for a heart-to-heart. And I didn't say it earlier, but I'm so sorry about your mom. I sure loved meeting her. I remember her fondly," Jackie said to Elvis.

He squeezed Jackie closer. "Yes, she was a gem."

"Well, I need a drink," Maggie announced. "If you'll excuse me. I'm going to leave the two of you to do whatever it is the two of you do."

Jackie hadn't felt her mood this elevated and relaxed in years. She and Elvis walked to the edge of the patio to stare at the stars. Knowing it was going to end, the safe thing to do would be to stop the intensity growing between them and not let him work his way into her soul. There were events in his life pushing forward that would take him away from her, but it was a time for healing and releasing the bitterness she had let fester over many years. Locking him out was a thought she couldn't fathom.

"What a stunning view," Jackie said, her back against Elvis's chest.

"I'll fear not the darkness when my flame shall dim. I know not what the future holds." Elvis's voice waxed lyrical even when he spoke, not only when he sang.

"That's beautiful. What is it?" Jackie asked.

"It's from my favorite hymn," he said.

"It's a perfect hymn," Jackie murmured.

"As incredible as Maggie is to talk to, I enjoy talking to you about my life," Elvis said.

Elvis turned Jackie to face him and kiss her again, drawing out emotion from the depths of her soul, leaving her breathless once more, her desire to stay with him growing stronger with each touch of his fingers on her skin and each time his lips found hers.

He lifted her chin, lacing his lips with hers one more time, delivering a long, drawn out, luscious kiss. Jackie clung to Elvis's embrace and lost herself in the kiss, her senses consumed and intoxicated by his touch. She wanted the world to go away, both worlds, leaving her and Elvis on their own. She didn't want to worry about anyone else's fate. All she cared about was that she and Elvis stayed together. It had been such a long time since her heart had been open to feeling love, she urgently wanted to nurture it and enjoy what was happening, pushing out the reality looming in the background, ready to destroy her happiness.

"You see those stars? I want you to believe that when I'm not here, if ever I go back to my life again, that each night I'll be looking at those stars and thinking of you," Jackie promised.

"Are you saying you're going to leave again?" Elvis continued, staring at the stars.

"I'll stay as long as I possibly can and as long as you want me here." She stared at him, which was dangerous.

Illogically, Jackie believed being armed with the knowledge their love was finite would make the heartbreak easier when it came. She could prepare herself, unlike her past relationships, when the end slammed her into a wall. But realistically she knew being prepared for endings often times was not easier, like when a loved one passed away after a long illness, telling yourself you're ready, they're ready, it's for the best, all the proper words and comforts to help you through, but as much as you pretend to be prepared, you never are. The Earth shatters, your heart breaks, endless tears pour out on the pillow, night after night. She wanted to believe this was different and would make her time with Elvis sweeter. The truth was, standing next to him with his arms around her, she didn't want to think of endings because it felt too much like a beginning.

He looked down at her, telling her, "I want you here for always. In fact, come to the studio tomorrow. I'm laying down some tracks, but it will only take a couple of hours, then you and me and Maggie can go spend the day together."

"That sounds wonderful. We'd love to." She stood on her tippy-toes and kissed his cheek.

"I can send a car if you want."

"Are you kidding? Maggie is champing at the bit to get behind the wheel of Eleanor."

Elvis raised his eyebrow, then curled his lip, saying, "I need to see this car. I might want to buy it?"

Jackie laughed. "No, you are saving your money for a rainy day, remember? Did you take my advice and invest money like I suggested?"

Elvis groaned. "You didn't think I would, did you? Yes, My Lady Lawyer, I did what you asked. Nobody knows about it. It's our little secret."

With that tidbit, Jackie didn't want to talk anymore. She was tired of being practical and logical. She was young again and wanted to feel every emotion she'd been too busy to feel, or too scared to feel, or too stubborn to feel. Her past relationships had been limiting, she'd been unable to share her true self and pure love with the life-partner she'd chosen, but with Elvis she spoke her mind and didn't try to tamp down her true emotional self, if she could confess the rest of her truth, she would never leave.

The world had delivered a gift to her, allowing her to be thirty-one again, staring into the eyes of a man who had captured her heart. She wanted to soak it in, to feel every prickling of emotion, whether it was joyous or painful, to touch his skin and feel her nerves come to life when he touched her back. To absorb his kiss and let it open her soul and pull desire back into her heart. She didn't want to stop what had started, right or wrong. Wanting only to let her heart escape.

Jackie looked at Elvis, who was staring back at her with more emotion than she'd known in her lifetime. She felt lucky to have a second chance at discovering the expanse of her heart. She touched his cheek and wrapped her arms around his neck; he responded and pulled her tightly against his strong body. She could feel how much he wanted her, and she acknowledged it with a pleasant moan of delight.

They lost themselves in each other beneath the stars as he tenderly kissed her with a love that was clothed in desire as they promised to share forever, no matter how much distance might separate them. Only Jackie knew that true distance. He thought it was only geography; she knew it was dimensions cast against them. If only it could be for always. Knowing how it was going to end was something she wished she didn't know.

Chapter 22
Burn Baby Burn

The party wrapped up around one a.m., far past Jackie's normal hours, but she didn't feel sleepy and the thought of leaving Elvis was something she didn't want to entertain, even if it was only for the night. Plans were set for Elvis to take time off for a day of fun with her and Maggie after his ten o'clock set call to lay down the soundtrack. He'd invited them to watch the recording, setting off giddy giggles in anticipation.

By the time the final goodnights were said, it was after two a.m. before they returned to the hotel and their heads hit their sumptuous Wilshire pillows. However, even in the plushest of beds, sleep wouldn't come to the women. Enthusiasm filled the room as they recounted the evening, remembering the tiniest details with great impression, like the shrimp on gold toothpicks.

"I didn't know they made gold toothpicks," Maggie squealed. "And the food, it's the best I've ever had. The bacon and asparagus roll with the sauteed onion strips were to die for. I'm going to have to make those. Charlie will love them."

"I have to order some gold toothpicks," Jackie added, wishing she could check Amazon, alternatively wondering what type of business she would look under in the Yellow Pages to buy gold toothpicks. She contemplated this trivial thought more than was warranted.

Full party mode had been engaged at three a.m. as Maggie and Jackie plowed through the night like lovestruck teenagers, overly excited after a stimulating party. By four a.m. they were still consumed with light and happy conversation as they ate popcorn on their luxurious mattresses covered with Egyptian cotton sheets. Jackie was counting the hours until morning arrived, excited to head back to the studio and spend the day with the King.

"So, in the true spirit of a slumber party, since that is what we are apparently having," Maggie joked with Jackie, "truth or dare?"

"Truth," Jackie stated firmly.

Past experience with Maggie's college dares, gave her the wisdom to know better than to agree to one at four in the morning, mostly because the odds of her performing it were much too high and getting arrested in 1966 might prove to be more than difficult with no proof of her actual existence, plus the energy required was not something she possessed at this late hour.

"Who was the best kisser in your life? And you can't say Elvis. I know that's what you're going to say."

Jackie laughed. "Yes, I was going to say that." She thought hard about the men she had kissed over the years. There were many when she was young, but since marrying and divorcing Bob, there had only been Elvis. Narrowing it down to the top two was easy. "It would have to be Deke."

Maggie looked a bit shocked at Jackie's answer. "Deke? Guy's BBQ, Deke? The hot, steamy, brooding young man who barely spoke and hummed endlessly? That Deke?" Maggie described him perfectly.

"Yes, that Deke. He wins as the most sensuous kisser I've ever laid my lips on until Elvis, of course. They are neck-n-neck as contenders with those killer blue eyes that I could get lost in all night long," Jackie confirmed dreamily.

"Really, that's hard to believe, but it must be true if you say so. And I agree, he had gorgeous blue eyes."

195

"I'd ask you the same question, but it would be a waste of breath because I know you're going to say Charlie." Jackie laid back on the bed and fluffed her pillows. She could feel the late hour settling in as the vibrations of the evening began to smooth out.

"Of course, it's Charlie. I can't even remember any other kisses so they must not have been that great." Maggie laid back too.

Unable to stifle a yawn, Jackie said, "Oh, good grief, I can't believe I didn't tell you. I think I know the key to getting back to 2023 and what happened when I went to Memphis."

"Oh, really? That's valuable information. What's the secret? I spiraled into stress-thinking about this earlier today, wondering if we could get ourselves home. As much as I like being thirty-one again, I miss Charlie."

Jackie knew Maggie would be ready to go home by Monday, even if she wasn't sure she would be. "I know. I started to tell you earlier and I don't know what happened. Sorry."

"I can guess what happened," Maggie said, mimicking kissing sounds amongst her giggles.

"Most likely," Jackie said with a grin. "Elvis reminded me that when I disappeared, we were talking about where I came from. I had planned to tell him the truth. I do remember that. He said the last sound I made was the sound "f." What he doesn't know is the f was for the word f-u-t-u-r-e." Jackie wasn't sure if saying it out loud was enough to send her back to 2023, but to be safe, she spelled it out.

"So, we must not say the F-word!" Maggie said as she sat up in her bed, then plopped back down on the mattress in laughter.

"Yes, like our mothers always said," Jackie added between uncontrollable late-night giggles.

Bouncing off high and happy moods, coupled with the lack of sleep, everything was funny even if it wasn't. When the laughter finally subsided, Jackie smiled uncontrollably, she thought it felt healthy and real to laugh so hard and to be "simpled out," a feat she thought was only achievable when she was young and carefree, knowing she hadn't outgrown the ability to reach that level of disconnect to the serious world washed over her. The reconnection to a safer and happier time with a more honest and less burdened part of who she used to be settled her mind and reinforced new priorities for her: laughter, enjoyment, friends who care about her, and love. The important things.

It was hard to ignore that the past thirty-plus years were driven by making money, sometimes out of necessity and sometimes out of fear of facing a day without it, the world making it a necessary evil to reach a certain social status and to provide for a comfortable living, one she wouldn't apologize for wanting and needing. She melted deeper into the sheets and stared at her panoramic penthouse view of twinkling lights across the city and thought of Elvis.

It was time for a shift, certainly an easier feat in her 2023 life, since she had plenty of money and no work obligations. Though the anxiety of those beginning lean years as a baby lawyer with only debt to her name and the financial minefield of the divorce could never be forgotten. Like Maggie said, she did what needed to be done, but she had let it consume and define her, leaving her a bit unbalanced. When she finally settled her mind, sleep came upon her smoothly and rescued her from her thoughts. Maggie snored peacefully.

Arriving at the sound stage promptly at ten, Georgie met them and guided them to the recording studio. Elvis sat inside the sound booth with headphones on. Jackie caught her breath, unable to stop herself from examining him head to toe as she would any fine work of art. Admiring every stich on his body, she took inventory; a navy-blue silk shirt with tiny white polka dots unbuttoned just enough to make her heart jump, slim white hip-hugging trousers, and white brogues. Drop-dead gorgeous, as usual. Jackie thought she could stare at him twenty-four hours a day and never tire of his chiseled face, debonair smile, and fit physique.

Her heart exploded as he waved and blew a kiss to her through the wide glass partition between the sound studio and the control room. She reciprocated; he caught it in the air, adding a clever smile. She savored their corny playfulness. His sense of humor was relaxing.

Elvis masterfully sang the tracks for the movie, restarting and massaging the sound until his artistic prowess was satisfied. To Jackie's untrained ear it seemed perfect ten takes ago, but she didn't share the expert and well-tuned musical ear of Elvis Presley who by the last take contorted the track to a higher plateau of perfection than she ever imagined, it was masterful and proof why he was the King. Just as Elvis signaled his acceptance of the final run and pulled his headphones off and set them on his stool, the Colonel came bursting into the studio.

"Why are you here?" He glared at Jackie with his beady little mole-eyes, sweat dotting his forehead.

"I was invited," she responded without hesitation, matching his glare with her own. If it was a fight he wanted, Jackie was ready and would happily take it on. She suddenly felt sixty, protective, and like the legal beast she was.

The Colonel ignored her and continued moving pointedly across the room, flanked by two men in suits. All entered the sound studio and shut the door with a bang. Jackie thought it intentional, the Colonel always needing to be the most notable man in the room whether the attention was bad or good. As the men spoke, Elvis looked at Jackie from time to time. The discussion seemed to be annoying Elvis, even though he maintained a neutral expression. His body said more as he gripped the microphone stand and shifted uncomfortably. The smile that sat on his face minutes earlier slipped away. When the conversation ended, the Colonel pulled the door to the sound room open and held it as each man exited single file. The men in suits were all smiles, Elvis was not.

"Good morning," Elvis said to Jackie as he entered the control room, planting a kiss on her cheek.

"Everything okay?" she asked.

"No, the record label is here. They want me to record a new song this afternoon so it can be released before the end of the year. I'm not sure why it has to be done today. I was looking forward to spending time with you. I specifically told the Colonel that earlier this morning," he explained.

Jackie knew exactly what the Colonel was up to. She asked, "Are you contractually obligated to do that? You need to take care of yourself, Elvis. If you're feeling like you need time off, then take it. You are the star, after all." Jackie tried to encourage him to control his own schedule.

"I'm under contract to do this according to the Colonel. I think he wants to keep me away from you, honey." Elvis wrapped his arms around Jackie's waist.

It seemed Elvis was catching onto the Colonel's manipulations. She told him quietly, "I need to look over those contracts. I don't trust the Colonel and I don't believe he has your best interest at heart."

She knew the truth and wished she could show him proof of how the Colonel had bilked him out of millions over the years. As tempting as it was to blow it all up, it would be a reckless move.

"How about you and Maggie go get some lunch, go to the beach, go shopping, and then I'll send the car for you around seven? We can have dinner at the house and a small cocktail party," Elvis responded, changing the subject from the Colonel. He reached into his pocket and peeled off several hundred-dollar bills and tucked them in Jackie's hand.

"Seven is perfect. The money is not necessary, I have plenty," Jackie protested.

"Don't argue with me, honey. I want to take care of you today since I can't be there. Go have fun. I'll get this done and tomorrow, I promise, we'll spend the entire day together. In fact, pack your bags and you and Maggie stay at the house from now on. There's no reason for you to be at a hotel, even if it is The Wilshire. You can each have a private suite if you want, but you're sleeping in my bed." He raised his eyebrows and smiled.

"I would hope so," Jackie said, smiling back, feeling her face flush with anticipation.

"I want you to be with me tonight and we can talk about the days after that. Be prepared though, I'm going to talk you into staying longer than Monday," he told her and sealed the deal with his come-hither grin that couldn't be refused, kissing her tenderly with the exact touch of passion to make sure she'd return this evening.

Jackie was confident he knew exactly what he was doing to her as he nibbled her ear making it difficult for her to stay focused and fight the urge to close her eyes and moan in delight, but the room was full of men watching them, so she maintained her decorum.

"Okay, but tonight, I want to look over those contracts and see what you're obligated to," she whispered as the Colonel moved closer to intervene and pull Elvis away.

With a kiss on the cheek, she reminded him not to work too hard, then reciprocated the ear nibble. Two could play this dangerous game. Knowing he didn't have her discipline, she waited for his reaction; he emitted a low groan. Mission accomplished, Jackie thought. She sweetly waved goodbye to the Colonel.

"So, what was all of that about? I thought Elvis was going to take a day off," Maggie questioned on the walk to the car.

"He planned to, but the Colonel and the record label had different ideas. Evidently, he's obligated to record a new song. But he's sending the car for us tonight and we'll have dinner at his house. He wants us to stay there also, we can check out of the hotel later. And he gave me money for us to go to lunch and shopping and suggested we go to the beach, which is a great idea, don't you think?" Jackie tried to hide her disappointment at Elvis not joining them, but the thought of the beach sounded heavenly, and she knew fighting with the Colonel would get her nowhere. Elvis would have to draw that line.

"Wonderful. Guess we better start shopping for swimsuits. I didn't bring one. Did you?" Maggie asked.

"No, I didn't think about it, not that I own a swimsuit. It's been years since I've been to the beach. I think the kids were in high school when I took them down to San Diego for Spring Break, but as I recall, it wasn't that warm. But it's warm today and I can't wait to relax on the beach and listen to the waves. Guess we better go find us some itsy bitsy teenie weenie yellow polka-dot bikinis," she said. The laughter returned as they pulled into a parking spot on Rodeo Drive with Maggie at the wheel.

The women ducked into the first store they saw with swimwear. They were on a mission to find the smallest bikini they could. It had been a long time since either had been excited to venture out in a teeny bikini.

Jackie thought it ironic that looking at her thirty-one-year-old figure now, it seemed perfect. Thinking back to the age of thirty-one the first time around, she had been hard on herself, judging her body with intensity the rest of the world would never impose. She'd been insecure, self-focused on the smallest negative attribute, having the sense of never being able to achieve perfection. Not long after, she became pregnant with Susan, which afterwards further altered her body perception even more. Whether the source of that was her own internal manifestation of what the world viewed as perfection from magazines and images of supermodels, she didn't know.

Fortunately, she only had magazines to inflict those unattainable images when she was growing up. Today's kids are bombarded with unrealistic, unattainable body images from every direction. Now, with the wisdom of living sixty years, she could look at her thirty-one-year-old body and be proud and truly see its beauty. It wasn't perfect, but every curve, every dimple, even the little stretch marks added to who she was. All it took for her to come to that realization was living life for three more decades and looking back through eyes of wisdom and years.

She promised herself if, and it was a big if, she arrived back in her world, to stop the harsh judgment of herself when she assessed the effects of time and gravity imposed on her sixty-year-old body and try to look at herself with the same adoration she felt now.

"Don't they have anything a little more teenie-weenie?" Maggie asked Jackie.

Jackie hung the high-cut, mid-waist suit back on the rack. "I know. I distinctly remember the sixties being the time of free love, rock-n-roll, sex-love-drugs!"

"Do you have any string bikinis?" Jackie asked the salesclerk.

"No, I'm sorry. Our buyer insists these are the most popular styles," the girl responded.

"It's only, we are looking for something smaller, better tans, less coverage," Maggie chimed in.

"I don't think you're going to find those here. You might try the little surf shop down in Malibu. They carry those types of suits, but here, we have respectable, expensive, and modest suits," she advised, as if repeating a sales pitch with a bit of sarcasm thrown in.

"Okay, I guess I'll get this one." Maggie placed the two-piece with bright yellow daisies on the counter. Jackie joined her and bought a red two-piece with a high-waist bottom.

"We better get sunscreen. What's the highest SPF you have?" Jackie asked.

"I'm sorry, the highest what? SPF?" the girl replied with confusion.

Jackie picked up a bottle of suntan lotion, the one from her childhood with the picture of the little girl and the dog pulling her bottoms down so you could see the impressive tan line. Jackie examined the bottle, finding there was no mention of SPF. The instructions said, "for the best tan, reapply after swimming."

"Guess we better get two bottles," Jackie said, placing the lotion among their purchases.

"You know, if you're looking for a little fun and want to really feel free and get an all-over tan, you could go to the nude beach," the salesgirl suggested, smacking her gum rhythmically as she rang up the items.

"Nude beach?" Jackie looked at Maggie with a wide, evil smile.

"Yes, that's where we should go. I've always wanted to go to a nude beach." Maggie offered with unexpected eagerness.

"Seriously? You've always wanted to go to a nude beach? I do believe I've never seen this side of you, Maggie. I mean, me going to a nude beach would not be a surprise, but you, miss conservative who dresses properly all the time?" Jackie found herself pleasantly shocked and amused.

"Well, maybe you used to be the girl that would go to the nude beach way back when, but when was the last time you felt free and young?" Maggie kidded Jackie, who didn't disagree.

The salesgirl drew a map to the beach located a few miles away, tucked inside a private cove. Armed with their map and a plan, the women went to the hotel to get ready for the beach.

Maggie packed the book she bought, a nice summer romance beach read, hopefully loaded with plenty of hot and steamy encounters. She'd been stuck in a non-fiction mode for years, she needed a change, reality had become boring. Being lost in a hot dream of torrid love sounded much more entertaining, especially since present life felt like a fantasy. She couldn't wait to relax and read on the beach, the nude beach.

"This is going to be so much fun," Jackie told Maggie as she stuffed all the beach gear she purchased in the new beach bag. "I can't believe you're game for this."

"I know. I don't know why. Somehow, reliving this age again has given me a freedom I was afraid to express the first time around. I was always worried about what the world thought of me. I kept myself prim and proper. You know, we were raised with that 'good girl' mentality and the notion there were certain things you did not do as a good girl. I'm nearly sixty and looking back on how benign this is and truly not caring what anyone thinks of me here in this day and time, I feel liberated. I want to try life out, experience things I passed by the first time around," Maggie said happily.

"Did you ever have to take those etiquette classes when you were young to learn to be a 'proper' lady?" Jackie asked.

Maggie recounted her childhood lessons. "Yes, instructions on setting the table properly, greeting strangers, exuding politeness and charm?"

"Exactly. I was the master of walking across the room with a book on my head, chin up, back straight." Jackie stood straighter, instinctively.

"Wow, I'd forgotten about that. Maybe that should be a new course in the school curriculum," Maggie joked.

"I think being concerned about how we were perceived by others was probably engrained in us, so don't be too hard on yourself. I was too busy having children and building my career to even imagine sitting on a nude beach, or even a beach for that matter, the first time around. I was trying to keep Bob happy, the partners happy, the clients happy, and turns out that all of that keeping everyone happy didn't stop bad things from happening. I thought if I kept everything in order, then life would stay in place too," Jackie said with irritation as she tossed the rest of the items in the beach bag. "The truth of it is, life is messy and there's only so much that's in our control. But I still can't shake the feeling that I should have made better decisions and I'm having a hard time accepting those decisions and moving forward." Jackie shrugged.

"We're caught in a trap. I've worked the same job, at the same school, for over thirty years. I could have retired years ago, but if I'm honest, there's a fear of fading away without a purpose. I'd love to retire and for Charlie to retire and spend our time enjoying each other, traveling, doing all those projects we talk about but never tackle. Maybe get an RV. I've been afraid if the motion stopped, we'd get old before our time."

"You and Charlie will never grow old. You two are timeless," Jackie told her. But she understood the fear of fading away. Her retirement brought that front and center to her awareness. She had wondered for a while why Maggie kept working, now she knew.

For herself, juggling life's demands didn't leave much room for relaxation and time to enjoy the good moments, and she'd been conditioned that work had to be the priority forcing her to direct her time and energy there. Before she knew it, all the special moments became secondary and when she finally slowed down, looked around, and realized the world was spinning more slowly, those moments were gone.

"The other option, for both of us, is to do something about what we don't like about our current lives," Maggie replied.

"Which current life is what I'm trying to figure out. I'd be a fool to refuse this gift the universe has given me of being thirty-one again and the opportunity to live life over and not make stupid mistakes, and there's Elvis. I never thought I'd be heading into the retirement phase of life alone. It all looked much different when I was young, and retirement felt unobtainable and eons away. It has passed too quickly, Maggie. I want it to slow down. It's frightening how fast life passes."

"It has, but do you really think you'd be happy if you lived it over? And what about Elvis? You don't know if you can save him. If he's gone in ten years, will you regret giving up what you've built? Do you really want to start your career over because you think you made a bad decision marrying Bob? I think you should evaluate what has you stuck in this mindset a bit deeper," Maggie imparted her opinion, whether Jackie wanted it or not.

"It's more than marrying Bob. I stopped living. I'm happy now and feel alive and it's been a long time since I felt like I'm living life and not merely going through the motions. When it comes down to it, I only have myself to blame. I let the years slip away. I took it all on and let the work overshadow too much of my life," Jackie admitted.

"At least you know how to set boundaries and say no to social commitments." Maggie laughed, knowing she was a perpetual over-committer, never saying no and volunteering to do things to avoid hurting someone's feelings.

"Never change. That's what I love about you. I know if I ask you to do something, you'll say yes," Jackie told her with a laugh. "I'm not sure I set boundaries. I just never had time for anything else. My schedule was crazy, so nobody ever asked me to do anything," Jackie added.

"You did a good job, Jackie. Your kids are happy and well-adjusted," Maggie reinforced.

"You think so? I hope so, but they haven't needed me for a long time." Jackie reflected.

Maggie had always been confused by Jackie's lack of confidence as a mom. She was certain there was more to it. "You don't give yourself enough credit. All that means is you did a good job raising them, and they will need you forever, no matter how old they are."

"Don't get me wrong, I'm proud of my family and building my business. It's given me prosperity and happiness on many levels, but I disregarded that I was a consideration and that doesn't sit well with me. What's worse, I didn't even notice."

Maggie smiled at Jackie and hugged her. "You're always a consideration."

"Enough of this drivel. Let's go get nude!" Jackie squealed.

Jackie and Maggie found the beach without a problem, hidden from view from the coastal highway as the salesgirl described. They parked, hiked down to the water's edge, and climbed over the man-made rock wall, stepping into a new world where at least fifty people dotted the shoreline. All nude.

There were small and large bodies, men, women, old and young adults, all hanging free. The women found a location away from the main groups of sunbathers who had set up camp along the shore. A handful of people were playing frisbee, something Jackie didn't want to watch, and others were lounging and taking in the sun. A couple of elderly men stood in the shallow waves wearing nothing but sailor hats, chatting up a storm without a care in the world. Probably reminiscing of some long-forgotten war, the Navy maybe, as they stared intensely out to sea, pointing at ships moving across the water in the distance.

Jackie glanced at Maggie, who was staring down at the white sandy beach as she followed closely behind. She teased, "Lost your nerve?"

"I guess I didn't realize there would be this many people. I didn't know so many people liked to take their clothes off in public," Maggie told her. She walked a little faster to catch up to Jackie, directing her as she closed the gap. "Let's go over there, away from the crowd."

Jackie could sense Maggie was having second thoughts, but she gave her credit for pushing on with determination. They found a secluded spot and set up their towels and beach gear and the takeout food, which Jackie was now second-guessing as a bad idea as she juggled the container. But she wanted to worship the sun as long as possible before the night's events, imagining a sun-kissed glow would make her look particularly sexy when she saw Elvis, especially in the mint green chiffon, A-line mini-dress she planned on wowing him with. A tan would pop against the color.

"Jackie, there's a man coming to talk to us. He's naked," Maggie whispered in a hushed voice, then put her new sunglasses on as she settled on her towel.

"It's a nude beach, everyone is naked except us." They'd opted to wear their new swimsuits in case they couldn't find the nude beach. They were determined to get some sun.

"Hello," the man called out with a friendly wave.

Jackie put her sunglasses on too. No point taking the chance he'd see her staring at things. "Hello," she replied.

"Welcome to Be Free Beach," he said, sticking his hand out to shake.

Maggie froze, looking away as he parked himself in front of her. Jackie shook his hand quickly. Maggie was right, trying to hold a conversation with a nude stranger was more than off-putting, especially since she was kneeling, and he was standing.

"Thank you." Jackie refused to engage.

After an awkward silence, the man deciphered he was not welcome. Regardless, he told them with neighborly inflection, "If you need anything, holler. My name is Chad. We're camped about thirty yards that way." He pointed to a small campfire where people were roasting hot dogs.

"Thank you," Jackie replied with no commentary.

"Okay, I'll let you enjoy your day," he said before walking away.

"That was so weird," Maggie exclaimed when the man was out of earshot. "I didn't know where to look!"

Jackie attempted to muffle her laugh, not wanting the man to know they were laughing at him. She removed her swimsuit, applied the non-SPF suntan lotion, and tried to get comfortable. The nudist she once fancied herself being in her younger years had grown up. Maggie followed and took her swimsuit off but kept it close at hand, reapplying suntan lotion twice, unsure of how her fair skin would handle lotion that was supposed to make you tan evenly without sunburn protection.

"I'm lying on my stomach. Even though I really wanted to do this, I don't feel as brave now," Maggie admitted as she rolled over and smashed and smushed the sand until it reached an acceptable comfort level.

Jackie shielded her eyes and looked at Maggie. The sunglasses had no polarity, and the sun was blinding. "We can go if you want."

"No, I don't want to go. I just need to take a moment to relax and remember that none of these people are from our world and will never see me again. I mean, I guess they won't. Do you think there are others who have time traveled like us?"

Jackie never considered that as she looked around at the other people on the beach. "I have no idea. I guess there could be others. It would be presumptuous to think we're the only ones capable."

"All of this is so bizarre. How did we even get here? I've been so caught up in you and Elvis that I keep pushing out of my mind that we are in 1966. How, Jackie?" Maggie sat up and took a couple bites of her food before closing the lid and putting it back in the bag, turning again to her stomach to sunbathe.

"I don't know. There's a purpose for all of this, but I can't seem to figure out exactly what it is. I've been caught up in it too and forgot about the why. I know I was sent here to help Elvis, we both were." Jackie bit her lip, not wanting to think about it. "What I do know, is that you look Far Out, Baby," Jackie said, imposing the only vernacular from the sixties she could recall, hoping to shift Maggie's mood and bring levity back to the day.

"Well, you should be proud to Let It All Hang Out," Maggie responded in-kind, enjoying getting caught up in the sixties banter, a time warp she appreciated.

Jackie followed Maggie's lead and rolled over to her stomach, but not before applying more suntan lotion, especially to the most sensitive spots of her body that were about to be exposed to the sun for the first time, ever, and congratulating herself about what a good idea the spa had been.

Maggie relaxed into her nudity and began reading her book. Jackie closed her eyes. The warm California sun pulsed over her skin, her muscles relaxed with the sound of the surf washing back and forth in perfect rhythm, the whooshing sound overpowering the thoughts in her mind and luring her into a deep sleep. Jackie didn't know it, but Maggie's head dropped into her book, and she joined Jackie in slumberland. They were both out of practice in attending slumber parties.

"Excuse me! Excuse me!" Chad had returned.

Jackie could hear a sound growing louder as her consciousness slowly awakened. She couldn't understand the words, but she was aware it was a sound outside of her own dream. With stiff arms frozen above her head, she pulled them down, breaking the tightness from the position she'd been lying in for over two hours before rolling over to see who was talking to her.

"Sorry, Miss, but I thought I should tell you, both of you have been asleep a long time and you're getting a terrible sunburn," Chad said, half smiling as Jackie sat up.

Jackie came to a full state of awareness, suddenly remembering she was nude as her senses engaged and her modesty took over. She looked over at Maggie, whose bottom was bright red, her poor fair skin was scorched. The suntan lotion failed to provide much protection from the intense UV rays of the California sun. Jackie felt her own backside begin to sting as she grabbed her coverup and pulled it on. Chad stood, watching her, clearly waiting for an acknowledgment of his good deed.

"Thank you," Jackie managed to say. "Maggie, wake up." She reached over and shook Maggie's shoulder. "You're getting burned."

Maggie moved slowly, partly from the sleep and partly because the burn had already set in. "Oh, my gosh. Did we really fall asleep?" Maggie grabbed her coverup also when she saw the man standing and staring.

"You can go now." Jackie dismissed the good Samaritan. Chad turned and left for the second time without a word.

"Jackie, what were we thinking? We needed SPF 50 or 100 for this, something that doesn't exist these days."

"I know. How did we survive our childhood and teen years without it? Remember when we used to lay out and use baby oil to cook ourselves?" Jackie shook her head in disbelief.

"We were idiots, everyone was. Nobody knew about skin cancer. And if you recall, you were the only one that tanned. I turned varying levels of pink to red. I believe this red is the winner," she moaned. Maggie stood gingerly as she assessed the damage, her frontside white as snow, her backside bright as fire. "This is going to hurt so much in a few hours. It's already burning. I swear, looking at you, you're red, but it's already starting to turn brown. It's not fair," Maggie protested.

"Let's go find a grocery store and some aloe vera and take a cold bath. Tonight's going to be 'on fire,'" Jackie half-joked. Maggie winced.

Maggie and Jackie packed up and headed back to the hotel to take care of their sunburns and get their luggage so they could go to Elvis's house. They agreed there would be no storytelling about their trip to the nude beach.

"You have to admit Jackie, the sunburn was worth it," Maggie said as they hiked to the car.

Surprised, Jackie said, "I never thought I'd see the day when Maggie Roberts thought getting her ass burned was worth it! It's been a fun day of adventure, that's for sure."

Chapter 23
Lady Lawyer

Between aloe vera and other remedies, the women temporarily soothed their burning backsides, determined to keep their exploits a secret. Jackie wasn't sure how she was going to pull off hiding her burned ass if things went like she hoped, since she was staying at Elvis's house for the night. She had dreamed about sleeping next to him for many nights, now that dream was about to come true. Jackie examined her posterior for the tenth time as she dressed. Maggie was right, the burn was already turning to a tan; it was a blessing she had fallen asleep on her stomach. The car soon arrived, and they waved goodbye to The Wilshire and skirted off to Beverly Hills, relaxed and eager to have fun.

Elvis stood waiting as the car slowly pulled through the massive circular stone driveway. Even Maggie took a deep breath when he opened the door to help them from the car, taken aback by his striking looks. He looked every part the movie star wearing a dark green, silk shirt unbuttoned to his mid-chest, gold chains hanging low, dark slacks outlined his fit physique and revealed the strong muscles of his thighs, the entire ensemble topped off by his signature 'come hither' expression perfectly placed on his exquisite face. Jackie caught herself staring dreamily before she was greeted with a hungry kiss. She matched the intensity.

"Did you two have a fun day?" Elvis asked as he led the women inside where a small party was already underway.

"Yes, it was indescribable," Maggie replied, walking tenderly, trying to keep the fabric of her dress from touching her rear and igniting the pain.

"Dinner's ready for the three of us in the dining room. We can join the party in a while, if you don't mind. I want to hear about your day." Elvis closed the glass doors to the dining room to ensure privacy.

The women spilled the details of their day, truthfully saying they went to the beach without disclosing the type of beach, vaguely talking about their sunburns. They had to, considering the way they were tenderly sitting. Elvis promised with a naughty smile to apply aloe vera to Jackie's burn later. Jackie was ready to run up the stairs and get the rubdown started for multiple reasons, including the increasing uncomfortable feeling of her singed derriere and the stiff chair it was perched upon. She reminded herself to be patient.

The electricity that surged through her soul surprised her. It had been years since she'd allowed herself to feel anything romantic, much less the burning love for Elvis she felt every second she was near him. Now that the floodgates had been opened, she couldn't stop the rush. She once heard a therapist on some talk show say if you had loved once, you were more likely to love again. Maybe it wasn't a talk show she heard it on, or a therapist, maybe it was some movie, or maybe her mom said it when Jackie's marriage capsized and was trying unsuccessfully to reassure Jackie that life moved on. She couldn't recall where she heard it, but at this moment, she wanted to believe it.

"Before we go join the party, my Lady Lawyer made a request earlier today," Elvis announced.

Jackie tingled all over when he called her 'Lady Lawyer' and the sexy way it rolled off his tongue. Maggie looked puzzled, uncertain if she wanted to hear the request, thinking Elvis and Jackie should go upstairs and forego the party.

"A request?" Maggie asked hesitantly.

"Yes, she wants to look over some contracts," Elvis said.

Maggie exhaled and smiled. "Well, that sounds like the Jackie I know. I'll let you two deal with business. I'm going to find Georgie. Thank you for this excellent dinner. It was delicious."

"You're most welcome. We won't be long, but I promised her she could do this to ease her mind." Elvis stood and helped Maggie with the chair, walked her to the door, and opened it for her.

"You mean, get her off your case." Maggie patted Elvis on the cheek, telling him, "Good luck."

Watching Elvis walk Maggie to the door, Jackie realized that a southern gentleman was both endearing and stimulating, and suddenly reviewing contracts seemed insignificant. But he was right. She did want to look over the contracts.

She and Elvis made their way through the doors on the opposite side of the room and through the back hallway to his office so nobody would know they were doing business. The last thing she needed was the Colonel lurking around. She had gotten a glimpse of him as they walked through the living room earlier, piquing her curiosity, it was atypical for him to attend an after-hour party. Jackie felt uneasy about his presence, which was not atypical.

Elvis seated Jackie at his desk and laid out the contracts in front of her. He went to the sofa and reclined, watching her while she looked at the papers. Jackie could feel his gorgeous eyes locked on her while she tried to focus on the task at hand. It was more than distracting. Even from across the room, the heat sizzled between them. She reluctantly pushed it away, knowing the sooner she barreled through the contracts, the sooner she could get to the sofa.

"You make it hard to concentrate sitting over their looking so damn sexy," Jackie remarked.

"Honey, I hope you're a fast reader and get through those papers quickly," he told her and raised one eyebrow, followed by his million-dollar, sexy smile that sent women screaming and collapsing into weepy heaps, an effect she fully sympathized with. Jackie cleared her throat and refocused.

Elvis watched as her expression changed from a smile to a serious look, and finally settled into a frown as she flipped through pages. Now he was concerned. "So? What's the verdict?" Elvis asked.

Jackie put the papers down and sat back with a sigh, and told him flatly, "You're being ripped off."

Elvis stood and came over to the desk and pulled a chair beside her. "Show me."

"The percentages the Colonel is getting as your manager are far above the industry standard and he built-in automatic increases based on your escalating income. He's taking more than fifty percent of the revenue from merchandising, yet charging you a hundred percent of the cost, and in five years, he'll be getting at least fifty percent from your performances. He can commit you to contracts and not give you any artistic control, and so much more. Did you have an attorney look this over at all when you signed it?" Jackie tried to deliver the news thoughtfully.

"Hmm." Elvis looked at the contract as Jackie pointed to section after section.

"The only saving grace is that this contract expires at the conclusion of the last movie commitment. And there's a termination clause, requiring ninety-day advance notice, in writing, with your intent to terminate or it automatically renews at the higher percentages. If you don't terminate and renegotiate a new contract, that thirty-five percent commission he's currently receiving will escalate to fifty percent and extend the contract period for five more years. It also talks about loans you may owe the Colonel for merchandise."

Jackie wasn't happy as she continued moving through the documents, each clause written to benefit the Colonel more than the last one. Her brow furrowed, deepening the nagging crinkle before she reminded herself for the millionth time that one day it would become a permanent wrinkle, and she should stop letting the stress settle on her face. She stretched her jaw to relax.

"Okay, so it sounds like I can fix it."

"Yes, but you need to give notice to terminate this contract. You can give that notice in advance of ninety-days, which I would suggest, so there's no room for error or misinterpretation of your intent. This contract terminates officially at year end of 1967 with notice. Have your attorneys draft the notice now and hold it until the first of January and then give an early notice. Also, have your attorneys draft a new contract with a lower fee and cut those commissions back or apply some to past money borrowed and don't let him front anything and add it to a loan," Jackie said emphatically.

"I don't have an attorney. I've been trusting my dad and the Colonel to work out the business details," Elvis explained.

"Look, I'm going to talk to you like I would one of my clients. You're the star in this relationship with the Colonel. He didn't make you Elvis, God made you, and your hard work made you. Yes, he secured performances and made connections, but any good manager would have done that. That's his job. There are a dozen competent and honest managers that will take your career higher and take it in the direction you want to go, like back to live performances. I know you love performing for an audience, that you hate these movies, and you want to get back to singing and recording," Jackie told him, feeling her frustration for his situation rising.

"How do you know all of that?"

"Just a guess," she said, ignoring the fact that she'd seen his entire life and death play out before her.

"It's true. I'm a bit bored with these movies. I want to sing to an audience. It's exhilarating. I want to make my fans happy, excited; it thrills me. They're the people who made me." Elvis was up on his feet, pacing.

Jackie watched him, knowing that in two years he would be back on the stage, which created additional problems. The Colonel would overwork him and drive him to his death, and there would be more loans. There had to be a way to get the Colonel out of the picture. Jackie hoped that Elvis truly had been saving money and had a back-up plan. She'd done what she could and said as much as she could without revealing his life to him. Nobody should know how their life would unfold, particularly when that life was going to be cut short. Jackie was thinking about that on the beach today before she fell asleep. She couldn't tell Elvis the perils that lay ahead. He had to live without that knowledge, like everyone else. But she could put subtle suggestions into his head.

She continued explaining to him ways to legally shield his assets and income from theft by anyone around him who was trying to take advantage of his generous heart. He agreed with the suggestions when they finally decided to take a break and have some fun. Before they joined the others, they drew to each other, their lips connecting their hearts as their hands caressed and teased each other into a heated frenzy.

"I want you to stay as long as you can. It's lonely dreaming of a girl a thousand miles away. I don't want you to leave," Elvis whispered in Jackie's ear.

"Elvis, what about your current involvement? Aren't marriage and a family in those plans?" Jackie spoke evenly. She didn't want it to be true, but there was no denying that was the course his life had to take, and it had to be discussed.

Elvis didn't respond. His eyes were closed. Jackie watched him disappear into his thoughts, obligations, responsibilities, and promises…as much as they would both like to, it couldn't be ignored.

Jackie didn't want to complicate his life. His struggle was obvious. "Let's enjoy the time we have and not overthink it tonight. I'm here now. We have a couple of days before I'm scheduled to go home.

Let's love each other until we can't anymore." Jackie laid her cheek against his strong shoulder.

Elvis pulled her close, his arm resting over his eyes. "I want more," he said. "I want us."

"I want us too." She sighed, knowing it would never be.

Maggie was having the time of her life. She was beginning to miss Charlie, but the trip to another dimension had sparked an energy she'd been missing for several years, forcing her to reluctantly accept that she and Charlie had settled into a rut. It was comfortable and predictable, but she didn't want to get old before her time. They were still young. Sixty was the new forty, right? That's what everyone kept telling her as she approached her big birthday. If only they could see her now at thirty-one again, they wouldn't recognize her.

She searched her memory for what she was doing at thirty-one the first time around. She and Charlie had married when she was twenty-six. Year five of her marriage was spent thinking about having babies, but it wasn't in the cards. Years of sadness followed the doctor's news, then years of balancing joy and sorrow when Jackie had Susan and Toby. Secretly she had clung to the hope of a child until she turned forty-five and let it go, adjusting her plans, dreams, and reality, and becoming the best "Auntie" to Jackie's kids that she could be. It took work to heal, but soon she was happy again and her thoughts were focused on the good parts of her life: her job, the school children she helped, Jackie and her kids, and the best part – Charlie. Her life made her happy.

"How's the sunburn?" Jackie asked.

"Burning, and yours? Did Dr. Presley doctor it for you?" Maggie laughed.

Jackie smiled. "I wish! Maybe later. I'm so happy we're staying here tonight, although I don't know about you, but I'm ready to hit the sack." It was already past two a.m.; these late nights were draining her.

"I'm with you. How do they do this day in and day out? It's exhausting, even if I am thirty-one. I couldn't even do this pace when I was twenty-one," Maggie exclaimed.

"Me either. My sleepless nights were when the kids were babies. Those were my party days." Jackie smiled. "We sound old."

"We are," Maggie agreed.

Sweet notes slowly filled the air. Elvis was sitting at the piano, lightly touching the keys, having been encouraged by a small group of young women who were hanging on his every word and following him from corner to corner of the room. Jackie watched in amusement. They all wanted him.

"Can you imagine how it would feel if everywhere you went, women were falling in love with you instantly?" Jackie asked Maggie.

"How does he know who really loves him? It must be a lonely feeling having to question everyone's motives. He seems sure of you, though. And who knows what the true situation is with his love-life? I've read so much about that relationship, good, bad, contradictions, even retractions of some of the things written in tell-all books. I feel for him. He's a good man, and he manages the fame and fortune damn well. And he's a better host than I would be, too. I'd kick everyone out of my house," Maggie said with sincerity.

"I'm sure I didn't help that insecurity. I just lectured him on not letting people take advantage of him or use him," Jackie said apologetically.

Quiet fell over the room as Elvis began singing. Maggie grabbed Jackie's hand in amazement. His voice filled the air and expanded the space. Beautiful notes coated with deep emotion stopped every movement. Jackie watched the pleasure on his face as he sang for the crowd, losing himself in the lyrics and lifting every syllable to a higher place. The magic combination of his soulful voice and the heart wrenching lyrics froze time as the listeners waited for the next note to take them even higher. The smooth sound of artful notes tugged at emotions and awakened them. When he finished the song and the last piano key dropped its bright tone into silence, he looked straight at Jackie.

"I hope he kicks out all these people. I'm ready for this party to end," Jackie whispered to Maggie, who nodded emphatically in agreement.

"That was beautiful," Maggie told Elvis when he walked up and took Jackie's hand.

"Thanks, Maggie. I don't know about you guys, but for once, I'm ready for this party to be over. How about you, honey, ready for bed?" Elvis asked.

"Yes, most ready," Jackie eagerly agreed.

"I have a special surprise for you two. Tomorrow we're going horseback riding. I have horses stabled on a remote piece of property I bought a few years ago. I have a caregiver living up there that takes care of them. It's secluded, so we'll have lots of privacy. We can go out in the morning and eat lunch out there. It's a beautiful valley," Elvis said, his excitement obvious.

"I love to ride. It's been years since I have though. I had a horse when I was a kid up until I was about fifteen and discovered boys and cheerleading," Jackie commented. "Except I don't have clothes for riding."

"Don't worry about that. I had clothes delivered today for both of you. I had to guess on the boot sizes, so I had them send out each size from six to nine."

Jackie smiled in appreciation at his thoughtfulness.

"That sounds like a perfect day, but I'm going to opt out due to a badly placed sunburn. But you kids have a great time," Maggie said, knowing Jackie and Elvis would be happy to spend time alone.

Elvis understood. Jackie had forgotten about her sunburn, but she would suffer through simply to have a full, uninterrupted day with Elvis, possibly the last day she would spend with him for the rest of their lives.

After making excuses for leaving the party, Elvis and Jackie practically ran up the stairs to the bedroom, eager to finally be alone. Watching Elvis turn down the sheets, Jackie was overcome with insecurity. It had been a long time since she'd contemplated getting in bed with a man and sleeping next to him. She busied herself looking in her suitcase for the baby-doll pajamas she packed for this exact moment and miraculously, they'd survived the trip intact. This was the moment she'd pictured for the past several hours and many days and nights before that. Now she was halted by nerves, much like the first time she saw Elvis in 1956 getting a parking ticket.

Elvis crossed the room, taking her in his strong arms and pulling her close, but he didn't kiss her. He hugged her tightly, wrapping his arms around her as if his life depended on keeping her body next to his as securely as possible. It was abrupt. Jackie assumed it was fueled by guilt, perhaps or confusion, possibly. Confusion she could understand as she was battling it herself. She wanted him, wanted to make love to him all night long, but knew it could open a Pandora's box. They stood together, holding each other for what seemed to be an eternity.

"What's on your mind?" Jackie finally asked.

Elvis sighed, and said, "I'm struggling. I want you and have wanted you since 1956, but you left, and I was alone. By the time my heart healed, I was off to the Army, Germany, and I thought of you all the time, but you were gone, and I couldn't find you, so I let go. And many girls came after you. I'm not going to lie about that. Now there are expectations, demands, people I must answer to, when everything in me wants to stay with you." Elvis stood still, holding Jackie tightly against him.

"I understand. We don't have to do anything. Let's focus on spending right now together. That's all I want, and you should be cautious with your heart. You have a life you're supposed to live, and it doesn't include me. Your place is with someone else." Jackie tried to comfort him, knowing that if she altered his world, it could be catastrophic. And also facing the real possibility that the only way to save him - was to leave him.

"What if I want my place to be with you?" He released his grip on Jackie just long enough to look into her eyes.

It was difficult to fight the hungered need she felt peering into those eyes. They pierced her soul each time she saw them, but she knew she would have to, at least for tonight. There was too much uncertainty, too much room for the world to turn askew with a wrong decision. She looked up at him and said the only thing that made sense, "Let's go to bed, Elvis. We can hold each other all night and talk about it tomorrow in the light of day. Somehow, when the day comes, things that look bleak at night become crystal clear in the morning."

Elvis kissed her, scooped her up and carried her to bed. There was no need for the baby-doll pajamas after all.

Chapter 24
Ride 'Em Cowboy

Jackie was awake before Elvis. She dressed in her new riding outfit and planned to find Maggie before she and Elvis left for the ranch. She was still troubled by the contracts she'd reviewed; it was a miracle she slept soundly. Normally solving legal matters was her demon that scared sleep away. It was a good sign that she hadn't let it. Knowing the secret to her restful sleep was the fact that Elvis kept her tucked next to him all night. Elvis had slept well too, another good sign.

She sat on the edge of the bed watching Elvis sleep peacefully. A slight thrill ran through her thinking of his muscular body she couldn't help ogling last night when he'd stripped down before bed, every part of him exceeding perfection. What she saw indicated he was the epitome of fitness. Much to her regret, they'd done nothing but held each other all night, but under the circumstances, it was probably wise.

With his leg out, lying on top of the covers, she stopped to admire his muscles. All the dancing kept him in great shape, the karate helped too. When would it change? She wondered. Thinking of the years ahead that were coming for him. Reluctantly, she finally admitted to herself that her attempts to gently guide him to better choices to protect himself were not having a noticeable impact. She wanted to blurt out a warning...*you're going to be taken advantage of, driven into the ground by performing, touring, the weight of the world on your shoulders...* but that wouldn't be fair. Maybe she should write a note and leave it for him, then after she left, if the stars were aligned, he would find it and read it. If he didn't find it until after she left, it couldn't change things, could it?

Jackie held her breath as Elvis shifted on the bed. She didn't want to wake him yet; he needed sleep, and she wanted to talk to Maggie. She quietly left the room and went downstairs to the kitchen. Mary, Elvis's skillful chef, told Jackie that Miss Maggie was eating her breakfast by the pool, then hurried Jackie out of her kitchen with the promise of bringing breakfast to her.

"Good morning," Jackie greeted Maggie, who was in her swimsuit, her face shaded with a large brim hat, looking pure Hollywood and chic, reclining in the plush chaise lounge chair with a mimosa in hand. "So, this is how the other half lives?" Jackie teased.

"Yes, and it's a good life." Maggie smiled. "I see you're ready to ride!"

"I am. Elvis is still sleeping. I wanted to talk to you before we left. What's our plan? Are we leaving tomorrow?" Jackie wasn't ready to go, and she was hoping against hope that Maggie wanted to stay, too.

"I am leaving tomorrow. As much fun as this has been, I want to return to our dimension, or whatever it is, and I miss Charlie. I can't stay here in this world. Although, I plan to enjoy this day by the pool before I zap back home, wherever it may be," Maggie said, pointing to the cloudless blue sky.

"I figured you were ready. I don't want to go back yet, and Elvis asked me to stay. Can you let the kids know that I'm okay when you get back? Tell them I'm at a wellness spa and have no cell service. I don't want them worrying," Jackie asked, knowing it was an awkward request.

"Sure, I'll do that. I don't like lying to them, but this is one case where it's necessary. Beyond that, what's the plan? How do I get back without you? Can I get back?" Maggie suddenly panicked.

"I have no idea. I don't know how all this works. We'll have to figure it out in the morning. Elvis is having Georgie pick up the car at the hotel today and bring it here. I'll take you to the airport and we'll hope for the best," Jackie explained. "What's this suntan lotion?" Jackie picked up a bottle on the table beside Maggie.

"I don't know. Mary said Elvis told her to give it to me. It's tanning lotion from Hawaii. It's supposed to provide full protection, it's sunscreen of some sort. But my backside will not be seeing the light of day, I assure you," Maggie said with a giggle.

Mary walked up with a mimosa and an omelet for Jackie, saying, "It's the best sunscreen. It's a special blend the Hawaiians made for Elvis when he was filming there so he wouldn't get burned being on set in the sun hour after hour."

Jackie took a whiff. "Oh, wow, this lotion smells like coconut and plumeria, it's delightful." Jackie took the drink and the omelet from Mary. "Thank you, Mary. This looks delicious."

"I just took Elvis his breakfast. He said he'd be ready to leave in fifteen minutes. Your lunch is packed for the day as well," Mary told her, leaving her and Maggie to enjoy their drinks.

Jackie took a quick bite of her breakfast. "What's your plan for the day, Maggie?"

"I'm going to sit here by the pool while you go get dusty and dirty on horses. Speaking of getting dirty, how was the night with Elvis?" Maggie grinned.

"You are terrible. It wasn't what you think, it was more, well it was an emotional bonding. It was special. He's struggling with a lot. I mean, can you blame him? The man has so many people depending on him. Every choice he makes, every decision affects not only himself, but a ton of people. There're different opinions flying at him from all directions. Plus, who am I to come in and tell him what to do or how to do it? I know what happens to his life, so it makes sense that I could affect the outcome, but he doesn't know that. He's such a good man, and he's doing what he thinks is right for everyone else, even if it's not for him." Jackie felt her heart break a little as she spoke.

"That's all any of us can do. Try to make the best choices with the information we have in our life and accept those decisions. He doesn't know what lies ahead any more than we do for our own lives. You know what your life held for the first sixty years. Are you sure you want to change anything?" Maggie asked Jackie.

"That's just the thing, Maggie. I don't want to know what the f-word—you know what I mean—holds for me. I want to live my life and enjoy it in the present. The uncertainty is which present I want, with Elvis or my real life. I spent far too many years regretting the past and being frustrated and trapped by it and wishing I would have made better decisions. It took me away from the present. I want to recapture the time I wasted. It's a question of which present life do I fight for?" Jackie exhaled in resignation. It felt good to acknowledge the truth about herself.

"I think that's simply human nature. Trust me, Charlie and I spent many nights dwelling on things that Bob did and how we could have missed it all. We let it take over our lives for months, making it feel like we weren't even living anymore. Which present time you choose is up to you, but I hope you choose your life back in Seattle. I think when we get home, we both need to promise to live in the present and not dwell on the past or the. . .you-know-what. I'm going to start right now by enjoying this sunny day, with this beautiful view, and my exciting romance novel which I'm half-way through. Tulsa, the hot Rodeo star, is about to have an encounter of the sexual nature with a flirty Buckle-Bunny." Maggie raised her eyebrows and smiled, sinking back into the chaise.

Jackie laughed warmly. "You enjoy yourself. I like this side of you, Maggie. It's entertaining."

Elvis joined the ladies by the pool. He leaned down and kissed Jackie, then placed a cowboy hat on her head. "You don't need more sun." He grinned and added, "That hat looks good on you. I'd swear you're a real cowgirl from Texas!"

"I am, kind Sir."

Jackie stood to leave with Elvis, full of excitement for the day ahead. Maggie was right. Focusing on the present was the only way not to let time pass you by. She planned on making the most of the time she had left with Elvis, sensing it was coming to an end sooner than she wanted, but until it did, she was here, and he was here; they were together…right or wrong.

"Bye, Maggie, enjoy your day." Elvis waved.

Maggie feigned a wave, already focused on Tulsa and the Buckle Bunny.

The drive to the horse property wasn't far. Elvis assured Jackie the horses would be saddled and ready when they arrived. He insisted on driving them to the ranch himself, but had multiple cars leave at the same time so the fans outside on the road at the end of the property wouldn't know who to follow. The truck Jackie and Elvis were in sported darkly tinted windows and was a bit rickety with rust popping through the paint in spots. "It's road-worthy, don't worry," Elvis commented as he shut her door. Jackie wasn't as confident.

Elvis wore a cowboy hat to cover his recognizable hair, adding non-descript sunglasses, not his standard flashy bling, and tried to disappear. Nobody was expecting him to be driving, much less driving a truck badly in need of a paint job. As predicted, the fans opted to follow the black limousine that was ahead of them. Clearly, his use of decoy cars was something he and his team were skilled at executing.

"I don't see anyone following us," Jackie reported as she checked the mirror, then turned to look behind them to double-check.

"That's because they weren't expecting me to be in a broken-down old truck. They probably thought I was the gardener." Elvis smiled a crafty smile.

"Brilliant." Jackie laughed.

"Sometimes, you have to hide in plain sight," he told her.

"If anyone would know about that, it would be you. I'm sure you've had to employ all sorts of methods to avoid fans and reporters over the years. Your fans can be a little obsessed, you know. I mean, you are the King of Rock-n-Roll after all," Jackie teased.

"I need to get back to doing what I love. I owe it to my fans. Even I'm getting bored by my movies," he said, staring straight ahead.

"Elvis, your movies are incredibly popular and will be for decades. You are loved. I keep telling you that, but you don't seem to believe it. Look what you've accomplished since the last time I saw you. Give yourself credit," Jackie implored.

"Thank you," he politely replied. He didn't seem convinced.

"I bet it's hard not having any privacy," Jackie sympathized.

"I love my fans. I do this for them. Sometimes it's hard, but I'm so grateful for what my fans have given me, it's an incredible life and I'm not sure why I was chosen to be this person, but I'm grateful to God." Elvis squeezed Jackie's hand.

As they went through the security gate at the ranch, Elvis waved to his caregiver, who knew they were coming. As promised, the horses were saddled, standing patiently outside the massive red barn. There was a small brick home situated next to it and a trailer house next to that. Jackie assumed the caregiver lived there. She wondered if Elvis ever escaped his life and stayed at the quaint little house. It looked like a perfect getaway spot.

Jackie hadn't ridden in a while, but as a kid rode often, so she wasn't nervous about this expedition. In fact, she was exhilarated. Riding horses had been a fun time in her life and a big part of her world until she exchanged it for high school activities, cheerleading, all sorts of boys, and crushes galore, part of her short attention span in those days.

It wasn't until she met Bob that she'd decided it was time to settle down and unwisely ignored the things about him that bugged her as she defiantly waved off all the red flags. Before she knew it, they had married. To this day, she wasn't sure how it happened. She said yes to the question little girls dream of hearing and with the proposal accepted, the next thing she recalls was walking down the aisle telling herself that it was the adult thing to do. She didn't want to be a spinster after all, her mother said. If she had listened to her dad, she would have passed on Bob and kept looking, but at the time it all made sense and fit into her life plan: career, marriage, kids, retirement, and grow old with Bob. Even though there was always a nagging feeling that he wasn't honest, she'd ignored her intuition. Her doubts about his character began the moment they met, but she pushed it away and pursued her well-laid plans, eyeing the outcome more than the substance.

Now that time had caught up to her, slowed down again, and thrown her back to a place she could reflect and think, she wanted to believe she was about to live her best life. That had to be the focus from now on, not the lost years or the years ahead, but the present years. Today was the only guaranteed moment.

"Race you," Jackie shouted, giving her horse a kick and getting a jump start, lurching quickly ahead of Elvis.

"That's cheating," Elvis hollered, urging his horse as he caught Jackie.

"My hat," Jackie called out as her hat flew from her head.

Elvis slowed his horse and circled back to retrieve it. "You're a great rider, but a cheater," Elvis complimented Jackie as he came up beside her. "Your hat, my lady."

"Thank you, you're a good sport. Sorry you lost," Jackie goaded him.

"In my eyes, this day has been perfect so far, so I've won," Elvis told her.

They slowed the horses as they came over the ridge, which crescendoed, then flattened and dropped into the valley, revealing acres of billowing dark green grass swaying across the massive meadow. Jackie was taken aback by the peacefulness. The freeway stood only a few miles from where they were, but the low valley gave the sense they were far removed from civilization.

"This is breathtaking," she told Elvis.

"It's one of my favorite escapes," he confided.

"I can see why. What a great place to ride. Have you ridden all your life?" Jackie was curious.

"No, I only learned when I started filming movies. They had to teach me when I made my first film, *Love Me Tender*. Once they heard I loved riding horses, it seemed they were putting me on one as much as they could. I don't mind that at all."

"It's an incredible way to relieve stress and being out in nature is calming," she told him.

"I have more horses back in Memphis," Elvis said as the horses stepped gingerly down the rocky edge to the open field.

"I haven't ridden in so long. I'm going to be saddle sore tomorrow. Can I ask you something? Do you enjoy acting?" Jackie had read several accounts about how Elvis hated the movies they forced him to make.

"I do. I'm grateful for the opportunities I've been given, but I always wanted to be a serious actor and sometimes I think I'm a joke and my movies are a joke," Elvis replied, dismounting to come help Jackie.

"Take my hand." Elvis reached up to help Jackie dismount. She knew she could manage alone, but she appreciated the gesture and let him help.

"For what it's worth, I love all your movies. Especially *King Creole* and *Jailhouse Rock*, such a great performance, you're a wonderful actor, dancer, and singer. It's really impressive," Jackie told him. It was something she had wanted to say in 1956, but he hadn't made any of the movies then.

Elvis kissed her and whispered, "thank you" before tying up the horses and spreading out the blanket. There were no people for miles and no schedules to be beholden to. Glancing around, she took in the beauty of the area. One side of the meadow was surrounded by tall trees, revealing one way in with rugged terrain as the boundary on the other side of the property beyond the trees. Jackie was certain there would be no paparazzi snapping photos today. With time as their friend, they turned their focus to each other.

"Maybe performing on stage again would be enjoyable. I'll never forget watching you in Memphis ten years ago. I know a lot has happened in your life, but you're a talented singer and dancer. You seem so alive when you perform on stage." Jackie knew in a couple of years he was going to do just that, but she had to get the conversation started so she could caution him as well.

"There's something in the works. The Colonel doesn't know about it, but I am going back. It's what makes me happy. But first, I have contracts and movies I'm committed to see through."

"Can I say one thing, though?" Jackie wanted to be sensitive to his ego.

"Sure, my Lady Lawyer, you can say anything you want." He pulled her down to him and started kissing her.

"I can't talk if you're kissing me," Jackie said between kisses.

"That's the point," Elvis replied with a snarled smile.

Jackie chose to enjoy the moment and met his passion and then surpassed it, moving on top of him and deepening the kisses. Elvis moaned happily. Living in the moment might be the best decision Jackie had made in years.

Chapter 25
Say the "F" Word

Monday morning arrived far sooner than Jackie wanted it to, souring her bright mood that remained after riding horses and enjoying a quiet evening with Elvis and Maggie. It was decision time for her and Maggie, though. So far, all that had been decided was that Maggie would be leaving alone if fate was on their side. She hadn't prepared Elvis about the real possibility that she could disappear again. In fact, between kisses in the meadow, she'd agreed to stay with him for as long as possible. Her ability to think clearly was lost when Elvis was kissing her, leaving emotions as the critical decision maker, with reason and logic flying right out the window, replaced by a raging desire to never let him go.

She wasn't sure how long the world would let her remain in 1966, and she hadn't figured out her true purpose for being here, she and Maggie had run through all the possibilities last night, and without clues on how to proceed, she simply needed more time. Maggie had suggested that perhaps it had nothing to do with Elvis at all, which Jackie immediately rejected, instead focusing on wanting to understand how she could save Elvis, certain it was the reason she'd been inserted into his world. It had to be. It was her birthday wish, after all. What other reason could there be?

"Are you all packed up?" Jackie met Maggie in the living room. "We should leave in about fifteen minutes to get to the airport on time."

"Sounds good. I'm ready," she replied. "I never asked, how did the talk with Elvis go yesterday?"

"Honestly, we were caught up in a make-out session, but I did drop some hints about him taking care of himself when he tours again. He doesn't like talking about himself," Jackie said.

"Charlie's that way too. I think it's a man thing, but sometimes even when it seems they aren't listening, they take mental notes," Maggie offered.

"We did talk about work-life balance vaguely. I tried to use myself as an example. I felt like I was preaching to him. Cleverly, he started kissing me, so I'd shut up and I let it go."

"I'm sure that was difficult," Maggie joked.

"It was torture, pure and simple. Hopefully, I'll have more of that torture tonight," Jackie said, winking at Maggie.

Jackie knew firsthand the guilt she felt when trying to balance life and work could be overwhelming, and she was sympathetic. Countless times Maggie had tried to get her to stop working ungodly hours and devote more time to herself and her kids. Jackie had shrugged it off, telling Maggie time and time again that she didn't understand the demands and expectations of owning a law practice. Perhaps it was her own ego that drove her so hard all those years, causing her to miss recitals, baseball games, and soccer games. The nanny took care of homework and projects. Jackie tried to stay informed, but she knew it wasn't the same as being involved.

Fortunately, Maggie and Charlie had picked up the slack for her. Looking back, she knew she could have taken more time for the kids and for herself. It was hard to admit, but she'd been afraid to let go. Afraid her law practice and her life as she wanted it would disintegrate right in front of her eyes if she didn't show the world how dedicated she was to "the work." For years, she rationalized and buried her thoughts, but in her soul, she felt regret, and it gnawed at her daily, reminding her she had failed her children. She accepted it as a fact last night as she watched Elvis sleep.

"Did you tell Georgie goodbye?" Jackie asked.

"Yes, Georgie was sad but excited you're staying. He thinks you're good for Elvis, that you calm him, whatever that means. All I've seen is that you get him worked up," Maggie said, before bursting into laughter.

Jackie pulled herself out of her contemplation. "You're hilarious, Maggie. Not wrong, mind you, but hilarious," Jackie said with a content smile.

"I told Elvis goodbye earlier too, before his early set call to finish the movie. He said he's here another week, then back to Memphis," Maggie told Jackie.

"Yes, I'm not sure if he wants me to go with him or stay until he gets back. It's going to be a conversation tonight," Jackie responded.

"Between kisses, of course." Maggie grinned.

"Definitely! We better get going," Jackie said as she picked up Maggie's bag to take it to the car. "Honestly, Maggie, I'm not sure why I was sent here. I thought it was to warn Elvis, but every time I try to talk to him without coming right out and saying, you're going to die, it feels like I'm criticizing him, and I don't want to do that."

"Then find a gentle way to persuade him without telling him what to do," Maggie suggested.

Finding a gentle way was not as easy as it sounded. She'd been softly direct so far but agreed she needed to alter her method, as Maggie suggested. This morning, the tough self-recriminations had settled in her heart; *who was she to be judging Elvis for his dedication to his fans and trying to be the best performer he could?* She'd been no better at striking a balance between work and life. Now here she was looking back at her own life, wanting to do it over, to do it better. If she stayed in this world with Elvis, maybe she could have a child with Elvis and give him or her a better life, be a better mom than what she'd been to Susan and Toby.

Maybe she could keep Elvis from making the same mistakes he was going to make. There were a lot of maybes. Perhaps her real purpose in being sent to Elvis was to change both their lives.

"Let's do this," Jackie said, heaving Maggie's suitcase into the car.

Maggie took a long look at the house and told Jackie, "It's been a once-in-a-lifetime experience. Thank you for bringing me here and showing me this world, his world."

"He's quite a man," Jackie admitted, fighting back tears, wondering if she would see him again if this experiment to return Maggie home alone didn't work.

Thinking of Elvis, his touch, his kiss, sent Jackie's heart soaring. So much time had passed since she visited those emotions, to know that a man found her attractive and responded to her with strong passion. Sure, she was thirty-one and in a thirty-one-year-old body, but it was still her. She was the person connecting to Elvis with her innate wit and charm. She fully believed if they were both older, they would have the same reaction, even in her sixty-year-old body. The confidence she once enjoyed in herself was pleasantly seeping back into her mind. Maybe it was never gone, only dormant, but it was awakened now and she wanted to stay immersed in the journey.

Jackie shifted Eleanor's gears and accelerated as she sped down the California highway to the airport. The traffic was nothing like it was in 2023. There weren't as many twisting and confusing highways and byways and exits. It was an easier drive, for which Jackie was grateful. Powering the sports car through the maze of traffic was thrilling and gave Jackie a feeling of freedom as she jetted through Los Angeles. It helped redirect her thoughts that seemed to be tumbling over her faster than the cars passing her by.

"So, do we have a plan?" Maggie asked, turning the radio down, cutting into their loud and off-key singing of California Dreaming by the Mamas and the Papas. It was number one on the Billboard. Elvis's songs had dropped from the top 100 since he had not recorded and released any new albums for many years. Jackie knew that would change in 1968 when he made his comeback, her excitement for that event barely containable, in fact on the way home from the valley she almost blurted out the concept of the special, how it would happen and what a smashing success it would be. She caught herself just in time. Hopefully, after Maggie went back, she and Elvis would have more time to talk about his next career move. She didn't want Maggie to leave, but she understood the reason and the internal pull between worlds. There was never any question about Maggie's choice of lives.

Without GPS, Jackie watched the freeway signs carefully for directions, decelerating to a respectable speed to enter the off-ramp as the airport exit signs popped up. "I'm going to go to the parking garage area and see if we can find a secluded section to attempt this. If it doesn't work and we are both sent forward, then nobody will see us, and perhaps we'll know where the rental car is if we arrive at the LA airport in 2023. I think." Jackie looked at Maggie, her face conveying she had no idea what was going to happen.

"So, no plan really, we're relying on blind hope?" Maggie gave Jackie a pessimistic look in return.

Jackie sighed. "Pretty much. But I did leave a note for Elvis just in case I get sent home. If I don't, then I'll get the note before he gets home, and he won't be any the wiser about it."

"What kind of note?" Maggie was concerned.

"It explains all of it. The time travel and the reason I'm here. I didn't tell him what happens in the…you-know-what, but I did tell him he has to take care of himself and not let the Colonel drive him into the ground with a grueling performance schedule. That his health is going to fail if he doesn't make himself a priority," Jackie told her. She hoped she hadn't said too much, for all intents and purposes, she'd alerted him she was not of his dimension and from another time.

"Georgie will be happy. Elvis was angry and upset when you disappeared ten years ago. He was worried someone kidnapped you and was going to harm you. He kept waiting for the ransom demand, but it never came. But he was prepared to pay whatever they wanted," Maggie relayed.

"Really? Elvis never told me that. He would pay a ransom for me?" Jackie was flattered. "Bob would never have paid a ransom for me." Jackie snickered.

"Bob is an idiot!" Maggie added.

The women arrived at the parking garage, circling through the levels until they ended up on the top, where fewer cars were parked. They unloaded Maggie's bags and stood behind the car. Jackie dug the gorget from her purse and held it in her hand.

"Maggie, to be honest, I don't want to go back. What if we never see each other again?" Jackie felt tears begin.

She was caught between lives, but this one felt like it offered more, and it had been a long time since all the pieces of her life stacked nicely and orderly. In her world, she ran madly from one thing to the next, going through the motions to keep it all balanced. Thoughts of not staying with Elvis brought a fear akin to a rug being pulled out from under her and ultimately falling into an abyss. The kids were grown and didn't need her. The law practice was gone. And a harsh reality smothered her, driving home that she was alone in her real world. But in this world, she felt alive, desired, needed, and the opportunity in front of her was a life with Elvis. Even with the knowledge she had, it was intriguing and tempting.

"Jackie, I know you love Elvis. I know you're having the time of your life with him and this exciting world of his suits you in some ways, but don't forget what you'll sacrifice. You built a good life back home. And your kids still need you despite what you think. You have the most precious granddaughter. Would you really want to turn your back on that?" Maggie held Jackie's hands.

"I don't want to be alone anymore, Maggie. It's confusing. What am I supposed to do? Choose me or everyone else? I've always chosen everyone else. When is it my turn?" Jackie wiped a tear. "I want my do-over."

"Only you can make this decision, Jackie. I can't tell you how to live your life. That's your choice. And honestly, Jackie, only Elvis can decide how he's going to live his life. I know you want to save him, but that's something only he can do," Maggie reasoned. "I hope you come back, but if not, you know I love you."

"I know. And I love you too. If I don't come back, will you please watch out for the kids?"

"Of course. I always have and I always will. Although, I really don't know what I'll tell them if you don't. That's going to be difficult to explain and it will be a pain I'm not sure I can heal," Maggie said sincerely. She hugged Jackie tightly, praying she'd come home.

Jackie pulled an envelope from her purse and handed it to Maggie, telling her, "This will explain everything to them. But don't give it to them for a few weeks. If I'm not back in three weeks, that will be thirty years in this world, then you'll know I accomplished what I set out to do and saved Elvis." Jackie half-smiled.

"Okay, Jackie. I'll take care of them. You take care of yourself," she choked out the words. Maggie felt the tears burn her cheeks. She never thought Jackie would give up the kids and her life and stay in this world. She had been in denial, underestimating Jackie's regrets and needs. How could she have missed Jackie's loneliness? She was a trained counselor, after all.

Clearing her throat, Jackie tried to push off her emotions. "Before we dissolve into puddles of tears, nothing is decided, so let's not get too emotional. I wrote you a letter too. But don't open it until you're sure I'm not coming back."

Maggie wiped her tears. "I don't want to read it."

"For Pete's sake, we don't even know if this will work. I may be sent forward with you right now and all this blubbering is for nothing." Jackie cleared her throat, cutting off the emotions and turning the gorget over in her hand to look at the words even though she had them memorized. "I'm not going to touch you. I'll read the inscription and tell it to take you to the…you-know-what," Jackie explained.

"Okay, let's give it a try. I'm ready to get home and to be sixty again. As much as I liked being thirty-one, I like my life and the years I've lived. Surprisingly, I feel more confident at sixty. It's been a fresh perspective and, in a way, given me a new lease on life with a full belief that I don't have to please anyone and don't care if I do. Meaning, I will start saying 'no' more often. We have wisdom Jackie. Wisdom we didn't have at thirty-one. And it feels good," Maggie stated.

"It's funny, I've imagined what it would be like to be young again, but when I went back to 1956 and was twenty-one, I found myself feeling self-conscious of everything I said, how I looked, whether Elvis liked me or not, and wanting to make sure I did things he liked even knowing I was an accomplished grown-ass woman. It was a bit exhausting. It's weird how you fall back into that pattern of negative self-talk when you're young and insecure." Until now, Jackie hadn't had time to reflect.

"For me, since I didn't go back to being twenty-one and, quite honestly, never want to, being thirty-one again has been a mixed bag. On one hand, it feels great to be healthy and feel like you have years to tackle things you've finally discovered you're interested in and didn't do the first time around. But, on the other hand, and maybe it's because we've already lived it, it's also hard work. Building your life, your career, family, all the things that take so much energy and dedication. It was a fun adventure, but I like being sixty. I know myself and I like me. I hope you make that realization and come home," Maggie explained, stepping over to her luggage to bring it closer, readying to return to her true life.

"Thanks. I need to sort out my thoughts and evaluate a few more things about myself before I have the same confidence you do," Jackie said. She hugged Maggie as they prepared to send her home. "Okay, here we go." Jackie held the gorget and read the inscription.

There is no death, only a change of worlds,
with some lost in between.
Send Maggie home to the future.

As expected, the thunder boomed, and the sky flashed. Jackie covered her head with her arms until it stopped. She opened her eyes and looked around. Maggie was gone and Jackie was still standing in 1966 next to her candy apple red dream car. Maybe the universe had given her a sign that she should choose the do-over and stay with Elvis. She hoped Maggie was safe and back in Seattle.

Chapter 26
Do-Over

After walking the perimeter of the car, and looking around the parking level to make sure Maggie had truly gone to the other side, she checked her watch. It was already late afternoon. The day felt like it was moving quickly, with clouds rapidly streaming past her, casting eerie shadows all around. Time seemed to be accelerating unnaturally. She felt an urgency to get back to Elvis's house and retrieve the letter before he arrived home. She wanted to see Elvis and wanted to stay with him, but now, with Maggie gone, she could feel her real life tugging heavily at her heart.

Rounding the long circle to the front of the house, Jackie could see Elvis's car in the drive. Fearing he'd found the note already, her heart hitched a little as she exited the car, imagining a conversation with no logical explanation.

"Hey, Georgie, you guys are back early, aren't you?" She tried to sound casual as she walked toward him. He was standing in the foyer, looking bored.

"Elvis told them he would wrap everything tomorrow and then take the rest of the week off. He didn't give them a choice, it was entertaining to watch," Georgie explained.

"Where is he?" Jackie's nerves were exploding.

"He's out by the pool looking over the final scene and the production schedule, and a new script for the next movie. He's not thrilled about it," Georgie warned.

"Okay, I'm going to change my shoes and then I'll join him," Jackie replied, making an excuse to get upstairs.

"Did Maggie get off?" Georgie asked.

"Yes, she's headed home." Jackie thought Georgie had a bit of a crush on Maggie and who could blame him? Maggie was the best. Jackie missed her already. Staying in this world might be harder than she thought.

Jackie sprinted up the stairs, stumbling a bit in her rush to get to the note. She exhaled in relief when she saw it still sitting on the dresser where she left it, grabbing it and stuffing it in her pocket quickly, even though nobody was around. Irrationally, she felt the uncontrollable urge that it be hidden from sight. She moved the curtain aside slightly and peeked out to ensure Elvis was still on the patio. She watched him flip through pages of the script, moving each page with irritation. With a few minutes to take care of the note, she pulled it from her pocket with the plan to destroy it, but first she re-read it. After the third reading, instead of tearing it up and flushing it so it would never be found, she changed her mind.

A big part of her wanted Elvis to know the truth. Keeping it from him had been something that didn't sit well with her. That's when she made the decision to hide the note, hoping one day he would find it and understand. Tonight, they would talk about her staying, even though in her mind her decision was made that she would stay with Elvis and continue her mission to save him. If their worlds were altered, then so be it. But letting him go was not something she could live with. First, she had to handle the matter of the note in case something should go wrong.

The adjacent sitting room held bookcases stacked with Elvis's favorite books. He'd recently developed an interest in metaphysical concepts, and the shelves were lined with books on spiritual topics. The titles seemed to blend into each other until she arrived at a book called *Making Your Fate*. She pulled it from the shelf, slipped the letter in the middle of the pages and was about to reshelve it when the handwriting on one of the pages caught her eye. It had to be Elvis's. The script was small and tucked into the margin of the pages. It read, "Evil is only Good tortured by its own hunger and greed."

She'd heard that Elvis often made notes in his books and wondered why and when he'd made this notation and what it meant. Was it a conclusion that everyone was born good with the potential to be evil? That evil was a part of goodness, hidden away until it was fed by the dark side of life, pushing people to the opposite side of themselves, away from goodness to the point where they became evil.

Maybe some people had lower thresholds to be drawn to the other side, although she couldn't think of anything that would drive her to be evil. Her life hadn't been a bed of roses necessarily, but she still had freewill to make right and wrong decisions and not let it change her. She wondered if her kids would look at her as selfish or even as evil if she stayed with Elvis. Was making a decision that solely served her needs and disregarded those she loved, evil? Jackie snapped the book shut and slipped it back on the shelf and headed to the pool.

"Hello, gorgeous. Georgie says you're taking time off," Jackie said as she joined Elvis outside.

The afternoon sun was perfectly positioned, the heat of the day having subsided. Jackie slipped down onto the chaise and finally relaxed, releasing the thoughts circling in her mind since Maggie left.

"Yes, and they gave me a new script," Elvis said, tossing it across the table towards Jackie.

"I take it you don't like it?" Jackie picked it up, curious about which movie it was. "*Easy Come, Easy Go*. That looks like a fun movie," Jackie said as she read the synopsis. She recalled seeing the film not that long ago. It was a cute movie, but she knew Elvis was tired of making "cute" movies and had lost hope that he'd ever be seen as a serious actor.

"It's going to start filming in October. The Colonel wants me to go back to Memphis the day after tomorrow. I told him I was staying until the end of the week." Elvis exhaled in frustration.

"I understand. You have a job to do, responsibilities, and a life. Does that mean you need me to leave?" Jackie tried not to sound upset as she picked at a thread on her shorts. She knew Elvis had bundles of pressure from all sides, more than she could understand.

"No, I don't want you to leave. I want you to stay. I'll be here until the end of the week, then I'll go back to Memphis and take care of some business and personal matters. I'd like for you to wait here since I'll be back in two weeks," Elvis conveyed his plan.

"What if I come to Memphis?" she asked.

Elvis looked back at the script before he answered, "I think it's better if you stay here."

Jackie smiled, knowing the reason why. Flashes of his life played through her mind, mostly from movies she had seen over the years. Images which she couldn't ignore. Perhaps Maggie was right, maybe Elvis was the only person that could save himself. Who was she to interfere with what destiny had ordained?

She stood and walked behind Elvis's chair and wrapped her arms around his neck. His broad shoulders felt strong, as if he could handle all that he was given and then some. Being close to him made her skin prickle with delight, forcing adrenalin to speed through her veins. She kissed his neck and whispered, "It's okay, we weren't meant to be. Go do your life. Let's enjoy this week and each other. We have to let go. There's too much that's happened these past ten years that has set your life on a path you have to continue."

Jackie didn't know why she said it. She wanted to stay, had firmly planned to stay and leave her life behind, and now she willingly offered to leave and give up everything she convinced herself she wanted. To give up her do-over. To go back and accept the decisions she'd made in her life and to continue to live the life she created and face it all, the good and the bad. Everything inside her was draped in immense sorrow. Internally, she silently wept as she forced a smile on the outside and let go of the chance in front of her. *Why had she said it? She didn't mean one word of it.*

Elvis didn't respond, sitting silently as Jackie held him, knowing it was the right thing to do but not wanting to admit it out loud and make it real. Lives would be upended if he stayed with Jackie. He'd made commitments when he thought she was gone for good. Now it was all topsy-turvy, but he was a man of principal and in his heart, he knew he would fulfill his obligations. There was no choice and no guarantee Jackie wouldn't abruptly leave him again. For now, he wanted to stay in the thrill of their love, to escape his life for a little while before they had to move forward with separate lives.

Maybe if he had down time with Jackie, he would be ready and refreshed and could take on the world once again as the King of Rock-n-Roll. All he really knew was that for a few days, he wanted to be a man in love with a woman who loved him back for who he truly was. Their fate was decided and sadly, in their silence, had been agreed to by both of them. Jackie would leave Thursday. Elvis would go back to Memphis, and they would never see each other again. It was fated without any fanfare or tears, just logic and maturity.

Thursday came much too quickly. Jackie had decided this time she would let Elvis leave her instead of her leaving him as she'd done before. She stood on the front porch of his Beverly Hills house and watched the crew load up the bus to travel back to Memphis. Elvis stopped to kiss her every trip in and out of the house as he supervised the guys loading equipment, clothes, and personal items, including his books. Before he left, he pulled Jackie inside the house and into his office. They sat on the sofa; he looked as if he'd lost his last friend.

"Tell me again why we are doing this?" he asked.

"Because you are Elvis Presley and people are depending on you." Knowing it wasn't fair to put the blame on him alone, she added, "It's not only your obligations. I have a life to get back to. People depend on me too. And we both know you have…other commitments, marriage, possibly." Jackie was stern. She hadn't brought up the talk of other women because she already knew he would be married soon, even if he was unaware.

"We don't 'both' know anything. I'm not thinking about marriage. I don't know how to fix this."

"I know. So, I'm fixing it for both of us. Just promise me you'll take care of yourself. I know you'll take care of everyone else, but take care of yourself too, and I mean physically, financially, and emotionally, and get your career back on track. Be happy Elvis."

"I am happy," he protested.

"I know. Hell, I don't know what I mean. Stay happy, okay," she said.

Jackie couldn't argue. He did seem happy most of the time and when he restored his career, then he would really be on his destined path. But Jackie knew too much, or at least she thought she did. Who knew what the full truth of his life was? What she'd seen was a man who was kind, funny, healthy, and had talent beyond anything she'd ever known.

"I'll remember you," Elvis told her.

He kissed Jackie as if it were the last time they'd ever see each other because they both knew it would be. He held her face in his hands, deepening his kiss. This time, he sent her a message of love into her soul. He pulled her into him, kissing her neck. She wiped her tears over his shoulder so he wouldn't see them. He'd know she was lying about wanting to leave if he did. The sweet fragrance of his cologne burned

246

into her senses. Breathing slowly, she tried to absorb the slight musky scent, never wanting to forget it. Fighting the urge to undo all she had said, she steeled herself, forcing her will to be strong, though she really wanted to weep and beg him not to go. She felt his tears on her neck as he hugged her tighter.

Too many times in her life, Jackie felt as if the world's timing wasn't right, and she couldn't get her life to flow as she thought it should. This was the most painful of those times. She watched others live their life in harmony and wondered how they did it. And now, even in this world, the timing was doomed.

Elvis kissed her one last time as they begrudgingly said their goodbyes, hearts longing to be one, ripping apart as they faced the truth.

Jackie watched the entourage caravan away and felt the ground drop out from beneath her as Elvis disappeared from sight. *Why was doing the right thing so damn hard?* The question tumbled through her mind as she climbed in her fancy sport car for a last race to the airport and her return home, but predictably, she had no answer to her own question.

Chapter 27
Mom Duty

When Jackie made it back to 2023, her phone was blowing up; text messages, missed calls, voicemails, all from her daughter Susan. Jackie panicked at first, but then read the text messages and realized her daughter was simply in need of her mom. Nobody was hurt or sick, which was her first motherly instinct, along with accompanying fear and panic. She couldn't recall the last time she and Susan had talked for more than a brief minute. Susan's life had been hectic between Rosie, Rusty, and her job, not leaving much time for anything else. For months, it had felt like *Cats in the Cradle* playing out in real life.

Jackie replied with a text that she was boarding a flight and would call as soon as she landed. They could talk it through when she was firmly home and grounded. She didn't tell Susan, but she needed time to get her own emotions in check.

"Hi, honey, I'm back home. What's going on? It sounded like you were crying on your last voicemail," Jackie asked Susan.

"Oh, Mom, it's so hard. I'm trying to juggle my job and take care of the baby. I can't seem to get it together. Everything is falling apart. My house is a wreck. I can't keep up. I'm so tired," Susan said, bursting into tears again.

"I know, sweetheart. It's expected, you have a two-year-old. It's a challenging time. Where is Rosie now? Is she asleep?" Jackie asked. The hour was late. Hopefully Rosie was sleeping.

"Yes, Rusty put her to bed. He seems to have more patience at night than I do. Last week we transitioned her from the crib to a toddler bed and she doesn't want to stay in it," Susan explained between sniffles.

Jackie smiled to herself, remembering how difficult two-year-olds were and being quite relieved she wasn't still struggling with those baby years. Years that were trying and magical all in the same moment, bringing laughter and tears simultaneously some days.

"Then you need to go to bed. It's late, and you sound exhausted. And it's no wonder you are juggling a job with being a mom and working from home with a two-year-old under foot."

"I can't go to bed. I have a project due, and I'm still not finished." Susan cried harder.

"When is it due?" Jackie asked.

"Not until the end of the day tomorrow. I have about four hours of edits to finish, but I'm afraid to wait until tomorrow because the baby will be awake. It's easier to do it when she's asleep, which seems like is never anymore."

Jackie listened to Susan and flashed back to those long days of trying to work to meet deadlines after the children were asleep. "Rusty has a flexible schedule. Can't he stay home tomorrow and help while you finish the project? Have you asked him?"

"No, I can't stop crying to do anything," Susan managed between uncontrolled sobs.

Jackie knew it was one of those emotional, hormonal days for her daughter and she felt her pain as if it were her own. She had many of those days over the years herself and offered what consolation she could.

"Okay, all of this is quite normal, Susan. You can't do everything. You have a helpful husband, talk to him and let him help. It's okay to ask for help."

"But Mom, you did it alone. You made it look easy. I only have one child, and I can't even do it. And Rusty wants to have another baby. It's too much." Susan forced the words out.

"First of all, I appreciate that you think I made it look easy, but you were too young to know differently. And I'm glad you didn't know, and Rosie won't know either. Sometimes it's easier with two as they get older, but it was crazy hard with two babies when you were little." Jackie could remember thinking when the kids were around five or six, looking back on the toddler years, that she had never been so tired in her entire life. She chose not to tell Susan that.

"How did you manage, then?" Susan was trying to stop crying.

"I had help, your daycare, then the nanny, and Maggie and Charlie. How about trying to get Rosie into a daycare for the three days you are working," Jackie suggested. "I'll be happy to help pay for the daycare."

"Mom, you know Rusty won't take money from you. And it's not just Rosie, it's my work too. My part-time work has turned into full-time. I'm working five days a week for the most part even though it's supposed to be part-time."

"There's the first problem you need to solve. Set your boundaries, Susan. You are working remotely; it doesn't mean you aren't working. I know it's hard to tell people that you're not available because you have that work ethic and drive of your mother, which is not a bad thing. But also, I'm sorry. Having managed that all my life, if there's one thing I've learned, especially recently, is you are important and you deserve to live the life you and Rusty planned. You can't let other people's priorities become your priorities. Tell them no." Jackie was trying not to lecture, but she saw too much of herself in Susan and hoped her advice would help keep her on-track for what she and Rusty planned when they decided to have a baby.

"That's what Rusty said too, and Aunt Maggie."

Jackie smiled when the kids called Maggie their aunt. Even though, technically, it wasn't true, but she and Maggie felt like sisters.

"Then maybe listen to us. We can't all be wrong," Jackie proposed.

Susan's tears slowed and her breath evened. "Rusty and I have been fighting about it. I know I've been letting my clients push me more and more, and it's not what I want. I want to take care of Rosie and only work three days." Susan stopped crying.

"Then do that. She's only going to be a baby once. You have the support of your husband, and it was your agreement when you planned your family. If Rusty wants another baby and you do too, then learn to draw those lines. If you want to work full time, then find full-time daycare for Rosie. You and Toby went to daycare, and you loved it. Do you think I could have done my job with both of you underfoot?"

Jackie had mixed thoughts about the new work-from-home set up circulating the country. Her job never would have lent itself to such a situation, but the pandemic even changed how attorneys and courts operated for a while. With the exception of the mandatory, "stay-at-home" time period, she never worked from home after that. She was in the office every day and found it difficult to understand why everyone wasn't.

"I want to have another baby, but not right now. I'm building my contracting business, but don't want to work more than three days," Susan explained.

"Then don't. Be grateful you have choices. Many women don't. Susan, you and Rusty need to sit down and talk about your budget and your schedules and make a plan that works for both of you. And set expectations for your customers about your availability. Each time you let them push you into working five days a week, they will know they can and will continue doing it."

It was a life lesson she wished she'd learned - boundaries. Her mother's advice when Jackie had similar conversations was for her to quit her job, which, as a single mother, wasn't a possibility. Jackie knew Susan was good at what she did, and Jackie thought it was important for women to work and have skills, because you never knew when the responsibility for your life would fall squarely in your lap. Sometimes it can happen overnight. God forbid anything should ever happen to Rusty.

"You're right, Mom. Thank you. I hope you've been having fun on your trips. You deserve to have fun. I know what you sacrificed for me and Toby. We do appreciate it, even if my lame brother is unable to express any emotion."

Jackie smiled. No matter how old they were, the sibling sparring lingered. "I think he's getting better at it. I don't talk to him frequently, but he's growing up."

"If you say so. I'm going to email the customer and let them know I can't work on the project tomorrow. I'm sure it's a false deadline anyway and my contract with them says I'll work Tuesday, Wednesday, and Thursday. Tomorrow is Friday and my day off," she assured Jackie.

Susan sounded determined and stronger. Jackie relaxed; sometimes a girl just needs a good heart-to-heart with her mom and this one had been long overdue.

"I think that's a great idea. I may have work for you in a month or two. I'm starting a foundation for musical development to provide scholarships for lessons, clubs, camps, for underserved children to introduce them to music. It will be in Elvis's memory, of course." Jackie thought it sounded a little silly when she explained it, but it was meaningful to her, especially now that he was gone from her life for good.

"That's amazing, Mom. There are so many children that never get to be exposed to music. It's expensive, and I heard that last year they voted to eliminate music and art in the schools due to a budget shortfall," Susan said.

"Then this is perfect timing." Jackie couldn't wait to get started helping the community and it would help her ease into her new life.

"Goodnight, Mom. I love you. Thanks for being a great mom," Susan mumbled through a yawn.

"I love you too. You need to go to bed, you're worn out. And thank you, you make being your mom easy. And thanks for being a wonderful mom to my sweet little granddaughter. Why don't you let me watch her next Saturday for a few hours and you and Rusty go out and have some fun," Jackie offered.

"Thank you, Mom. That would be heavenly. We haven't had any alone time in a while," Susan said.

"Goodnight, sweetheart. Talk to you tomorrow."

Jackie hung up with a new sense of appreciation for her years of hard work. What the kids felt was the only thing that mattered to her, and maybe she had done a few things right after all. She dialed Toby's number, knowing he would be awake. She needed to touch base with him too; it had been weeks since they had a real conversation.

"Hello, sweetheart," Jackie greeted her son.

"Hi, Mom. You're up late," he replied.

"I got back tonight and just got off the phone with your sister," Jackie told him.

"Oh, cool. Did you have fun?"

"I did. It was definitely interesting. I thought I'd check in to see how you are and let you know I'm back in town." Jackie knew the conversation with her son would be much shorter than with her daughter.

"Great. I have news. I've met someone. She's amazing, smarter than me for sure, and beautiful. I'll tell you more about her later, but I was hoping you could have lunch with us and meet her," Toby sputtered with excitement.

Jackie was surprised by the invitation. Usually, Toby kept his girlfriends far away from her and Maggie. Most, they never met, others they probably never knew about.

"That sounds delightful. Let me know when. I'm going to watch Rosie next Saturday and this weekend I'm hoping to get organized. But we'll get a date set. That will be fun," Jackie responded.

"Really? Okay. No lecture on settling down, picking the right girl, keeping this one this time?" Toby laughed.

"No, Toby, you are grown. It's your job to figure out your relationships and do what's right for you. You're the only one that knows who makes you happy and I only want you to be happy," Jackie told Toby honestly.

In the past she would have grilled Toby on the new girlfriend, wanting to assess whether this one was going to last past his usual six-month expiration. But over the past couple of weeks, Jackie realized she had to let go of those expectations and the pressure she put on Toby. It was time to focus on her life and she didn't want to control Toby's decisions, or lack thereof. It was his journey, not hers. It felt good to let go of one worry she had no control over.

"Okay, Mom. Thanks for trusting me. I do want you to meet her. I think you'll like her."

"I'm sure I will. I love you. Goodnight." Jackie smiled as she hung up the phone.

And now, after doling out sage motherly wisdom, she was going to take her own advice and go to bed and get some much-needed sleep. The week had been full of emotion, happiness, love, confusion, heartbreak, and sorrow, leaving her heart filled with pain after all was said and done. As the week ended and her dreams of a life with Elvis faded away, Jackie reassured herself it was time to start building her new life and new dreams.

Chapter 28
Down by the Boardwalk

The next day was a perfect summer day in Seattle, drawing tourists and locals alike out to enjoy the weather and mill around Pike's Place, purchasing fresh flowers and eating oysters by the water. Maggie and Jackie met on the boardwalk in their favorite spot they'd been visiting for the past thirty years for their lazy Sunday brunch. Today was Friday, but Maggie knew Jackie needed some support after returning and leaving Elvis behind.

It was busy as usual, but they found a table near the railing with a perfect view of the water. It was the best prescription for rejuvenating the soul, complete with squawks of seagulls flying overhead, calling out and diving for fish and scraps from tourists. The muted horns of the distant ships in the background wailed a low melody to complement the shrill voice of the seagull. It was calming and something Jackie desperately needed. Her heart was still stuck in a time that had passed and mourning for something that could never be.

"How are the kids? Did you talk to them last night?" Maggie asked.

Jackie nodded. "Yes, they are doing great. Susan sent a million text messages while I was gone, so we had a long talk last night. She was having a meltdown and decided she didn't know how to be a mother and succeed at her job simultaneously. She actually asked how I had done it and told me I made it look easy. I couldn't believe it,

Maggie. Here I was thinking I'd screwed up my kids for life and was going to have to hire you for counseling, and she was thinking she was screwing up her kid for life."

"I took her and Rosie to lunch while you were gone. She seemed frazzled that day and was working on a big project. She told me the same thing, wondering how she was ever going to meet up to her mom's example," Maggie gladly told Jackie.

"Did you tell her she's my hero? She and Rusty are the ones that make it look easy. You know what they say, the grass is always greener." Jackie couldn't force a smile for other reasons weighing on her mind, but she was happy Susan had Rusty and was confident they would work through the challenges as a new family.

"Of course I did," Maggie said, smiling at Jackie, knowing her heart was breaking.

"I never expected to hear that from her, but I guess it's universal. All mothers at some point think they are failing. Fortunately, we talked it through, and I assured her she was an incredible mom. Maybe I need to let my own mother off the hook a bit and quit blaming her for not being the mother I thought I needed."

"Your mom loved you, that's all that is important," Maggie said. "I think it's going to be helpful for you to spend more time with Susan and Rosie," Maggie encouraged.

"True." Jackie had already started to make plans to do just that, she said. "I told her I would keep the baby next weekend for a few hours so she and Rusty can go have some fun."

"I've heard being a grandmother is much easier than being a mother," Maggie quipped.

"Yes, it is. That's a confirmed rumor. You can come help me next weekend and find out," Jackie taunted.

Maggie laughed and happily agreed. She loved baby time. "I'm sorry about Elvis, Jackie. I know leaving him was a hard thing to do. How was your week with him? Did you have fun?" Maggie asked.

"Honestly, I didn't have much of a choice."

"By the way, here are those letters you wrote." Maggie slid the envelopes across the table. "Did you destroy the letter to Elvis?"

"Thanks, I guess I should get rid of these. And, no, I didn't destroy the letter to Elvis, I hid it in a book. Maybe one day he'll find it and understand." Jackie shrugged.

"Oh, wow!" Maggie was surprised.

"But, to answer your other question, we had a wonderful week. We laid by the pool and relaxed and rode horses. He needed that and so did I. There were no parties, it was just the two of us. He serenaded me every night," Jackie told her, sighing at the memory and remembering his voice. She felt her heart crumble as the lyrics to *Can't Help Falling in Love* repeated in her mind.

"Good, hang on to those memories, but don't get stuck in them either," Maggie counseled.

"He's so talented, as you know. We read books to each other, talked for hours about his big dreams. I wanted to tell him he would achieve them all." Jackie was glad to talk to Maggie about Elvis, it helped. She smiled the smile of a woman in love and then it disappeared as the heartbreak edged its way back in, pushing the happiness away.

"Were you able to talk to him about taking care of himself?" Maggie pressed.

"I didn't want to scold him or talk down to him, so I tried to use myself as an example about how I overwork. At some point, I forgot about eternity. Enjoying him became the priority and then I got swept up in our conversations about everything under the sun. He's intelligent, but we both know he didn't figure it out," Jackie added, her words dripping with sadness.

"Oh, by the way, here's your book. I've tried to remember to give it back to you. It's a fascinating read, well researched, and talks about the extensive health problems Elvis had. You know Jackie, I'm not sure anyone could have saved him. Did you know he suffered from Glaucoma?"

Jackie looked surprised. "No, I didn't. That would explain why his eyes were constantly bothering him when we were outside. He tried several pairs of sunglasses before he felt comfortable. It was probably beginning."

"You should look up the information about Alpha-1 and his family history. It's all in the book." Maggie slid the book across the table to Jackie.

Jackie picked up the book. "I'm not sure it matters now. I'm not going back, and he's gone. What's the point? Obviously, I didn't save him." Jackie shifted and didn't want to talk about Elvis anymore, it was too hard. She knew it was time to let go and changed the subject.

"You tried," Maggie told her.

"I'm working on a local program for the arts, specifically music scholarships for the underserved children in Seattle. It will be dedicated to Elvis. It's the least I can do to try to keep his memory alive. His contributions were earth-shattering when you think about it. He crossed so many barriers and launched a new genre of music. It was the original movement of inclusivity if you want to get right down to it," Jackie told Maggie all the details.

"You're right. And as John Lennon said, 'Before Elvis, there was nothing!'"

Jackie nodded in agreement as she looked out at the water, forcing herself to be content being back in her world. She had plans to spend more time with her granddaughter, knowing how keeping busy would pass the time and distract her from her pain. Time healed all wounds; she kept reminding herself when the lump in her throat appeared from nowhere.

In an effort to heal her heart, she had already booked her second spa appointment and looked up dance classes. Only one day back and she wasted no time getting her calendar filled, even scheduling time for her roses. The music scholarship program was going to require a chunk of dedicated time, and Jackie was thankful for that. Powering down after so many years of maintaining an intense schedule was a challenge. The difference now was she was pursuing activities that interested her and not for the kids or the law practice.

"Hey, Maggie, look over there, is that Garon?" Jackie asked, nudging Maggie and pointing to the sidewalk on the other side of the patio where they sat.

"I think so. He's in a hurry if it is. Looks like he's headed to the Bainbridge Ferry," Maggie replied.

"I need to talk to him. Wait here," she said, jumping up from the table.

Jackie ran as fast as she could manage, trying to dodge the tourists wandering about on the sidewalk, but Garon was moving too quickly, and she lost sight of him. She ran a little faster, finally catching a glimpse of his baseball cap as he entered the ferry loading dock.

"Garon!" she shouted.

She thought he momentarily turned and saw her, then he was gone. Disappearing through the entry gate to board the ferry. She headed back to the patio deck, knowing the ferry was visible from there. Keeping her eye on the ferry trying to will it to slow down, she darted through tourists, determined to find Garon. Panting heavily, she rejoined Maggie, who was watching the ferry begin its trek across the sound. Jackie scanned the railing, searching, hoping Garon would come out on the deck.

"Garon," she shouted. "Maggie, do you see him?"

"I don't. I'll check the upper deck you look on the lower deck," Maggie suggested. Both women scoured the decks.

"There," Maggie said excitedly, "on the upper deck. He's up there at the railing."

"Garon!" Jackie screamed.

He looked up, instantly recognizing the women. "Jackie, Maggie," Garon hollered and waved.

"How do we know each other?" Jackie screamed at him. She could see Garon's smile from where she was.

"I changed your tire. We were fifteen, in Texas," he shouted back.

"What?" Jackie said to Maggie. "Changed my tire? Is that what he said?"

Maggie confirmed what Jackie heard.

Garon shouted again to Jackie, "Don't give up, Jackie! Finish it!"

Jackie and Maggie waved as the ferry moved too far to hear more.

"What does that mean, finish it?" Jackie was perplexed.

"He said he changed your tire when you were fifteen?" Maggie questioned.

Jackie and Maggie went back to their table. Jackie thought for a moment, searching her memory from decades ago, telling Maggie, "There was a boy, a handsome boy, blonde hair, blue eyes, who did change a tire for me on the side of the road. I remember because I only had a driving permit, no real license, and I was worried a cop was going to stop and help me. I had taken my friends to the fair, and I wasn't supposed to be driving without a parent. But that helpful boy's name was Chad, not Garon. I remember that distinctly. I was late to meet my boyfriend at the time, Lonnie. We ended up breaking up because of Chad. He overheard me tell a girlfriend that the boy that changed my tire was the most handsome boy I'd ever seen. Lonnie couldn't stop harassing me. It was so obnoxious."

Jackie recalled that day and that moment with clarity. She'd been hysterical, and the boy calmed her down instantly with his patient demeanor and reassurance that it would be all right. He drove a rusty pickup truck and wore blue jeans and looked like he'd been farming.

He sported a trucker cap pulled down low, but Jackie could see his blonde curls sticking out from under the cap. She'd never seen eyes so blue until recently.

"That's odd. I can't believe he remembers you from that day. He must have developed quite the crush. Seems he may still have it," Maggie kidded.

"I was a hysterical, teenage nightmare. My plans were wrecked, Lonnie was a real jerk, and I knew he would be angry that I was late for this stupid dinner he was throwing for his lame friends. He had a hot temper. I'm not sure why I even went out with him other than he was the quarterback, and I was a cheerleader, the perfect cliché. Anyway, that night I saw who Lonnie really was when he accused me of cheating on him. It was a great lesson if you want to learn how to deal with a moron. I was proud of myself for telling him off and never letting him speak to me that way again."

"Sounds like Garon did you a favor," Maggie added.

"But that's the thing. Like I said, the boy that helped me that evening was not named Garon. I remember clearly because Lonnie kept shouting the name over and over, Chad this, Chad that. It was a boatload of drama," Jackie explained.

"Maybe he changed his name, or it's a middle name." Maggie paused; her eyes widened with realization. "Jackie, hand me that book."

Jackie passed the book to Maggie, who flipped the pages until she found what she was looking for. "Look, here it is, Garon. I don't know why I didn't think of this. It's Elvis's brother's middle name: Jesse Garon Presley."

Jackie grabbed the book from Maggie and stared at the name in print. "What the hell, Maggie? What's going on?" She watched the ferry as it scooted further away, moving toward Bainbridge, searching for Garon and trying to understand what he meant.

"I don't know, but Garon said you needed to finish it."

"What does that even mean? Finish what?" Jackie questioned.

"Saving Elvis. You have to go back and give it one more try. There's more information he needs. You have to warn him about the health issues and his family history, he may not know. Read the book Jackie and go tell him what you found out."

Jackie took the book and stuffed it in her purse. "I don't even know where to find him. The first time was by accident. And the second time, I was eighty percent sure it wouldn't work, and you were going to lock me in a looney bin."

Maggie pulled out her phone. "It seems every week in our world has been ten years in his, so it would be 1976 based on the years you've jumped to. One year before he dies."

Jackie ran a search on her phone for 1976. She showed it to Maggie. "It says he was still performing in Vegas that year in the spring only and was starting a tour in July. Oh, look at this Maggie. He went to Vegas for a business meeting in July 1976 before the tour started." She looked at Maggie.

"That's it. You have to go to Vegas," Maggie urged excitedly.

"Okay, but I have one question. Are you coming?" Jackie asked.

Maggie shook her head. "No, I'm staying here. You need to do this on your own. Finish it, Jackie."

Jackie logged on to her flight app and booked the next available flight to Vegas, the red eye. Maggie was right. She had to finish this, and after she did, she would find Garon.

Chapter 29
Viva Las Vegas

Exasperation surged through Jackie as she tried to get comfortable on the flight and avoid the elbow of the man sleeping next to her as he shifted and snored, both preventing her from sleeping for any length of time. She finally gave up and turned to the book, trying to read it as best she could through blurry eyes. When the descent to Vegas was announced, she excitedly put away the book and readied for the landing. Thrilled to be getting some distance between her and her seatmate and get to her hotel for a nap.

After landing and grabbing her bag, which she had stuffed in the overhead compartment since she was worried about making time and getting to the hotel to find Elvis and "finish it," even though she had no idea what that meant or how this would play out. Instead of summoning an Uber, she opted for a taxi. Her brief removal from technology had been a welcome break, and weary from the flight, it felt simpler to let someone else summon a car.

The minute she stepped out of the taxi at the hotel she was swarmed by dozens of men dressed in jumpsuits, draped in bling, wearing large gold sunglasses perched on their noses, and sporting awful dark wigs with extreme sideburns. There was an Elvis impersonator contest underway, the taxi driver informed her as he unloaded her bags. Jackie smiled internally, wishing the real Elvis could see how his legacy lived on and witness grown men making a living trying to embody the magic persona of Elvis. She hated to tell them they were never going to be Elvis, but she appreciated their dedication and love for the King.

Fortunately, her room was clean and available, a small miracle given the impersonator mayhem unfolding all over the hotel. Tickets were sold out for the event and crowds were gathering in bars as some performers tried to hype-up their version of Elvis and gain followers on social media, which was evidently part of the contest. The competition was being held in the theater, lanes were roped off and long lines of people snaked through the hotel even though the first round wouldn't begin until ten that morning. Jackie pushed her way through to find the elevators and collapse in her bed for as long as possible before calling Maggie.

"I'm not sure where to go, Maggie. Did you find anything on the Internet that might give me a clue about where he would be?" Jackie was perplexed.

"All I found was Elvis stayed at the hotel next to yours to meet with management about his contract and his residency. I haven't found anything else," Maggie told Jackie.

"There are so many Elvis impersonators running around here, it's so bizarre." Jackie yawned as she spoke, barely coherent after her quick nap.

It was almost noon now, and she needed to find Elvis. There were only two days before he was supposed to be in concert half-way across the country, at least on the 1976 schedule.

"What if we don't have the year, right?" Maggie asked.

"I don't know, but I'm going to take a shower and grab lunch and try to find something that makes sense. I'll start at the hotel he might have been at in 1976."

"Do you have the gorget?" Maggie reminded Jackie.

"Yes, I have it. Let's hope this works, Maggie. I read a lot of that book on the plane; I couldn't sleep. It's well researched and explains so much about his health. He must have been in great pain with his body failing, if it's true. He was keeping a pace that nobody could withstand. And you may be right, I'm not sure anyone could have diverted him from what he believed was his path, to serve his fans. It's sad that the world tells us if we don't gather things, money, fame, and fortune, then we don't have value. Or our value is less than others who achieve more. It's a false narrative, and it's taken me this long to figure it out. As far as I'm concerned, the value of a person has many other measures," Jackie said, exasperated by societal pressure, demanding we work ourselves to the death. For what?

Maggie had been preaching to Jackie for years, trying to encourage her to have more balance in her life, but for all her efforts, it had fallen on deaf ears. It was reassuring to hear Jackie's new perspective. Maggie added to it while she had the chance. "We were raised in a different era and Elvis was, too. He grew up in a post-depression society and during a World War, you had to work hard to survive and not starve, and the hard work was to take care of your family. The way social media has exploded and created this generation with influencers and instant celebrity, making obscene amounts of money. It really sets false ideas of how to make a living and the expectations of success in a flash. There needs to be a balance between overworking and not working at all."

"Both chasing the tail of the tiger," Jackie chimed in.

"Yes, I'm glad you've stopped the chase," Maggie told her.

"I don't know, Maggie. I'm not sure I understand the world today and what people want. How will this culture sustain itself and where will it all end up?" Jackie felt the conversation becoming too large, and she was too sleepy to be this philosophical, and pulled back. "I guess we need to solve one problem at a time, and my current problem is to figure out where Elvis was in 1976 and see if I can get transported back. Time is closing in with one last shot before it slips away and he's gone for good."

"You'll figure it out. I'll be happy if I don't hear from you for a couple of days." Maggie grinned to herself.

"Any last words of advice?" Jackie was hoping for wisdom.

"Tell him I miss him and tell Georgie, too. And tell Elvis I said thank you for all he's given us. He has no idea the long-lasting impact and the positive change he brought to our world, or how much we needed him." In retrospect, Maggie wished she'd joined Jackie for this last attempt at saving Elvis. She would love to hug his neck one last time.

"Thanks. Maggie. I can't wait to see him again."

"I know, make it worthwhile," Maggie suggested.

"I will." Jackie hung up the phone.

She couldn't get the conversation out of her mind. How society had changed so drastically year after year, sexualized advertising, risqué entertainers, graphic movies and books, the breakdown of cultural norms. How hate and anger seemed to be at an all-time high. Criticizing everyone for no reason other than anonymity behind a keyboard. And cancel culture. It was synonymous with the persecution and criticism Elvis was subjected to in the 50s.

Comparing the loose morals of today, even thinking about what Elvis was judged for back then, some leg shaking and hip-thrusting, it was laughable. When Elvis erupted on the music scene, there were protests and naysayers that thought he was destroying morality. "Elvis the Pelvis," was causing young women to lose their minds.

Jackie thought about her own sexuality and how she'd been boy crazy all her life and most of the women she knew were the same way. But it wasn't Elvis's doing, it was part of being a human being. Elvis happened to be the perfect man to dream about, and having seen him in concert, it was no wonder he caused small riots of screaming fans. Women have been fantasizing about that perfect face, perfect body, and angelic voice for decades, because he was stylish, sexy, masculine, and not weird, fanatical, or deviant. He loved and admired women and made women feel desirable, beautiful, aroused, and confident. Jackie knew this because she'd felt the arousal and lifting of her own confidence. The world needed Elvis then and still does, for so many reasons.

"Hello, there, honey." An impersonator stepped into the elevator.

"Hello," Jackie replied, amused and impressed by the voice, even though it wasn't quite right. She knew because she'd had the pleasure of hearing the original sultry voice whisper in her ear, but it was close.

Jackie exited the elevator and made her way to the hotel next door. There were countless Elvis look-alike's running around, many overweight and sweating profusely as they stood in the Vegas sun covered in polyester and thick wigs, looking like they might fall over at any minute. She side-stepped them and entered the mega hotel next to hers.

Large signs were posted inside the hotel entry with arrows saying, "This Way to Elvis." Was it really this easy? Jackie wondered as she laughed to herself, hoping she was headed in the right direction. The signs snaked around hallway after hallway, through the main casino, and continued to the convention center at the back of the hotel where she anticipated crowds of people watching performances and standing in line for Elvis memorabilia, but it was the opposite. The crowds thinned until she was the only person walking down the quiet hallway toward the great hall, the two-story ceilings accentuating that she was alone on this journey.

Continuing to the end of the hallway, she reached a tall, exquisitely carved wooden door. Pulling it open, she found herself in a pass-through leading to another door. She opened the second door and stepped onto concrete floors, the plush fleur-de-lis carpeting ending as it transitioned to a maintenance entry in the bowels of the hotel. The ceilings were shortened to normal height, with fluorescent yellow lights illuminating her path. There was only one way to go, the other direction a dead-end cinder block wall. Where she was headed, she had no idea.

Once she reached the end of the hall, she noticed a small, oddly placed water fountain, a remnant from another decade. It reminded her of the fountains in her elementary school back in the 60s, looking misplaced in this modern day. A hallway past the fountain led to the right, forcing her to make a choice; continue straight on the path of the endless concrete hall or take the right and end at another door thirty feet away. Turning right, she found herself at the doorway with her hand on the doorknob. She turned it slowly.

The room smelled of must, time gone by, and dregs of an ancient cologne which long ago lost its charm. One wall was flush with mirrors, surrounded with bright light bulbs, two were completely burned out, the interior of the bulbs a dark, charcoal black. She ran her finger across the antiquated linoleum countertop, leaving a path of cleanliness through the dust that had been deposited there and ignored.

Her reflection in the mirror caught her eye, as she evaluated the woman staring back at her, it was obvious. There was a marked difference from a couple of weeks ago when she first looked at herself with any discernment, before she went to Memphis, before Hollywood, before Elvis. Then she saw herself as beat-up, battered by life, and ignored by the most important critic in her life...herself. Now, as she met herself again, she saw someone lighter, someone who had paid attention to herself, had taken time to love and care for herself. Someone with softer features and lips not constantly pursed, a brow not set with horizontal wrinkles, her fight-or-flight instinct not on guard anymore as she opened her heart to life again. Maybe this journey had been for both her and Elvis, though regrettably, she feared only one of them would make the trip to the other side.

Jackie pulled her lipstick from her purse, the red lipstick from Memphis, a part of who she was now. She expertly lined her outer lips as her mother had taught her as a teen, then filled in the rest and popped them together to make sure every bit was covered, admiring the color and smiling at herself, loving the woman staring back at her. It was going to be a pleasure hanging out with her for a couple of more decades.

Looking at the room in the mirror, she knew it was once a stunning space where great entertainers prepped for their performances, readying their makeup and costumes, running their lines, warming their voices, and preparing to wow crowds of fans. The old, dusty sofa against the wall with torn upholstery and faded colors must have been opulent long ago with famous derrieres plopped upon it. The dark cherry arms were scratched and chipped by time and neglect.

As she turned and scanned the room, she spotted a round wooden inset at the base of the front of the sofa; it drew her attention with its familiarity. Jackie kneeled down to examine it, tracing the carved pattern to remove the dust, realizing it resembled the carving on the gorget. Jackie grabbed the gorget from her purse and held it next to the inset on the wood of the sofa. They were identical. How did this find its way onto a sofa in the middle of Vegas? Holding the gorget and closing her eyes, she grasped her purse tightly as she repeated the familiar epitaph and waited for the thunder.

When the clanging of metal carts and banging of pans became louder and louder, Jackie knew it had worked. She opened her eyes and saw people in the hallway wearing uniforms, hustling with intent to get to important destinations. Down the hallway, sounds of drums and trumpets tuning up filled the air. Guitars played, not in concert, but prepping for some spectacular performance. The laughter from the next room warmed her heart. It was deep and soothing; she knew it well. Jackie stepped through the door into the hallway, led by the comforting sound, drawing her further down the hall to a large practice room where the door was propped open. She stood in the doorway, watching the chaos until their eyes met.

He dropped the guitar when he saw her; it hit the floor with a thud causing everyone to stop, a hush fell over the room. He rose from the stool and crossed the room in what seemed like one step; she met him on the way. He placed his fingers lightly on her cheeks with tears in his eyes; hers responded in kind. Without hesitation or a word between them, with everyone in the rehearsal room watching, he found her lips with his.

"I recall all the good times we shared," Elvis told Jackie. "I missed you."

"I missed you too. I had to come see you." She had to finish it, take one last shot at saving him.

Chapter 30
Save Yourself

Elvis pushed the door to his hotel suite open, only pausing their kissing long enough to move through the doorway.

"You look good, Elvis," Jackie said.

"You taste good," Elvis replied with a smirk.

Jackie felt the familiar thrill run through her, activated by the sound of his melodic voice and flirtatious comment. It was good to be back in his arms. It had only been a few days for her, but she confirmed as they came up the elevator that it was 1976. Elvis looked at her with skepticism when she asked what year it was. The hourglass sand was spilling through faster than she could bear. Time was running out.

"I thought I'd never see you again." Elvis guided her to the sofa in the sitting room adjacent to the bedroom.

Jackie thought she spied women's clothing hanging in the closet. The door was slightly ajar. She tried to look around casually to see if there was more evidence of someone, but Elvis was too distracting. He had aged, but it served him well with a marked sense of maturity and worldliness and still the most stunning man she'd ever known. He held her focus as she absorbed every curve of his face, every touch of his hand, every kiss of his perfect lips, knowing these would truly be the final moments she would enjoy with him since he'd be gone in a little over a year. It was one reason she never wanted to come back after she left him in California, fearing the pain and heartbreak.

Sometimes it was easier to turn away and protect yourself by running away, but it was time to face her pain and her love.

What she was finally realizing was the truth about life, that pain and love balanced the teeter-totter of a heart. The sadness of life on one side fighting against happiness on the other. Maybe that's how good became evil, mulling over the notation Elvis made in the book. Contemplating whether life could tilt a person from good to evil because of disappointment, heartbreak, pain, or loss. Jackie had pushed love away because the pain was too much in the past. It took away too much of who she was, and it was easier to ignore it than face it and fight, letting evil take over good. What she now recognized was that both were necessary to keep a balance. Each making the other more recognizable in the most drastic ways.

It was a hard lesson to know her joy came with pain and that to experience one, you inevitably experienced the other. Maybe she'd been too busy, or too weak, or too stubborn, to let happiness back in her life after Bob scammed her out of years of living, shutting down except for loving the kids. She'd kept men at arms-length, kept her social world tight, limiting it to Maggie and Charlie and some superficial friendships with a few women, but nothing like she and Maggie shared.

She trusted few. Burying herself in her work, reinforcing that if she allowed herself to take time to be a priority, to live her life, that the careful balance would fall apart with her law practice suffering, her finances drying up, and her and the kids would be destitute. None of that was completely true.

In the beginning years of the law practice, money fears were real. It took long hours to cover the expenses. She could have taken a job with a law firm and not having ownership might have allowed for more freedom, but that was questionable, knowing she would have driven herself no matter what. The safest path was to own her firm and make the rules, sadly the fear of not setting a good example and being a workhorse led to long hours and late nights. The thrill of putting her dreams into action were a driving force in the beginning, but somewhere along the way things shifted, and she lost sight of why she built the practice in the first place with the priority of the clients and growing the bank accounts redirecting the focus, when that happened it was hard to change course.

"Did I interrupt your vacation with someone?" Jackie saw a pair of high heels under the desk. "I'm sorry for showing up out of the blue. I should leave." Jackie knew Elvis had divorced some time ago.

"If you haven't noticed, you've always shown up out of the blue. And yes, the woman I've been seeing is here in Vegas, and no, you didn't interrupt anything. How long are you planning on being here this time?" Elvis crossed the room and picked up the heels and tossed them in the direction of the bedroom.

"I won't be here long, but I had to see you. I wanted to give you information about your health." Jackie had written down the description of Alpha-1 and handed it to him. "I want you to ask your doctors about this hereditary condition that can cause many health problems. Your mother may have had it and your uncles, too. I'm not a doctor and it's only recently been discovered, but it could explain a lot," she told him. Jackie stared at Elvis, noticing a dark mood settling in his eyes.

"How would you know anything about my health? I haven't seen you in ten years," Elvis said defensively.

Jackie could see he was angered as he stood and began pacing before leaning against the grand piano and staring out the window over the Strip. She went to him, putting her hand on his shoulder. He made no acknowledgment of her presence, which broke her heart even more. It had already been crumbling since California, despite desperately fighting to put it back together. His anger was apparent as she studied his face and recognized the scowl, signaling she had come on too strong.

"I've heard you've been having some health issues. Just because I haven't been here doesn't mean I don't keep up with you the best I can." Jackie tried to diffuse what she lit, withdrawing her hand from his shoulder.

"I am in fine health. I perform two shows a day for six weeks here at this hotel in the Spring then go on the road performing live venues, more than any other singer ever has. A man in poor health could not do that, honey," he grumbled, continuing to stare out the window.

"That's a lot of performances, Elvis. It would destroy most people. And I know why you do it, for the fans, you love them. I'm not saying stop doing what you love. I'm saying, talk to your doctors, have some tests run and see if there is a treatment that can help so you can stay on this Earth as long as possible," Jackie pled her point.

Elvis finally broke his stare out the window and looked at her. "Is this why you came? To lecture me about my health?"

"I came because it was my last chance to try to save you," Jackie blurted out in frustration.

She saw disappointment and anger flash in his eyes as they stared at each other. It wasn't what she expected, but she hadn't thought it through. Of course, he was irritated. If someone had come to her trying to change her life, she wouldn't have taken it well and would have reacted the exact same way.

"You've said something similar before. Did it occur to you that I don't need saving? I'm capable of managing my own life," he replied, turning back to the window.

Jackie cleared her throat. The last thing she wanted to do was insult and upset him. Their last time together could not be spent in a fight. She wouldn't waste this time. She wanted their time to be a memory to stay with her for the rest of her life, though he had every right to be angry with her.

"You're right, I'm sorry. Standing here now, having said all of this and the other things over the years, I realize it's not my place. You are a grown man and have your own life, which I'm not a part of, and you're capable of handling that life. You make decisions about your life as I do about mine, right or wrong. And we both must accept our own decisions and live with the consequences. But please know, I came here because I care. I believe you're the most talented, funniest, kindest, and unique man I've ever met. I think you know what you've given your fans and how much you mean to people. People love you. They want you to stay around for many years."

Elvis made no movement, refusing to look at her or respond.

Jackie tried again. "I came here because I love you. Nothing would make me happier than listening to an eighty-year-old Elvis doing a live performance of one of your iconic songs." She moved to him and stared at his blue eyes, spying a smile slowly forming at the corner of his mouth as his anger eased. "I'm so sorry I overstepped. It's not what I intended."

Jackie watched his chest rise and fall with a heavy sigh as he finally slowly said, "I don't know about being eighty and doing any hip thrusts unless I get a new hip, but how about watching a forty-one-year-old do a live performance tonight? I'm only here to do a special appearance for a friend's birthday. He's in residence at the hotel. They paid me to come for his special day, but I would have come for free. Of course, the Colonel would never allow that." Elvis half-smiled. She thought it was a reluctant smile, but it was a move in the right direction.

"So, the Colonel is still around?" Jackie silently cringed but tried to not use a critical tone.

"Not for long. I'm making plans to get rid of him. And I did do what you asked the last time I saw you and I renegotiated his contract. I'm getting more money in my pocket. So, thank you, my Lady Lawyer." Elvis moved toward Jackie and stared at her for a minute, then relaxed and smiled. Wrapping his arms around her waist, his irritated mood dissolved.

"I'd love to see you perform, but I don't want to cause any problems with your girlfriend."

"Don't worry about her. I'm sending her home. I'm back on the road in two days. I don't guess there's any chance you'd come with me?" Elvis said half-heartedly as he pulled her closer to him, wrapping his arms tightly around her.

Jackie melted into him as she'd done dozens of times before. It felt as if she was supposed to be there forever, but she knew she wouldn't be.

"I wish I could, but I can't." Regret swallowed her words.

At twenty-one, Jackie had jumped at Elvis's offer to follow him across the country and the chance to stay with him. She felt young and free, with an exciting new future waiting for her to take it on. A second chance to live her life again and make different choices, maybe not be a lawyer after all, but fate had intervened and taken her back to where she belonged to remind her that the life she built was good and decent. She cried when she lost him and lost the chance to do it all over again, to do it right and better.

She considered his offer to stay with him at thirty-one in 1966 and did stay for a while, and it was heaven. Never feeling so loved by a man and so excited and stimulated by someone's heart, experiences, and knowledge. It was another chance to erase her life and go down a new path, but between the path she knew he was on and the cost of leaving her kids behind, the weight of it was too heavy for her heart and she made the choice to return to her children and her prior life, it was the right thing to do for him and for her.

How do you give up the best part of yourself - your children - in order to grant yourself a reprieve from bad mistakes? You don't. You simply face them and learn from those mistakes, then graciously count the blessings that arose from them. And you vow to make yourself a smarter person and give yourself a break.

Now being here and being forty-one, knowing the life she had ahead of her and watching this man standing in front of her, this beautiful and perfect man who wanted her and wanted her to stay with him, she knew the only choice she could make was to leave, once again. There were people relying on her, children that even though they were grown, still needed her and wanted her words of wisdom, and there was herself. She'd not done a bad job after all, finally consoling herself, knowing it was the best she could do at the time. She battled demons she never dreamed existed and waded through the muck and mire that we call life, and fortunately, she hadn't drowned in it or let it force her to become evil.

Holding Elvis, feeling him caress her hair, and listening to his heart beat with her head against his chest, she realized it was judgmental and selfish to keep asking him to live his life differently. This man, this King, had taken on a life at the young age of nineteen that most people couldn't even imagine. He'd handled performances, fame, interviews, persecution, slander, fortune, criticism, poverty, heartbreak, pain, responsibility, an ever-changing music terrain, and the ultimate loss of those he loved with the public watching his every move and some sneering at his downfalls and envying his joys, and others like her, pledging eternal adoration and love.

He'd been used and manipulated by those interested in his fortune and disinterested in his health. All he'd endured was for love, the love of the people who depended on him, the love of the music, and the love of the fans. He had given his all for everyone else. It was his destiny, and she couldn't alter that. All she could do was give him love. She knew he would pay the ultimate price with his life and all Jackie hoped right now, in the presence she was embracing, was that he knew how much he was loved and would be loved for generations to come.

277

"Let's live in this moment and not worry about tomorrow or the time after and enjoy each other tonight. I can't wait to see you perform. And after, we don't have to talk about anything you don't want to discuss. If you want to talk all night, then I want to listen. I would love to hear you tell me what you've enjoyed most over the years. It's been an amazing ride Elvis and you've done it well," she said. Looking up at him as she spoke, every emotion she could muster rose to the surface as she met his gaze. She kissed him, knowing that he was the best kiss she'd ever had in both worlds.

He stared into her green eyes, kissed her, and agreed. "That sounds like the best plan we've had in a long time. I have business to take care of first. I'm going to send the boys for some dinner and then I need to be downstairs by eight-thirty to get ready for the surprise." He stopped kissing her and leaned his head back in resignation of obligations he had to fulfill.

"Before we get caught up in the celebration and are joined by your team, there's something I want to give you. It belongs to you." Jackie left Elvis's embrace and went to her purse and pulled the gorget from it. "This is something I found back in Memphis. It's what brought me to you in 1956. It also brought me to you in 1966 and again today. Somehow, it let me find you. I believe it belonged to your great-great-great-grandmother. It's a medallion, a gorget, with some mystical powers. I want you to take it. You can destroy it, keep it, bury it, or do whatever you would like, but it's yours." Jackie took his hand and dropped it in it.

Elvis examined the gorget and the design on it. "You see that eagle?" he asked.

"Yes, it's quite an eagle and I think the other symbol is a snake," she told him.

"Take a look." Elvis went to a large closet and opened it and shuffled the hanging jumpsuits until he came to a white suit with a large multi-colored sequined eagle on the back. "It's the same eagle. It's

278

positioned the same, with the same claws, it's identical. I designed this eagle. I dreamed it one night, a dream you were in. I had to have the design."

Jackie examined both eagles, agreeing they were identical. How could he have known? Jackie felt that familiar chill run down her spine.

"Elvis, where are you?" the high-pitched voice chimed.

Elvis stood still, putting the gorget safely in his pocket. "I'm in here," he shouted, his demeanor instantly soured.

The door burst open and a young and pretty lady wearing stiletto heels walked in carrying multiple shopping bags, no doubt full of designer clothes. "Who are you?" the woman demanded, casting a piercing glare at Jackie.

Jackie could see the flash of jealousy. She started to explain but Elvis cut her short.

"She's a dear friend of mine." Elvis turned the girl around and led her into the other room.

Jackie could hear loud voices and a foot stomp when Elvis told her she was being sent back to Memphis. Jackie moved into the sitting room and watched the lights on the Strip pop to life as the evening descended on Vegas. People on the streets looked like ants darting here and there, in one direction first and then another, several slowly traversing while others moved at the speed of light. Jackie came back to the presence of the room when the door to the suite slammed.

"We have a performance to get to." Elvis took her hand. Not a word was spoken about the woman as the room filled with his team bustling about and demanding Elvis go to the dressing room and get ready. He kissed Jackie on the cheek, telling her, "Georgie will take care of you, and he has your dinner."

Jackie was left standing alone in the suite until Georgie showed up with a gourmet dinner for her.

"Maggie said to tell you hi." Jackie hugged Georgie.

"I miss her. And we both miss you." Referring to him and Elvis. "He talks about you from time to time, mostly when he's looking up at the stars and rambling about angels that watch over him."

"I do the same," she admitted. Every night without him, she had looked up at the stars, knowing they shared the same sky once upon a time. "I won't be back again, Georgie. Elvis is not well. He pretends that he is, but he's not. I'm afraid he doesn't have too many days on this earth," she confided, not knowing if it would cause any problems in her world or his, but she didn't care. She had to finish it.

"I'll take care of him," Georgie promised.

She kissed him on the cheek. "I know you will. Thank you!"

Georgie took Jackie to the theater where the show was underway, straight to a special seat saved for her. Flashes of 1956 surged through her heart. Elvis wasn't the headline show, he was the surprise guest and would perform one song, a special birthday song, and then leave while the show continued so he wouldn't become a distraction to the crowd.

Jackie watched in awe, as she had the first time she saw him on stage when she was twenty-one and fell in love. She fell in love all over again as she took in every part of him. Even though he was forty-one, he moved like a man half his age. His maturity accentuated his handsome stature. The years had come upon him gracefully. His voice never faltered but had grown even more rich and sultry as he belted out full round notes that hung in the air and kept her captive until it rolled to the next one and drew her in deeper. It was not just a concert, but an experience of a lifetime, one you'd have regretted missing if the stars of your life never aligned correctly to put you in the dimension where you could witness his magic.

Jackie felt flush after the concert, her emotions riding high, knowing that once again the goodbye was coming. The night would be perfect, and she'd be back in her world before he woke the next day. She would kiss him until the light of day, sleep contently for a few hours, profess their love for each other, then depart to continue the life she built, and he would fly away to finish the life he built for the time he had left. What was in between it all was something that only magical worlds could create.

She knew as she watched him sleep that night, there had never really been any chance for her to save him. She'd given him what clues she could and the little advice possible without trampling on his ego and altering lives. He was a good man. He had his flaws as we all do, but he did good. Jackie settled her emotions and reminded herself that we all simply do the best we can. And now, it was up to him alone; he was the only one that could save himself.

Chapter 31
Finding Garon

Miraculously, Jackie made it back to 2023 without any issues other than her predicted broken heart, but this time she knew it was the right choice as much as she didn't want to admit it to herself. She cried herself to sleep the first night and several nights thereafter until she had no more tears. There was no denying Elvis was gone by now. It had been two weeks since she left him. That was a good twenty years in his world. There was no going back now or ever.

Over the past two weeks since she had been home, she tried ferociously to move forward, but before she could, she needed to locate Garon White and finish that puzzle, and then continue to build her new life. Her search had been futile thus far.

She had all but given up, thinking it was never to be, and shifted her focus back to herself and living her best life. Making an adventurous decision, she had booked a trip to Hawaii set a few months away, wanting to stay around a while before she started traveling again, determined to be present to help her daughter with Rosie. Susan and Rusty found out they were pregnant with baby number two not long after she returned from Vegas. Jackie was thrilled for them and their blossoming family. They adjusted their schedules, and Susan had stuck to her guns and cut back on work. Rusty increased his hours to make up the difference. They were doing well and working it out. Jackie smiled at the thought of them, knowing they would be all right.

Maggie walked into Jackie's house, carrying an envelope and a box from the printer she told Jackie she would pick up.

"Great, you're here. I was about to take the wine out of the fridge."

"How did it go today looking at buildings for the music center?" Maggie asked.

"Good, I think I found a place. Susan went with me for a little while but her morning sickness was bothering her," Jackie told Maggie, pulling the wineglasses from the cabinet.

"I can only stay for a minute, but I wanted to stop by and drop off that information for the event company you wanted to look at for the grand opening and the flyers for the fundraiser." Maggie set the box on the counter and the brochures on top of the box.

"Thank you so much." Jackie poured the wine and settled in to unwind with Maggie.

"How do you like Toby's new girlfriend?" Maggie asked.

"She's actually quite delightful, smart, funny. I think Toby's met his match. She seems to hold his feet to the fire. He's quite happy."

Toby had been true to his word and brought the new girlfriend around to meet her, and for once, Jackie was impressed.

"I liked her too. Hopefully, they will stay together for a while." Maggie also worried about Toby.

"He has to figure it out. I will show up for dinner and pay the bill when I'm invited. So far, we've met for lunch and dinner twice. I don't know if they like my company or my credit card." Jackie laughed.

"Charlie and I are going dancing this weekend. Do you want to come?" Maggie asked.

"Yes, we had so much fun last weekend, and I found a new pair of shoes I need an excuse to buy. I can't wait. I'm so glad you and Charlie are getting out more. It feels like it's been a positive lift for you." Jackie smiled.

Maggie and Charlie suddenly turned up the heat in their relationship. They had taken up dancing and started going on dates, each having to plan the date each week for the other. If ever there was a "cute" couple, it was Maggie and Charlie.

She loved that they included her on their dance night. She'd forgotten what rhythm she had and how she could boogie on the dance floor. All it took was a part as an extra in a 1966 Elvis movie to remind her she still had a bit of American Bandstand in her bones. She felt as if she had emerged from a cocoon as a beautiful butterfly and was flitting about, soaring above the world, stopping on each flower to notice its beauty. It felt nice.

"Life is good. I even started painting again, so you'll be getting a present soon. In fact, you're going to be sorry that you got me back into it. Soon your walls will be full of new artwork, whether you like it or not." Maggie giggled.

"I love your artwork. I can't wait to hang them proudly. I have a spot in the garage waiting for them," Jackie joked. "No, truly, it makes me so happy. You look good, Maggie, and seem really happy these days."

"I feel really happy these days. Thanks for the reminder about living life," she said. "And how are you doing? I know you're busy with the foundation, but how's your heart doing? Feeling any better?"

"I still miss him terribly and think of him often, if you can't tell by the record playing right now," Jackie replied.

"I'm so sorry. I know it's been hard, but you do seem better. How about Garon, any luck finding him?" Maggie asked.

"No, it's been a dead end. I'm not proud to admit it, but I sat down by the ferry for over four hours this past Sunday after our brunch hoping to see him, but nothing. I thought about going to Bainbridge and asking around, but that seemed a bit like a stalker when I put my legal mind to work," she admitted.

"Well, hopefully, you will run into him again soon. I looked online but didn't find anything. It's like he disappeared."

Maggie had hoped that Jackie would find Garon, certain there was a spark between them that could turn into something more. Even though Jackie seemed less lonely and more content with her life as she sank into retirement, Maggie knew Jackie was ready for a relationship. Elvis had brought her back to life. Maybe she hadn't saved him, but he had saved her.

"If the world wants it to be, then it will happen. If I've learned one thing these past few weeks, is that we don't necessarily control our own destiny. Do you want to stay for dinner?" Jackie asked, searching her iPad for her nightly cooking show.

Looking at the menu for tonight's meal, she pulled the ingredients from the refrigerator. Learning to cook was on her new life agenda, a skill she was certain her children had wished she tackled years ago. Her instruction was from the Internet and consisted of watching cooking shows and experimenting with new recipes. There was a ton of experimenting. She wasn't great at it, but she was making progress. Besides, she was only cooking for herself, so the quality didn't have to be five-star...yet.

"No, Charlie is waiting for me. He wants to try that new Thai restaurant that opened. I know you dislike Thai, or we would have asked you to go." Maggie finished her wine.

"That's okay. I am looking forward to a quiet evening. It's been a bit hectic getting everything up and running for the music foundation, and I kept Rosie a few hours this week." Jackie smiled.

"I've got to run, but I'll talk to you tomorrow and will see you Sunday for brunch. Enjoy your evening." Maggie hugged Jackie, relieved that life was sinking into a blissful rhythm.

"I will." Jackie shut the door behind Maggie, feeling content as she returned to the kitchen.

Her heart surged as Elvis belted out the alluring and flawless, heart wrenching lyrics of *It's Now or Never*. It was the last song he sang at the piano at the Beverly Hills house before they left each other. The memories would never leave her.

When she felt her heart would burst with regret, she let her thoughts drift to Garon and hummed along with the loving lyrics Elvis delivered majestically. She couldn't help but mull over what Garon said the last time she saw him. "He changed her tire when they were fifteen."

That day was clear in her mind, and she knew the boy was named Chad. It had been the first time since she returned and caught up on sleep and planning her life that she decided to turn it over in her mind. In her memory she could clearly see his blue eyes, his blonde hair, his crooked little lip-curled smile. Jackie let her imagination go in various directions before she shut it down again, knowing it was pointless.

She was in the middle of cutting cucumbers when she heard a knock on her door. "Is that you, Maggie? Did you forget something?" she said loudly, wiping her hands on a cup towel before making her way to the entry.

Looking through the sidelights of the front door, she saw it wasn't Maggie, but a man standing on the other side. He wasn't facing the house, but she could make out his gray hair and tall build. She opened the door cautiously.

"Can I help you?" She asked the man as he turned around to greet her. "Garon?" Jackie gasped.

"Hi, Jackie. Can we talk?" He stood, smiling a familiar smile.

"Sure, come on in," she said, opening the door wider. "You're a hard man to find." She saw no point in pretending she wasn't happy to see him. She was thrilled, a fact that her stomach confirmed with a flutter. Maybe she would get some answers.

"Yes, I know. Guess we have that in common," he said, a gentle smile affixed on his handsome face. "Did you figure it out yet?" he asked.

Jackie was confused and curious by what Garon was asking. "Figure it out? You mean when you changed my tire? I've thought about that a lot, but that boy was named Chad, not Garon. That's an unusual name, isn't it?"

"It's a name I use from time to time. It's not my real name."

Jackie wasn't sure what game Garon was playing, but she knew she deserved straight answers. "What's the real name?" Jackie asked impatiently.

"Let's sit down and I'll tell you everything." He took her hand and led her to the living room.

Feeling his hand in hers, she was struck by the thought that it had been there before. Garon led her to the sofa. His knee brushed against hers as they sat next to each other. A familiar surge darted through Jackie, she'd been next to him before, she was certain.

He said, "I hope you'll understand why it took this long for me to find you. I had to wait until you finished it before I could tell you."

"Tell me what?" She looked at him closely. She had only seen him in quick spurts the few times she ran into him, but as she studied his face, she saw something new. Thinking it was her heart's hopeful wish, she sat and listened, repressing her instinct to cross-examine him.

"Do you remember a tree at Graceland with initials EP plus JS? Or spraining your ankle in a theater and being carried to the car in the pouring rain? And how mad I was when I saw you on the set of my movie and I almost fell off that bench. Or when your cowboy hat I bought you flew off when we were racing to the meadow in California? Or how you disappeared in 1976 while I slept, but not before you gave me this?" He reached in his pocket and pulled out the gorget and placed it in her hand.

Jackie could feel the heat of tears welling up in her eyes. She remembered it all, every detail he had described and more. The last time she'd seen the gorget was when she placed it in Elvis's hand in Vegas and he stuck it in his pocket, he knew that she remembered.

"But how? When? How did you figure it out?"

She felt a tear escape and run down her cheek. Instinctively, he reached up and wiped it away. She didn't want to look him in the eyes in case what she was thinking was wrong.

"When you gave me the gorget, you said it was how you were able to find me, which I didn't understand at the time. And as usual, you left, so I couldn't ask you more about it and we were too preoccupied before that for me to think about it." Elvis grinned at the memory.

Jackie blushed.

Elvis continued, "I showed it to Georgie, and he seemed to know everything."

Jackie stammered, "But how, I didn't tell him. How did he know?"

"Years earlier, my team was worried about me always looking up to the stars for you. I knew you were out there, but I didn't know where. They thought I was reading too many spiritual books and decided to burn them. Georgie was helping bring them downstairs when he found your note. He kept it hidden for over seven years. But when I showed him the gorget, he gave it to me. It explained it all," Elvis told her quietly.

"I hoped someone would find my note." Jackie touched his hand. "But how and when did you get here?"

"It was August 1977. I was in pain all the time. I was sick like you said, but I didn't want to admit it then. I tried to get the doctors to do the research on Alpha-1, but they said I was overworked and gave me more pain pills and recommended stopping the tour and resting, which I did from time to time. I tried to manage it all, but it was too much. So, one night when I couldn't sleep, I pulled out your note and the gorget and read the inscription. I ended up in your world in 1977 and I was fifteen years old, the same age as you."

Jackie was in shock. He should be eighty-eight now, but he was here and sixty years old, like she'd been his age when she went to his world. She stared in his eyes and finally saw it all, the same smile, same dazzling blue eyes, she knew she recognized the features, but she would never have known if he hadn't shared the truth, not that the same glint in his eyes wasn't there, but she had never looked for it.

"So, you've been living a second life all these years?"

"I didn't have any home to go back to. I was blessed, really. I was given a second chance, and it was a starkly different life from the first one and it's been good. The hard part was watching the people I love and not being able to be part of it and waiting for you. I knew you had to go to my world a last time, otherwise I couldn't have arrived in your world."

"The reverse grandfather paradox."

"The, what?" Elvis asked.

"Never mind, it's something Maggie said a while back," Jackie murmured.

"I've watched you over the years. When you got married, I left and went to Europe for many years. I didn't want to watch you with him. Europe had always been a dream for me," he explained.

"But how? How did you get a passport?" she asked.

"It was easier back then, before the Internet. And when you have money, you can get pretty much anything you need, like silence, anonymity." He laughed.

"You saved your money, after all. You did take my advice?" Jackie grinned.

"Yes, I withdrew it the day before I took the gorget out that fateful night. I don't know what I was planning on doing with the money, but something nagged me, so I went and got it. Nobody ever knew about it except my friends Joe and Georgie, who handled things at Graceland after I left. And I've worked all these years in this world and saved a bit. I've enjoyed a lucrative career in both worlds. I've been smarter in the second life than I was in the first in some ways." He smiled and held Jackie's hand in his.

So, Joe really was an Elvis expert, she thought. "I can't believe you've been here this entire time. Didn't anyone recognize you?" Jackie was surprised by the revelations, but happy.

"Yes, when I was younger, I made my way across the country working on ranches as a ranch hand, taking care of the horses. On occasion, I'd miss singing and would go play in some small, dusty old bar. Every once in a while, someone would ask if I was Elvis. When they did, I would laugh, pack up, and move on to the next ranch. There's a lot of ranches in this country. I followed your career later when the Internet came about, saw you were still in Seattle and moved out here when I read about your divorce, then decided to stay and wait."

It was difficult to grasp that he'd been living near her for so many years, a lifetime really, and she never knew. "I can't believe you weren't recognized. But it makes sense. You were hiding in plain sight, something you were always skilled at doing."

"Yes, I was. You didn't even know when our paths crossed. You didn't recognize me the day I changed your tire. My hair was blonde, I wore caps often, and nobody was looking for a fifteen-year-old blonde boy. They were looking for forty-two-year-old Elvis, who they knew was gone. As the years passed and cell phones became the way of the world, it was loads easier with everyone in a cellphone trance, rarely looking up to see what's in front of them. They don't make small talk or eye contact with strangers like they did years earlier."

Jackie couldn't disagree. She had witnessed families sit at dinner and never engage in conversation, with kids attached to their iPads and parents distracted by their phones, creating little individual self-absorbed worlds instead of a community. Sadly, those conversations with family, neighbors, and friends were the things that made life worth living. They were the substance that enriched and expanded the soul. She'd been guilty of it herself over the years, getting lost in the digital world to avoid the human world. But it wasn't that way anymore, living in the present and paying attention to the people around her who mean the world to her had pulled her back to a balanced way of life.

"Wait, what do you mean 'the times we met'? You mean on the plane and at the airport?" Jackie wanted all the truth.

"I mean back in Lubbock, Texas. Do you remember a boy named Deke?" He smiled dangerously.

"That was you?" Jackie's eyes were wide.

It shot through her, his reluctance to take the cap off or to engage with anyone, her deep infatuation, the thrill of his kiss. She'd never known that kiss again until Elvis, she never put it together. Why would she? She had no way of knowing any of it could be possible back then.

Elvis explained further, "Deke was my character from the movie *Loving You*."

Jackie stared at Elvis, seeing it all now. "The song you hummed all the time." She was overcome with emotion at the realization that all the pieces were falling into place, finally.

Elvis smiled. "And I was at the reception for your award for 'Attorney of the Year' several years ago. I signed the registry using the name Mike McCoy." Elvis's sly grin showed he was proud of that little inside humor.

Mike McCoy, the character Elvis played in *Spinout*. She'd missed the connection when she read the registry, and why wouldn't she? *Spinout* wasn't in her mind at all during that time period and Elvis was dead as far as she knew.

"Why didn't you tell me?" Jackie wanted to understand.

"The same reason you didn't tell me. You wouldn't have believed me. I would have been called a crazy person, telling you I was

Elvis, and that you had given me a gorget in 1976, and I used it to time travel. And, by the way, I'm twenty-seven years younger than I should be. I would have been cuffed, arrested, and locked up within minutes. I couldn't tell anyone. All I could do was watch from afar and wait," he explained. "I knew eventually you had to travel back and find me. How else could I have the gorget? It was a matter of time and patience. Something I wasn't sure about year after year. When I saw you and Maggie at the airport headed to Hollywood, I knew it wouldn't be long."

Jackie knew he was right. She wouldn't have given him the time of day. Her mind and heart were shut to anything but logical law, work, and success. She wouldn't have believed there was a world between worlds, or a parallel universe, or time warps, or even good fortune.

"You're right, I would have thought you mad. Maggie thought I lost my mind the first time I came back. But how do I know you're really Elvis? How do I know you're not an imposter? There are dozens of them out there if you haven't noticed that fact over the years." She stared at his blue eyes, knowing in her heart it was him.

A crooked smile crossed his face, he told her, "I guess you'll have to trust me, like you told me once. And I've given you many details that nobody but the two of us could know. But how about this as the ultimate confirmation?"

Elvis cupped her face with his hands, leaned her back on the sofa and kissed her as he had done many times before, but this time was different. It was connected to a power she couldn't deny. It was a deep, wanting kiss, which burned hot beneath her skin. The kind of kiss that left her grappling for more. A kiss that spanned lifetimes, connecting them in a way only the magic of the universe had the power to do. She knew that kiss. Nobody in her life had kissed her like that but him. And there was no reason now there couldn't be more to follow that enticing kiss.

"I think we have some unfinished business, Mr. Presley. Something I've waited a lifetime or two to do," she whispered, trying to catch her breath. Jackie stood up, took his hand, and led him to her bedroom. The record continued playing in the background as he crooned poetically. Jackie grinned... *Welcome to My World.*

When they arrived in the bedroom, Elvis kissed her with an eagerness he'd never known. They were not going to be separated again; he was sure of it. He deepened the kiss until Jackie moaned for more. Elvis smiled with satisfaction... he knew he was home to stay.

"Mmm... My Lady Lawyer!"

The End... and the beginning!

About The Author
Leslie Asbill Prichard

 Leslie was born and raised in Texas but now resides in New Mexico. Leslie has spent many years as a marketing and technical writer, but her passion lies in storytelling. Finding Elvis is her debut fiction novel, with several more publications to follow. Coming soon: *Betrayed by Blood.* Her children's books, *Brat the Pirate* and *But, Where is God?* are also available online.

Leslie has four adult children and four adorable grandchildren. Leslie enjoys spending time in her yard, playing tennis, traveling, and writing. She hopes you enjoy reading her stories as much as she loves writing them. To sign up for her mailing list to receive new release information, please visit her website at www.onenoseybroad.com or follow her on social media @onenoseybroad on FB, Instagram, and TikTok.

Fun Facts for Elvis Fans

♪ There are 31 chapters in this book because Elvis made 31 films.

♪ All the male names in this book, except for Vernon and Georgie, are character names from Elvis's movies.

♪ I did see Elvis in concert in 1975. I was 13 years old. My heart was broken when he died.

♪ When researching this book, I visited Graceland and Tupelo, MS, and had the time of my life. If you haven't gone…GO!